COMING HOME TO HOLLY CLOSE FARM

JULIE HOUSTON is the author of *The One Saving Grace*, *Goodness*, *Grace and Me* and *Looking for Lucy*, a Kindle top 100 general bestseller and a Kindle Number 1 bestseller. She is married, with two teenage children and a mad cockerpoo and, like her heroine, lives in a West Yorkshire village. She is also a teacher and a magistrate.

COMING HOME TO HOLLY CLOSE FARM

Julie Houston

First published in the United Kingdom in 2019 by Aria, an imprint of
Head of Zeus Ltd

9 7 5 3 1 2 4 6 8

A CIP catalogue record for this book is available from the British Library.

ISBN 9781788549813

Aria
an imprint of Head of Zeus
First Floor East
5–8 Hardwick Street
London EC1R 4RG

Prologue

July 1953

From each observation point across the rough-grassed terrain, all approaches were covered. Anyone arriving or leaving, any movement, whether human or otherwise, could be monitored by at least one of them. Although the moon was a newly formed sliver, visibility across the acre or so of land was good.

No light was seen from any of the farm's many windows; no smoke rose negligently from a single one of its four huge stone chimneys on this chilly July night.

The waiting continued, until suddenly, in the early hours of the new day, the stillness was shattered by gunshot.

A volley of five shots in rapid succession blasted the cool summer-night air and was immediately succeeded by what seemed, to those waiting stiff and rendered almost lifeless in the long grass, a yawning silence.

And then they rose, almost as one, darkly spectral figures of a childhood nightmare, scrambling, slipping and falling down the hill towards the direction from which the shots had come.

I

Friday evening and I could almost taste the gin and tonic waiting for me as I dragged the carrier bags of shopping up to my flat on the second floor. Wincing as the plastic cut into both hands, I dumped the bags onto the floor with relief and had a good scrabble round in my shoulder bag for the door key. Dominic always laughed at what regularly surfaced from the depths of the Tardis: sketches and notes for the new designs I was working on, fabric and flooring samples, an over-ripe banana and the usual make-up and Oyster card.

What the hell was wrong with the key? I peered at it, scrutinising the tarnished metal before attempting to ram it once more into the Yale lock of the flat door.

No go. Bugger. Had I got the wrong key? No, it was the one I always used: the key Dominic had fastened onto my bunch when he'd suggested we make our relationship rather more permanent. I'd been over the moon – more than happy to leave the cramped flat I shared in Bayswater with a rather strange girl from Lancashire who very rarely socialised, and who thought a good night's entertainment consisted of the sofa pulled up in front of *Strictly* while making her way stolidly through an entire half-pound tub of Philadelphia cream cheese.

It was definitely the right key. I peered again, turned it over and tried again. Nope. Had I bent it, put it out of service somehow earlier in the day when my bag had collided with that cyclist on the Old Kent Road as I rushed, late as usual, for an initial consultation on this morning's new job? I rubbed tentatively at my leg where the bike's front wheel had caught my foot as I stepped onto the zebra crossing, flooring me physically while its owner had attempted to do the same mentally, pouring vitriol onto my head as I lay, speechless in the road.

'Having problems?' A tall, very attractive blonde appeared at my side and I started at her words.

'Yes, the damned lock appears to be jammed. I don't know what the hell's wrong with it...'

The woman, older than me but far more glamorous, scrutinised me carefully, taking in every aspect of my sweating face and, after an afternoon on a building site, my creased and dusty jeans, denim jacket and scuffed heavy-duty boots.

She smiled. 'Here. Try this one. I think you'll have more success.'

'Sorry?' I took a step away from my front door, tripped over the bags of shopping and looked at the woman full on as she stood, eyebrows raised, offering me the key. 'So, what are you?' I laughed. 'The fairy godmother of knackered keys?'

'Gosh, no, nothing as imaginative as that.' She smiled again. 'How about the gullible wife of a cheating bastard husband?'

'Aw, that's awful for you. I'm so sorry. And didn't you know?'

'I do now.' She was no longer smiling. 'Look, are you being deliberately obtuse or are you just thick?' She tutted, brushed past me and inserted her key into my door. 'Your stuff's all packed up. I'd like you out in ten minutes: the estate agent will be here to value the place...' she scrutinised her little gold wrist watch, '... in half an hour.'

Five black bin bags, the sum total, it appeared, of my life, were heaped in disarray in the tiny hallway. My heart revved uncomfortably and I felt a trickle of sweat start under my arms. Surreptitiously wiping the film of moisture from my top lip, I pushed the stray lock of hair that regularly went AWOL from my one plait and searched in the depths of the Tardis for my phone.

'It's no good ringing him,' the woman said. 'Dom knows I've found out.'

I ignored her, immediately finding Dominic's number, and pressed the usual button. 'This is my flat,' I snapped, glaring at her as I waited for Dominic to answer. 'I share the rent, I pay the bills. I pay my bloody way.'

Three little beeps on my phone heralded an unrecognised number. I tried again.

'*My* flat,' she countered. 'Every bit of it, *mine*. Bought for me by my father for my twenty-first birthday.' She actually laughed. 'I would imagine the money you gave to

Dom each month went straight into his children's pockets for spending money. You know: little treats, trips to the cinema. Good old dad. I bet he always insisted you pay your share in cash…'

'He's got children?' I stared at her. 'Dominic's got children?'

'Three. And, if you still haven't worked it out, one very alive, still very married wife. Me.'

'He told me he was divorced.'

'And I suppose he also told you, on the nights and weekends he wasn't with you that he was in the Manchester or Paris office? You've been had, darling. He has a very much alive and extremely kicking wife as well as three kids away at school to support and pay for.'

'You can't do this!' I shouted, but one look at her calm features and I saw that she jolly well could do it. And had.

'I can, and I am,' the blonde confirmed. 'Out, now, you trollop. Come on, out. I want to lock up.'

'You can't just turf me out like this. Where the hell am I supposed to go at…' I glanced at the clock on the wall – a horrible art-deco thing I'd always hated… 'seven o'clock on a Friday evening?'

'Your problem, not mine.'

'I didn't know,' I pleaded. 'I really didn't know he was married and had kids.'

'Well, you do now. Dom is well and truly married and living in Haslemere with me, two dogs and, when they're back from school, three children.'

'The bastard. The absolute bastard.' I started grabbing two of the black bin bags.

'Yes, well, that's one thing we can agree on. Now, if you don't mind.' She started throwing the remaining bin bags out into the corridor. 'Oh, and if you have any idea that he's going to leave us and whisk you off to become the second Mrs Abraham, you can forget it.'

'He's due back from his trip to the States this evening,' I said defiantly, still hanging on to the two bin bags in my sweaty hands, but not making those final steps outside with them.

Dominic's wife snorted at this. 'The States? As in the *United* States?' She laughed almost gleefully. 'The only *state* he's been in this week is one of grovelling servitude, begging my forgiveness at every turn. When he's in "*The States*" or in "*Europe*" or "*Out of Town*" as the sod euphemistically calls it, he's actually working from home in the studio he had built in the garden several years ago.' She picked up the last of the bags, wrenching the ones from my clenched fists, before hurling each one with well-aimed fury outside. 'Oh,' she added as the last one hit the corridor, 'and as I and my father are the major shareholders in Abraham Developments, your service in the company is, from this moment, well and truly terminated.'

I found myself on the wet, miserable streets of London in mid-November, visions of having to make my way to Oxford Street or Covent Garden to grab a pitch to sleep rough skittering through my mind, as I paused for a while to collect myself.

I stood outside one of North London's ubiquitous coffee houses and made the decision to go in. I needed a strong coffee to clear my head and think who to call to beg a bed for the night, although I had a horrible feeling my phone was running out of charge. So much for the gin and tonic and its accompanying cosy night in.

'Oy, lady, you can't bring all that rubbish in here with you.' The young Eastern European barista glared at me as I opened the door and hauled in my life in five bags after me. 'Health and Safety. You order and sit outside and I bring it out to you.'

'It's raining,' I said. 'In fact, it's bloody pouring down.'

And with that all the fight went out of me as I balanced a bin bag under each arm and bent to grasp the remaining three. There was, I realised, only one option.

'Mum?'

'Charlie? Hello, darling. Dad and I were just talking about you.'

'Mum, can I come home for a bit?'

'What, for the weekend you mean?'

'A bit longer than that, possibly. Probably.'

'Of course you can come home. You know that.' Mum sounded surprised as well she might. I suddenly realised with a slight jolt that not only had I not been back to Yorkshire for a good six months, I'd not rung home for ages either. 'Dad and I were only just saying we needed to have a trip down to London to see you. How's Dominic? Is everything OK?'

'I'll tell you when I see you.'

'So, when are you thinking of coming up then?'

'Er, like now?'

'Now? Today? This evening? Oh, right. Lovely. And is Dominic with you? Are you both up for the weekend?'

'Oh, Mum.'

'Charlie, what is it?'

'Mum, can you pick me up? The train gets in at ten thirty.' I paused. 'And can you come in Dad's car rather than yours? I've got rather a lot of stuff with me.' I glanced at the bin bags perched in a neat row on the overhead luggage rack like a flock of particularly malevolent crows.

'Right, darling. What time did you say? I was just about to watch that new drama with Cummerbund Benderbatch...' She paused and I could almost hear her brain clicking into gear. 'That's not right, is it? Oh, you know who I mean. I'll go and make sure your bed's made up. Will you have eaten?'

I didn't think I'd ever be able to eat again. I could certainly drink, though. I rang off and made my way down the carriages until I found the buffet bar and bought three little plastic bottles of wine.

I worked my way methodically down all three bottles, glaring at the man opposite so that he gets the message that conversation was definitely not on the menu. I tried Dominic's number again and again, only to hear the three little beeps verifying no such number was in existence. Well, I could still email him. I couldn't see him getting rid of that so easily: he'd need it for work.

You bastard, Dominic Abraham.

That was after the first bottle of wine...

You lying, cheating, tosser bastard.

Two down and I was on a roll.

And yes, Dominic, size does matter. It must be down to all the double exercise it's been getting lately. Obviously wearing away.

That little drunken tirade accompanied the final plastic bottle.

I finally drained my glass and looked tipsily out of the window. We were heading towards Doncaster and, as we went through a tunnel, my reflection stared back at me. Is this what I'd come to? Several years in London doing a job I loved and had trained for and I was heading back home to Midhope, tail between my legs. Nearly thirty and back home to my mum and dad. No home, no job, no man but, instead, five black bin bags to show for seven years' training as an architect. And then another three in London working for one architectural company before being interviewed by Dominic Abraham eleven months ago and landing the job in property development which I loved and which I was jolly good at.

As we pulled into Wakefield, I stood on my seat and started hauling down my bags.

'Here, love, let me help you.' The man opposite stood and pulled down the last two bags but the final and fullest bag split, its innards of unwashed bras, pants and work shirts, obviously scooped up from the laundry basket, spilling onto the floor, the seats below and, unfortunately, the balding heads of two elderly men nodding their way towards Leeds.

2

'We're going to have a full house,' Mum said more cheerfully than she obviously felt as she manoeuvred the last of the five bin bags into the battered Volvo's boot.

'Oh? Who else is staying?'

'Well, Vivienne appears to have taken root in the spare bedroom, and Daisy's home as well.'

'Granny Vivienne? And *Daisy*?' I perked up a bit. 'How come? Is she just home for the weekend?'

'Don't think so. She says she's had enough of being a trolley dolly and is going to use her degree for what it was meant for.'

'Which is? Mum, be careful, you nearly knocked that man down.' I had to grasp the dashboard as she braked sharply. My years living in London obviously hadn't improved my mother's driving ability.

'Sorry, darling, forgot my glasses. Blind as a bat without them. Well, obviously her degree in landscape architecture means she can *be* a landscape architect. After three years of travelling, working in bars all round the world and now with this job as an air hostess out of Liverpool suddenly coming to an end, she's decided enough is enough and she wants to have a proper job.'

'Right.' I couldn't see my younger sister settling down to anything, particularly back home in Midhope, where there wasn't a huge amount of opportunity for setting up a new business in landscape architecture, especially when the only real work experience she'd had, apart from on the flights, was working on a sheep farm in New Zealand and pulling pints in Australia.

I could sense Mum glancing in my direction as I stared through the windscreen, scowling into the night as I bit my nails, a habit I thought I'd overcome.

'So, are you going to tell me what's happened? I'm assuming, with all those bags with you, you've decided to give London a rest for a while?'

'I love London, Mum. I love my job.' I could feel the traitorous tears begin to gather once more. '*Loved* it...' I trailed off, my voice wobbling as I slid down into the seat in an attempt to get warm. 'God, I'd forgotten how bloody cold it is up here.'

'Where's your coat? It is November, you know.'

Hell, where *was* my lovely sheepskin coat? Not in the black bags, I was certain. A sudden vision of it hanging on its usual peg in my office swam before my eyes. Well, that was obviously gone. I couldn't see anyone bothering to parcel it up and send it on to me. Good job I always carried my phone and laptop in the Tardis with me. I gave its voluminous contents on my knee a reassuring pat.

'So, I've got both my daughters home for a while, have I?' Mum stopped at a red light and turned once more in my direction.

'Is that OK? I mean, you'll enjoy having us both to feed and fuss over, won't you? Look how much you missed us when we went off to uni.'

Mum laughed. 'One very quickly gets used to having a tidy house and *not* having to feed and fuss over one's kids. It's quite blissful not having to think about what to have for supper. Dad and I can have a glass of wine and just saunter down to the village for a "two for £13 meal deal" at the Jolly Sailor. Quite liberating really.'

'Oh, so you're not happy about having us back then?' I felt the tears that had been threatening all evening start once more. Rejected now by my own mother as well as that bastard Dominic.

'Oh dear, something *has* happened, hasn't it?' Mum set off at speed once the lights turned to her advantage, totally oblivious of the woman in the Evoque to her left, mouthing some obscenity as Mum cut her up. 'So, Dominic? I assume he's got another woman – or even another man, what with all this gender fluidity – and as he's your boss that means you're out of a job as well?'

'He's married, Mum.'

'Doesn't surprise me, darling.' Mum gave my arm a little squeeze of sympathy.

'I thought you liked him?' I turned and stared at her.

'We only met him once, Charlie,' Mum protested. 'And yes, Dad and I both liked him enormously... but...'

'But? But what?' Even though Dominic was a cheating bastard, I still wanted my mother's approval of him.

'Oh, maybe he was just *too* good-looking, *too* worldly-wise. To get to almost forty and *not* have a wife somewhere tucked away… And you did say he was away an awful lot. You were supposed to be sharing that flat with him, but you spent a hell of a lot of the time on your own.'

'I really like being on my own,' I protested crossly, stung by her words.

'I'm not saying you don't. But every time I rang you, Dominic appeared to be away in the States, or Paris…'

'Or Haslemere. God, I don't even know where Haslemere is.'

Mum frowned. 'I'm not sure I do either. Can't be that great a place if we've never heard of it. Anyway, you're home now, darling.'

We continued in silence through Westenbury, the village on the outskirts of Midhope where I'd lived all my life until leaving for university and then London. Slowing down and indicating right, Mum pulled into the drive of our Victorian detached house. It seemed smaller somehow, not quite as I remembered it. But then, I guess, being away for some time does that to you.

'And it's lovely to have you, you know that,' Mum said, patting my arm. 'Come on, Dad and Daisy are waiting for us.'

I opened the car door and stretched, yawning. I felt grubby, hungover and thoroughly depressed. If, when I'd galloped off down the road to the tube that morning, slice of toast and Marmite in one hand, trusty Tardis in the other, someone had told me that, fifteen hours later, I'd be back with my mum and dad in Westenbury village with no job and no flat, I'd have laughed at their idiocy.

'It won't be for long, Mum.' I said, feeling slightly panicky at being back at the starting line once again. 'A couple of days, a week at the most to sort myself a new job and somewhere to live in London, and I'll be off back down again.'

'So, what happened to your career as waitress in the sky?' I hugged my younger sister before flopping down onto her bed and, closing my eyes, tried to shut out the awful events of the day.

'Cunnilingus finished me off.'

'Sorry?' I opened one eye and squinted at Daisy. 'I can't take you seriously with that purple stuff on your hair and white stuff above your lips.'

'I've no money to get my hair done at the hairdresser so I'm touching up the roots myself – I borrowed Vivienne's toothbrush to do the job: she's the only one without an electric one round here – and for some reason I seem to be sprouting a moustache suddenly, so I'm bleaching that as well. I blame all the fumes I've had to breathe in while walking up and down that damned cabin.'

I looked at Daisy doubtfully. 'Fumes give you a moustache? Never heard that one before. You're just getting old. By the time you're thirty you'll probably have a beard that'll give Rip Van Winkle a run for his money.'

'Shit, do you think so?' Daisy felt her chin before scrutinising her face in the mirror. 'My eyebrows are sprouting as well. Raphael said to me the other week, "Eets like being in bed wiz Denees Healey."'

I tutted. 'Cheeky sod. You should have asked the little frog how *he* knew what being in bed *wiz Denees Healey* was like.'

We both cackled at that and I felt a bit better that Daisy was having a few problems on the man front too. No matter how much you might adore your sister, you don't want her to be one up on you, especially when she's two years younger than you.

'You do know you can't call the French *Frogs* any more,' Daisy tutted in turn. 'I thought you'd have learned that, living in London. Totally and utterly not PC. Anyway, the little frog's on the way out, I reckon, especially as I'll no longer be meeting up with him at Charles De Gaulle: Terminal 2D. He'll have to concentrate on handling baggage rather than me in future.' Daisy lay down on the bed beside me, shoving me up towards the wall as she did so. 'Blimey, it's jolly hard work keeping your face tilted upwards so this vile-smelling stuff doesn't slide down into your mouth.'

'And the cunnilingus?' I closed my eyes again and snuggled under Daisy's duvet. It felt warm and safe and I wanted to hide there for ever, shutting out the events of the past few hours.

Daisy laughed. 'It was so boring up there in the sky that, once we'd served the drinks, food, duty free and slapped down the wandering drunks and gropers, we'd come up with ways to entertain ourselves.'

'Couldn't you just strap yourself in and have a snooze?'

Daisy tutted. 'Having a kip thirty-five thousand feet up is hardly professional.'

'And indulging in a mile-high sex act is? So, you entertained yourselves with a bit of covert oral sex? With whom? Not the pilot, I hope?'

Daisy laughed. 'Don't be ridiculous. Have you seen the size of a cockpit on a charter plane to Malaga?'

'It wasn't the cock *pit* I was imagining.' I opened one eye and raised its eyebrow in her direction.

Daisy laughed again. 'If living in London has given you such a vivid imagination, it's probably time you came back north. Anyway, in order to overcome the total monotony of trailing up and down the aisle, we set ourselves little tasks. The task for the day was for a crew member to get the word *cunnilingus* into a sentence over the public-address system.'

'Right.' I yawned. It all sounded terribly juvenile. 'As in, please be aware that cunnilingus, like smoking, is not permitted in the aircraft toilet?'

'Do you want to hear how clever I was, or not?'

'Sorry, go on.'

'So, over the speaker I said, "Good afternoon, ladies and gentlemen. The seat belt sign is still illuminated so please ensure you're strapped in. There does appear to be some turbulence, which may give a bit of a bumpy ride. It could be there for a while as it appears to be the sort that *kinda lingers...*'

I laughed despite myself. 'Oh, well done. Ten out of ten.'

'Yes, I was so pleased with my quick wit. Unfortunately, while most of the crew thought it was brilliant, one of the stewards, who was teed off with me because the co-pilot he'd fancied for ages had chatted me up in Liverpool, reported me to my line manager.'

'The traitor. And you were in trouble?'

'Sacked,' Daisy sniffed, jumping off the bed and examining her now quite purple roots in the mirror. 'I don't really care, because the season was coming to an end and I'd totally had enough of the whole damned circus of arm waving the safety stuff when nobody takes any notice because they know it's all a farce anyway, and a mask and yellow rubber dinghy and abandoning high heels isn't going to save them from the sharks below.'

'Sharks? In Malaga?'

'You know what I mean.'

I yawned. God, I was tired. And depressed. 'So, what now? You can't stay here for ever.'

'I don't plan to.' Daisy checked her watch before wiping the white cream off her top lip with a couple of quick moves before squinting in the mirror above her dressing table once more. 'There, that's better. Ready to face the world now.'

'I don't imagine there's much of the world to face round here. There never was before, so I don't see why there should be now.'

'Oh, I don't know,' Daisy frowned. 'I'm actually enjoying being back. Having both feet on the ground all the time.'

'Yes, but what are you going to *do*? You can't just sit around all day doing nothing.'

'Hey, I've not stopped since I came home three days ago. I'm already earning my keep by giving the garden a makeover. And Westenbury's becoming quite trendy, you know. There's Clementine's restaurant down the road. I thought I might see if they need any kitchen or waiting staff. Just until I find some more landscaping work.'

'Do people want their gardens doing in November? I thought it was a miserable time of year for gardens?'

'That's where you're wrong,' Daisy said enthusiastically, warming to her theme. 'Dahlias need lifting, new bulbs need planting, the ground needs to be prepared for planting hedges, trees and shrubs…'

'Fine, fine, enough,' I groaned, burying my head under her pillow. 'Spare me the details; I've got one hell of a headache. You won't catch me staying round here longer than I have to. As soon as I've sorted myself a new job, I'll be back in London. I sort of panicked. You know, there I was, on the streets of Bloomsbury, five bin bags around my feet and I just headed for King's Cross and the train home. I should have gone to stay with someone in London really, but to be honest I was too embarrassed to ring anyone.'

'Embarrassed?' Why? Because that wanker was married all along?'

'No, not because of that,' I managed to articulate from the muffled depths of the pillow before surfacing fully and sitting up. 'I suppose I've not been the best friend since moving in with Dominic. I was just so happy to come home and be with him – when he actually *was* at the flat – that I'd not really wanted to socialise with friends.'

'That's really poor of you, Charlie.' Daisy sounded cross. 'You really shouldn't give up your friends just because you've moved in with some man.'

'Anyway,' I went on, not really listening, 'when Dominic finds out I've left London, he might realise just what he's missing and...'

'Oh, don't be so wet, Charlie. He's had you over, good and proper. And yes,' Daisy went on, 'I totally understand what you saw in him and that you were taken in by him. He was charming *and* pretty gorgeous to boot.'

'Oh, he was, he was.' I lashed out furiously at the pillow.

'But you're better off up here for a while,' Daisy affected a broad Yorkshire accent. 'Oop North wi yer mam and dad, yer gran and yer little sister.'

3

'God, Dad, it's bloody freezing in here.' I felt the radiator underneath the kitchen window; it was stone cold. 'Can't we have some heat on?'

'Heat? What's the matter with you?' Dad grinned as he unclipped Malvolio, his black Lab from his leash, wet and smelling highly of dog after his morning walk across Norman's Meadow – a local beauty spot – and the woods beyond. 'Pass me that towel, Charlie, would you? Heat?' he repeated. 'It's not winter yet. Go and put another sweater on.'

'Since when has the middle of November not been winter?' I said crossly. 'It's like the sodding Arctic in here.' I scraped the remains from a jar of Marmite and smeared it onto a slice of toast. 'And we need more Marmite.'

'Darling girl, there are lots of things we need in this world but are very unlikely to get. Such is life.' I was enveloped in a flurry of trailing silk scarves, a plethora of cold metallic bangles and the overpowering, almost nauseating smell of Givenchy, all of which had defined my granny Maddison – or Vivienne, as she insisted on being called – for as long as I could remember.

'Hi, Vivienne, how come you're camping out here too? What's wrong with your place?'

'Decorators, darling. I've just had to have them in and I cannot *cope* with their endless mugs of Builders' Bum tea and their constant need for Radio One that sets my nerves on edge. But it's the terrible fumes from the paint that play absolute havoc with one's sinuses and complexion. Your father very kindly suggested I come and stay here for the duration.'

'Did I? Are you sure about that?' Dad winked at me.

'And now we're all here. How simply marvellous. We shall have such a good Christmas.'

Christmas? I hadn't intended still being back in the north for Christmas. It suddenly occurred to me why, only a couple of days ago, Dominic had said he would have to spend most of Christmas with his elderly parents. They were terribly possessive of him, he'd said, and he would have to go alone to stay with them in his family home in Cornwall. When I'd protested, said I was already planning Christmas for just the two of us in the apartment, he'd taken me in his arms and said there was absolutely nothing he could do about it, that he would give anything to be just with me but that surely my family would want me back in Yorkshire with them anyway? Dominic had stopped my protestations with his mouth, kissing me softly and then with some urgency until any thoughts of turkeys and tinsel were obliterated.

What a loser. And that was me, not him.

Seeing that I was near to tears, Vivienne stroked my hair, pulling loose strands back into my blonde plait.

'*By all the vows that ever men have broke, In number, more than ever women spoke.* I was Hermia once, darling,' she trilled, pouring muesli into her bowl and then immediately abandoning it as she warmed to her theme. '*A Midsummer Night's Dream* in Morecambe...' – she pronounced it Morry Cambie – '... 1962, I believe it was, just before I met your grandfather.' She paused dramatically, flinging a long scarlet scarf over one shoulder, catching Malvolio's nose with one of its metallic embellishments. 'Men will always deceive women.'

Vivienne had been quite famous in her day. Against her parents' wishes, she'd applied for and won a place at LAMDA in London before touring in rep up and down the country in the early sixties. Her big break had come when the BBC, desperate to come up with something to rival *Coronation Street*, had launched *Emergency!* and given the part of the sexy little blonde nurse, with whom all the doctors and patients were in love, to Vivienne McMaster, my gran.

'Mum told you, did she?' I was embarrassed and looked away, concentrating on chewing my toast, which appeared to have turned to ashes in my mouth. I poured tea from the giant brown teapot of my childhood and drank the stewed dark liquid gratefully.

'Well, of course, darling. Why wouldn't she? I'd have come and talked to you last night but I'd been learning my lines all evening and must have fallen asleep, exhausted.'

'Your lines? What are you doing now?'

'A rather amateurish production of darling Oscar's *Earnest*. I am, of course, Lady Bracknell.'

I smiled. 'Where is it on? Westenbury village hall? I bet you're the only one who's been a professional actor, aren't you?'

Vivienne sighed. 'Of course, darling. There really is very little talent in this backwater. Now, your father is playing Jack Worthing and, I have to say, is quite marvellous in the role.' She glanced over at Dad, who was examining Malvolio's nose. 'Your grandfather got it so wrong, not allowing your father to act. Such a terrible waste.'

'I bet all the farmers round here don't think it's a waste when he's out with them in the middle of the night pulling foals and calves out of their labouring mothers.' Dad was a vet, very much in the manner of *All Creatures Great and Small*, and a pretty good one if the huge number of bottles of whisky and wine that came our way each Christmas from grateful farmers was anything to go by.

Vivienne nodded sadly. 'Yes, I'm sure your father is a jolly good vet – look at him now with that dog of his – but he would have made a brilliant actor had he been allowed to follow in *my* footsteps rather than his father's. He could have been a northern George Clooney with that chest hair and those eyebrows.' She looked me up and down. 'And *you* still haven't any inclination…?'

'None whatsoever,' I said firmly, shaking my head so she was in no doubt that I might ever abandon my career and start treading the boards. 'I absolutely love what I'm doing in London. What I *was* doing.'

'And this, this *lothario* of yours? Surely, darling, you must have had a tiny smidgen of an idea that he was married?' Vivienne raised an eyebrow.

Had I? Part of me had perhaps wondered if he had another woman somewhere when he was always off, particularly at weekends, but I was so in love with him that I suppose I'd just buried my head and didn't question him or the situation.

'Vivienne, I promise you, I had absolutely no idea he was married. I don't *do* married men.'

'But, if you worked for him as well, surely the other people in the office would have known? Surely one has some inkling whether the boss is married or not?'

I shook my head. 'I'm obviously one thick woman.' I felt the tears start once more and swallowed them down. 'Dominic said to keep it quiet at the office that we were an item. That the others wouldn't like it that the new girl was living with the boss. So, I did.'

Vivienne tutted. 'Oh, dearie, dearie me. And you fell for that one?'

'Vivienne, stop it, leave her alone.' Mum came into the kitchen and filled the kettle. 'Charlie appears to have been had over good and proper. I can't see it would have gone on for much longer, had his wife not got in there first.'

'You didn't suspect anything, did you, Mum? When you met him?' I pleaded, not wanting to be the only one who'd been taken in.

Mum shook her head and I smiled gratefully at her. 'No, Dad and I both thought he was charming. We had absolutely no reason to think he was married with – how many kids is it, Charlie?' When I couldn't reply, Mum went on, 'If you want acting ability, Vivienne, there's your man.'

I put my head on the breakfast table. 'What am I going to do now?' I wailed into the crumbs left behind from Dad's toast and marmalade. They tasted sweet and buttery on my cheeks and lips as my tongue sought them out. 'My life is over at the age of twenty-eight. I don't have a job, a home or a man.'

Vivienne took my hand, pulling me up from the breakfast table and, aping Ethel Merman, began to sing lines from *Annie Get Your Gun*. Daisy, trailing dirt and wet in from the garden, where she'd obviously been doing something gardenerish, joined in singing right on cue with Dad and Vivienne while Malvolio, used to such bursting forth of song, slunk despondently towards his basket, tail between his legs, as the three of them went for it. I looked at the dog, at Mum, in a world of her own clearing the breakfast table, and at Vivienne, Dad and Daisy united in their love of drama and musicals, and wished I had a tail and basket of my own.

I knew I was home.

Over the next couple of hours, I must have called Dominic's mobile ten times, all to no avail. I sent as many emails, my tone ranging from jolly and friendly, so as not to frighten him into not replying, to pleading with him just to ring and talk to me, and then downright murderous where I left him in no doubt as to the state of his manly bits and pieces were he ever to cross my path in the future. And then, worried that I might be accused of stalking and sending threatening letters, reverted to jolly and friendly once more. At the end of the day I needed a reference from him. I couldn't envisage applying to top architectural and property development companies back in London for a job and, when asked to supply references from my present post, have to say sorry, can't do that, I was shagging the boss and his wife found out. Not overly professional. I wrote a final, grovelling email to Dominic saying that the least he could supply – if his tanned lithesome body was no longer on the menu – was a glowing reference as to my experience, capabilities and downright brilliance as a property developer.

And I *was* good. I knew I had an eye for finding the right property, haggling the price and then drawing up the plans for developments. Problem was that although *I* knew I was pretty good, and Dominic, having taken me on in the first place after seeing the projects I'd worked on previously, knew I was pretty good, I'd only done a couple of internships and temporary work before landing my dream job with Abraham Developments. Any prospective employer worth their salt would want to know what I'd been doing in the past eighteen months and why there was no one willing to back my application.

'Right, Charlie, come on, you can't stay up here all day hiding away.' Mum bustled in, her arms full of clean towels and spare loo rolls. 'Unpack these black bin bags, let's get the dirty things washed and the rest hung in your wardrobe and then I have a couple of jobs for you.'

I groaned inwardly. Hell, this was like being a teenager again when I used to hide in my room.

'Jobs?' I frowned up at Mum from the depths of my bed and laptop. 'I'm actually doing some work, Mum.'

She laughed. 'Yes, you used to say that when you were sixteen, too. Revising, doing homework: anything to get out of peeling the potatoes or hanging up your wet towels.'

I sighed. 'OK. What is it?'

'We need to sort Granddad.'

I stared at her. 'Which one? Aren't they both, you know, *dead*?'

Mum tutted. 'Of course they are, and Grandpa Maddison well and truly with his maker, I should hope, these past ten years, but Granddad Black is still in the utility.'

'The utility? What's he doing there? Has he come back to haunt us? He's been dead two years now, hasn't he?'

'I feel so guilty every time I look up at the top of the utility units, Charlie.' Mum pulled a face. 'He's up there with Gin and Tonic.'

I stared at her. 'You've put Granddad in the utility and you leave him a gin and tonic? What every night? Or on his birthday and Christmas? What?'

Mum tutted. 'Oh, you haven't met the kittens, have you? Well, not so much kittens now, actually. Brother and sister, and feral little things they are too. They spend most of the time out in the paddock but come into the utility at night. They go up on top of the units to get out of the way and to sleep, but my father's up there, too. I put him up there after the cremation. I didn't like to put him in the garage; it gets nippy out there in winter and full of fumes too. He was always a bit asthmatic.'

'Mum, you're not telling me Granddad's been roosting up on the top of the cupboards with two cats for the last two years?'

'Well, no, the cats have only been with us a few months: your dad rescued them from some farmyard in the summer. Anyway, I don't think the cats mind, darling,' Mum said seriously. 'In fact, I think they quite enjoy his company. Cats have this spiritual connection with the dead, don't they? Wasn't it the Egyptians who thought so? Anyway, my father, from what I knew of him, was a rather nice man. Quiet, but intelligent. I'm sure the cats haven't been spooked with him sharing their bedroom.'

She broke off as Daisy came into my room, red faced and glowing from two hours in the garden, 'Did *you* know Granddad was still up in the utility?' I asked.

'Still? Mum, you promised you'd do something with him when I was home at Easter.' She shivered. 'I really think it's weird he's still in the house. It probably means he's in purgatory, unable to go up or down, suspended in a world of Persil, Kitekat and muddy wellingtons.'

'Why have you never scattered him?' I asked Mum as she fiddled with tying curtains and smoothing my duvet cover.

'It's your Granny Nancy's fault really. You know what she's like.' Granny Nancy was Mum's mum, and she and Mum had, allegedly, never been close, my mum being brought up, for much of the time, by her own grandmother, Granny Madge. God, all these grandmothers and not one grandfather left – apart from Granddad Black, forever trapped in his box in the utility...

'Your granny Nancy and my father were divorced years ago when I was still a little girl – she'd have driven him into an even earlier grave if he'd continued to be married to her – and she denied all responsibility for his ashes. She told me, as his only next of kin, that I should do with him as I felt fit, and I really wanted to scatter his ashes where he'd always been happiest.'

'The golf course,' Daisy and I chorused in unison.

'Absolutely.'

'So, why haven't you?' I asked.

'Because your granddad's golf course committee have a policy of not allowing it. I asked, immediately after the funeral, and they said no way.'

'Oh, come on, Mum, who's to know?' Daisy frowned.

'How about the golfers whose way we obstruct just as they are about to get a hole in one?' she said tartly. 'You know what golfers are like about their precious greens. So, Charlie, that's job number one for you today. I want you to come with me to scatter Granddad's ashes. Take your mind off things.'

'I doubt it,' I muttered. 'Probably make me wish you were scattering me as well, seeing my life is over.'

'Oh, for God's sake,' Daisy frowned. 'It's just one adulterous bastard man. Get over it. Wash your hair, get your lippy on and get out there. And if you're as good as you say you are, you'll soon find another job. And this time don't bother with the man. Concentrate on the job.'

'Like you, you mean?' I said somewhat sourly, looking at the dirt under Daisy's fingernails and her glowing face.

'I've not been dumped on from a great height. I don't *need* to take my mind off things. I just love being outside.'

'Right, girls, while you're arguing about whose job is more fulfilling, Granddad is languishing another day with the cats.'

'And the other job?' I asked, heading, without any enthusiasm, for the bathroom and a shower.

'Great-granny Madge.' Mum said firmly. 'It's Saturday and I've not been to visit her for over a week. She'd love to see both you girls.'

So, instead of spending Saturday in bed with Dominic in London, licking croissant crumbs from his neck and chest before sliding myself onto him once more, I was scattering one grandparent on a golf course and then spending what remained of the afternoon in the old folks' home with another. Great stuff. I glanced out at the rain, at the dark clouds gathering on the northern hills, and made it all even worse by realising that, as far as I could remember, Dominic had never spent more than a handful of Saturdays at the flat with me in Bloomsbury anyway.

'We can't leave him here,' Mum frowned as Daisy instructed her to pull in at the gates of Midhope Golf Club. 'It's not allowed, I told you.'

'Mum, where did Granddad spend all his time?' Daisy reached for the box beside her on the back seat.

'Well, here…'

'Exactly. The golf course. We *have* to leave him here. Gosh, I never realised he'd be so heavy,' she added, pulling him onto her knee. 'Do you reckon big fat people's ashes are heavier than little slim ones?'

'Daisy, do you mind?' Mum was beginning to look a bit weepy. 'I've got to know my father a lot better these past couple of years than I ever did when he was alive.'

I glanced behind me at Daisy, who was cradling Granddad Black with some reverence. What was Mum going on about?

'I've spent quite some time with him in the utility,' she went on. 'We've discussed whether to come out of Europe – he'd have definitely voted to stay in – and what Zimbabwe should do about Mugabe. He wasn't very good at deciding what to have for supper, but...'

'Mum,' I said gently, taking her arm and indicating she should stop the engine. 'I know he wasn't a huge part of your life when you were growing up, but you obviously did get to know him a little better recently.' I turned once more to Daisy, who was trying not to laugh. 'Now, you want to leave him where he's been happy, don't you? He spent virtually every day here after he retired and moved back to Midhope. We're going to leave him here. Come on.'

Somewhat reluctantly, Mum followed Daisy and me as we skirted the perimeter wall with Granddad, looking for a way in. The rain was becoming more persistent. I pulled up the hood of Mum's plum-coloured quilted dog-walking coat I'd borrowed, seeing my own coat was still on the peg in the office. It made me look like the Queen: a headscarf and a couple of corgis and I'd be a dead ringer. I bet anything Milly Taylor, whose desk was next to mine, would filch my lovely sheepskin once she knew I wasn't coming back.

'Charlie? Charlie, are you listening?' Daisy pulled at the hood covering my head. 'We're going to have to go back to the car and drive him round to the far edge of the golf course. We can't just blatantly walk up the drive, and there's no other way in from this side.'

We retraced our steps back to the car, Granddad becoming decidedly soggy as the heavens opened.

'Maybe we should leave it for a better day,' Mum said. 'You know, wait until the sun comes out.'

'Mum, this isn't an outing to the seaside,' Daisy snapped. She was obviously getting thoroughly fed up and thrust Granddad towards me. The cardboard-taped box was beginning to lose its rigidity as it soaked up the rain; all we needed was for it to split and Granddad to be spilled unceremoniously onto the pavement amongst the crisp packets, fag ends and dog shit.

Five minutes later we were back where we started. Mum drove for ten minutes through the next few villages before taking a couple of right-hand turns down bumpy lanes and overgrown farm tracks, pulling up on the edge of a large coppice of trees that abutted the golf course.

'Perfect,' Daisy smiled. 'Come on.'

'You don't think he'll be a bit lonely out here all by himself?' I said doubtfully as we stood amongst the giant oaks and sycamores and I opened the box to reveal a plastic bag of grey lumpy ash. 'I'd be really scared out here by myself at night.'

'He'll miss the cats,' Mum added.

'There'll be foxes,' Daisy said somewhat impatiently. 'And squirrels and birds... Oh, and golfers.' She attempted nonchalance as three hearty-looking women in waterproofs suddenly appeared in front of us.

'Afternoon,' one trilled in our direction. 'Lovely day for it.'

'Does she mean for scattering granddads?' Daisy asked, giggling.

'I think she's being ironic,' I said sarcastically. 'OK, they've gone. Is the coast clear?'

I took a handful of the ashes, my black leather gloves turning white in the process, and looked around for a good place to scatter.

'Hang on,' Mum said suddenly, staying my hand. 'Shouldn't we sing something?'

'What?' Daisy asked. '"So long, farewell, auf Wiedersehen, goodbye?"'

Mum stared at her. 'He wasn't German.'

Daisy tutted. 'OK, Queen's "Another One Bites the Dust"?'

'"Going Underground"?' by The Jam,' I sang, giggling.

'Now I think you're both being disrespectful,' Mum tutted in turn.

'And you weren't, putting him on a shelf with feral cats?' Daisy said indignantly.

In the end, we sang four verses of 'Fight the Good Fight', scattering a handful of ashes on the downbeat at the end of each line. Never having done anything like it before, I was amazed at just how much there was; it seemed never ending, but we did manage to get quite a bit of him onto the actual green, which pleased Mum.

Once we'd finished it was mid-afternoon and growing dark and miserable in the way only a November day can. The day reflected my mood. I was shattered and beginning to feel depressed again as the reality of my situation hit me once more now that the excitement of sending Granddad to that great golf course in the sky was over. I wanted to go home.

'No, no,' Mum said firmly. 'Job number two, if you remember. We're off to see Great-granny Madge.'

4

Great-granny Madge, Mum's gran, was, at the last count, ninety-four and still going strong. She'd lived alone – apart from various moth-eaten cats and dogs – as long as I could remember in an untidy bungalow on the other side of Midhope, perhaps fifteen minutes or so from where we lived in the village of Westenbury. While the bungalow had always been in need of a good dust round, according to Granny Nancy – my Mum's mum and Madge's only daughter – the garden, where Granny Madge had spent much of her day, regardless of the weather, could have been a model for the lid of one of those chocolate boxes full of strawberry creams and sickly Turkish Delight. It was obvious from which gene pool Daisy had been handed her love of, and ability for, gardening.

To my shame, I'd not seen Madge since Granny Nancy and Mum had moved her from her bungalow into a care home, six months previously when it became obvious, after breaking her femur falling off a ladder as she pruned her wisteria, she was no longer capable of living alone.

'I'm not intending to stay here for ever, you know,' Granny Madge stated crossly as soon as the three of us trooped in and found her staring out of the window at the rain and gathering dark, an abandoned gardening book on her knee 'They're all so bloody *old* in here. Old codgers who sit watching TV all day or sleeping. I need to be getting back to my garden. There's jobs to be done.'

'Hello, Granny Madge,' Daisy said, sitting down beside her and giving her a kiss. 'I shouldn't worry too much about your garden – there's not a great deal to be done this time of year.'

'I thought you said there was loads...' I trailed off as Daisy glared at me.

'Would you like me to go over there next week and see what's needed?' Daisy asked. 'In fact, can't we take you home for the afternoon and you can show me?' It was Mum's turn to glare at Daisy.

'You can all stop glaring at each other,' Granny Madge said crossly. 'I'm not in my dotage yet even though you've put me in here. I'm fully aware that you,' she nodded towards Mum, who had the grace to look embarrassed, 'and especially Nancy, are wanting to sell the bungalow from under my feet. But you can't. You do know that. I'm perfectly capable, once this damned leg is up and running again, of returning home, and I fully intend to do so.'

'Look, Granny,' Mum said, placating, 'why don't we see what happens once you're all mended?'

'Kate,' Granny spoke in measured tones, 'I'm not a child so stop treating me like one.'

'I'm well aware you're not a child,' Mum said gently, 'but it's not safe, you going back to the bungalow by yourself. And you'd hate having someone to live in with you.'

'Hell, I certainly would. I've lived far too long by myself to consider flat sharing.'

Daisy and I both looked at each other and giggled. Granny Madge laughed too. 'God, you two girls, don't ever get to my age. It's bloody awful. And avoid hellholes like this. They're determined to call me *Poppet* or *Dearie* and feed me mush on a spoon. I'm dying for a decent steak and a good bottle of red. If you want to bring me anything, girls, a bottle of Merlot would be very much appreciated. And then there's the damned singalongs, for heaven's sake and the woman who comes to do our hair once a week. She ended up giving me a lacquered helmet; so ageing.' Granny Madge patted Daisy's knee and then looked hard at me. 'Not seen you for a while, Charlotte. Been busy in London?' Before I could reply, she went on, 'Some man, I suppose? Yes, I know what that's like. Nothing else matters when you're feeling so in love that you forget everyone else. Being in love makes one terribly selfish, of course, but better to have known that passion than not.' She looked at me intently as I sat, embarrassed, unable to speak, wanting to cry and, for some reason, tell her everything, but then she smiled and the moment passed.

'You've a couple more visitors, Madge.' The woman who'd opened the door to us earlier popped her head round the door. 'You *are* popular today, lovey.' The opening bars from some popular TV quiz show followed by a burst of canned laughter, plus what was presumably the lingering smell of the residents' lunch came into the room with her.

An attractive blonde woman, in her early forties, was walking towards us, ushering forwards a young girl who was much younger than either Daisy or me, but who was carrying a very tiny baby in her arms. Granny Madge frowned, peering over her spectacles as she appeared to work out whether she knew them. Mum didn't seem to know who they were but stood up smiling as the older woman stopped in front of Granny.

'Auntie Madge?'

Granny peered closely at the woman, scrutinising her features for clues as to who she might be.

'I'm sorry...?'

'It's Harriet,' the woman smiled a little nervously. 'Lydia's granddaughter.'

'My Lydia? My sister, Lydia?' Madge seemed puzzled.

'Oh,' Mum said. 'You're Keturah's daughter?' She turned to Madge. 'It's one of Keturah's daughters, Granny. You *know*. Gosh, Harriet, I've not seen you for years.' She paused. 'It must have been at Aunt Lydia's funeral, what, ten years ago?'

Daisy and I exchanged looks. Blimey, how many more grannies and aunties were there? They seemed to be coming out of the woodwork at an amazing rate. I was totally lost as to who they all were.

'Lydia's been dead twelve years now,' Harriet said, reaching for the bundle of baby from the younger woman as it began to make snuffling noises.

'My great-aunt Lydia was your Granny Madge's older sister,' Mum explained, pulling up a chair for Harriet and the baby. 'She was quite a bit older than you wasn't she, Granny?'

'Oh, yes, much older. There were five of us: Lydia was the eldest and I was the youngest. There was a good twelve years between us. By the time I was eight or nine, Lydia was newly married and living over towards Colnefirth.'

'I'm trying to work out how we're all related,' I said, smiling at the younger woman, who was looking as perplexed as I felt.

'Oh, sorry, how rude of me.' Harriet laughed. 'This is my daughter, Liberty… Libby.'

'So, you girls and Liberty must be eighth cousins loads of times removed then. Sorry, can't work it all out,' Mum smiled. 'I was never very good at maths.'

'We're vaguely related. Probably best if we leave it at that.' Liberty grinned at Daisy and Me. 'Oh, and this is Lysander.' She took the baby back from her mother and pointed him proudly in our direction.

'Lysander? Golly, that's a good strong noble name,' I said. 'What's that song we used to sing at school? *Some talk of Alexander, and some of Hercules; Of Hector and Lysander diddle um tum diddle iddle um…* Sorry, can't remember the rest.'

'"The British Grenadiers",' Granny Madge tutted crossly before launching loudly and tunefully into song: '*But of all the world's great heroes, there's none that can compare, With a tow, row, row, row, row, row, to the British Grenadier.*'

The old chap who, up until then, had been nodding peacefully in his armchair in the far corner of the residents' lounge, suddenly shot out of his chair, saluted Granny, shouted, 'Damn good soldiers. Bless 'em all,' and then, just as suddenly, sat back down and began to snore loudly.

'Silly old fool,' Granny Madge tutted again. 'I tell you, they're all mad in here. I need to get out before I become as crackers as they are. I'm sure it must be catching.'

Harriet smiled and cleared her throat. 'There's something we, well, Liberty really, wanted to ask you.'

'You know, Harriet, one of the last times I saw your granny Lydia was one Monday night at bingo. Can't abide the game myself, but Lydia went every week without fail. Her neighbour who usually drove her there was ill, so I said I'd drive her there and drop her off.'

'Are you still driving now?' Liberty asked, surprised.

'Of course,' Granny Madge said firmly. 'Why wouldn't I be? And this was twelve years ago when I was a mere youngster. Anyway, I didn't like to leave Lydia by herself, so I went in with her. "I can't get comfortable, Madge," she kept saying. "I can't concentrate on the numbers…" She was up and down in her seat like a lousy stocking. People behind were tutting at her, telling her to be quiet and sit down. "I'm going to have to go home, Madge," she said – she was almost in tears. "I think I've got something wrong with me: I can feel a huge lump." Well, as soon as the first game was over I took her down to the Ladies. "What is it, Madge?" she kept asking, obviously frightened. "Have I got a growth? Our Isaac died of a growth, you know." She had so many layers on: vest, petticoat, corset, blouse…

Anyway, I had a good root around her back and yes, there was something.'

'I didn't know Great-aunt Lydia died of some sort of growth,' Mum said sympathetically. 'Poor thing.'

'It was her bloody slipper,' Granny Madge hooted in great delight. 'She'd obviously sat on the chair to pull on her corset and her slipper had caught in it and when she pulled it up, her slipper doubled up and came too. We laughed until we cried – actually, I seem to remember Lydia wetting her pants; she was prone to that. I do miss her.'

'So, Auntie Madge, the thing is…' Harriet stopped again, flustered.

'It's about your house,' Liberty said, obviously embarrassed, but with a steely determination to say what she and Harriet had come for.

'My house?' Granny Madge sat still and looked intently at Liberty. She was a pretty girl with long blond hair and huge eyes and, despite having a tiny baby, immaculately dressed. I felt quite scruffy in my pink Timberlands and Mum's dog-walking jacket, my face devoid of any make-up. The last thing I'd wanted to do, once Mum had decreed the day ahead of us, was tart myself up. For whom? I'd asked myself bad-temperedly. Granddad's ashes and the mumbling inmates of some care home? 'What about my house?' Granny Madge was continuing to look calmly at Liberty and I could see she was beginning to struggle under her close scrutiny.

'I love it… *we* love it,' Liberty said somewhat breathlessly. 'We're really hoping you might consider selling it to us.'

Granny Madge's bungalow? Daisy and I exchanged glances and then stared at Liberty and Harriet, who were both leaning forwards, waiting intently for Granny to speak. Why on would anyone fall in love with that horrible bungalow? OK, it was in a rather upmarket village and the garden was wonderful. Maybe that was Liberty's plan? To knock the bungalow down and develop the land?

'I'm sorry, Liberty, there's absolutely no way I'm giving up my bungalow and garden. I'm only here, in this place, temporarily. I shall be returning home in the next few months.' Madge smiled rather grandly. 'Once I'm in that great garden in the sky, then of course you're free to make an offer to my daughter, Nancy. I'm sure Nancy would be absolutely delighted to get rid of it without the bother of going through an estate agent.'

'Oh...' Liberty tried to interrupt but was browbeaten into silence by Granny patting her hand rather patronisingly.

'But, as I have absolutely *no intention* of giving St Peter any of my gardening tips for at least another ten years,' Madge went on. 'I'm afraid you're going to have to be patient or look elsewhere.'

'Oh no, Auntie Madge, it's not the *bungalow* Liberty and Seb have fallen in love with.' Harriet was shaking her head.

'Seb?'

'My partner, Lysander's father.' Liberty took over from her mother. 'It's not the *bungalow* we're *desperate* to have.' She spoke with the passion and excitement of a child eliciting her Christmas present list.

'The garden and land then, presumably?' I can see why you might want to knock down the bungalow.'

'No, really. I don't even know where your bungalow is. It's your *house* we love. You know, your *other* house.'

Granny Madge sat back in her chair, placing her hands neatly in her lap. She might have been over ninety but she was as alert and shrewd as she'd always been, contemplating the rest of us with an inscrutable gaze as we sat uncomfortably in front of her. At last, she said calmly and clearly, 'I'm sorry, Liberty. My house will *never* be for sale while I'm alive. And there's an end to it.'

'What house, Mum? What was Granny Madge talking about?' Daisy, Mum and I had spent another half-hour with Granny, making small talk over a cup of quite revolting weak tea and hard, dry scones, once Harriet and Liberty had left. Liberty had been near to tears but had shaken Granny Madge's hand politely as she stood. Granny had patted her hand once more, but seemingly been unable to give Liberty any hope that what she and Harriet had come to see her about could ever be resolved.

Mum frowned as she reversed her car into the dark of a wet, misty November afternoon, narrowly missing the back of a black Mini. 'Jesus, why do people have black cars in November? How the hell are you supposed to see them?'

'Presumably they're OK in December when it snows?' Daisy murmured idly. 'Come on, Mum, what house? Did Granny Madge mean the bungalow?'

'Darling, I really don't know what the three of them were talking about. They obviously know something we don't. My mum has hinted at something over the years, but then refused to divulge any more. You know what she's like. She'll offer so much and then keep you guessing. I always got the impression that there was some big family secret she was ashamed of.' Mum took her eyes from the road and turned to where I was sitting in the back. 'She didn't have it easy, you know.'

'Neither did you,' I protested. 'She almost abandoned you to Madge once she and your father divorced when you were little.'

Mum smiled at me through the driving mirror. 'Well, that's the way she was. She was single once my father had left and gone to Manchester. She needed to get out and about with people; she'd have loved to have married again really. My mum was a real party animal in the early seventies and there were always lots of different boyfriends.'

'I'm amazed she didn't remarry then if that's what she was after.'

'I'm not sure why Mum married my father in the first place – they really had very little in common – and then, according to Granny Madge, she was never overly impressed with the men from round here. I think she thought they were beneath her, so any chance she had, she'd be off to London; Paris even. My junior school was very near to Madge's bungalow so it was easier just to have my tea with her and then, if my mum was going out or was abroad with one of her men friends, it made more sense to sleep at the bungalow. I didn't feel I missed out; I loved being with Granny Madge – she taught me a lot.'

'Well, she's certainly a lot less scratchy than Granny Nancy, who really, let's face it, is a bit of a snob, isn't she?' I'd always found my mum's mum hard work. Whereas Madge would hug you to death and have you out in the garden, getting dirty, Granny Nancy was terrified you'd ladder her tights or smudge her nail varnish. Now in her mid-seventies, she still spent a lot of time away from Midhope, rarely getting in touch with either her mother – Granny Madge – or her daughter – my mum.

'So,' Daisy turned to me as Mum pulled into our drive, 'shall we hit the town tonight, you and me? It's ages since we've had a night out together?'

'We were out a couple of weeks ago when you flew into Gatwick.' The last thing I wanted was to get dressed up and pretend I was having a good time. Depression seemed to be descending once more with the lowering November teatime skies. What the hell was I going to do with the rest of my life?

'Well, yes, but you had Dominic in tow then.'

'And that's supposed to make me feel better?' I just wanted to go to my room and curl up and think of him and let the tears that had been about to fall all day have their head.

'Not at all,' Daisy said seriously. 'I just think lying on your bed all evening thinking of that...' Daisy lowered her voice '...that *wanker* ...'

'Oy, do you mind, Daisy Maddison?' Mum opened the car door. 'I can hear you.'

'You need to get out and forget him. I'm going to pop down to Clementine's and see if she has any temporary work for me – just until I decide what I'm going to do next – and then I thought we could have a drink at the Jolly Sailor?'

I groaned. 'Oh God, Daisy, that's the *last* thing I want to do...'

'Well, maybe the *first* thing you can do is peel some potatoes for supper?' Mum smiled encouragingly. 'We have to eat, you know.'

'Madge has just phoned, Kate.' Dad, watching some vet programme on the tiny TV set in the kitchen while sharing a packet of Hobnobs with Malvolio, shouted to Mum as she made to go into the downstairs loo to take off her coat.

Mum turned, surprised. 'We've only just come from there. What did she want?'

'Charlie, apparently.'

'Charlie?'

'Yep.' Dad was watching the TV screen with mounting incredulity.

'Charlie's just been with us.' Mum said. 'We've all just been to see her.'

'Oh, for God's sake, don't handle that bloody cow like that,' Dad shouted in disgust at the screen. He turned from the TV. 'I don't know, Kate. She just said she wanted to speak to Charlie and said to give her a ring when you got in.'

I frowned. 'She was all right when we left, wasn't she?'

'Give her a ring, darling,' Mum said, reaching for a bag of potatoes.

I walked back down the hall to the telephone, which had sat on the same polished walnut table ever since I could remember, and dialled the number Mum shouted from the kitchen. When I was eventually put through to Granny Madge, she said, almost immediately, 'Are you insured to drive your mother's car?'

'Yes, I think so. Why?'

'Well, darling, I'd like you to come and pick me up tomorrow, if you would, and then take me out for a little drive. Don't tell anyone where you're going, but I'd like to show you something. About ten thirty, after breakfast?'

Before I could answer she'd hung up, leaving me looking at the phone like some ham actor in one of Vivienne's amateur productions down at Westenbury village hall.

5

I'd loved Sunday mornings in London, with or without Dominic. Before I moved into the flat with him, I'd relished the luxury of being able to stay in bed with a good book and endless mugs of tea. Once I'd packed up my few things and moved from my flat in Bayswater to his place in Bloomsbury, it wasn't books that kept me awake on those – admittedly few – long, languorous, Sunday mornings, but Dominic and his magic hands and wonderful body.

But how the hell had he managed to spend even that many weekends of the summer just gone with me when he had a wife and kids waiting in the wings? Why hadn't his wife kicked off when he wasn't at home with her and the children? Oh, silly me. What do middle-class families *do* once the children have broken up from school? Of course, they decamp to their place in Cornwall, or Devon, or Norfolk or somewhere for eight weeks. But didn't the dads usually escape the dirt and stress of London and join their families for the weekends for a couple of days *en famille* before heading back to the grindstone – and their waiting illicit lovers – just forty-eight hours later? Dominic had spent a couple weekends away in the summer – on business, he'd said – but most week nights had been spent with me.

How did you manage it, Dominic?

Where was your wife all summer? Abersoch? Rock?

I emailed, before heading for the shower.

Twenty minutes later I'd washed the last of the London dirt out of my hair and was back in my bedroom, towelling it dry. I really couldn't be arsed to start blow-drying it, seeing as I was only taking Granny Madge out for a Sunday spin in the country.

Daisy was lying on my bed, my laptop on her knee.

'Oy, do you mind? Do you always read people's emails?' I snapped crossly, pulling the laptop from out of her reach.

'Only when they're corkers like this one,' Daisy retorted, eyebrows raised.

I grabbed the laptop, feverishly reading Dominic's reply:

Turkey, actually. My parents own a wonderful place in Kalkan. Now, would you please stop emailing my husband and get it into your thick head that he's been well and truly caught with his pants down. No more emails, or I'll have you for harassment.

Ah, so not from Dominic then.

'Let me reply to her,' Daisy was saying as I read it for a second time. 'I'm sure we can think of something suitably cutting. Something like: "Instead of sending threatening emails why don't you make sure you know where your husband is at night?"'

'Don't even think about it, Daisy,' I said, my voice wobbling slightly as I tried not to cry. 'I have some dignity, you know.'

'OK, OK. Well, let's do something to take your mind off it. I'm glad to see you've finally had a shower; we could go into Leeds for the afternoon. It is nearly Christmas and I bet you've not done any Christmas shopping yet?'

'Daisy, the last thing I want to do is Christmas shopping.'

'But I bet you *haven't* done any, have you?'

Only the beautiful gold cufflinks on which I'd spent an obscene amount of last month's salary and which were, even now, nestling in their little blue box wrapped in dark-red paper with green ribbon in the bottom drawer of my desk in the office. What a waste of my hard-earned cash.

'I'm already going out,' I said, taking a deep breath and rubbing my hair furiously while desperately trying to eradicate a seemingly indelible picture of Dominic and me exchanging Christmas presents under a huge Christmas tree from my mind. Was that a beautiful ring in the little box he'd just handed to me while kissing me…?

'Charlie…?'

'What?' I surfaced from the towel to find Daisy shaking one end of it at me.

'Oh my God, you have got it bad, haven't you? I said, "Where?"'

'Where what?'

Daisy sighed crossly, slapping the wet towel round my bare backside. 'Where are you *going*?'

I had to think for a split second. 'Out with Granny Madge. You know, she rang me yesterday as soon as we got in?'

'Where does she want you to take her?'

'I really don't know, Daisy. Probably to the bungalow to pick up a few things. Can't be anything to do with her garden – she'd have wanted you to take her for that, I suppose.'

'OK, well, if you're not coming to Leeds with me, then you can join me tomorrow night. I've booked us into an evening of delight and excitement.'

'Oh God, Daisy. What? What is it?'

Daisy screwed up her face and then started to laugh. 'Apparently the third Monday in the month is speed dating at the Jolly Sailor. Now, I'm not promising you an 'andsome admiral or even a sexy submariner – and what's better than some man who's professionally trained to go down…' Daisy began to laugh again as she saw the look on my face '… but I got us the last two places.'

'No, absolutely not. No way. No. *Non, nada.* On your bike.'

'I'll take it that's a "no" then?' Daisy grinned.

'Daisy, it's the sort of thing we'd have done in the sixth form. In fact, we *did* do it in the sixth form. I ended up with Bradley Beaumont.'

'*Bad Breath* Bradley?' Daisy hesitated for a second.

'The very same.'

'Really?' Daisy frowned. 'In that case, I can understand your slight misgivings.'

'Daisy, it's bad enough having to come back up north, tail between my legs, without having to speed-date spotty men smelling of cheese and onion crisps.'

'Oh, I'm sure he'll have moved on to eating something a little more sophisticated.'

'I really can't believe anybody still *does* speed dating anyway. That is *so* ten years ago.'

'Well, yes, but I bet Tinder hasn't got as far as Westenbury yet.' Daisy frowned. 'What am I going to do with this spare ticket now?'

'Vivienne will go with you. She'll get all dolled up and interrogate all the men as to whether they've seen any of the past episodes of *Emergency!* She'd love it: take *her* with you.'

'So where do you want to go, Granny Madge?' With the help of two of the home's care workers, who'd fussed over Madge as if she were as fragile as an egg, I manoeuvred her into the front seat of Mum's car.

'I'm fine,' she said crossly, waving her stick and shaking off the care workers with an impatient shrug of her shoulder. 'Good God, they do fuss. Anyone would think I was ninety.'

Granny Madge turned and grinned. She could be very naughty when she wanted. She was still an extremely handsome woman – I'd seen photos of her in her younger days, particularly in the 1950s when she resembled

Princess Grace of Monaco, silvery-blond hair swept up into a chignon, wearing Norman Hartnell ball gowns and draped in expensive furs.

'Right, darling, take the road to the bungalow if you would.' Madge patted my arm as we pulled out of the small car park, full, it seemed, with families on visiting duty. I wondered how many were actually being taken back home for Sunday lunch or out for a drive and resolved to ask Mum, once I returned, how often she went to pick up Madge.

'I'm sorry I've not been in touch, Granny,' I said, feeling horribly guilty. 'I should have come up to see you when you first broke your leg.'

'Oh, don't be ridiculous, Charlotte. That was six months ago and it's mending very well now. Look.' She stretched her right leg in its rather gaily-patterned (no elasticated-waisted beige polyester slacks for Madge) trouser. 'The plaster came off weeks ago and a *very* nice young man comes to manhandle me a couple of times a week. I'm not sure what he is – physio or osteopath – but he's *very* lovely.' Madge turned to look at me. 'He's probably your age. Haven't noticed any wedding ring.'

'Stop matchmaking, Granny,' I smiled at her. 'I've given up men for ever. But I really am sorry I didn't come and see you, you know.'

Madge gave a snort of derision. 'You're young, you were in London and in love. Why on earth would you be thinking of me? And that's not me being martyrish, you know, darling. The *last* thing I was thinking about when I was your age was my great-grandmother.' She paused and frowned. 'To be fair, I never even knew my great-grandmother. Popped her clogs long before I was born. And the one grandmother I did know was a fearsome old biddy. Came to live with us on the farm during the war and spent her last years having us all running after her. I was glad when I joined up and got away from it all. Right, here we are, darling.' Madge sat up in her seat as I pulled into the drive of her bungalow. 'Now, if you'll just come round…' she began to take off her seatbelt '… help me out of the car and into the house, and then when I've found what I'm looking for we can be off.'

I looked at her in surprise. 'Off? Off where? I thought this was it?'

'No, no. You'll see.' She frowned. 'This bloody leg, it's a bit stiff today.'

I jumped out and manoeuvred Madge out of the passenger seat, handed over her stick and, taking her arm, assisted her up to the front door of the bungalow.

'Poor old garden,' she sighed, obviously upset at its overgrown and unkempt appearance. 'I will get Daisy to give it the once-over.'

'She will, you know; she's very good. I'm sure she'd love to get stuck in. Gosh, I always forget how huge a garden you have. There must be a good couple of acres?'

'Almost three if you include the paddock,' Madge said proudly. 'And I miss it so much.' She took her front door key from the pocket of her camel trench coat. 'Right, you wait there. I know exactly where it is; I won't be a tick.' She set off, limping slightly, down the hall and disappeared into her bedroom.

The bungalow was icy and smelled musty and stale. I looked round. Someone, either Mum or Nancy, presumably, had obviously been round in Madge's absence and the sitting room was neat and tidy, the tapestry cushions standing to attention on the sofa and chairs, and when I wandered into the kitchen I saw that the work surfaces were clean and the parquet-floor polished. A weak sunshine had broken through the gloom of the last couple of days, refracting light through drops of water held static on abandoned spiders' webs. The juniper, directly in front of the kitchen window, glistened with myriad jewels.

'Come on, I've got it.' Madge reappeared at my side.

'Do you want a cup of tea or something while we're here? It seems a shame to go straight back, although it is absolutely freezing in here.' I shivered, banging my gloved hands together in order to get the circulation moving.

'No, no, we haven't time for that.' Madge was impatient. 'Anyway, the water and electricity will be off.'

My phone beeped an incoming message and my heart did the thumping thing it had become accustomed to doing ever since Friday. God, was it only two days ago?

Madge looked at me with some sympathy. 'Your young man?'

I scrabbled in my hoody pocket. 'No,' I managed to smile. 'Mum, telling me to bring you back to eat with us.'

'That's very kind of her. Your mother does do a lot for me.'

'But it's because she wants to, you know, not from any sense of duty.' I hated the idea that Madge thought we might be feeling sorry for her and that she might consider herself a burden.

'I know that, darling.' She smiled and picked up her gloves and stick. 'I'm not quite at the dribbling stage yet; I'm still able to feed myself. And I fully intend coming back here once the weather gets better.'

'I'm sure you do. I can't see any reason not to. OK, where next? Some shopping? Church? The garden centre?' I waited while Madge made the bungalow secure once more and then led the way down the path. It was slippery with wet November leaves and I was terrified she'd fall. She didn't speak, concentrating on planting her heeled and booted feet securely with each step until we reached the car.

She grinned at me as she fastened her seat belt. 'There. You see? Fit as a flea. Right, take the Midhope road and I'll direct you from there.'

As we drove through the town centre, thronged with what I assumed must be Christmas shoppers, Madge tutted. 'Look at this lot. What's the matter with them, shopping as though their life depended on it, and on a Sunday morning?'

I glanced at her. 'You'd rather they were in church?'

'Church? Certainly not. Why aren't they in *bed*, making *love*, instead of spending money on tat in an overheated shopping centre?'

I laughed, slightly embarrassed at my great-grandmother's referral to sex. 'Maybe those without children are. Once you have kids, I would think such luxuries as Sundays in bed go right out of the window.'

'Depends on who you're with, darling… Now, take the road out towards Heath Green.'

I indicated, taking the road out of town and we drove in silence, both obviously lost in thoughts of other, more amatory Sunday mornings, for another ten minutes or so, until Madge suddenly sat up in her seat, peering through the windscreen. 'Left here,' she barked.

I braked. 'Here? There is no turning here, Granny.' I peered through the windscreen at the dense stretch of overgrown hawthorns weaving thickly amidst lines of woodland allowed to run wild.

'Yes, there is. Here, here.' Madge grabbed her stick, indicating, with several taps on her window, where I should turn.

An unmade lane, thick with mud, fallen leaves and the dendritic limbs of untamed oak and beech lay to the left and I hesitated, worried that the car would get stuck.

'Down here?' I asked. 'Are you sure?'

'Definitely.' Madge raised her eyebrows. 'And presumably Harriet's daughter has been down here in the past few weeks? It'll be fine. Go on.' She was growing impatient and I could see tracks ahead where other vehicles had disturbed the vegetation. Cautiously, I drove down the lane, concentrating on keeping the little Corsa on track, but also aware of Madge sitting gripping the crook of her stick in total silence, at my side. She seemed to be rather agitated and I was beginning to wonder if I'd done the right thing, agreeing to this jaunt. Round a bend and then another, and there, in front of me, dozing in the very lee of the valley, was a long, low farmhouse, the glass of its windows long since gone, and what was left of its stone-tiled roof an obvious target for marauding scavengers.

'Blimey.' I pulled the Corsa over to a scrubby area of grassland and killed the engine. I turned to Madge. 'You're not going to tell me this is all yours? This is what Harriet and Liberty came to see you about yesterday?'

'All mine, Charlotte. Every little bit of it.' Madge stared out of her window at the ivy-clad walls of the house and, for a good minute, didn't say another word.

'I don't understand, Granny,' I said eventually. 'I mean, I *can* understand you not wanting to live down here now. It's miles from anywhere and far too big for one person to manage. But it looks as if it's not been lived in for years.'

'Sixty-five.'

'Sorry?'

'My house hasn't been lived in for sixty-five years.' Granny turned from staring out of the window and, instead, looked me full in the face. I was horrified to see tears in her eyes. One spilt down her lined cheek, making a furrow through her face powder, but she hurriedly wiped it away with her leather-gloved hand and smiled before attempting to open the car door.

'Hang on,' I said, unbuckling my seat belt. 'I'll come round and get you out. Do you *want* to get out?'

'I want *you* to see the place, Charlie. I've not been down here for years and years. I should have realised the state it would be in after all this time.'

The late morning had morphed into one of those totally unexpected November days where a weak sun breaks through the depressing mist and drizzle and, although the skeletal trees around the house were divested of virtually all their leaves as they awaited the real blasts of winter, one could almost imagine for a moment that spring had fought winter, trouncing it before it had managed to take hold its grip.

'I'm glad the sun's come out,' Madge smiled as she stood with her stick. 'Let me show you the view.'

'I've never been here before, have I?' I asked as I followed Madge down an overgrown path, a couple of raucous blackbirds cutting across the dark canopy of the huge beech trees ahead.

'No, absolutely not. Neither has your mother.'

I stopped, but Madge carried on, determined to get where she had planned to go, and I hurried after her. 'What? Mum doesn't know about this place either?'

'No. There was never any need to tell her,' Madge said, turning slightly to answer before stopping at the periphery of the garden. She raised her stick. 'There now, did you ever see anything like that?' Madge had come to a standstill, rather breathless as she leaned on a broken-down and rotting fence.

'Careful,' I warned. 'That doesn't look safe. Oh, my goodness...' I stared down at the valley of which the house was part. 'What a view. This house must have the best position in Midhope.' The land below, consisting of untold acres of farmland interspersed with woodland, bridle paths and footpaths stretching as far as the eye could see, was dotted every now and then with farmhouses from whose chimneys wreathes of smoke ascended lazily in the still air. A plethora of sheep, the black and white Friesian cows that symbolised much of the Yorkshire farming round here, and one field given over to rather splendid-looking horses were proof that this valley was working. I turned to look back at the garden. The autumn had been mild and the last of a spray of rusting yellow roses, totally gone wild and choked by avaricious brambles, was still visible.

'I think it probably does,' Madge smiled. 'I can't tell you the amount of people who have approached me over the years wanting to buy it from me. If Nancy had her way, it would have gone to developers years ago.'

'Oh, Granny Nancy knows about this place?'

Madge smiled. 'She lived here until she was about nine.'

'Right... but she never told Mum?'

'She had her reasons. Look, come on, let me show you the house.'

'I think it's too dangerous to go in, Granny.' The last thing I wanted was Madge slipping and falling. I felt for my mobile in my jacket pocket and gave thanks I'd remembered to charge it before I set off.

But Madge was already off, planting her stick firmly in the overgrown garden as she went, thrashing the long, wet grass, weeds and brambles in front of her as she headed for the house. The huge oak front door, although cracked and weather-beaten, had stood firm against decades of rain and wind and Madge stopped in front of it, leaning against the wall as she scrabbled in her coat pocket.

'Right, Charlie.' She handed me a huge key. 'Have a go with that.'

'Granny, I can't even see a keyhole.' There was no way the door would open after all this time.

'Here, here, let me,' Madge said impatiently. 'It's here, look.'

She took the key back from me and attempted to insert it into the black hole that must have once been the keyhole, almost collapsing against the door as she did so.

'Granny, stop it. You're going to fall. There's no way that's going to open. Look, you can see the door is swollen; the lock will have rusted up as well. If we walk round here, we can see through the windows. All the glass has gone.' I took her arm, thankful that she seemed to realise how reckless she was being in her eagerness to show me the interior, and we walked slowly round to the side of the house. The remains of a stone seat, although damp and covered in a green moss, looked fairly stable and Madge sat down for a couple of minutes to get her breath back.

'I'm fine, I'm fine,' she said crossly. 'Go and look through the kitchen window. Go on. I'm fine here.'

With the help of an ancient wisteria on which I was able to get a foothold, I levered myself up and, steadying myself on the thick stone mullion, peered in through the overgrown void that had once been the kitchen window. I was relieved we'd not been able to gain access through the front door as it was very obvious the ceilings were down, piles of dusty, cracked plaster lying in heaps along the stone-flagged kitchen floor. While heavy beams, black and broken, had collapsed and were hanging dejectedly towards the floor, a wooden creel was somewhat incongruously still hanging tenaciously to what remained of the crumbling plastered ceiling.

Poor old house. It must have been beautiful when Madge lived here. No wonder Libby and her partner wanted to get their hands on it. I pulled my head back out of the window and, missing my foothold on the wisteria, swore aloud as I scraped my wrist and fell to the ground.

6

I could get very little out of Madge on the journey back into Westenbury village. She'd agreed to come back home with me and stay for lunch and, although she'd also agreed that I could tell Mum and Daisy about the house and told me she was in fact seriously thinking of letting Harriet's daughter buy it from her if Liberty was still interested, she seemed reticent to explain further as to why she'd abandoned the house and kept it such a secret all these years.

'You've got another house, Granny?' Mum, in the middle of beating batter for Yorkshire puddings, stopped mid-beat. 'Where is it? Why've you never told us about it?'

Granny shrugged. 'Long, long story, Kate, which I didn't actually anticipate ever having to tell. It's such an age ago now, you see. I sort of assumed, once I passed on, Nancy would sell it and nobody would be any the wiser. She'd pocket her inheritance, probably spend it all on cruises and handbags, and that would be that.'

'My mum knows about it?' Mum asked, wiping her hands on her pinny. 'Lay the table, Daisy, would you?

Well, she's certainly never said anything to me. What is it? A little cottage you lived in when you were first married?'

I laughed at that. 'Little cottage? Mum, just wait until you see it. It's the most beautiful house – pretty derelict now – in probably the best position in all of Midhope. Honestly, Granny, it'll be worth a small fortune now.'

'Well, that's what Nancy's been banking on. She's been badgering me to let her sell it for years.'

'And why haven't you let her?' Daisy, in the process of laying the dining-room table for lunch stopped in the middle of rooting in a drawer for table mats and came back over to where Granny was holding court as we sat around the kitchen table.

'Oh, lots of reasons, Daisy darling, but the main one being I know Nancy wouldn't care who bought it and what they did with it, as long as she got the best price for it. I couldn't bear to think of the house being flattened and fifty houses being built there instead.'

'I don't think anyone could get permission to flatten it,' I said. 'The house must be listed?'

Madge laughed. 'Well it certainly wasn't when I lived there.'

'So, what's made you change your mind about selling it after all these years?' Mum came to sit with us at the table. 'Shall we have a sherry, girls?'

Daisy pulled a face. 'I'd rather have gin, Mum.'

'Me too,' Madge pulled a similar expression to Daisy. 'Sherry's for old ladies who smell of pee. Believe me, there are plenty of 'em in Almost Heaven.'

Daisy giggled. 'That place we went to yesterday? It's not called Almost Heaven?'

Mum laughed too as she poured the drinks. 'She's having you on, Daisy. It's called Almast Haven, presumably because it's on the outskirts of Almast village. Well, I'm having sherry and I bet Vivienne will have one too once she gets back from her rehearsal.'

Madge pulled another face. 'I forgot you had the diva staying with you.'

'Ssh,' Mum warned. 'She'll be back anytime. So, come on, Granny, why've you suddenly decided to let us in on this house secret?'

Madge sipped her gin. 'I suppose it's with Harriet and… what was the girl's name? Lottie…?'

'Liberty,' we all chorused.

'… Liberty coming to see me yesterday. The last thing I was expecting was a visit from Lydia's granddaughter and *her* daughter. Over the years – and there have been literally hundreds who've managed to work out that I own the place – I've simply turned down out of hand those who've come around wanting to buy Holly Close Farm.'

'You didn't say that's what the house was called, Granny,' I interrupted her. 'That is such a wonderful name for it; it totally encapsulates the whole feeling of the place.'

'Oh God, she's off,' Daisy sighed.

'So, was it a working farm, then?' Mum frowned as she finished her sherry and poured herself another large one. I grinned across at Daisy. At this rate, we'd be pouring Yorkshire pudding batter on our apple pie and Mum would be wondering why the crème-anglaise- tasting

Yorkshire puds hadn't risen. 'I knew *you* were brought up on a farm but I didn't realise you'd lived on one when my mum was a little girl. Granddad Arthur wasn't a farmer, was he?'

'Don't get any idea that *I* was brought up on a big farm, Kate. My dad worked for the Co-op as a tenant farmer and milkman, and the Co-op moved him – and us – from farm to farm in the area whenever a new manager was needed. We kids all went into the mill as soon as we left school at fourteen: Goodners and Sons' Mills on the outskirts of Midhope. Holly Close Farm was a smallholding – your grandfather Arthur had always wanted to raise poultry; he certainly didn't want to go back into the mill when the war was over – and with some help from his mother who'd saved up every bit of money he'd sent back to her from his army pay, we managed to buy it straight after the war.'

'But you left? Wasn't it successful?' I was sure Madge had said no one had lived at Holly Close Farm for over sixty years.

'My husband – your great-grandfather – wasn't the most talented of men when it came to business…' Madge hesitated. 'Nancy and I left in 1953.'

'Not with Granddad Arthur then?' Daisy glanced across at me. Had Madge left him? This must have been a bit of a scandal just after the war. As far as I knew from my scant knowledge of social history, divorce, particularly away from London in some northern backwater, wasn't ever the done thing.

'Arthur died in 1953. Much as I adored the house, it…' Madge hesitated again, '… it just wasn't… *appropriate* for

Nancy and me to carry on living there. What did *I* know about turkeys?' Madge, who was generally exceptionally self-assured, appeared to flounder as she spoke and she reached for her gin, her arthritic fingers grasping tightly around the glass.

'Appropriate?' Mum frowned. 'What do you mean *appropriate*? I assume, seeing the house still belongs to you, that you didn't have to sell up when Granddad Arthur died?'

'No, I didn't need to sell it. I didn't *want* to sell it. Arthur had left us reasonably well provided for and I think, at the time, I probably thought I might go back there one day.'

'He must have been very young to die,' I said gently. 'What was it? Some sort of accident?'

Madge didn't say anything but twisted the plain band of gold on her right hand. Her ring finger on her left hand was, I noticed, ringless. 'If I'm going to give Holly Close Farm up, Charlie – and it really is silly, I should have done so years ago, I suppose – then the whole story will come out.'

'Whole story?' Mum, Daisy and I all leaned forward to catch what Madge was saying.

'Not now, not now,' Madge whispered as the kitchen door banged open and Dad and Vivienne came in.

'Ah, sherry, marvellous,' Vivienne said, rubbing her hands theatrically. 'Madge, dear, how *are* you? You look wonderful. How's the leg?' She poured herself a generous sherry, took a large sip and stood back, giving Madge a long appraising glance. 'Now, Madge, I have a *darling* little crepe-de-Chine scarf, in a shade somewhere between amethyst and lavender, that would go *marvellously* with that jumper of yours. I shall search it out for you after luncheon.' Vivienne paused for breath only to imbibe more sherry and then launched once more. 'My God, I need something to drink after that rehearsal. The director is a *total* amateur.'

'Yes, Vivienne,' Mum tutted, 'John Wright's the butcher in the village.'

'Yes, well,' Vivienne sniffed. 'Let's hope he handles his steak and kidney rather more professionally than he handles his cast of players. And as for the woman who is trying to be the young Honourable Gwendolen Fairfax – well, she must be fifty if she's a day, and with a huge bust Mae West would have envied. And that accent.' Vivienne shuddered. '*Oh! Ah 'ope Am not that, luv.*' Vivienne affected a broad Yorkshire accent. '*It'd leave no room for t' developments, and Ah intend to develop in many directions...* And then she thrusts that great bosom of hers in the direction of the family butcher. I think she's after more than his half-pound of shin beef. Must be something going on between them or he'd have brought in her understudy weeks ago: can't act her way out of a paper bag.' Vivienne laughed and downed her sherry. 'Just got a couple of emails to write, Kate. Shout me when luncheon is ready. Smells marvellous, darling.'

'Where's everybody gone now?' Mum, red-faced both from the sherry and unsuccessfully juggling the oven space for roast potatoes, Yorkshire puddings and the beef she'd forgotten to actually put in until an hour previously, was stressed. Cooking wasn't her strong point and I knew she'd be itching to get back up into the attic, which she'd converted into her studio. Mum was a brilliant potter and, with one of the attics done out years ago – the floor reinforced to take her wheel and clay – she spent as much time as she possibly could away from domestic duties, creating the most wonderful plates and pots for which she was beginning to make a name for herself.

'Sprouts, Mum! I'll get them.' I dashed over to the hob where a sulphurous smell of overcooked veg was beginning to emanate from one of the pans. 'These are done now. Well, overdone, really.' I eyed the watery green liquid in which myriad sprout leaves were floating and boiling. 'What do you want me to do with them?' My ability in the kitchen was worse than Mum's and I gave the contents an exploratory poke with a knife. At least Mum had had thirty years of marriage to hone her culinary skills whereas, living alone, I'd been happy with a baked potato and a tub of cottage cheese. Once I'd moved in with Dominic I'd made an effort, watching *MasterChef* and devouring the Saturday *Guardian*'s cooking supplement, but Dominic had laughed, thrown my inedible pastry to the poor birds – I suspect there were a lot of grounded starlings in Bloomsbury – and taken me out for dinner.

'Oh, God knows,' Mum sighed. 'How anyone can enjoy sprouts is beyond me, but I suppose they're good for you.'

'I think you've boiled any nutritional value out of them.' I held up the pan.

'Look, stick the little green bastards in that tureen on the side. We can microwave them back to life a bit when we're ready to eat.' Mum put down her oven gloves. 'How are you feeling now, Charlie? Pretty fed up?'

'Hmm. Not wonderful. I just keep thinking of Dominic and his wife and three kids all sitting down to Sunday lunch. You know, one big happy family.'

'I doubt very much either Dominic or his wife will be feeling on top of the world, you know. I'm sure he'll be missing you, and his wife most certainly won't be giving him an easy time of it.'

'Suppose. So, what happened to Granny Madge's husband, Arthur? He must have died pretty young for Madge to have brought up Granny Nancy all by herself.'

'Whenever I asked my mum what her father had died of – I know she was only about nine when he died – she said I was too young to understand and that she'd tell me when I was older. I've always thought he must have taken his own life, you know, Charlie, and in the early fifties, of course, it was a crime. If you survived a suicide attempt you were prosecuted and probably ended up with a prison sentence, and if you did succeed in ending it all, you couldn't be buried in consecrated ground. There's no grave anywhere, as far as I know. Granny Madge has been just as unforthcoming over the years.'

'Mum, what's this supposed to be?' I dipped my finger into a jug of yellow lumpy gunge and licked.

'What do you think it is? It's custard.'

'It's full of cornflour lumps and it's salty. You've added salt instead of sugar.'

'Bugger. Stick some of your dad's toffees in and we can call it salted caramel sauce. No, better still, chuck it and open a tin of Ambrosia. Where is everyone? We're going to eat soon.'

'Dad was called out to a cow in labour, Daisy's doing something with your geraniums, Vivienne is answering her fan mail and Granny Madge has gone for a lie-down in the sitting room.'

'Well, can you round them all up and tell them food is just about ready? I want to finish off a ceramic I'm working on before the light goes.'

'It really is so much colder up here than in the south,' Vivienne was saying as she helped herself to cremated roast parsnips. 'It's such a shame Graham decided that farm animals were his forte...' Vivienne raised her manicured fingers to air quote the word '... after he'd graduated from vet school and thus ended up in the north.'

'Just be thankful he didn't make *penguins* his forte...' Mum, fed up after a morning spent in the heat of the kitchen, used her knife and fork in order to raise her own – extended – quotation marks, sending, in the process, a shower of still semi-frozen peas from her plate '... or you'd be having luncheon with the Inuits. Anyway, he followed *me* north after university rather than a herd of Friesians, Vivienne.' Mum was beginning to lose her rag.

'Ah, here's the intrepid vet now.' Vivienne made it sound as if Dad had been exploring the Amazon instead of some poor cow's nether regions. 'Come on, darling, your food's in the oven. Were you successful? Have you brought forth new life once more?'

Dad grinned as he took his plate from the oven. 'God, that's hot. Well, it wasn't exactly me doing the pushing.'

'No, darling, but I'm sure you were doing the pulling.' Vivienne patted his hand before attempting– and failing – to pour the now congealed gravy over his somewhat fossilised- looking lunch.

Mum threw her a dessert spoon. 'Try *spooning* it out, Vivienne.'

'Dad, you stink.' Daisy pulled her chair away from Dad's.

'I was just saying, Graham, how cold it is up here in Yorkshire,' Vivienne trilled.

Granny Madge, who'd said very little so far over lunch, arched an eyebrow in my direction and I grinned back at her.

'I really do think, once *Earnest* has been put to bed, I might explore warmer climes.'

'Costa Rica,' Mum said dreamily. 'I've always fancied Costa Rica.'

'Oh, I don't think so, Kate,' Vivienne smiled somewhat patronisingly. '*Spain* in winter won't be overly warm and the Costas will be full of retired couples in shell suits, drinking their duty free and indulging in swinging parties.'

'Sounds like my kind of fun,' Granny Madge said drily, and Daisy and I giggled.

'No,' Vivienne went on, 'I think Spain is out of the equation. Now, if Santa comes prematurely...'

She looked hopefully at Dad as Daisy muttered, 'Raphael's problem, too, when he'd had a drink.'

'... then maybe he'll bring me a little surprise voucher for a Thomson's holiday and I could pop down to the travel agents in town and book something for late January after the performance. Be out of your hair...?'

'Get your cheque book out, Graham,' Mum muttered grimly. 'Right now.'

'So, Vivienne,' Daisy said, after chewing with some difficulty, and swallowing the tough beef, 'I've a spare ticket for speed dating at the Jolly Sailor tomorrow evening. Apparently, it's a charity do – raising money for Help the Aged, I think. Charlie won't come with me. Are you up for it?'

Vivienne laughed theatrically. 'Me, darling? I do hope you're not implying I'm *Aged* myself?' Vivienne laughed again at the very idea that anyone might think she was old.

'Not at all.' Daisy said smoothly. 'You're the very vision of youth and loveliness, Vivienne. And, yes, I'm sure there'll be someone your age.'

'Oh, I doubt that anyone would be interested in a fading ex-TV star.' Vivienne pouted with the hidden implication that the whole of Westenbury, if not Midhope itself, would, in reality, be ready to sweep her off on a date.

'Too right,' Mum sniffed. 'Charlie'll go with you, Daisy.'

'No, I won't.' Perish the thought.

'Yes, you will. That's all settled. My house, my rules.' Mum's tone softened as she said, 'You have to get out there, Charlie. Show the world you don't care you've been dumped.'

I felt my throat constrict and had to concentrate on the food on my plate before I could speak. 'But I'll be off back to London by the end of the week.'

'Charlotte, that's what I want to talk to you about.' Granny Madge, suddenly alert, put down her knife and fork neatly on her plate and took hold of my hand across the untouched sprout dish. 'I'm hoping you won't go back to London. Before I get in touch with Harriet and her daughter and negotiate a price, I'd like to be able to tell them that I will sell, but on the proviso that you will be the project manager. I believe that's the term used these days? And that you will draw up plans and work with them on Holly Close Farm.' Madge never once took her eyes off my face as she spoke.

'Granny, I don't think you can do that,' I said gently. 'You, as a seller, can't stipulate who a prospective purchaser must use to develop the property.'

'Oh, I think I can,' Madge said stoutly. 'If they want the house badly enough – and to be honest I'm not sure they'll have the money, I mean Liberty is just a slip of a girl – then I will suggest that having you to oversee it all would be part of the deal.'

'I think you're living in a bit of a fairy tale here, Granny,' I smiled.

'No, I'm not. I actually would really like Lydia's great-granddaughter to have my house. That's why I changed my mind about selling: it's keeping it all in the family. I'd hate the idea of Holly Close Farm going to strangers. So, Charlie, what do you think?'

7

'Let's do it, Charlie. Let's do it together.' Daisy was beside herself with excitement. 'You and me together. We'd make a great team.'

'I can't *ever* remember you and me being a great team.' I pulled a face. 'We could never agree on *anything*: whose turn it was to sit in the front seat of the car with Mum, who was going to hoover and who was going to dust, which one of us was washing up or drying.'

'You're going back over twenty years, for heaven's sake,' Daisy laughed, lifting the kettle and pouring boiling water onto instant coffee.

'Well, that's where we disagree to begin with,' I said, pointing a spoon at her mug. 'How can you drink that instant crap when there's such fabulous proper coffee to be drunk?'

'Oh, that's Dominic talking. You *loved* a mug of Nescafé until you met that pretentious wanker.'

'And who refused to unload the dishwasher after lunch yesterday? Said it wasn't their turn, *they'd* done it after breakfast?'

'Well it *wasn't* my turn. You'd done nothing but fanny around taking Granny Madge to visit her old house while

I'd spent all morning working my backside off in the garden. Those two have absolutely no idea about how to put a garden to bed for the winter.'

'But you've not even *seen* the house yet, Daisy. I know Granny's got this mad idea that she'll only let Libby and her partner have the house if they'll agree to me project managing the renovations and you sorting the garden, but the plot is huge – there must be eight or ten acres at least – and as far as I saw yesterday a good part of it used to be given over to being a smallholding. There's broken-down sheds that will need clearing. It's a huge job.'

'Why is it that you think yourself capable of planning the renovations of the house and yet you don't think I'd be up to sorting the garden?' Daisy was getting cross. 'Just because your architectural degree took you seven years and you're a "professional" doesn't mean you can belittle my work as a landscape gardener.'

'I'm sorry, Daisy, I know you're really good at what you do. But what experience have you had? You've spent the last few years either travelling, doing a ski season, pulling pints or walking up and down the aisle of a cabin flogging duty free and handing out sick bags?'

'You really can be sodding supercilious when you want to be, can't you, Charlie?' Daisy attempted to scrape burned bits from her toast into the kitchen bin, scattering flecks of black onto the surfaces and floor.

'Look, I'm not planning staying up here much longer than a week,' I said. 'Pass me that coffee jar, would you – I do drink this stuff when I have to. I don't want to be back in Midhope, I want to be back in London. Dominic might—'

'Dominic might *what*?' Daisy raised an eyebrow. 'Dominic might tell you he's left his wife and kids and he's coming back to live with you? In what? A bedsit? He won't have his wife's flat in which to carry on his extra-marital affairs any longer.' She looked at me in disgust. 'Get real, Charlie, for heaven's sake. Have a bit of pride.'

'I *was* going to say Dominic might give me my job back. Once all the furore has died down.'

'No, he won't, you daft bint. You said his wife and her father are the major shareholders of Abraham Developments.'

'She could have been lying.' I was grasping at straws, wishing I'd not told Mum and Daisy what his wife had almost laughed into my face. 'You know, just saying that so I wouldn't turn up for work again.' I trailed off as Daisy tutted, sat down at her laptop at the kitchen table, where she'd been working earlier, and tapped away in silence before folding her arms and concentrating on the screen in front of her.

'OK? Will that do you?' Daisy turned her laptop towards me.

Companies House

Abraham Developments:
Primary business: Architectural and Property
Development
Company directors: Michael Pennington, Arabella
Pennington-Abraham, Dominic Abraham

'Well, at least I know her name now,' I snapped. 'She *had* to be Arabella Double-Barrelled, didn't she? Not simple Vera Higginbotham or... or Hilda Smith... or...' I tailed off, defeated.

'Annette Curtain?' Daisy ventured. 'Carrie Oakey?'

'Heidi Clare?'

'Barbara Seville?'

We both started giggling. 'Do you know,' I chortled, 'there was actually a girl on my course called Fonda Dicks?'

'No. Oh my goodness, the poor thing.' Daisy stopped laughing, horrified, and then we both started again. I'd forgotten how much Daisy and I used to giggle. It used to drive Dad mad, especially if we were in the back seat of his car and he was driving. 'There, you see,' Daisy said comfortably. 'Stick with me, kiddo, and we'll have a great time. Come on, at least show me Granny Madge's house. I'm dying to see it.'

An hour later, Daisy and I were following the same wooded path Madge had taken me down the previous morning. It had taken me a while to find the overgrown opening and we'd driven backwards and forwards across the same bit of road until I spotted the virtually concealed entrance to the lane.

'Down here?' Daisy asked dubiously. 'Are you sure?'

'I told you it was secluded,' I said. 'Tell you what, close your eyes until we drive round the bend and first see the house. Go on,' I urged, 'close them.' I suddenly felt ridiculously proud of the place and wanted Daisy to be as transfixed as I'd been the day before...

'No way.' Daisy opened her eyes and stared as I braked and pulled into the side of the lane in order to see Holly Close Farm from its best vantage point. 'And this is all Granny Madge's?'

'Apparently.'

'But why hasn't Madge ever said anything? Even to Mum?'

I shrugged. 'Granny Nancy lived here as a little girl and Madge and Nancy left when Great-grandpa Arthur died in 1953, I think Mum said.'

'And it's just been left like this for...' Daisy did her maths '... sixty-five years? That's ridiculous. Madge could have sold it years ago and done up her bungalow and gone on cruises and things.'

'That's the point. Madge's never wanted to go on big holidays or have lots of material things, but she knew Granny Nancy, if she ever got her hands on the place, would flog it all for development and buy as many designer clothes as she could fit in her wardrobe. You know what's she's like.'

I started the car once more and we drove down the lane, pulling up in the same place Madge and I had parked the day before. It was sunny but frosty and Daisy and I put on hats, scarves and gloves before taking the plunge from the warmth of the heated car seats into the cold morning air. 'It is *definitely* colder up here in the Frozen North,' I grumbled, wishing I'd put on my Uggs rather than my work boots.

'Yes, but could you *ever* get a glorious view like this in London?' Daisy had almost run over to the remaining bits of the rotten wooden fence that separated the actual garden from the land belonging to Holly Close Farm in the valley below. 'Oh my God, Charlie. I never, for one minute, imagined this. And you are even *considering* missing the opportunity to do up this place to go back to... what? A tiny shared flat with people who'll nick your milk from the fridge and leave dripping pants in the bathroom? Sending countless CV and application forms off to property development companies to try and get yourself back on the ladder?'

I didn't say anything but as Daisy set off down the gardens and paddocks, stopping occasionally to examine the remains of various plants or stroke the trunks of trees and the black, spiny hawthorn and already bare branches of blackthorn, I retraced the path I'd taken the previous day, climbing still fairly solid, but rusting, drainpipes in order to peer in through the gaping black mouths of windows, their glass long since a victim to vandals and weather.

Could I do this? Could I move back home, live with Mum, Dad, Daisy and the dog, not to mention Vivienne, who seemed to have her feet neatly under the table for the duration? Was I up to such a mammoth project as this? I'd be my own boss, not able to run for advice to Dominic, who might be an out-and-out philandering bastard but, I would be the first to concede, was a brilliant architect and developer? I stroked the creamily mellow stonework of the house in much the same way Daisy was touching the various leaves and winter-flowering shrubs in her path and felt a stirring of excitement. Daisy was right. I'd lived in London, loved the fast pace of living, the bars, the clubs, the big red buses – *there are big red buses here in Midhope, you daft thing* – but what would I be going back to? Dominic and my work had been the total focus of my life down there. I couldn't have Dominic back, it seemed, but I would still have my work if I moved back north. And what work! Once I was back on my feet, I wouldn't actually need to live at home. Renting a place here had to be *much* cheaper than London. I might even be able to buy somewhere – get myself on the property ladder. Temporarily, of course. Just for the time it would take to do up Holly Close Farm. I couldn't envisage my moving back here permanently.

'Charlie. Charl-ee.' Daisy, shouting and waving her hands, brought me back to the present. I jumped down from the drainpipe and it shook ominously, sending a shower of rusting paint to the flagstones below. Hmm, not so solid, then. I took a couple of steps back, looking skywards to where the drainpipe was clinging precariously to the wall, noted the dangerously listing chimney pot and realised the whole place was probably a death-trap. First thing I'd need was my hard hat. 'Charlie, come and look at *this*.' Daisy was almost jumping up and down in her excitement.

'Be careful what you're *doing*, Daisy. We really shouldn't be here without protective work gear.' I looked down at my steel-capped work boots, grateful now that I'd donned them almost automatically, as I did virtually every morning in London, before setting off. 'What have you found?'

'Come on, down here.' Daisy led the way down another overgrown path until the roof of another building hove into view. The stone tiles were long since gone, leaving a skeleton roof, its bones blackened timbers that, although laid bare to the elements, looked solid enough.

'What is it? A shed of some sort?' I climbed down through the overgrown bushes and trees and joined Daisy, who was almost jumping up and down in her excitement.

'A cottage,' Daisy said, eyes saucers. 'The most beautiful romantic cottage, sitting bang in the middle of the view.'

'The *remains* of a cottage,' I frowned. 'I wonder who it belongs to. My God, you're right. What a position. I wonder why no one has ever developed it?'

'I would think because it's part of the estate.'

'Really?' I said doubtfully. 'Madge never mentioned it yesterday. She didn't even bring me down here.'

'It's well within the boundary of Madge's land. Look, you can see where the perimeter fence is – well, what's left of it. And look,' Daisy went on, excitedly, 'it has its own garden. A real cottage garden.' She bent down, crushing something between her gloved fingers and sniffing. 'Lavender.' She bent again. 'Sage and thyme. See? Totally run wild now but I bet this was a beautiful place years ago. It's even more south-facing than the main house.'

The cottage was built of the same mellow stone as the farmhouse, but considerably smaller. 'Give me a leg up, Daisy,' I said, Daisy's excitement becoming infectious. 'I want to see inside.' She bent down, made a sling with her hands and I hauled myself up to look through the first of the three downstairs windows.

'Bloody hell, Charlie, you weigh a ton. I can't hold you up much longer. What is there? Come on, you're breaking my back.' Daisy's muffled voice came from below me. She suddenly collapsed and we both tumbled to the ground. 'Weight Watchers for you,' she said crossly as we brushed ourselves off.

'It's just perfect,' I gasped. 'There's room for a huge kitchen… and I'd put French windows from it, right out into this herb garden.' I ran round the side of the cottage, stumbling through dead undergrowth and ancient thorny rose bushes. 'And look,' I shouted back over my shoulder to Daisy, who was still on the ground rubbing the small of her back, 'look, it's really quite deep: plenty of room for a sitting room, study and snug.' I was already mentally drawing up plans for its renovation.

'There's someone here.' Daisy, now upright and attempting to walk through the overgrown bracken and bushes that had greedily consumed what had once been the cottage garden, stopped and shaded her eyes against the low winter sunlight towards the lane we'd just come down. 'In a car.' I jumped down from the rotting window ledge and made my way back to her.

'I think it's the girl that wants the house,' Daisy said. 'What was she called, you know, the girl that was at Almost Heaven on Saturday?'

'Almast Haven,' I giggled. 'Yes, it is. Liberty.'

The girl, wrapped up against the cold in a long blond shearling coat that matched her hair, and a man walked towards us. 'We saw your car...' she smiled as soon as we were in hailing distance. She trailed off, seemingly not knowing what to say next. 'This is Seb, my partner,' she finally said, almost shyly. 'Lysander's father.' I glanced over at Daisy, knowing exactly what she was thinking. There was only one word for Seb: devastating, and I could feel Daisy almost wilting under his gaze. He was, I guessed, probably in his late twenties – but Libby was younger.

From beneath his flat cap, dark, almost black, hair curled into his huge brown eyes. He grinned, a perfect white-toothed grin and held out his hand. 'This is so fortuitous that you two are actually here,' he said.

'Is it? Why?' I frowned and glanced towards Daisy once more, who seemed to have been struck dumb in the presence of such beauty. I glared at her, wanting some back-up, but she seemed unable to stop staring at him.

'Mrs Booth – your granny Madge – rang Harriet last night.'

'Oh?'

'Yes.'

'I'm amazed Madge knew how to contact her,' I said crossly. Why the hell was I feeling so cross? Daisy finally glanced my way, her trance-like state broken by my tone of voice.

'Mum left her phone number with Mrs Booth,' Liberty said, slightly pink in the face, whether from the cold or embarrassment I wasn't sure. 'I know your granny Madge said there was absolutely no way the house would be for sale while she was still alive, but Mum didn't want to lose touch with her again after all these years.'

'As well as you hoping she might change her mind about Holly Close Farm?' I almost snapped. I knew I was being abrupt, and Daisy frowned in my direction.

'As we're led to believe she now *has*,' Seb said, smiling winningly at us both. Daisy crumbled under his warm smile.

'With one proviso,' I retorted. 'I'm sure she explained to your mum,' I nodded towards Libby, who was almost holding her breath as she looked hopefully at Daisy and me, 'that she would only allow Holly Close Farm to be sold and developed if the architectural plans and the project management of the house were left to me?'

'Absolutely,' Seb said firmly. 'I have no experience whatsoever of drawing up plans, and I'm so busy with work that I certainly don't have the time to take it over. Libby is due to start back at Med School in Leeds next September so she'll have plenty on her plate as well. We would need someone to do it all for us, and what better than keeping it in the family?'

'Where's little Lysander?' Daisy asked, in a daft cooing voice. 'He was *gorgeous*. I could have adopted him on the spot and taken him home with me when I saw him on Saturday.'

Gorgeous? I glared at Daisy once more. Since when had Daisy started liking *babies*, for heaven's sake? She'd called them horrible rug rats up until now, and yet, here she was, making out she was the Angelina Jolie of the North.

'We've left him with Seb's mother,' Libby smiled. 'She's always desperate to get her hands on him.'

'I'm not surprised,' Daisy gushed.

'So, Charlotte – Charlie, isn't it?' Seb turned his charm on me – 'what do you think? We're totally in your hands. Without you, we can do nothing.'

'I'm sure, now that she's seen all of this, Charlie will be dying to get her hands on it.' Daisy glared at me.

'Look, I don't mean to be rude, but you're both so... *young*. Once this place, along with the cottage down here...' I indicated, with a slight nod of my head, the newly discovered wreck of the cottage behind us '... is valued, I would have thought you'd need to be a lottery winner to take on a project like this. I've valued a lot of places, and with all of this, you're not going to have much change out of a million. Add another hefty sum for all the renovations.'

'Charlie, I don't wish to appear rude either.' Seb continued to smile, but I could tell he was embarrassed, if not a little cross with my bringing up his finances, or what I perceived to be a lack of them. 'All I will say is that whatever Mrs Booth wants for the place, we'll be in a position to pay it. My father is behind us with the whole project.'

'Who's your father?' I raised an eyebrow. 'Santa Claus?'

'David Henderson,' Seb said calmly. 'I'm sure, with you living in Westenbury, you'll know of him.' It was a statement rather than a question.

Daisy whistled. 'David Henderson? *The* David Henderson? The Richard Branson of the North?' Daisy whistled again.

'The very same.' Seb smiled at Daisy. 'He's been down here a couple of times with us and he's fallen in love with the place, too. He'll be more than happy backing us in the project.'

'Not that I've ever met him,' I said somewhat sourly, 'but I'd have thought if David Henderson was helping you out, he'd have wanted to bring in his own project manager?'

'He probably would really,' Seb agreed, nodding. 'But if we're to buy the place we obviously need to abide by Mrs Booth's rules. There's clearly some history here. We've just been to see her now before coming down here and I get the impression she still loves the house very much.'

'Well, if she does, she's kept it very well hidden from the rest of us,' I snapped.

'So, Charlie, what do you think? Will you do it for us?' Liberty was pleading, her face full of hope.

'Daisy and I are on our way to see Granny Madge now.'

'We are?' Daisy looked surprised.

'Definitely. Come on. We'll be in touch.' I held out my hand formally. 'We'll let you know our decision in a couple of days.'

'What *is* your problem?' Daisy was cross. 'Those two are lovely, and you came over as an arrogant, supercilious know-it-all.' Daisy slammed the car door behind her and headed for the main door of Almast Haven. 'You've been offered this wonderful opportunity to develop the most heavenly house I've ever seen – and probably with *carte blanche* to spend as much money as you want now that you know your customer is David Henderson's son.' Daisy stomped towards reception and I had to hurry to keep up. 'And yet you were bad tempered, miserable, inflated with your own importance.'

'Anything else?' I snapped back. 'Anything else you'd like to add?'

'Oh, how about condescending – I can't believe you asked David Henderson's son if he had enough money, for heaven's sake.'

'I've told you, Daisy, I wasn't planning on staying back in Westenbury.'

'Well, in that case, put those poor people out of their misery and bugger off back down south. If Granny Madge will let someone else develop and project manage it for them, then I'll certainly take over the gardens.' Daisy glared at me. 'If they'll even *consider* a Maddison sister now after your little performance back there.'

I *was* feeling guilty. As we walked in stony silence along the corridor towards Granny Madge's room, I tried to work out why I'd been so awful.

'I was jealous,' I muttered to Daisy's back.

'Sorry?'

'I was jealous. I'm sorry.'

Daisy stopped walking and faced me. 'I'm not even going to ask what you were jealous of,' she said, a little more gently.

'He's gorgeous, so is she. They have a beautiful baby. She's going to be a doctor, for heaven's sake. And they want the house as well?' Daisy shook her head as I counted off all their attributes on my fingers. 'And they're in love. I don't think Dominic ever looked at me the way Seb was looking at Libby.'

Daisy smiled. 'I rather thought it might be me he was looking at.'

'In your dreams,' I managed to smile back.

'Charlie, you have everything too – OK, OK, you don't have wanker Dominic – but you have your talent, your sister wot loves you and, although it kills me to admit this, you scrub up pretty well, too. You're pretty gorgeous yourself, you know.'

'Thanks, Daise.' I went to hug her. She was right: I needed to start feeling better about myself and regain some of the confidence and self-esteem Dominic's defection had chiselled away. 'OK, then, shall we tell Granny Madge we'll go ahead?' I suddenly felt a stirring of real excitement at the prospect. 'Come on, you're right, let's do it.

8

'They've smartened this place up a bit, haven't they?' I looked round the pastel-walled interior of the Jolly Sailor with its contemporary décor and upbeat lighting. What had become of the gloomily sombre taproom with the sticky garishly patterned carpet where, at the age of not quite sixteen, I'd experienced not only my first vodka and lime but a beery tongue shoved between my lips by one Josh Lee, the catch of the upper sixth?

'Gone the way of all traditional pubs,' Daisy shrugged. 'It's called a "kitchen and bottlery" now; you'll be lucky if you get a pint of Timothy Taylor's. It's really a wine bar with tables that leave your legs dangling with pins and needles, and your food served on a piece of driftwood – I suppose the nautical connection – and your chips in jam jars.'

'Daisy, what are we *doing* here?' I took a gulp of my wine, which tasted cheaply acidic.

'Celebrating? Oh, and by the way...' Daisy added, peering over the bar area to the room beyond, 'not only do you scrub up pretty well once you're out of your work clothes, but Josh Lee is over there.'

'No? Really? I was just thinking about him.'

'Don't look,' Daisy hissed. 'Don't appear too eager.'

'Eager…? Daisy, I can assure you—'

'Charlie,' Daisy went on, ignoring my protestations, 'did you have any idea what Granny had in mind before we went to see her this morning after seeing Libby and Seb at Holly Close Farm?'

'No, absolutely not. When Madge first showed me the house yesterday, she didn't even mention the cottage, let alone suggest I go down and have a look at it.'

After Daisy had totally – and, OK, I admit correctly – bollocked me for my rudeness to Libby and Seb back at the farm, we'd gone to find Granny Madge, who was in her room.

'Hello, my darlings,' she'd welcomed us. 'Do come on in. What a treat – I wasn't expecting another visit from you both so soon. Are you alright sitting up here with me or would you prefer to go down to the lounge? It'll be either full of cleaners hoovering – they're always damn-well hoovering around your chair when you're trying to read – or dribbling old dears mumbling at the TV.' She'd smiled and patted the bed. 'Sorry, girls, only one chair.'

'Granny,' I'd said. 'I… *we* want to do up Holly Close Farm.' Madge hadn't said anything but just looked at us with her bright, intelligent eyes. She waited – it was a bit like being interviewed for a new job – and I went on quickly, 'We've just been down there again; I took Daisy, of course, and Libby and Seb were there. They said you'd spoken to Harriet last night? Anyway, we'd like to take on the project.'

Granny smiled and her whole face lit up. She was still a very beautiful woman and, dressed in a smart tweed skirt and crimson cashmere sweater that matched her lipstick, her abundant hair newly set, she looked a good twenty years younger than her actual age. 'I'm so pleased, girls. I really should have done something with the place years ago, but with you being an architect now, Charlotte, and you, Daisy, able to take on the gardens, well, it's time, I think, don't you? Time to let it go.'

'You never mentioned the cottage yesterday,' I continued, spurred on by Madge's apparent pleasure that her plans looked like being realised. 'We went exploring and came across it this morning. Is that all part of the sale? Will Libby be allowed to demolish it?'

Madge leaned forwards towards the bed and took Daisy's and my hand in her own. It felt warm but dry, papery almost. 'Well now, there's the thing,' she smiled. 'The cottage is *yours*.'

'Ours?' I caught Daisy's eye. She was as wide-eyed as me.

'Look, girls, if I do nothing with Holly Close Farm – as was my intention until Harriet and Libby came here on Saturday – then basically, once I'm dead, the whole place – the farm, the cottage and the acres of land – will pass to Nancy, who'll immediately pass it on to developers.' Granny sat back in her chair and rubbed her leg. 'I've known this all along, of course, but until now I've buried my head…' She trailed off and looked at us both in silence for a few seconds but then smiled again. 'However, I love the idea of Libby and Seb – I think that's what Harriet said Liberty's young man was called – bringing life back to Holly Close Farm. It deserves to be loved again. And Nancy, you know, quite understandably, hated the place.'

'Really?' I glanced across at Daisy. 'Why would Granny Nancy hate it?'

'Long story, darling. Anyway, as you two have agreed to be the ones in charge of renovating the whole place then I'm giving you both the cottage. My will states that you would have inherited, along with your mother, a share of the money once I was dead. Well, I'm hoping to be around for a few more years yet and what better than for you to inherit the money now when you need it to get yourselves on the housing ladder? I mean, girls, you're both pushing thirty. Goodness, I'd been married and Nancy was at school by the time I was your age.'

'It's not for want of trying, Granny,' I smiled ruefully.

'Speak for yourself,' Daisy frowned. 'I'm far too young to be married with kids.'

'Anyway, darlings, here's the plan.' Madge folded her arms and reached for a pad on which she'd obviously been making copious notes and jottings. 'We'll get the whole place valued in lots – the farm, the cottage and the land: you do know there's around thirteen acres that go with the place? – and come to an agreement with Libby and... Seb ... as to what they will pay for the farm and the majority of the land. The cottage and several acres surrounding it will then be put into your two names and, once I get the money from the sale, you will be given enough for its renovation, your mother will get her share and the rest will go to Nancy.' She looked at us seriously, scrutinising our faces. 'So, what do you think? Is that fair, do you think?'

'Fair?' Daisy almost shouted. 'It's wonderful, Granny. Thank you so much.'

Madge glanced over at me. 'I think, Charlotte,' she said slowly, smiling, 'that you're actually contemplating whether, not only do you want to be living back up here, but also do you want to end up living with your sister? Am I right?'

I reddened slightly, embarrassed. Much as I loved Daisy, I wasn't sure I actually wanted to live with her. And what happened when one of us moved a man in? Had children even?

Granny had laughed. 'I loved my sister Lydia, but couldn't have envisaged living with her.' She sat back in her chair and took up her notepad. 'It's a large cottage and I see no reason why you wouldn't be able to develop it into two separate places. There's certainly enough land surrounding it to extend the footfall. I'm not stipulating you *have* to live there, girls – I wouldn't be so controlling. It's entirely up to you. You might want to do it up and then sell it and split the profit. Buy yourself that tiny apartment in London, Charlotte?'

So, there we were, almost home owners the pair of us, overnight. And as Daisy and I stood at the new, long and shiny metallic bar in the Jolly Sailor, I felt slightly more cheerful than I had for the past couple of days. Only slightly, mind you. I still had to get through this ridiculous speed dating folly.

I was amazed how busy the Jolly Sailor was. It had totally reinvented itself since I'd been away but there were several people with whom Daisy and I had been at school, drinking wine from ridiculously large glasses and laughing in one corner of the room, plus a whole load of people I didn't recognise.

'Is that Stacey Anderson over there?' I nudged Daisy.

'Stacey Anderson who was in your year?' Daisy twisted round and peered past me in the direction of the large, rather blousy blonde. 'Blimey, she's put some weight on, if it is. Or is she pregnant?'

'Why would you come speed dating if you were pregnant? Actually, why would you come speed dating at all?' I was beginning to feel depressed all over again. 'Can we drink up and go home, Daisy? We can pinch one of Dad's bottles of wine and watch *Outlander* instead?'

'Charlie?' The blonde had made her way through the crowd and now stood in front of me. 'Gosh, you haven't changed a bit. I thought you were living in London?'

'I am.'

'She *was*,' Daisy interrupted. 'We're both back now for a while and going into business together.'

'Oh?' Stacey looked me up and down. I'd never much liked her at school and, as she launched into what she'd been up to since I'd last seen her, totally uninterested in what Daisy and I might be doing, I realised I probably wouldn't like her any better now. 'Well, *I'm* married. That's my hubby, Jed, over there; been married four years now. Met him at university and never looked at another man after that. We were so lucky, *soul mates* right from the start. It's wonderful when that happens to you, isn't it? Anyway, Jed's in the police – working for his sergeant's exams – I reckon he'll be chief inspector one day, he's that sort of chap. I said I wanted to move back to Midhope and he was more than happy to move with me and find work here. I'm in banking. Got a job straight away in Leeds. We live on the new development over the other side of Westenbury – saved like mad and got onto the housing ladder. We won't stay there, though, you know; I get a good mortgage rate working at the bank and we'll soon be able to have the four-bedroomed rather than the three-bedroomed that we're in now. Not that there's anything wrong with a three-bedroomed but...'

'You'll need it for the baby?' Daisy asked politely while I stood, unable to say a word as Stacey's life story threatened to engulf me.

'Baby? What baby?' Stacey's small blue eyes narrowed for a second and then she laughed gaily. 'Bless you, baby won't be here for another three years.'

Was this the longest pregnancy on record? Daisy glanced at me and crossed her eyes while Stacey continued her monologue.

'You have to plan these things, you know. Make sure baby comes along at the right time.'

'Right,' I interrupted. 'So, no speed dating for you tonight then?'

'*Moi?*' Stacey tinkled. 'Good gracious me no. I'm long since done with anything so juvenile as speed dating, thank goodness.' She glanced at both Daisy and my ringless fingers. 'I'll leave that up to you singletons. Hope you find yourselves a man tonight. It really is so fulfilling, so *right*, when "*two become one*".' Stacey shot two fingers towards us, rapidly becoming one, à la Spice Girls. 'Well, must be going. Jed doesn't like me to leave his side for too long. Been lovely catching up with you, Charlie, and hearing *all* about what you've been up to. *Ciao.*'

'Right, that's it, Daisy, I'm off.' The utter depression that was hanging over me was in danger of flattening me onto the authentic plastic decking underneath my feet.

'No, you're not. Come on.' Daisy grabbed my arm. 'It's upstairs in the function room.'

I remembered it from a friend of Mum's silver wedding do where Daisy and I were so excited about being included in adult celebrations, and where we overdosed on toxic-looking Sunny Delight and white bread rolls filled with flabby damp ham and synthetic cupcakes. It didn't look any different twenty years on. The same nicotine-stained Artex-covered walls, fake wooden beams and overly short red polyester curtains.

Long trestle tables with chairs facing across from one another were arranged in a rectangle around the room, and on each table was a couple of pencils. Daisy handed in our tickets and we were each given a sheet of paper and assigned the number of a table. Even Daisy quailed somewhat as she surveyed the function room and saw the women settling themselves down at the tables, hanging coats on the backs of chairs and shoving bags under feet as if they meant business.

'Come on, you're table eleven and I'm twenty.' Daisy suddenly grinned at me. 'For God's sake, smile, Charlie. Relax, enjoy.'

'Can't I come and sit next to you?'

'No, you're over there. Go on, they're waiting to start.'

Jesus.

I walked quickly over to my allotted table, head down, thoroughly embarrassed. I would have loved all this when I was eighteen, but ten years on, in a function room smelling of the trendy falafel and chicken kebabs that were, apparently, being cooked in the kitchen to one side of us, I was determined not to.

'So,' a woman of around Mum's age, wearing skin-tight leather trousers and a leopard- print top, tapped on her microphone, sending static round the room and making the potential speed-daters wince. 'Sorry about that... Right, there are twenty men and twenty women. You lovely ladies are seated and *you* don't move. The men, on the other hand, are going to come and sit opposite you and then when I ring my bell...' she proceeded to ring the bell loudly as if she were on duty in a school playground and we all winced once more '... after five minutes, you men will move once to your left. Both men and women have a tick sheet. Look and see what table you are visiting, men, and you women, you have a look at the number badge pinned to the men. After each bell ring, you must decide whether it's a "yes" for a future date, or "no" for "not on your nelly".' She laughed uproariously at her own wit and then continued. 'At the end of the session you'll be asked to write down both your email addresses and mobile numbers and these will then be shared with those you fancy the pants off.' More ribald laughter. I downed my wine in one and glared across at

Daisy, who was already chatting to the dark-haired man standing behind her ready to take his place on one of the chairs.

I took a surreptitious glance both at the competition and at the hovering men who, the majority, it was obvious, were already planning to make a beeline for the bubbly pretty blonde on table fifteen. You'll all get your turn, I thought sourly. I looked at my watch. Twenty men, five minutes apiece. One hundred minutes. In two hours' time, I could be home, tucked up in bed with a hot-water bottle, *Outlander* and Jamie Fraser.

And we were off.

'Smile, it might never happen.' Oh, not that old chestnut, please. The man – Number 18 – who'd sat down heavily in front of me was not, by any stretch of the imagination, Jamie Fraser, and the last thing I was going to do was smile at him. 'Have we met before?' he asked, puzzled. 'Only, you're glaring at me with such dislike, I can only assume I've crossed you some time in the past.'

'You mean, like time travelling?' I was still in *Outlander* mode.

'Time travelling?' The man stared. 'I actually meant last week. Maybe in Tesco? Or Aldi...?'

I shook my head.

'But talking of time travellers, are you into *Dr Who*?'

''Fraid not. *Outlander*?' I asked hopefully.

'Oh, you're another one, are you?' he snapped, sitting back in his chair with folded arms. 'My wife – my ex-wife, I should say, could only, you know, *come* –' he leaned forward and whispered the word – 'if I said, "Ah want ye so much, Sassenach, I can barely breathe…"' He affected a rather terrible Highland accent and I began to laugh. He didn't.

I was grateful when the bell rang and Number 18, giving me a funny look, stood and moved one to the left.

I caught Daisy's eye and glared once more. 'Don't be a party pooper,' she mouthed back, and then smiled winningly at the man about to sit down across from her. That was Daisy all over: she'd always been able to wrap men – Dad included – round her little finger.

'Sorry?' I said as Number 2 repeated something as he sat down. Nothing to write home about: probably a couple of years older than me, but already showing the beginnings of both a slight paunch and receding hairline.

'I *said*, "When I was christened my fairy godmother offered me two choices: one was to have a perfect memory and the other to have a huge penis. Unfortunately…' He stopped and smiled, wilting somewhat as I stared stonily at him, but then carried on bravely, '…unfortunately, I can't remember which one I chose.'

I wanted one of those buzzers they have on *Britain's Got Talent*. One quick descent of my hand and he'd be off before he started. Oh, Dominic, where are you, you bastard? Come and rescue me from this hell on earth.

'Actually,' Number 2 went on, obviously determined to have another go, 'you look a lot like my second wife.'

'Oh?' I was interested to know what she looked like. And to already have been married twice at his age. 'How many times have you been married then?'

'Just the once,' he grinned.

Beam me up, Scotty.

Number 2 slid a card across the table. 'I'm just practising some new material,' he said seriously. 'If you fancy coming to see me in stand up, I'm on at The George down in Midhope next Saturday night. Do you fancy it?'

'I think I'm washing my hair next Saturday.'

'Sunday then? I've got a double slot.'

And so, it went on. There was the sixth former whose mum was pulling pints downstairs and who'd snuck in while he waited for a lift home from football practice; the guy whose eyes filled with tears as he talked about his ex-girlfriend who'd gone off with his best friend; and a rather jolly red-haired guy called Neil who'd been in the year below me at school and who, apparently, had had a thing about me on the school bus, found out my address and sent me a Valentine.

'Was that you?' I laughed, remembering how I'd prayed it was from Josh Lee of beery-tongue fame.

''Fraid so.' He grinned back. 'Don't tell the leopard-skin queen, but I'm only here to make up numbers. I leave for Sydney at the weekend. Got a job with KRBM Holdings, starting after Christmas.'

'Oh.' I'd finally found someone who might have become a mate if I were to take on Madge's project and be holed up here in the North, but he was off to see the world while I was stuck back in Westenbury. Depression descended once more as Neil stood, leaned over and, still smiling, kissed my cheek – 'I always wanted to do that' – and moved on.

'Charlie. I thought it was you.' Josh Lee sat squarely in front of me, arms folded and leaned towards me. 'You're looking great. Daisy tells me you're back for good?'

'No. No, no...' I protested. 'I'm, well, I'm going to be here for a while as I project manage a renovation.'

Josh was instantly alert. 'A renovation? A building, you mean?'

'As opposed to what?'

'Well, you could be an art dealer? You know, renovating pictures? I seem to remember you were always known as the best artist in school?'

'Nope.'

'Oh, of course,' Josh interrupted. 'An architect. You went to do architecture, didn't you?'

'So, what did *you* end up doing?' Although I hadn't really given Josh Lee a second thought once I'd left home and immersed myself fully in uni life and then work, I was curious. He was still a good-looking guy and I was surprised he was still living round here.

Josh smiled. 'Did my first year at Exeter, decided academia wasn't for me and, instead, I came home and threw myself into my dad's business. I've taken it over fully now. Dad's gone to live the ex-pat life in Alicante with his new partner.'

'Oh, he was a builder, wasn't he? I remember now.'

'My company is responsible for most of the new development in Westenbury. We're just in the process of acquiring quite a bit of land from Edward Bamforth – the land he managed to get planning permission for last year – and so we're going to be busy.'

'Well done.' Josh was obviously very proud of what he'd achieved. I glanced at his ring finger. 'And no wife or partner?'

'Absolutely not. I'm far too happy with my life to want to be settling down.' He leaned forward and grinned. 'But, now you're back, Charlie, I can offer my services – building or, er, anything else you might have in mind?'

Despite myself, I smiled. 'Well, if you can point me in the right direction of good builders once we actually start renovating Holly Close Farm – that's my great-grandmother's house – then that would be really helpful. I'm obviously going to have to find a whole gang of people: builders, electricians, joiners.' I suddenly felt really excited at the prospect. This was what I was good at and I was starting to relish the challenge ahead.

'Oy, come on, love, it's not the bloody job centre here, you know.' The bell had gone while Josh and I were in discussion over builders, and the next man was hovering, waiting to take Josh's seat.

Josh grinned at me as he stood. 'How about dinner in the next couple of days to discuss?'

'Purely work,' I grinned back.

'Absolutely,' he said. 'What else were you thinking of?'

9

'So, was Arthur the love of your life?' I asked Madge. It was a couple of days after the speed dating and Daisy had dropped me off at Almast Haven before driving herself to Madge's bungalow to start attacking the garden there. I'd changed Madge's library books for her and brought a bottle of the Merlot she loved and the turmeric powder she insisted was keeping her free from dementia. I was in that mood that, if I couldn't have my own love of my life, I was more than happy to listen to someone else's. As long as it was in the past, mind you; anyone trying to shove any *current* wonderful love life down my throat would have got short shrift.

'Arthur? Love of my life?' Madge gave a wry smile. 'I married him.'

'Had you known him a long time?'

'Oh, yes, we grew up together. Joyce, Arthur's sister, was my best friend all through school and then we had our looms next to each other once we left school and went to work in the mill.'

'That must be strange, ending up with someone you went to school with,' I frowned. And then I pulled a face.

'Which is a daft thing for me to say – I've just agreed to go for a meal with someone I went to school with.'

'Oh?' Madge's eyes gleamed. 'That was quick work. You haven't been back a week and you've already got a hot date?'

'I don't know about hot.' I laughed at her turn of phrase. 'It's only Josh Lee. I did have a bit of a thing about him when I was seventeen, but I've agreed to meet up with him because he's a builder. He might be the one to use for the renovation. So, tell me about Arthur?'

'Well, darling, it was wartime, of course. Arthur was desperate to be in the RAF rather than be conscripted into the army like most of the boys round here. He had a notion that, once he was accepted by the RAF, he'd be flying planes and become a part of Bomber Command, but it didn't work out like that. You have to remember Arthur was just a local lad with only the minimum of education. He'd been a couple of years above me at school, but needs must and, like most of us, he had to leave school at fourteen and go to work to bring in money for the family. Arthur's family was particularly badly off because his dad had been wounded in the trenches during the First World War and, once home, never worked again. The pilots for training were your public school boys and grammar school boys, who understood advanced maths and science. Poor Arthur was accepted by the RAF but he didn't get a sniff of flying an actual plane all the time he was there. It did make him quite bitter: I could see him becoming like Herbert, his father, who was constantly aggressive and bitter because of what he'd gone through and how he'd ended up back in 1917. And that worried me.'

'So, what did Arthur do then?' I didn't know enough about the war and suddenly I was really interested.

'Well, as I say, he didn't have the education to get himself into pilot training so, instead, he was trained as a mechanic: "erks" they were known as for some reason. You know, he was able to grease and mend the planes but not allowed to fly them. I don't think he ever got over the disappointment of it all.' Madge looked sad for a moment as she remembered. 'And of course, Arthur didn't want me joining the air force as well.'

I stared at Madge. 'You joined up? I never knew that.'

She laughed. 'What did you think I did during the war?'

'I never thought about it really. I mean, it's such a long time ago.'

'Not to me it isn't. It seems like yesterday. Arthur didn't want me to join up and, because I was a weaver at Goodners and Sons – you know the old mill on the outskirts of Midhope? – and old Frank Goodners was given a government contract to make uniforms, we mill workers were seen as being in a reserved occupation and didn't have to join up.'

'Why didn't Arthur want you to join the RAF?'

'The WAAF, darling. Girls joined the WAAF. I suppose Arthur wanted me safely at home. He asked me to marry him one Sunday dinnertime when he was home on leave. Just before I joined up myself.'

'So how old were you then?'

'Just nineteen. I can see it as if it were yesterday. I was round at Arthur's house and I'd been really looking forward to seeing him as I'd not seen him since he'd gone off to Harrogate for his initial training two months earlier.' Madge sighed but didn't carry on.

'So, what was the problem? Had you gone off him?'

Madge laughed. 'Gone off him? Well, yes, I suppose I had. He'd always been a lot keener on me than I was on him, and I was young and wanted to get involved in the war.'

'I suppose you were about the age I went off to university,' I mused. 'The last thing I'd have wanted was some boy wanting me to stay at home here in Westenbury when I was off to Bath.'

Madge nodded in agreement. 'Although, you know, it really was the norm to get married in your teens in my day. It meant we could have sex.'

'Right.' I felt slightly embarrassed. 'Gosh, well, I'm glad I was born when I was. So, you said no to Arthur then even though you did end up married to him eventually?'

Madge nodded again. 'So, there I was at Arthur's house on that Sunday. I didn't really like going round there, even though Joyce, my best friend, being Arthur's sister, was there. His dad was a miserable old sod. I was actually quite frightened of him.

'"Look, Madge, I'm serious, let's get wed," Arthur said to me once he got me alone in the front parlour. I can still remember the feel of his battledress top as he pulled me into his arms. It was rough and felt horribly scratchy against my face. "They're not calling up married women, you know. You could stay here, then. Carry on working in t'mill, save up some money for us for when it's all over. And it will be one day, you know…"'

'Hard to turn someone down when they're away to war, I suppose,' I frowned. It was strange to think of ninety-four-year-old Madge as a young girl of nineteen.

'Yes, it was.' Madge looked down at her hands. 'Although, even in 1943, most of the boys were still in training and hadn't had a real look at any fighting. Unless you were a fighter pilot, of course – they'd been on bombing raids from the early days. So, anyway, I really didn't fancy sitting round the dinner table with Arthur's dad and, although I'd told my mum I probably would stay, I remember wanting to go home. Get married?' Madge snorted almost crossly. 'I was just nineteen, for heaven's sake, and I wanted to join up and be a part of the great exciting mess that was the war. I'd been itching to leave for months, fed up to the back teeth of working at that bloody loom all day long. I'd been in the mill for four years and I'd had enough. And then, by 1943, it had been made compulsory for single women my age to either join up to one of the forces or the Land Army and, I can tell you, Charlie, I was ready. My dad was a tenant farmer so if I'd wanted I could have stayed at home and been a land girl on his farm. Then there was a munitions factory over at Chorley in Lancashire, though I dreaded being sent there. No, it was the WAAF for me and the sooner I enlisted rather than wait for my call-up papers to come, the better. Was that terrible of me, do you think? Only thinking of what colour uniform was best going to suit me?' Madge grinned at me and was about to carry on when we were interrupted.

'Do you want coffee, lovey?' Janet, one of the more ingratiating care workers at the home, stood beaming in front of us.

'Don't suppose you've got any gin instead?' Madge raised an eyebrow.

'A gin, you naughty girl?' Janet simpered, spooning a particularly cheap brand of instant coffee into two cups. 'You'll get me fired.'

'Jesus,' Madge muttered under her breath, but took the coffee as well as a plaster-pink wafer biscuit. 'To be honest, darling, I remember feeling that particular Sunday dinnertime the same as I often do here in this place – you know, a bit stir-crazy. I tried to escape Arthur's family. "I think my mum's expecting me back for my dinner," I lied as the awful smell of overcooked cabbage drifted in from the kitchen, the windows steamed up and I had the urge to run away from it all.' Madge shuddered.

'"Come on, lass, come and sit down. Arthur's mum's laid a place for you at table." I can see Mr Booth now, towering over me, his collarless shirt open at the neck, showing a matt of greying hair, and, I could tell, in no mood to be contradicted. So I followed him into the kitchen and sat down opposite Arthur.'

Madge chewed on her pink biscuit and then put it down with distaste. 'I don't know why I eat these things, Charlie. Anyway, Arthur's mum – she was a pale, nervous little thing: years of living with Arthur's dad had sucked all the life out of her – served us the usual plates piled high with Yorkshire puddings and thick gravy. Probably every household in Midhope was eating the same thing. Certainly, if I'd been at home, that's what we'd have been eating as well.' Madge put down her coffee cup and assumed a man's broad Yorkshire accent once more. '"So, lass, our Arthur tells me you're thinking of joining up? Bloody mug's game. Why do it when you could stay on at Goodners? It's a reserved occupation for women, isn't it, making cloth for all the uniforms? Particularly when most of the men from round here have already been enlisted?"'

Madge now assumed a young girl's voice as she recalled the conversation from over seventy years ago. She either had a jolly good memory or she was having a great time making it all up. '"Oh, I want to do my bit," I twittered. It didn't do to argue with Herbert Booth. "And I want to see the world."'

I laughed. 'You sound like one of the Miss World contestants.'

Madge grinned back. 'And find a shelter for all the homeless pussies...?'

'You *are* naughty, you know. Anyway, go on.'

'Oh, don't you start, Charlie. So anyway, Mr Booth wipes gravy from his moustache and says "I saw the bloody *world* at Passchendaele and, I tell you now, it's not a world I'd ever want anyone to see again. I'd have stopped our Arthur going off if I could. And our Joyce is going nowhere. She's staying here where she's safe."

Joyce, who was always frightened of her dad, says, "I'm not going anywhere, Dad, I've told you. I'd be right homesick going away from home and having to share a room with a load of other girls. It was bad enough sharing with our Mary and our Ethel before they went and got wed." She was a bit of a ninny, was Joyce. Didn't join up and then found herself in the munitions over at Chorley. Never recovered, you know…'

'So, what was Arthur doing while all this was going on?'

'Getting stuck into his Yorkshire pudding. Actually, I did feel sorry for Arthur. He was embarrassed at his father's ranting and kept trying to catch my eye, but I was working my way stolidly through my own pudding and gravy, desperate to get through the meal so I could go home, and I just kept my eyes on my plate. I remember Mr Booth monopolising the whole dinnertime and me thinking, no way am I going to stay in Westenbury and get married to Arthur. If I had agreed to marry him, stayed as a weaver and then got pregnant, which was what Arthur really wanted, then I'd probably have had to go and live with Arthur's parents until after the war.' Madge shuddered once more.

'So, you joined up instead?'

'Absolutely.' Madge patted my hand. 'You *are* a good listener, darling. It's years since I've even thought about Arthur's parents. But Arthur was determined. As soon as I could make my excuses, he walked me the mile home. I remember it had started snowing while we'd been eating and the ground was slippery and slushy. "So, Madge, how about it then? How about we get wed?" He was still going on, all the way home.

'"Are you proposing?" I remember laughing, trying to make light of it, trying to make him see how daft he was being.

'"Aye, I am," Arthur said, and then, do you know what, Charlie, he suddenly gets down on one knee in the wet slush and fumbles in his battledress top pocket. He grabs at my cold hands, which I'd shoved deep into my coat, and tries to push a ring onto my finger.'

'Really? Gosh, I bet that frightened you.' I had a sudden vision of Josh Lee going down on one knee just as I was about to leave for Bath University and my architecture course. Not that he had. I wasn't even going out with him then. As far as I remember we'd had a couple of snogging sessions round the back of the Jolly Sailor and then he'd dumped me for Nicci Fellowes, a sophisticated undergraduate with a gamine hairdo and a non-existent bust. 'What's she got that I haven't?' I'd sobbed to Daisy as I played and replayed James Blunt's 'You're Beautiful' until even I was sick of it. 'A padded bra, perhaps?' Daisy had replied drily before drowning out James with Shakira and 'Hips Don't Lie' and belly dancing along the corridor to the bathroom.

'Totally frightened me, you're right,' Madge agreed. 'I know a lot of the girls in the mill would have loved it, but not me. Anyway, "Right, we're engaged," Arthur says. "I don't want to go back without you promising me you'll at least think about marrying me. It'd make it so much easier if I know you're wearing my ring and you're not going off with any other bloke. I really couldn't bear that, you know, Madge."

'And, Charlie, I remember looking down at the ring and then down at Arthur, who was still on one knee. I knew nothing about jewellery, but even I could tell this wasn't some ten-bob tat from Woolworths down in Midhope. It was a brilliantly cut ten-pointed diamond surrounded by two smaller unusual oblong diamonds and three round ones.'

I glanced down at Madge's ring finger. 'But you're not wearing it?'

'No, I'm not. Anyway, it was far too big for my frozen finger and kept slipping round. "For heaven's sake, Arthur," I said. "Get up. You're going to freeze to the ground down there," and I took off the ring and handed it back to him. I had to be quite cross with him, you know. "I don't want to get married to you or anyone," I said. "I'm going to join the WAAF."

'"Just wait until you're called up," Arthur kept on pleading. "Why not do that?" And he tried to put the ring back on my finger.

'"Arthur, where've you got this ring from?" I asked. I mean, Charlie, I'd never been given anything like that ring before.

'"I've been saving up," Arthur says to me. "I've been wanting to give you something ever since we started going round together."

'"But you did," I said. He'd given me the most beautiful little gold watch for my nineteenth birthday. Heaven knows where he'd got the money from for that.

'So, Arthur then says, "If we were married then you wouldn't have to join up. And we could have a baby."

'Well, I had to get a bit cross again then.

'So, then Arthur says to me, "Promise me you'll keep the ring? Keep it safe?"

'Well, what could I say? "But we're not engaged, Arthur," I finally said. "We're *not* getting married and don't you go telling anybody any different."'

I looked across at Madge. Her eyes were closing and her voice was becoming fainter. She'd obviously tired herself out with all this talk of the past. I gently took the blanket that had fallen to the floor and wrapped it round her knees.

'Thank you, Charlie,' she muttered. 'Thank you for listening to an old lady…' She smiled and her head moved slightly to one side. She was fast asleep.

10

'Darling, are you going out with a young man dressed like that?' Vivienne, sartorially elegant in flowing lavender for another Saturday afternoon rehearsal in the village hall, looked me up and down dubiously. 'I can lend you something to wear that might be more appropriate for a first date? I'm assuming most of your going-out clothes are still in London?' She stepped back to get another good look at my jeans and sweater.

'All my goods and chattels came back with me, Vivienne,' I said more cheerfully than I felt. Why on earth had I agreed to go out for lunch with Josh Lee? It was the last thing I was in the mood for. 'Anyway, it's a business meeting, not a date. Josh and I are going to discuss builders and who, if not himself and his workers, we might use for Madge's house.'

'It's all very *strange*, don't you think?' Vivienne sniffed. 'I can't imagine why your great- grandmother has kept this house of hers secret for so long. Is it a very elegant house? Would *I* like it?'

I shook my head. 'Elegant? Gosh, no, it's an old farmhouse.' I glanced at Vivienne's colour-coordinated lavender kitten heels – she was going to ruin those once she walked outside. 'Nothing *elegant* about it at all, really. It's all beams and low ceilings. You'd hate it.' I pictured Vivienne's upmarket little town house on the outskirts of Midhope, which was in the process of having a new kitchen and bathrooms, and knew that Vivienne would have found Holly Close Farm too rural, too *Yorkshire*.

'Well, how about a little chiffon scarf for that sweater? Or maybe a brooch to complement its colour?' Vivienne was determined to fix some adornment on me.

'I'm fine, really. Got to go, there's the bell.' I grabbed my bag and one of Daisy's coats – it was her new pink Hobbs boyfriend coat and she'd go mad once she found out I'd filched it – but it did go fantastically well with my black polo sweater and black skinny jeans. Anyway, I told myself, needs must.

'Hmm, not sure pink is going to be the best colour for that.' Josh, head to toe in black leathers, frowned and nodded towards the huge motorbike that sat squarely in the middle of Mum and Dad's drive. 'I've brought you a spare helmet but you might want to swap that coat for a leather jacket if you've got one? The roads will throw up some dirt and it will come back filthy if you go out in that.'

'Oh,' I said in delight. 'Wow, I never had you for a bike sort of person. You should have warned me we were going out on a bike.'

'I did.' Josh frowned. 'I sent you a text this morning.'

'My phone's knackered. It was on its last legs anyway, but I dropped it down the loo this morning. I'm just waiting for it to dry out and hoping it'll be OK.'

'What is it with women and dropping their phones down toilets? You'd never get a man doing that.'

I grinned. 'Search me. Right, give me two minutes.' I knew Daisy had a leather jacket somewhere. Good job she was out in Leeds.

I'd always loved speed. I reckoned I got the gene from Mum, who adored anything fast. Alton Towers, Blackpool Pleasure Beach, Lightwater Valley. She'd dragged Dad to every one over the years and, while he waited patiently beneath The Mouse Trap, Oblivion and Nemesis, knowing that he'd be throwing up even on so much as a simple merry-go-round, Mum had screamed and yelled her way round the pleasure parks of England. That was love for you.

I found Daisy's ancient black leather jacket, ran back down the stairs and fastened the helmet.

'Have you done this before?' Josh asked seriously. 'Do you know how to lean with me? If you don't, just stay still and try not to tense up when I accelerate. Oh, and it goes without saying, avoid putting your foot on the exhaust or you'll end up in A and E with third-degree burns. So, where are we going?'

'I thought you were taking me out? Lunch, remember?'

'That's fine. I thought we could go to the Coach and Horses at Upper Clawson. There's a great stretch of road out by the moors to give the bike its head. But how about you take me to see your grandmother's house first?'

'OK.' I was more than happy to have another trip out there. I particularly wanted to see the cottage again. I'd already attempted simple plans for it in my sketchbook and needed some actual measurements. 'Let's go before Daisy realises I've nicked her leather jacket and my dad sees me on a bike and tells me I can't go.' I laughed. 'It is a bit like being a kid again, being home.'

I pulled on my gloves and Josh moved closer – a bit closer than was strictly necessary – and helped me fasten the strap underneath my chin. He was wearing an aftershave I instantly recognised – Davidoff Horizon – and for a couple of seconds I had to close my eyes and fight the temptation to breathe it in and be instantly back with Dominic, my nose buried in his neck.

'Are you OK?' Josh looked concerned as I opened my eyes. 'I can go and get the car if you'd prefer?'

'I'm fine,' I said, trying to smile.

'So, this house is out on the Midhope road, isn't it? Once we get near you can indicate the directions by squeezing my waist. You know, if you want me to turn right…'

'Don't worry, I get it. Come on.'

I adored the sheer energy, joy and freedom of being on a bike, and the gloom and misery I seemed to have sunk back into that Saturday morning began to lift as we roared down the streets and out onto the main road. I loved the feel of the bike between my thighs and yes, cliché or not, a throbbing great bike between your legs is a total turn on when compounded with a feeling of danger and fear. I wrapped my arms around Josh's waist, smelled the leather and felt the kick of excitement flood through me.

Josh put the bike into low gear as I gave tactile instructions that he should turn and head down the lane leading to Holly Close Farm. He stopped at the end, spread his legs to keep the bike upright and just stared. He took off his helmet and turned. 'I imagined you to be taking on a little cottage,' he said finally. 'Nothing like this.'

I laughed. 'Well, there *is* a cottage that Madge is giving to Daisy and me. But the farm itself and most of the land is being bought by David Henderson's son. Do you know him?'

'Who? David Henderson or his son?'

'Either.'

'I've heard of David Henderson, of course, but I wasn't aware he had a son.'

'So, you can see, money will be no object. Mind you, I'm sure my granny Madge will do a fair deal with the Hendersons. She's not out to fleece anyone.'

'I can't believe I've not come across this place before,' Josh mused as he parked the bike and I pulled off my helmet and raked fingers through my hair. 'I really thought I knew most of any potential renovation sites round here.'

'I don't really understand it myself, Josh. Even my mum didn't know about it. She and Dad only came down for the first time yesterday and Dad was actually really miffed Granny has kept it to herself all these years; it's just the sort of place he'd have loved to live in when we were kids. He'd have had goats and horses and geese and a ton of dogs here and Mum could have had the cottage for her pottery. Anyway, too late now, but Granny is a bit *persona non grata* with my parents, particularly my dad, at the moment because of this.

Josh nodded. 'I can understand that. Come on, show me your new cottage.'

It was another mild, late November day, the temperature belying the fact that Christmas was just around the corner, and only the overgrown abundant holly bushes – exuberant with a glut of red berries – displaying the seasonal truth.

I took out the tape measure, paper and pencil I'd secured in Daisy's jacket pocket before we set off and, while Josh set about exploring, tapping walls and kicking wood and stone, I made some quick basic measurements of the place. By extending the footfall of the cottage, there was definite scope to create two separate semi-detached places and that's what both Daisy and I wanted. Much as we got on, living together, sharing a kitchen and bathroom, wouldn't work.

A good hour later and both Josh and I had been able to gather as much information as we needed for the moment. Josh had disappeared for most of the time, checking over the farm building as far as was possible without actually going in, examining the walls, the look of the foundations and finally spending a lot of time just standing back and staring skywards to see the state of the roof. I'd then gone to sit outside in what was originally the cottage garden, enjoying the weak sun on my face and being in the company of, let's face it, a very attractive man.

'What are you doing? Just sitting and thinking?' Josh appeared at my side, making me jump, my senses suddenly alert. He hunkered down on the dry-stone wall next to me and the smell of leather, lemony cologne and maleness assailed my nostrils. I remembered how I'd fancied him like mad but he'd gone off with Nicci Fellowes, who was home from university for the summer and, a year older than Josh, an obvious magnet as a sophisticated, living away from home, more sexually aware woman.

'I was just enjoying the view,' I lied and then conceded, 'and remembering how you went off with Nicci Fellowes when you were supposed to be meeting me and taking me to the school prom.'

'Who?' Josh looked genuinely puzzled.

'Nicci Fellowes? Her dad has the hardware shop down in Westenbury?'

Josh still looked unsure. 'I seem to remember something about her. Wasn't she a few years above us at school?' Josh didn't seem overly interested as he came to sit beside me. 'You've been given a wonderful opportunity here, Charlie.' He looked me full in the face, his leathers brushing my arm. 'I'd really like to be your builder on the whole project. By the time the sale has gone through and you've got planning permission and drawn up plans, I'll have finished most of the site work down in Westenbury and will be able to spare quite a few of the men. I'm going to be fully involved with Edward Bamforth's building project at some point, but if they cross over I can take on other labourers, brickies, sparkies and joiners, etc. I have a great site manager – a Lithuanian guy – who can always be relied on to find an extra gang if needs be. I'm assuming you'll be wanting to do this project fairly quickly so you can get yourself back to London?'

'That's the plan, yes. I know Seb Henderson is really wanting to get on with it. There's no chain involved so

I'm sure, especially with his father behind it, we should be able to move fairly quickly.'

'But meanwhile…' Josh grinned at me and moved closer and I felt slightly shocked at his nearness. 'Close your eyes and listen…'

I did as he said. 'I can't hear a thing.'

'Exactly. It's so wonderfully quiet down here. No, no, keep your eyes closed.'

I jumped as I felt his mouth on mine. Not the beery-tongue teenaged kiss I recalled from over ten years previously, but a man's kiss. How could I possibly be kissing another man – and Josh Lee from Westenbury High School, for heaven's sake – when I only wanted Dominic? Oh, but this was such a professional kiss from a man who'd obviously kissed a lot of women in his time. And, after rejection from Dominic, I was enjoying the contact with a warm-blooded male. Josh moved his legs closer to mine and I opened my eyes. If he'd had a soppy look on his face, I'd have been off, but he was lazily grinning down at me and, against my better judgement – let's face it, my judgement had been crap anyway for the past year or so – my arms came up and rested on his black leather jacket.

'There, that wasn't so bad, was it?' Josh smiled, but just as I was considering closing my eyes once again and carrying on where we'd left off, he jumped up. 'Come on, I'm starving. I only had a bowl of cornflakes for breakfast and I could murder a steak. They do pretty good ones at the Coach and Horses.'

'I'm almost vegetarian,' I said a little primly, slightly miffed that he had his mind set on food.

'Oh, we'll soon cure you of that,' Josh laughed. 'Tha's back in't North na, tha knows. None of that namby-pamby London vegan stuff up here.' He set off back to the bike and, realising I was also ravenously hungry for the first time in a week, I levered myself up from the garden and ran to catch him up.

As we neared the top of the lane that led back on to the main road, Josh slowed right down and stopped, indicating we take off our helmets just to admire the view down the valley. We must have sat there for a good ten minutes, enjoying the weak sunshine and the glorious countryside, when a rather flash silver car drove towards us and carried on past us down the lane. I turned to see who was heading down to the house – *our* house. Was it Seb's father, David Henderson, perhaps? I managed a good view of the man: youngish, around my age and one I was almost sure was from the speed dating at the Jolly Sailor. An extremely attractive man who'd stood at the back of the room for ten minutes or so, arms folded and slowly drinking a glass of wine but not taking an active part in any of the proceedings.

By the time Josh dropped me back at home, sated with the most deliciously tender fillet steak I think I'd ever eaten, it was dark.

'Oy, that's my jacket,' Daisy snapped as I attempted, and failed, to creep past the kitchen where she was watching

Saturday afternoon rugby with Dad and Malvolio. 'Dad, tell her, she's been wearing my leather jacket without asking.'

'Yes, but a very ancient specimen, I think you'll agree,' I said loftily. 'Not worth having a hissy fit over.'

'Well, you owe me one,' Daisy said, her eyes never leaving the TV and a particularly horny pair of muddy thighs attached to a New Zealand All Black. 'I should keep your eye on that lovely cream cashmere sweater of yours, if I were you.'

'Don't even think about it, Daisy,' I hissed. 'Dad, tell her, she's not to touch my new cream cashmere sweater.'

'Will the pair of you shut it? I'm trying to watch England being annihilated by these poncy down-under softies.'

'Ooh, nothing poncy about those bums,' Daisy grinned. 'Look at them in those white shorts: rock hard, all of them. Now, that jumper of yours will be perfect for me to wear tonight.'

'I mean it, Daisy. That jumper is the *only* good thing I've got left in my life.'

'Kate,' Dad shouted towards the kitchen. 'Come and tell these two to shut it. The dog and I can't get a minute's peace to watch the game living with all you women.'

'Mum'll be in the attic,' I said. 'No good trying to get help from her.' I left them to it, went to hide my best jumper and carried on up the next flight of stairs to find Mum.

'Hello, darling, just give me a sec and I'll be with you.'

'Gosh, Mum, these are really good. You are talented, you know.' I inspected the finished article – a christening cup in blue, by the look of it.

She smiled. 'Well, now that I'm teaching only two days a week, I've so much more time on my hands. Or at least I did until Vivienne, you and Daisy arrived back.'

'Don't you want us back?'

'Of course I do, darling. Although to be honest Vivienne is intent on outstaying her welcome. If I hear *A handbag* practised in her Lady Bracknell voice just one more time, I shall shove the sodding handbag where the sun don't shine. Once Christmas is over she will have to be on her way.' Mum scratched absentmindedly at the drying clay on her forehead. 'So, yes, now I have more time, I'm happy to accept commissions. What I'm on now has been ordered by Mandy Henderson – David Henderson's wife. It's for her new grandson, Lysander.'

'You do know that it's Seb Henderson who's buying Holly Close Farm with Libby?'

Mum looked at me. 'I do now. I didn't when I first took on the commission, but Mandy put me in the picture just this afternoon when she called round. Apparently, they're all very excited about the project.' Mum scratched again and examined the brown clay beneath her fingernails. 'As *I* would have been if Madge had given us the opportunity all those years ago when you girls were little. I'm absolutely furious with Madge, but also my mum for keeping the place under wraps. Once she's home I shall really have it out with her.'

'Where *is* Granny Nancy?'

'Living it large in South Africa with some new man. She's supposed to be here for Christmas, but whether she will arrive or not is anyone's guess. Oh, and while I remember, did Madge get hold of you? Something about a coat? I think she'd like you to go over to the bungalow and fetch it for her.'

'OK. It'll have to be tomorrow now. I've been drinking, so I can't drive. I'll pop over tomorrow.'

11

'Come on, Charlie, I want to take Mum's car over to Madge's bungalow to get stuck in to her garden and I can't if you need it to take Madge's coat over to Almast for her.' Daisy was in the process of pulling the bedcovers off me.

'For God's sake, Daisy. It's Sunday and it's...' I peered at my watch in the half-light ... 'not even eight o'clock yet.' I grabbed the duvet back from her and pulled it back up to my neck. 'What on earth's the matter with you?' I muttered. 'Get a life, or at least a bacon sandwich. And if I've got to get up, make one for me too and then I'll think about it.' I snuggled back down and tried to bring back the dream I'd been having of Dominic making love to me in the garden of the cottage at Holly Close Farm. Or was it Josh Lee? I screwed my eyes shut, slightly embarrassed at the vividness of the dream, trying to work out exactly who it was I'd been urging on. As far as I could recall, he'd had Dominic's face but Josh's black biker-leathers. Whoever it was, the dream had left me horny as hell. And hungry.

'I thought you were vegetarian?' Daisy grinned, pulling the duvet in her direction once more.

'I've been seduced over to the dark side by Mum's shepherd's pie and that fillet steak I had for lunch yesterday.' I frowned, sitting up. 'I'm a bit like a shark: I've got the taste for blood. You go and make bacon sandwiches, some proper coffee – Mum's got some somewhere – and I'll be with you. I'll drive us both over there, find Madge's coat, take it over to her and then come back for you. Do you want to look at the sketches I've done for the cottage so far?'

'I already have. While you were lying here snoring.'

'I don't snore.'

'They're fabulous, Charlie. You're very clever. Especially how you've managed to make two individual cottages out of the one. Have to say, I don't fancy living with you if you're going to snore like you just were doing.'

'I don't snore. I was actually in the throes of a very rampant dream.'

'Oh? Who with? *I* keep having fantasies about Seb Henderson. That is one gorgeous man. I wonder what his dad's like? I've always fancied having an older man.'

'Well, if Seb is our age, David Henderson must be in his fifties.' I grimaced at the thought. 'Forget it.' I put a tentative foot out of the duvet. 'Why is this house so damned cold?'

'Victorian, draughty, Dad economising. Always been the same.' Daisy shrugged her shoulders, encased in several layers of woollen sweaters. 'Right, get up now, come and have breakfast or I'm taking the car myself and you'll have to get Dad to drive you over. You know he won't let you take his car yourself in case he's called out to some cow or sheep.'

*

'It's a *red* coat Madge said she was after. I can't see it, can you?' I was thumbing through a whole plethora of coats hanging up in the utility while Daisy turned on the water and electricity and the bungalow slowly creaked back into life.

'Hang on, I'll come and help in a minute. I'm going to tell Madge she should keep the water and the heat running now. If we have a sudden cold snap she could end up with frozen pipes. She needs to keep the place warm and aired for when she gets out.'

'Sounds like she's in prison,' I laughed.

'Might as well be,' Daisy shuddered. 'Shall you and I make a pact?'

'A pact? What sort of pact? I remember your *pacts* from years ago – you never kept one of them.' I looked up from the pile of coats now on the floor – some must have been decades old – and glanced through the open utility door towards Daisy, who was filling the kettle at the kitchen sink.

'Whichever one of us becomes doolally first has to be looked after by the other so that the one who is losing her marbles doesn't end up in Almost Heaven making macramé egg warmers and boring the pants off their children – if we ever have any – going on about their past lovers.' Daisy gave me a meaningful look.

'Are you suggesting I'm already going on about past lovers?'

'You? Going on and on about wanker Dominic? Would I dare suggest that?'

I glared at her. 'No way am I having *you* look after me. As the oldest, I'll probably lose it first and you *wouldn't* look after me.'You'd dump me in Almost Heaven and run off with my cashmere sweaters. I really can't see any red coat even though Madge was convinced it was hanging up in here. This bungalow needs a huge clear out, you know. I wonder if Madge would like me to do that for her while you're tackling the garden?'

'Dunno. I wouldn't like anyone going through my things. But I suppose you could go and look in her wardrobe?'

I started hanging the coats, macs and hats back up on their pegs. 'Half of this stuff needs to go. I'll have a quick look in Madge's bedroom and see if I can find it.'

I walked across the hallway and into Madge's bedroom. All was neat and tidy, the bed made up, the few ornaments arranged symmetrically on the dressing table and the chintzy curtains standing almost regimentally to attention in their pink tie-backs. There was a whole bank of built in wardrobes running along the back wall but, as I tried the first door, I realised it was locked. Where was the key? It didn't appear to be in any of the other wardrobe doors. I could see I was going to have to ring Almast Haven and ask Madge. I looked along the dressing table where a glass tray held myriad earrings, lipsticks and perfume, but no wardrobe key. I didn't like to open Madge's bedside cabinet drawers, but quickly did so in the hope she'd secreted a key in one of them. In the drawer of the cabinet on the right side of the bed was a large shortbread tin, a rather jolly pair of black scotty dogs in tartan coats grinning up at me from the lid. Determined to find the key, I quickly took out the tin, placed it on the bed and took off the lid. Ah-ha. Several keys. I picked what appeared to be the most modern and immediately fitted it successfully into the lock and turned. As soon as I opened the first double door I saw what must be the red coat. It was cashmere and wool, a Max Mara full-length design, and I could see why Madge would be eager to have it with her in the home. There was a slight whiff of mothballs – what is it with old people and moths? A lingering smell of Opium, the perfume Madge had first used in the early eighties and continued to use ever since, was fighting a losing battle with the moth stuff.

The coat was beautiful but not my style. I locked the wardrobe back up and made to replace both the key and the tin when my eye was caught by a small black-and-white photograph and a metal badge.

'Charlie, you shouldn't be going through Madge's things.' I started guiltily as Daisy appeared at my side.

'I wasn't going through her things,' I said crossly. 'I needed to find the key to the wardrobe and I did.'

'I never knew Great-granddad Arthur was such an attractive man.' Daisy picked up the photo. 'Wow, look at him. He's a bit like a blond Seb Henderson.'

'Will you shut up about Seb Henderson?' I tutted, peering over Daisy's shoulder. 'Gosh, you're right, though; he's gorgeous. Hang on, that's not Arthur. You've seen Madge's wedding photo – it's in the sitting room.' I turned the photo over and read:

To my darling, darling Midge. Yours forever, James X

'He must have been a boyfriend of Madge's. Has he spelled her name wrongly or was it his pet name for her, do you think?' Daisy peered more closely at the photo.

'Look at those dark eyes with that fair hair. Quite a combination. Look, this must be Arthur's badge from the war.' She lifted the gold and blue enamel badge from the tin. '*Bomber Command Royal Air Force. Strike Hard Strike Sure.*' Daisy read the words from the badge, tracing the raised letters with a finger.

'I don't think it can be Arthur's.' I frowned, placing the badge back in the tin with the photo. 'I don't think he ever flew: he was a grease monkey, making sure the bombers were fit to fly.'

'Ask Madge when you take the coat. Ask her who James was.'

'But then I'd have to admit going through her drawers.'

'I really don't think Madge will mind. You had to find the key.' Daisy was beginning to sound slightly impatient. 'Come on, I've made some coffee. Drink that and then off you go. I need to start lifting the dahlias and it's back-breaking stuff. You've got it easy, swanning off to Heaven with a red coat for a cosy gossip about Madge's old boyfriends. I bet this James was just one of many: find out what you can, it'll be dead interesting.'

'Thanks, darling.' I found Madge still in her room although it was after eleven by the time I finally got to Almast Haven and handed her the coat. 'I love this coat,' Madge smiled, burying her nose in its warmth. 'Used to be Nancy's of course – I'd never have spent so much on a coat – but she was about to send it to Oxfam a couple of years ago and, as I said to her, "Charity begins at home. *I'll* have that, please." I knew it would be hanging up in the utility.'

'Actually, Madge, it wasn't.'

'Oh? Where was it then? Where'd I left it?' Madge looked puzzled.

'Well, I hope you don't mind but when I couldn't find it in the utility, I tried to see if it was in the wardrobe in your bedroom.'

'Why should I mind, Charlie?'

'Well, the wardrobe was locked so I had to search for a key in your bedside cabinet.'

'Oh, I'm sorry, darling. I should have told you that. I keep the key in a tin.'

'Yes, I know, I found it.'

Madge smiled and patted my hand. 'Of course you did or you wouldn't have been able to bring me the coat.'

'We're going to leave the water and electricity switched on in the bungalow, if that's OK?'

Madge didn't say anything for a while. 'Look,' she said finally, 'I'm determined to be back home once the weather starts improving – you know, in spring – but I've just had a thought. How about you – or both of you girls – moving into the bungalow and keeping it aired and lived in for me? Daisy's going to be there a lot anyway while she works on the garden.'

'Oh, gosh, I don't know.'

'Up to you, darling. The offer's there. My car's in the garage too, and if you pay for the insurance and promise me you won't give it too much hammer, you can both drive it. Now, have a think about it, but meanwhile do you fancy a walk round the grounds? I can put my lovely red coat on and give the old codgers in here something to talk about.' She laughed at the thought.

'Madge…' I hesitated. 'I found an old photo in the tin.'

'Did you, darling? Who was it of? Your mother or you two girls?' Madge looked at me expectantly, a smile on her face.

'Well, no, it was a man from years ago, I should think. Someone called James?'

Madge looked at me but didn't say anything.

'I didn't mean to pry, but I needed to find the key. I think he was probably very much in love with you?'

Madge reached for her stick and stood up. 'Help me on with the coat, Charlie, would you? And my leather gloves are over there. Come on, let's walk, and I'll tell you about the very first time I saw James Montgomery-West.'

12

'I was trained as a cook and sent to the Met training school on Oxford Street and actually, once I got into the swing of it all, I rather enjoyed it. I'm not convinced that my contribution helped defeat Hitler, but, like you, Charlie, I loved being in London, and because I had a fairly cushy number, enjoyed the whole war, really.' Madge shook her head and then pointed her stick in the direction of a wooden bench. 'Do you think it's warm enough to sit for a while?'

We walked the fifty or so yards and Madge sat down heavily. She looked pale. 'Do you want to go in?' I asked, concerned.

'No, no,' Madge said impatiently. 'Now I've started, I'd like to continue. And there is so much to tell.'

'Why now, Gran?' I asked. 'I mean, you seem to have kept it all to yourself all these years.'

Madge sighed and tapped somewhat impatiently at the ground in front of her with her stick. 'I don't suppose it really matters now. Constance is dead; I Googled her on my iPad.'

'Constance?'

Madge tutted. 'You're getting too far ahead. Let me concentrate on James and that wonderful, wonderful evening the very first time I clapped eyes on him.'

He was tall, with thick blond hair and the most amazing intelligent brown eyes, and had such an air of confidence about him that he must surely be an officer. Madge's eyes went to his uniform – always a giveaway – comparing unfavourably the thick, heavy fabric of Arthur's battledress with this man's individually cut and tailored jacket already bearing the two stripes of a flight lieutenant.

He was sitting at a table crowded with other RAF personnel and a couple of glamorous women in evening dresses, and although he appeared to be drinking fairly heavily he seemed a little distant from his rowdier companions, leaning backwards on his chair, his right arm flung carelessly along its back, his eyes focused on something or someone other than those he was with. Because she was shy she was able to stand slightly apart from the rest of them and had the opportunity to take in every bit of him before he was even aware that she was with Francesca.

'Darling James, how lovely to see you.' Francesca left Madge's side and almost ran towards his table, knocking into and cannoning off a couple of high-ranking army officers as she did so. 'Darling, I didn't know *you* were going to be here.' She flung her arms round him, hugging him, while Madge stood shyly to one side uncertain what to do. Shouldn't she be saluting all these officers?

'Madge, come and meet James.' Francesca turned to where Madge was rooted to the spot like some ancient oak tree and pulled her towards them. 'Madge, this is my cousin, James Montgomery-West. James, this is my fellow cook, Marjorie Gregory.'

'Shouldn't you two be saluting your superior officers?' the woman in mauve satin asked idly, echoing Madge's thoughts, while eyeing their uniform with some disdain.

'Shouldn't *you* be in uniform yourself?' Francesca immediately retorted, letting go of Madge's hand and hugging her cousin once more.

'Married woman, darling, with a child, so exempt. Besides, blue is so… so depressing, do you not think?' She sipped at her pink drink and winked at James, who didn't appear to notice. 'I'm bored with this place,' she went on petulantly. 'They appear to be letting anyone in these days.'

'Oh, are you going?' Francesca glared at the woman. 'Lovely, we'll have your chair.'

James, who up until then had said nothing, grinned and, turning to the rest of the table, introduced his cousin. 'This is my cousin, Lady Francesca Montgomery-West.'

Madge stared. Lady? She'd not known Francesca was a lady, for heaven's sake. Posh, yes – you only had to hear Francesca's cut-glass vowels to know she was a girl with breeding – but an actual lady? Francesca had certainly kept that to herself over the reconstituting of powdered egg for Madeira cake. They'd met on the corridor, both Madge and Francesca heading for the tiny bathroom that the six WAAF cooks shared. Dripping with wet stockings and pants, it was, nevertheless, the first indoor lav and plumbed-in bath that Madge had experienced, the Co-op not unduly concerned with its tenant farmers and their families having to retreat outside for the toilet, or in front of the fire in a tin bath for their Friday night soak. Francesca was twenty-one, a couple of years older than Madge and, as a result of six months spent at finishing school in Switzerland perfecting lemon soufflé as well as the correct way to serve it from the left, a favourite with Sergeant Briscoe.

James Montgomery-West stood, swaying slightly as he got to his feet, his brown eyes blinking slowly as he turned his attention and focus on Madge.

'Too much to drink, darling?' Francesca smiled indulgently at her cousin. 'I'm assuming you're not about to take your bombing machine anywhere across the Channel tonight?'

'We've forty-eight hours' leave,' the officer sitting across from James answered for him, his flat vowels indicating his northern origins.

James reached out a hand to Madge but, before they could connect, sat down heavily, his legs appearing to give way slightly beneath him. 'Sorry, girls. Too little sleep and too much of this.' James indicated the glass in front of him and then turned to Madge again, his eyes never once leaving her face.

'Eddie Wilson,' the other man smiled at Francesca and Madge before grabbing a vacant chair from the next table and lifting it towards them. 'I can see I'm going to have to introduce myself.'

'You sound like Madge here. She's from up north too.' Francesca took Madge's arm and swiftly sat both of them on the one chair next to the men, successfully eliminating the two other women from this inner circle of around ten RAF officers.

Eddie turned to Madge. 'You're from Lancashire?'

'No, Yorkshire.' Madge smiled shyly, conscious all the while of James's eyes on her face. 'The white rose rather than the red, I'm afraid.'

'Eddie is with me on *R-Rascal*,' James said. 'He's our wireless operator.' He smiled at Eddie and patted his arm affectionately before using his other hand to wave to a passing waiter. 'Gin, Francesca, or are you still into Daiquiris?'

'Gin, please. Lots of tonic. Madge?'

'I'll have the same please.' Madge had no idea what a Daiquiri was but had drunk gin on previous occasions. She wasn't that keen on its taste but the last thing she wanted to do was ask for a lemonade in such sophisticated company. She looked round the crowded room, at the sea of blue and khaki, and felt totally out of her depth. A band was playing over in the corner of the Palm Court, and while Eddie concentrated on clearing a space on the table for the drinks that the hovering waiter was intent on offloading, and James and Francesca caught up on news from some relative who was apparently at death's door, Madge let the music flood her senses. She'd adored Glenn Miller since being first introduced to 'In the Mood' by her big sister Lydia years earlier, and when the band – aping the great man and his music – struck up the first chords, Madge felt her feet start to tap almost involuntarily.

'Dance?' Eddie stood in front of her, grinning. 'We northerners need to show these southerners we're not just all Yorkshire pudding and Lancashire hotpot. Come on.'

Madge stood, straightened her skirt and took Eddie's hand as he led her onto the crowded dance floor. She was relieved to see most of the other women were also in uniform with the accompanying flat black lace-up shoes; indeed, the few women sporting silver and gold dance shoes and satin evening dresses were beginning to look overdressed. Having said that, Madge was glad that she'd spent time on washing and curling her blond hair and had borrowed Francesca's mascara to set off the new red lipstick she'd bought earlier that day in Selfridges on Oxford Street. Arthur had loved dancing as much as she did and together they'd spent most Saturday nights before they'd joined up down in Midhope at the Cambridge Road swimming baths, where a temporary wooden floor transformed the pool from swimming to dancing, perfecting their moves.

Eddie was also an able dancer and as he led her through various swing steps Madge began to relax and enjoy herself. She was at The Ritz, for heaven's sake, in London, dancing with Bomber Command officers. As she followed Eddie's lead she was already composing the letter she'd be sending to Lydia back home in Westenbury, but as the saxophones and trumpets brought the piece to its climax, all thoughts of her elder sister and previous life went from her mind as she concentrated on the here and now. Hot and sticky in the stifling June evening air, Madge felt her skin dampen and sweat trickle down her back and she longed to take off her uniform jacket and tie. As the band played the final notes, Eddie grinned down at her and nodded towards their group still sitting at the table to their right. She smiled back gratefully and was just about to follow him back when the band struck up once more: 'Moonlight Serenade'.

Madge thought at first it was Eddie who'd changed his mind about returning to their table, but the hand that was intent on steering her back towards the dance floor, where couples were now dancing to the much slower notes of the serenade, belonged to James. Madge looked up at him in surprise but knew then, from that first touch on her arm, things could never be the same. Later, much later, he told her that the minute he saw her face, he felt such a pull, such a force inside him that he knew – whereas previously he'd been somewhat cavalier about his sorties over the channel – he just had to survive any future bombing raids to make it back to her side.

James guided her back onto the dance floor, his eyes never once leaving her face until he took her in his arms and Madge lay her head against his chest. She held herself as still as she could, concentrating on following the slow music and his steps, but her heart was pounding at such a rate she seriously thought she must be experiencing a heart attack. Her grandfather had died of one just the year previously; maybe it ran in families. If she were to live just another hour before an ambulance was called to The Ritz and her body scraped off the floor, she was, she knew, from that moment on, spoiled for ever for Arthur. He didn't stand a chance.

James suddenly pulled her away from him but kept hold of her arms. 'I have to get out of here,' he said. 'I need fresh air. Will you walk with me?'

'A walk…? What about Francesca? I did come with her.' They both looked towards James's cousin, who was being chatted up by two high-ranking army personnel.

James grinned down at Madge. 'I think you'll find Francesca is more than able to look after herself.' He took Madge's hand and led her back to the table. Eddie had disappeared, but when Madge scanned the room, guilty that she and James appeared to be breaking up the party, she saw that he was deep in conversation with the woman in mauve satin and was in the process of walking behind her towards the bar. Francesca turned briefly from her conversation and waved. 'Give me a minute.' James left Madge by the table and she wasn't quite sure whether to relinquish the chairs to some hovering Wrens or sit down on them. She was saved from her indecision by Francesca appearing at her side.

'Darling, do take James out for some fresh air. I'm more than happy here with these two.' She grinned and nodded towards the men. 'Poor James has been having rather a rough time of it lately and crowded joints like this have never been his thing. I'm not going anywhere. I'll either see you back here or back on Oxford Street. You're perfectly safe with James, you know,' she added as she saw Madge hesitate. 'He's been brought up to be a gentleman.'

'Like you've been brought up to be a lady?' Madge said archly. 'You kept that one quiet, Fran.'

'Doesn't mean a thing, darling. Now, if you'd rather stay here with me, that's fine too, but it is getting hellishly hot in here.' She broke off as James appeared behind her, adjusting his cap as he did so.

They walked together in silence out of the palm tree-lined bar and James nodded towards the main entrance. Madge stopped to let four rather fey-looking men, all quite dashingly attired in pin-striped suits, cross her path before they headed as one towards the stairs to the lower floor.

'Ritzkrieg,' James muttered as Madge caught him up.

'Pardon?'

'Ritzkrieg – it's the term that's been cooked up to explain the recalcitrant profligacy of this place. It's all becoming a bit sordid in here; all rather rank and somewhat depressing.' He shook his head. 'Those men who didn't stop to let you through will be on their way down to The Pink Sink.'

'The Pink Sink?' Madge frowned as James ushered her forward.

'It's a homosexual pick-up joint.'

Madge felt herself redden at the very idea of homosexuality. She knew such a thing existed but, apart from her dad's bullocks experimenting in the fields below their farmhouse, she hadn't ever really given it much thought, let alone known any man who was openly... well, openly *that way* inclined.

'I'm sorry,' James smiled. 'I've embarrassed you and that wasn't my intention.'

'So, what *was* your intention?' Madge felt slightly cross that she'd been made to appear as a gauche country bumpkin.

'Oh, I'm just not really a city person,' James frowned. 'London is far too noisy and busy, even when there's not a war on. Now it's just hell on earth.' He turned to Madge as they were saluted by the doorman and stepped onto Piccadilly. 'But thank goodness I was persuaded by Eddie to celebrate our forty-eight hours' leave by having drinks at The Ritz.' James stood in front of Madge and smiled down at her from his six-foot height. 'Something good has finally come out of the place.' He offered her his arm. 'Shall we walk?'

13

'Granny Madge has suggested you and I move in here for the winter.' I found a sweating Daisy down in the bungalow's vegetable patch, stripped off to a grubby T-shirt and digging the contents of a compost heap into the newly dug trench in front of her. 'Gosh, you really know what you're doing, don't you?' I said in admiration. 'I wouldn't have a clue.'

Daisy straightened up and wiped her brow with a dirty glove. 'You just need to be systematic, forking over the bottom of the trench where the soil is very heavy and adding the organic matter in a generous layer before turning in the next spit. The worms will redistribute it to improve soil consistency.'

'Spit? I've no idea what you're talking about.' I frowned, eager to get off worms, spits and compost heaps and onto the idea of us moving into the bungalow. Madge had actually fallen asleep on me in the gardens of Almast Haven, tired out, I assumed, with the telling of her tale about meeting James for the first time. I'd wanted her to carry on, but she'd become reluctant to continue and, clutching the RAF badge in her gloved hand, had suddenly dozed off.

'Ooh, really? Did Granny really suggest that? It wasn't you putting the idea into her head? I'd love to live here for a few months. Vivienne is already driving me mad back at home.' Daisy beamed at the thought of moving into the bungalow, but then she frowned. 'But I thought Madge was hoping to be back herself after Christmas?'

'I'm not sure she's quite as fit as she thinks she is. She dozed off on me in Heaven's garden when we were out for a stroll. I had to get a couple of the carers to help her back in. Apparently, she's on some new medication for something and it's making her sleepy.'

'She'd be far better here, out in the garden, than being drugged up in Heaven. We could look after her here, you know.' Daisy took off her gloves. 'I need coffee and a big fat bun. Come on, let's go up to the house and put the kettle on.'

'Would you know what to do if she became ill?' I asked as I followed Daisy back up the garden. The path was slippery with moss and the drizzle that had started to fall as Daisy and I chatted in the vegetable garden. 'I wouldn't. And, don't forget, we're going to be over at Holly Close Farm most of the day soon; we'll need to start clearing the site as soon as the sale has gone through. We can't leave her by herself. What if she falls again?'

The bungalow was warm – very different from how it had been just the week previously when I'd called in with Madge to pick up the key for Holly Close Farm – and felt lived in once more. I could see myself living here.

'Won't Mum be upset if we move out again just as we've gone back home?' Daisy bit into one of the enormous chocolate muffins we'd brought with us. 'It's not a great compliment, is it?' she went on through a mouthful of crumbs. 'Moving straight out again, I mean.'

'I really don't think Mum will mind at all. She and Dad have got used to being by themselves and she's able to spend the time she used to spend on cooking and looking after us on her ceramics. She's beginning to make quite a name for herself, you know.'

'Do you think you could live just with me? Who's going to clean the toilet and wash the kitchen floor?'

'Oh, for heaven's sake, Daisy. We're adults.'

'Really?' Daisy obviously thought otherwise. 'No, I know that.' She frowned and slurped at her coffee. 'It's just that because we're sisters rather than flatmates, we'll end up leaving the housework to each other. You know we will. You can't afford to upset flatmates by not doing your own washing up or leaving your pants and pyjamas in the bathroom, but with sisters it doesn't matter. You can't throw your sister out.'

I laughed. 'Yes, OK, I know what you mean. We'll just have to be a bit grown-up about it: no leaving half-eaten pizzas under the sofa or not cleaning the bath after you. Bagsy have the biggest spare bedroom.'

'You see, you've started already. Being bossy and bagging the biggest room.'

'I'm the eldest.'

'Yes, and the bossiest.' Daisy popped the remaining bit of muffin into her mouth. 'Fine, fine. I *prefer* the little bedroom. It looks out onto the garden and the sun comes into it in the morning. Do we need to pay rent, do you think? I've got two months' wages still owing to me but I really am going to have to get bar work or some other gardening work to pay my way until Seb Henderson signs on the dotted line. Or do you think we can go back to Mum and Dad's to eat?'

'That's being really cheeky. I have a bit of money saved up. Not much, but it'll keep me going until the money comes through from the sale of Holly Close Farm. I bet Dad will sub you a loan.'

'Now, are we going to be on an equal footing over the farm? You know, you sort the house and the cottage and I'll be in charge of the land and gardens. I can't be doing with you telling me what to do all the time.'

'One of us has to be in charge. I'm project manager, Granny said; you know she did.'

'You're sounding a bit pompous, Charlie. You're not going to be my boss, you know.'

'I think you'll find I need to be. It *is* my area of expertise, after all, being project manager.'

'I tell you what you *need*.' Daisy folded her arms and glared.

'A bit of cooperation is what I *need*.'

'What you *need*, Charlie, is a right good seeing-to from Josh Lee. And the sooner the better.'

The 'right good seeing-to' prescribed by Daisy as a panacea for all of life's ills happened just a couple of weeks later. Daisy and I spent several days moving our stuff into Granny Madge's bungalow. Mum and Dad – professing much sorrow that we didn't want to stay in the family home with them but, we knew, secretly overjoyed that we were leaving – helped us move in, ferrying our bits and pieces as well as the loan of bedside lamps and extra plugs for the plethora of electrical gadgets Daisy and I insisted we needed to survive. Good old Mum, disinclined, as the world's worst cook, to fill Granny's fridge and freezer with home-made shepherd's pies, apple tarts, brownies and the like, did a massive shop at Sainsbury's and M&S as a starter pack for us both. I think it assuaged her guilt at feeling relief that we were to be no longer under her feet once more – and Daisy and I oohed and aahed over the contents of the myriad orange plastic bags in much the same way as we'd done every term on our return to university years before.

It was now early December, the weather had turned miserably cold and blustery, and Daisy and I were happy to light the wood-burning stove in the sitting room of an evening, draw the heavy Sanderson curtains against the pernicious damp and curl up on the floral chintz-covered sofas. Daisy, always a hard grafter, had done as she'd said she was going to do and found herself a temporary seasonal job as waitress down at Clementine's restaurant in the village. She was originally only supposed to be doing a couple of evenings a week plus one day over the weekend, but her phone was constantly ringing requesting that she cover staff who'd not turned up because of illness.

The dreaded winter-vomiting bug appeared to have struck with a vengeance in the area, but particularly at Almost Heaven where, because of fear of contagion and the possible subsequent sending of its residents one step nearer to their Maker, the home was off limits to visitors. Poor old Madge was beside herself and telephoned Mum as well as Daisy and me constantly, berating the fact that she was a virtual prisoner and that she'd end up as mad as the other silly old fools if she couldn't break out any day soon. I was dying to hear more of her and James's story, but she was disinclined to chat about her past over her mobile phone, saying that once she was 'out on parole' she'd tell me – and Daisy who was just as interested – more. Wonderful Granny that she was, she also phoned to say she'd deposited a sum of money in both our bank accounts and that we were to use it to keep our heads above water until the sale of Holly Close Farm went through.

I'd not heard a thing from Josh Lee since our bike ride a few weeks previously. I wasn't particularly bothered, being happy to hole up at the bungalow, enjoying my own company while Daisy worked in the garden or at Clementine's. I was getting stuck into the plans for the cottage and, as much as I could without any real idea of proper measurements or square footage or, indeed, what Seb and Liberty had in mind for their new house, for the farm itself. Thanking the God of Architectural Plans that I had my laptop with its PlanGrid app and computer-aided design and drafting software, I was able to fill my time sketching, measuring, drafting and making layouts of initial ideas for designs to create 3-D representations. With my trusty slide rule, compasses, rolls of tracing paper and my set of marker pens I was soon able to put my ideas onto paper and then progress, using graphics software that simulated building materials such as stone and wood, to experimenting with how different materials complemented my visions.

Late one afternoon I suddenly realised I'd had enough of being on my own, talking to myself and ranting at the designs if they weren't to my liking. I was both bored and lonely and in danger of becoming depressed. Daisy, if she wasn't working, was spending a lot of her time catching up with old school friends, as well as going out on dates with men she was swiping right on Tinder. I'd spent the day on my laptop, stopping only to make myself a cheese sandwich, and then another, and drinking endless cups of coffee. I felt jittery with too much caffeine, a definite lack of exercise or any meaningful conversation. I wandered into the bathroom and visibly blanched at my appearance in the mirror. Jesus, this was no way to make Dominic come back. My hair needed a good wash and, sniffing my armpits, I realised, so did I. What if he arrived out of the blue, begging me to go back with him to London? He'd take one look and scarper off the way he'd come. I needed taking in hand: a brisk walk followed by a shower, hair wash, leg shave and pedicure would sort me out.

I borrowed one of Granny's coats – remarkably similar, I mused, to the dog-walking one of Mum's I'd been forced into wearing on the ash-scattering afternoon – and set off. Almost dark at just half-past three in the afternoon: God, I hated winter. Young mums sporting winter coats, trendily tied scarves and myriad offspring dominated the pavements on their way back from the local school pick-up, and I had to step into the road to avoid them.

This was when I could have done with Malvolio with me: I always felt safer walking in woods and down dark country lanes with a dog, even a cowardy-custard like Malvolio, who would run from the tiniest yapping Yorkshire terrier, never mind a six-foot axe murderer intent on, well, murder.

Once I got into the swing of it, I really enjoyed tramping through the dank undergrowth, kicking up soggy dead leaves, leaping over the stream made fat with the recent rain and trailing a stick across the tree trunks as I walked. My spirits began to revive. By the time I'd done a circuit and arrived back at the bungalow it was fully dark, and I reckoned whatever it was that was supposed to be over the yardarm was definitely well over and poured myself a large glass of Sauvignon Blanc before heading for the bathroom to run a bath.

The minute I lowered myself into the warm water, scented with some rather revolting lavender stuff of Madge's, the doorbell rang. Jehovah's Witnesses or the six-foot axe murderer?

Josh Lee.

'Oh,' I said, surprised. 'What are *you* doing here?' I pulled Granny's towel that bit tighter round my top half.

'You shouldn't open the door to strangers. I could have been a six-foot axe murderer.'

'Hardly, seeing as you're only five-foot-ten.'

'Eleven, actually.'

'And no axe.'

'I'll go away and get one if you'd rather?'

'How did you know where I was?'

'I saw Daisy in the Jolly Sailor last night. She said you were both camping out here. She said you needed taking out of yourself.'

I glared at Josh. If Daisy had said I needed 'a good seeing-to' I'd have her.

'So, I thought I'd call round on my way home from work and invite you to my place for something to eat.'

'I've no transport.' Dad was in the process of sorting out Madge's car insurance so Daisy and I could drive Madge's little car. Neither of us could afford the exorbitant cost, but Dad had taken pity on us (probably realising he'd be otherwise hauled out of bed at midnight to pick us up, as had been the case when we were teenagers) and said it was an early Christmas present to insure Madge's car for us for six months.

'I'll wait for you.' Josh stamped his feet a bit on the doorstep and looked meaningfully past me. 'It is December out here, you know.'

'Hang on a minute.' I held up my hand like a traffic cop, preventing his crossing the threshold. 'I haven't accepted yet.'

'Probably best offer you'll get round here this evening,' Josh said archly as he rubbed his hands together against the cold, 'and there's spag bol for supper.'

'With mushrooms?' I asked suspiciously.

'Do you want there to be mushrooms?'

'No, I hate the slimy little beggars.'

'Definitely no mushrooms.'

'OK. Give me twenty minutes.' I opened the front door to let Josh pass, and his arm in its navy suit sleeve brushed my naked one sending a small *frisson* through me. 'Help yourself to wine,' I said over my shoulder as he made his way into the warmth of the sitting room and I scarpered back to the bathroom and my now-cooling bath water.

Why on earth was I shaving my legs, and giving my whole body the works? Because your poor old body needs it, I told myself. You've totally abandoned and mistreated it since Dominic buggered off. It was weeks since I'd bothered with anything more than a quick slash of lipstick and a bit of blusher, and it felt good to carefully smudge smoky eyeliner around my eyes and add a couple of coats of mascara. I finished off with a fabulous coral lipstick and, instead of replaiting my wet hair, dried it upside down so that it fanned out and framed my face in a mass of blond waves.

Oh God, was Josh Lee going to think this was his lucky night? I played down my appearance by pulling on a clean pair of faded jeans and my favourite navy polo-neck cashmere sweater. I was just about to add my work boots when, instead, I thought sod it, and scrabbled in a bag of still to be unpacked clothes and found my lovely suede ankle boots, which made my legs look so much longer.

'You're looking good, Maddison.' Josh smiled as he turned from where he'd been standing by the table. I remembered he'd always called me by my last name for some reason. 'I always said you were the most gorgeous girl in sixth form.'

'Not to me you didn't,' I said. 'And I'm only coming with you because I need to talk about Holly Close Farm with you. And I can't face another cheese sandwich.'

'Are these the plans?' Josh, I saw, had been having a good look at what I'd been working on. 'Bring them with you. Your ideas for the two cottages are stunning. Really.'

'Thank you.' I felt ridiculously pleased. 'Come on, you promised me food.'

Not being much of a cook, I'm constantly surprised by how good other people are.

'Where'd you learn to cook like this?' I mopped up the remains of the Bolognese sauce – sans mushrooms, as promised – and took a good look round Josh's kitchen. It was, as you'd expect from a professional builder and suave entrepreneur, ultra-modern. All stainless steel with huge fuck-off fridges and freezers: very masculine, very Josh Lee.

'I suppose I've just got into cooking over the years. Mum was a bit too busy with her own life to ensure there was always a proper meal on the table. We didn't starve, my brother and me, but it was usually a ready meal or a pizza or a takeaway. When Dad left us to be with Sally – his partner – we had to fend for ourselves a bit. Anyway, I enjoy putting together ingredients.' He grinned. 'It's a bit like building, starting with good materials and ending up with something whole.'

'I didn't realise,' I said. 'I didn't know your parents had split up.'

'Not unusual, really. Probably more unusual if your parents are still together. I suppose it has put me off long-term commitment...' Josh broke off. 'Or perhaps I was just waiting for you, Maddison, to reappear.' He grinned boyishly, reminding me so much of the sixth-former he once was. He'd had all the girls in the lower sixth – and probably the upper, too – drooling over him. He'd certainly done the rounds of us all, hopping from one to the next, playing us along.

'I doubt it very much,' I said archly, taking our plates over to the dishwasher. 'Gosh, this is some monster.' I opened up the machine, which was all shiny dials and flashing lights, and gazed in wonder: for a girl who was used to a yellow dishcloth, a pan-scrubber and a bottle of Fairy Liquid, this was pretty futuristic. Josh came up behind me as I looked for a seemingly non-existent place to stack the dirty knives and forks.

'Here.' He reached an arm in front of me, pressing something so that an empty cutlery tray suddenly shot towards me. I could feel the crisp cotton of his pink-striped shirt and the metal from his leather belt against my back and, remembering the dream from a few nights back, suddenly felt horribly randy. Embarrassed at his closeness, and convinced he'd be able to see my traitorous nipples, which had jumped to attention all on their own, I tried to back out, but Josh continued to load the dishwasher with me trapped between him and his shiny machine – '*You're telling me you were getting off on a bloody dishwasher?*' I could hear Daisy say scornfully. '*You need to get out more.*' I began to laugh at the very thought and stepped to one side out of both Josh and his dishwasher's way.

'What's so funny?' Josh smiled, reaching for the bottle of wine and refilling both our glasses.

'Oh, it all just seems ridiculous that ten years after I was snogging you in the Jolly Sailor, I'm back in Westenbury, trapped between you and your pan-scrubber.'

'I've never heard it call a pan-scrubber before,' Josh grinned, glancing down at his nether regions. 'And, for your information, I wouldn't dream of putting my precious pans in the dishwasher. They're soaking in the utility. OK, come on, into the sitting room where you can show me your plans properly.'

For a good half an hour Josh and I sat on his cream sitting-room carpet with the plans laid out in front of us as I explained my ideas for both the farm and the cottage. He was a good listener, genuinely interested in what I'd come up with, and said very little as I talked him through what I'd been working on all the previous week. It was strangely intimate and when he accidently touched my knee as he shifted to get a more detailed look, I moved it away.

It reminded me of a game of chess. We were studying the plans and I'd point something out and there'd be silence. Then he'd make a comment for or against my idea and I'd either accept his comment or shake my head and make a further move of my own by tracing a finger over something I was particularly pleased with. Then there'd be more silence; more studying of layouts, windows, new walls and then more comments. When he touched my knee once more with the stem of his wine glass, this time I didn't move away.

'Jesus, Maddison, I'm going to have to make love to you or call you a taxi.' Josh looked up from the chess game of plans and reached a hand for my face, stroking it with warm hands. 'Your call.'

My call? I was feeling so rampantly over the top from the wine, the heat of the room, the excitement of explaining my plans and Josh Lee himself there was no way I was going to call a cab.

14

'Wow, Granny, this James bloke sounds to have been an absolute blast.'

'Bloke? A blast?' Madge raised her eyebrows in Daisy's direction. 'Goodness, you girls do have the most extraordinary ways of describing men. In my day, it was smashing... a lovely person, a sweetheart ... a dreamboat even... Or was that in the fifties?' Madge closed her eyes slightly in an attempt to recall pertinent adjectives of the time. 'Anyway, yes, I was totally taken with James Montgomery-West from the very minute I met him.'

'Taken with him?' Daisy laughed. 'I can see why, looking at this photo.' I leaned across Daisy to take another look and studied the features of the exceptionally attractive man in the faded black-and-white image held in her hand. 'And you were still supposed to be seeing Arthur?' Daisy went on. 'That must have been a bit difficult?'

Madge frowned and, for a moment, looked almost distraught. Once the winter vomiting bug had passed and Almast Haven was open to visitors once more, I'd driven over, picked Madge up and brought her back to the bungalow for a change of scene as well as further instructions on sorting out the garden. Before we got stuck into our various tasks that Monday morning, we'd settled Madge in front of the fire with coffee and the date and walnut cake Mum had bought from some recent charity do.

'Difficult? Well, yes, I suppose it was rather difficult all round.'

Daisy cut herself a huge piece of cake and sat back on the sofa. It was sleeting outside and while it was the start of a new week and she and I should really be getting stuck in to our various jobs, it was very tempting to just stay put in the warmth and talk to Madge.

'So, you'd met him at The Ritz?' Daisy asked once she'd swallowed half her cake and recovered some crumbs from her sweater. 'What then? Did you start seeing him?'

Madge put down her own cake untouched and leaned forward. 'Well,' she smiled, her eyes bright, 'it was like this, girls…'

As Madge and James stepped out of the hotel and on to Piccadilly, James suddenly stopped and, much to both Madge and the doorman's surprise, stroked the carved stonework of the building. 'All a sham,' he smiled as Madge stood, wondering, at his side. 'This façade is just that. A façade. Take a pickaxe to this beautiful stonework and you'll soon expose the steel skeleton beneath it.'

'How on earth do you know that?' Madge laughed. 'And does it matter anyway?'

'I love buildings, love how the stones fit together. I was just really disappointed when I found out The Ritz isn't solid stone through and through.'

'So how *do* you know that?'

'Architecture,' James said, taking her arm and guiding her down the road and into Green Park. 'I managed two years at Cambridge before this all blew up in our faces. And also, the hotel management itself is constantly reminding the public how safe the hotel is because of its metal frame.' He laughed. 'They omit to mention that the steel was imported from Germany. Anyway, one day, when this is all over, I will go back to my studies… if I survive.'

'Oh, don't say that.' Madge shivered at the thought. She'd only just met this man but already she knew she couldn't bear to let him go.

'I'm probably living on borrowed time,' James smiled. 'Been incredibly bloody lucky so far. Anyway, I apologise, it's not my intention to be depressed tonight. Come on, let's breathe in this magical summer air.'

Madge had walked in Hyde Park a couple of times with Fran, but with the anti-aircraft guns mounted on their steel structures now the main feature of the area, rather than the grass, fields and flowers she was so missing from home, she'd not been inclined to venture in there by herself. Now, as they strolled through Green Park in the dusk and bosky light shed by the London trees, it felt wonderful to be seeing verdant green rather than the grey stone and concrete of the city.

'I just needed to get away from the madding crowd,' James smiled down at her as they walked beneath the giant plane and lime trees. Breathing in the scented night air, he appeared to be sobering up amazingly quickly.

'Thomas Hardy?' Madge was impressed. Not many men, particularly from back home, shared her love of reading.

'You like his novels?' James stopped walking. 'I've only just discovered them. There's a lot of hanging around back at base, waiting for the weather to break so we can be off. I've done an awful lot of reading lately.'

Madge stared up at him. 'Are you frightened? You know, when you set off?'

'Yes,' he said bleakly, starting to walk once more. 'Yes, every time. We're all a bit superstitious: the men all carry some good-luck charm or other, whether it be around their necks or in their top pockets.'

'What do you have? For good luck, I mean?' Madge suddenly really wanted to know what was going to keep this man she'd just met safe from oblivion.

James smiled. 'I don't have anything.'

'Then you must take this.' Madge sat down on one of the park benches and scrabbled around in the collar of her shirt, pulling out a chain with a tiny gold cross, which she unfastened. 'I'd really like you to have this,' she said shyly. 'My mum gave it to me the morning I left Yorkshire. She's very religious, is Mum: she and my brother, Isaac, are always at church. The rest of us aren't. I mean, we do go to church when it's Harvest Festival and Christmas… you know, we walk down into the village…' Madge knew she was talking too fast, and suddenly realised she must appear very forward to James, giving him this little piece of jewellery, the only piece her mum had ever given her. 'It's not particularly valuable.'

James took the chain and looked down at it as it lay in his hand, still warm from Madge's neck. Then he slid the tiny cross from its chain and placed it in his breast pocket. An old man was laying a huge bunch of yellow roses underneath one of the black poplar trees. Who was he remembering, Madge wondered as she breathed in James's smell of citrus, cigarettes and whisky as he reached forward. Her skin felt raw, inflamed, when he very gently unfastened the top button of her shirt and replaced the chain where it belonged. He fastened the button once again, straightened her tie and stroked her face with the ball of his thumb.

'Thank you, Madge. That will keep me safe, knowing you gave it to me.'

James stood and they continued to walk in silence through the park. He stopped at last at a park gate. 'Do you have to be back by a set time?'

'Yes, eleven o'clock. It's a bit strange, living on Oxford Street,' Madge smiled. 'Not really like being in the war at all.'

James glanced at his watch. 'Do you want to go back to The Ritz? I mean, I have dragged you away from Francesca?'

Oh heavens. Is that what he wanted? To go back there? Madge felt she would die if they just retraced their steps, went back and that was it. If he didn't ask to see her again. 'If that's what you want.' Madge could hear herself speaking almost sulkily. And she wasn't generally someone who sulked.

'Madge, I can't think of anything worse. I don't want any more to drink. I just want to walk with you. I want to know everything about you.'

Madge felt relief flood through her like a warm shower. 'Let's keep on walking then.'

They walked side by side up Pall Mall and through the surprisingly quiet streets, their hands touching occasionally but James making no attempt to take hers in his. As they passed the Phoenix Theatre where *Love for Love*, starring John Gielgud, was being played, Madge felt slightly embarrassed. Love? What was she feeling? It couldn't be love, she knew that. No one loved someone within an hour of meeting them. Maybe this was merely lust? She'd certainly never felt like this about Arthur, never wanted to melt into him as she'd wanted to dissolve into James in the park. 'Where are we going?' Madge turned to James, trying to take in everything about him: his tall stature, his blond hair, his brown eyes and the wonderful way he spoke. Cultured, educated, southern.

'I'm hoping... yes, it is... come on, it's still open, let's find ourselves a table at Elena's.'

'Elena's?'

'Elena Giacopazzi's café. We can drink coffee there, proper strong Italian stuff.' James suddenly looked worried. 'Unless you'd rather have gin, of course.'

She smiled. 'I don't really like gin that much – my mother always told me to stay away from it.'

'Wise woman.'

Elena's was only half full, mainly of after-theatre-goers as well as, Madge realised, American army personnel.

James easily found a table and ordered coffee for them both. 'This will keep me awake,' he grinned. 'I don't want to sleep and wake up to find I've dreamt you. That you weren't real after all.'

The coffee when it arrived was strong and unfamiliar to Madge, used as she was to mainly drinking tea or some revolting coffee substitute, but from then on strong coffee, its smell and taste, would forever remind her of James and this first evening with him.

'So, you studied at Cambridge?' Madge asked. James sat across from her, his fingers slowly stroking the back of her hand. It felt wonderful, rather like being bathed in warm sunshine, and she never wanted it to stop. James took her hand and brought it up to his mouth, kissing it before replacing it with her other.

'Yes, and funnily enough I'm back there now.'

'In Cambridge?' Madge's heart did a little somersault. Arthur was based in Cambridge. 'Whereabouts? Or is it a secret? There seems to be so much that mustn't be discussed.' She glanced round the café at the laughing, coffee-drinking crowd and tried to work out which, if any, could be a German spy intent on following James out, once they left, and finishing him off.

James laughed at her seriousness. 'I'm with Bomber Command at Bourn at the moment. See, look, no one's interested.' He turned to survey the other tables.

Madge felt herself pale. Arthur was at Bourn. She was his girlfriend. He'd given her that ring, for heaven's sake.

James didn't appear to notice her unease. 'Yes, we've been lucky devils. Chalked up fifty-two sorties so far and most of those with Eddie as wireless operator. He's bloody good at his job. You get used to flying with the same crew.'

'And are there a lot of you based there?' Did he know Arthur? was what she was really asking.

'A couple of thousand at least: RAF and WAAF, and the Americans now, of course. Thank goodness they've come in with us; we certainly wouldn't be anything without them.' James nodded towards one of the USAAF men, who nodded back but then carried on talking to the group he was with. 'Poor devils. Not their war, of course, and such a bloody long way from home.'

Still shaken that James was apparently at the same airbase as Arthur, Madge wasn't quite sure what to say. Should she say her boyfriend was there with him? Should she ask if he knew him? But, why would he? James was a flight lieutenant, flying the planes; poor Arthur, still in the lowest rank possible, simply serviced them. In the end, she said nothing.

'Madge, tell me everything. Tell me all about your family, your brothers and sisters, what you did before you joined up, what you want to do afterwards.'

Afterwards? Did he mean after the coffee? Madge knew she didn't want to have to say goodbye. She looked at her watch. It wasn't quite ten o'clock. She smiled at his enthusiasm. He really did want to know. 'Well, I live on a small tenanted farm up in Yorkshire where my dad does the milking and then takes some of it on his daily milk round. The rest is collected by the Co-op, who owns it all. I've three brothers and one sister. Lydia is the eldest and I'm closest to her although she's ten years older than me and married with children. Two of my brothers have joined the army, but Isaac, who isn't quite, well, quite the same as the others, he's still helping my dad on the farm...' She paused and glanced at his face to see how he was reacting to all this. Gosh, if his cousin was a lady, what did that make him? *And* he'd been at Cambridge studying architecture, for heaven's sake. 'I suppose it's all a bit different from what you're used to?'

'Totally, but it's all really fascinating.' James leaned forward and took her hand once more. 'And you, Madge, you must have a boyfriend?'

Madge felt herself redden. Was she going to tell a lie? Was she going to tell this gorgeous, heavenly man that, if it was up to Arthur, she'd actually be engaged to one of James's mechanics. In the end she simply said, 'There is someone from home, but nothing serious. How serious can you be when there's a war on?'

'And do you miss him?' James was looking at her with such intensity she simply and truthfully said, 'No, I don't miss him at all.'

'I couldn't bear it if you did,' James said quietly. 'When can I see you again, Madge?'

'Is it allowed?'

'Is what allowed?'

'A flight lieutenant being seen with a lowly aircraftwoman second class?'

James frowned. 'Goodness, I've no idea.'

'Maybe if I salute you constantly?' Madge began to laugh.

'I'd rather you didn't.' James laughed back before glancing at the clock on the wall. 'I think I need to get you back to Oxford Street. Shall we try for a taxi or are you happy to walk?'

Madge knew she wanted to prolong her time with James as long as she could and a taxi ride would mean only another ten minutes in his company. 'I don't mind walking at all,' she smiled, 'but will you be all right getting back? Where are you staying tonight?'

'Eaton Square. It's not a million miles from Oxford Street.' James stood, nodded once more to both the American and RAF officers with whom he was obviously acquainted and took Madge's arm, directing her towards the door and the London streets, still a long way from total darkness despite the blackout.

'Eaton Square? In a hotel?'

James looked slightly embarrassed. 'My family has a house there.'

'Your parents live here? In London?' Madge smiled at James in delight. 'Oh, your mum will be so pleased to see you, won't she?'

'They're not actually there. The place has been closed up for the duration; you know, dust sheets put over everything.'

'Oh.' Madge began to realise this man was very different from the boys back home.

'It's been in the family for years.' James took Madge's hand. 'My father doesn't really want to part with it.'

'But they're not there?'

'No, they're at home.'

'Home?'

'We live in Ascot.'

'Ascot?' Madge frowned. Wasn't Ascot something to do with horseracing?

'In Berkshire. It's where I grew up. Where my parents live. My mother comes up to London occasionally to shop but she doesn't often stay over. Dora, who's been with us for years, still comes in to do some cleaning and to make sure everything is as it should be. My father uses it when he's sitting.'

'Sitting?' Madge realised she must sound idiotic repeating everything James was saying. But sitting? Sitting where? She didn't like to ask for fear of being thought stupid.

James continued talking as they walked across Trafalgar Square, back through Piccadilly and followed the roads and streets towards Oxford Street. Madge knew she wouldn't have had a clue how to get back to base, but James seemed to know exactly where he was going. 'He's in the Lords,' James went on, 'although with the Commons being so badly bombed, Churchill and the other MPs tend to use it most these days, which annoys my father somewhat. He's a bit old school; likes things to be as they should be.'

'He sounds a bit scary,' Madge said without thinking.

'Well, he's getting on a bit now. He's quite a lot older than my mother, and I've three sisters, all older than I am, all doing various things to support the war effort. I suppose I was a bit of a surprise to the old man when I suddenly came along when he was in his forties.'

'Gosh, yes, you must have been. Do you get on with him?'

James frowned. 'To be honest, Madge, although I adore my mother, I don't feel I know my father that well. I was packed off to school when I was eight: I think he probably wanted me out of the way as I was a noisy kid, always zooming around the house and garden when he was trying to read his political papers or sort the estate out.'

'What do you mean, the estate?' Madge could only think of the estate of corporation houses that had been planned in the lower two fields of the farm at home. Maybe James's father had something to do with such an estate in Ascot.

'The house has... has, er... a few acres and he makes sure everything is as it should be...' James trailed off. He obviously didn't want to talk any more about his father. They walked on in silence for a couple of streets and then James suddenly stopped and took her hand. 'Can I see you again, Madge? I don't know when I'm going to be off next but as soon as I am, I can train it back down to London to see you; this damned withdrawal of all petrol for non-essential use means I can't drive any more.'

'I'd really like that,' Madge said shyly. 'There's a phone back at base that we can use out of office hours. I'll give you the number. Don't ring when I'm working or Sergeant Briscoe will go mad. She's already not very impressed with my heavy pastry. Francesca, of course, is her darling.'

James laughed. 'Yes, well, she's had a fortune thrown at her education in Switzerland. She *should* know what she's doing.'

'This is me. We're here. Thank you very much for walking me home.'

'I don't know what you've done to me, Madge.' Madge saw James swallow, his brown eyes so dark in contrast with his blond hair. She wasn't quite sure who moved first, but he broke off what he was saying about Francesca and her finishing school and, cupping Madge's face in both of his large warm hands, bent his fair head to hers and kissed her softly. Just once and so lightly that Madge almost wondered if she'd imagined it. He stood looking down at her, drinking in her features until Madge could stand it no longer and responded by bringing up her hands to his face and kissing him back. He gave a soft sigh before winding his fingers into her hair beneath her hat and kissing her again at length. She'd never been kissed like this before and she kissed him back, taking his lead, pushing herself against him.

'Oy, Gregory, enough of that on the streets of London. Get yourself in before Sergeant Briscoe sees you and has you over the coals.' Beryl, one of the other cooks based with them, grinned as she walked past and towards the double door that, in its heyday had led to the perfumery department of the store where they were based and then, realising Madge was with an officer, gave an embarrassed salute in James's direction and scuttled in.

'I'd better go,' James smiled down at her. 'Write down your address and telephone number for me so that I can contact you.'

Madge had both pencil and paper in her bag and quickly wrote down the required number and address.

James bent to kiss her once more, tipped her hat back slightly, saluted and grinned at her before turning on his heel, then glancing back for one last look.

Madge ran up the six flights of stairs on wings but hadn't been in the room she shared with Beryl more than a minute when Mary, Francesca's room-mate, knocked on her door. 'There's a rather gorgeous RAF man down on the street,' she grinned. 'Wants a quick word with you. I told him you'd be in trouble: it's after eleven. I've only just made it back in time and I bet Fran's not back yet.'

Madge grabbed her hat and, raking her fingers through her blond curls, dashed back down the way she'd just come. Had she not given him the correct phone number? She knew she shouldn't be out after eleven but oh, how lovely, he'd come back for something. Maybe just to say goodnight once more. Madge unlocked the door, stepped out onto the street and was immediately grabbed by a hand from out of the shadows.

'How could you, Madge? I saw you. I saw you kissing that officer. You're supposed to be engaged to *me*.'

'Arthur? Arthur, get your hands off me. What are *you* doing here?'

'Got a twenty-four-hour pass once work finished for the day. Not much you can do on that – most of the lads are just staying in Bourn and drinking themselves daft – but one of the mechanics was told to come up to London to fix some officer's car and given permission to take one of the motorbikes. I asked if I could ride pillion so I could see you.'

'But why didn't you ring? You know the number.'

'I bloody well did. Over and over, but no one knew where you were. And then someone said you'd gone off for the evening. So, I waited for you to come back.'

Madge felt herself go hot. Arthur must have seen everything. 'I'm sorry.'

'Aye, so you bloody well should be, making a fool of yourself with some officer. How could you, Madge? How could you do it to me?'

'I...' Madge didn't know what to say. The intensity and pain in Arthur's eyes frightened her.

'We're supposed to be getting wed and there you were, all over him, kissing him like there was no tomorrow. And do you know, for me, there might not be. God knows where I might be sent.'

'Why would you be? You're a mechanic on an air base. You're not going to be sent abroad. And, Arthur, I keep telling you, we're not engaged. I told you that when you insisted I keep that ring. I'm going to give it you back.'

'No, no, Madge don't do that. I can't bear it if you do that.' Arthur calmed down for a few seconds but then began to get angry again. 'So, who is he then? Who's the bloody officer you were at it with?'

Before Madge could say anything, a crisp, cultured voice rang out through the warm night air. 'Aircraftwoman Second Class Gregory, you'll be on a charge if you don't get inside this minute.'

'Yes, ma'am.' Madge saluted the woman standing in front of her and turned on her heel. The woman followed her inside.

'Thanks, Fran.'

'I could hear you both arguing a mile off. Arthur, I presume?'

Madge nodded. 'But not as much trouble as you're going to be in for being back half an hour late and impersonating an officer. Oh, Fran, what am I going to do?'

'So, what did you do, Granny?' Daisy brought Madge back to the present. 'I'm assuming because you married Arthur, you didn't see James again?'

'Well, I did, darling. How could I not? I'd fallen in love for the first time in my life.' Madge sighed, looked at her watch and glanced outside. 'It appears to have stopped sleeting, girls. Come on, there are jobs to be done.'

15

A wet Wednesday morning and, along with the damned cold miserable rain, came a damned miserable setback. I thought I'd been doing well with regards my broken heart. I *was* doing well: hadn't I had – rather energetic – sex with a man that wasn't Dominic and survived? More than survived. I felt my pulse quicken as I recalled Friday night, Josh Lee and his throbbing machine. That state-of-the-art dishwasher and its attempts at foreplay had a lot to answer for. So, yes, I'd thought I was picking up my life.

And when I decided I'd make an inroad into the day's ten thousand steps by walking down to the newsagent's for new pencils and chewing gum, I was actually feeling that maybe there was just a little thawing out of my frozen heart. So much so, I changed my mind about walking, donned my old tracksuit bottoms, which were as close as I had to running gear, and set off at a trot, taking the long way round to extend the distance.

By the time I reached the newsagent's, gasping for air like a landed fish and soggy from the persistent drizzle, I was feeling pretty happy. OK, maybe not happy – that was a bit over the top – but getting there. Sod you, Dominic

Abraham: since you buggered off, I've inherited a cottage, become my own boss, been turned on by a dishwasher and its owner and am now in training for my first marathon. Ha! Beat that, you bastard.

He did.

Concentrating on getting my breath back as I waited in the queue at the village newsagent, I took in the headlines of the papers. The usual stuff: Brexit, dire warnings of the ice age that was heading our way after Christmas; pensioners left on trolleys in A and E; and, with just a couple of column centimetres on the front of the *Telegraph*, right at the very bottom and only spied because the paper had been put into the rack upside down, Abraham Developments' success at the European Architectural Awards Ceremony. Abraham Developments? Success? My poor old heart, just about returned to its usual resting rate after the unaccustomed run, was once again racing, knocking painfully against my ribs as my trembling fingers picked up the paper and tried to find the business pages as directed. There, in all his glory, grinning as he held his award for innovative design aloft, was Dominic.

'Are you buying that, love?' The young shopkeeper looked meaningfully at the newspaper in my hand, several pages of which had come adrift and landed on my muddy trainers and the dirty wet floor.

'Bastard. Wanker.' I glared at the assistant.

'You do know I don't have to put up with harassment, alarm or distress in the workplace?' He glared back at me.

'Oh God, I'm so sorry,' I said, appalled as I realised I'd shouted my fury aloud. 'Not you, *you're* not a bastard...

Well, you could be, for all I know. It's *this* wanker here, I mean.' I turned the article towards the counter, shaking the paper in his face.

'Language! Do you mind?' An elderly woman, wet plastic Rainmate on her tight grey perm and an even wetter, shivering scrap of a dog on the end of her lead, tutted and glared at me in turn.

I burst into tears. 'Look, I'm really sorry,' I sniffed. 'Just had a bit of a shock, that's all. I don't normally harass newsagents and swear like a trooper.' Well, half of that wasn't a lie.

'That's all right,' the assistant grinned. 'I don't give a fuck really, but I'm supposed to quote that to anyone who might be giving me trouble. What's the bastard done?'

I shoved the article under his nose. 'That's my boyfriend. Well, my ex-boyfriend. He had a wife and three kids all along and didn't tell me. And now…' I was almost trembling with rage, '… now he's won an award for innovative design and, and… the fucking design… sorry, excuse me…' I nodded apologetically towards Rainmate woman as her Chihuahua or whatever it was, tail stuck determinedly between its legs against my tone, shivered uncontrollably, '… was mine. Mine!'

'Wanker!' the Rainmate bristled and drops fell onto the woman's already wet dog. 'What a wanker,' she growled. 'Don't you let him get away with that, love.'

Daisy and I had agreed to a planning meeting with Seb, Libby and Seb's father – Westenbury's local celebrity – David Henderson, that afternoon at David Henderson's house. He and his wife had lived in the village for years – everyone locally knew of them – and although I had gone past their gate every time Daisy and I had walked to our primary school, I never dreamt that I'd one day be working with him.

By the time I got home from the newsagent's, newspaper folded into my hoody pocket, I was seething. I'd take legal advice against Dominic, show him up for what he was. Daisy was back from the supermarket and, from the trail of crumbs, Marmite and peanut butter left on the kitchen worktop, had made and eaten breakfast and was already at work in the garden. I slammed her dirty plate and mug into the sink – no state-of-the-art pan-scrubber in this kitchen – and headed for the shower.

Funny how sorrow makes you slop around in old trackies, eschewing the shower and make-up, but fury has quite the opposite effect. I showered and scrubbed like there was no tomorrow, washed, conditioned and dried my hair, and by the time Daisy was kicking off her wellies and heading for the kettle and the remains of the date and walnut cake, I was fully made up and wearing the business suit I always wore for meeting new clients offsite.

Daisy frowned. 'Where are *you* off to?'

'*We*,' I emphasised, 'have a meeting with the Hendersons this afternoon, or had you forgotten?'

'No, of course not. But that's this afternoon.' She looked at the kitchen clock. 'It's only ten thirty. You're a bit premature, aren't you?'

I shoved the newspaper article in front of Daisy. 'This was in the paper this morning.'

Daisy abandoned the jar of coffee and read the article. 'So? You always said he was good. You should be proud you worked for his company; it'll look good on your CV now that he's won this award.' She reached for the coffee once more. 'Do you want one?'

'*My* design,' I snapped.

Daisy turned. 'What do you mean?'

'I mean, that when I read through the article, he's been given this award for a house design in Islington. The only work done in Islington by Abraham Developments was designed by me – it was one of the very first things I did when I went to work for him over a year ago.'

Daisy was quiet as she reread the article. 'To be fair, Charlie, it doesn't say that it was *his* design. Look, it just says an innovative design in Islington from Abraham Developments. I suppose it's the *firm* as a whole that's got the award, not one individual architect.'

I snatched back the paper and reread the column. Daisy was right: no one architect was actually named. 'I'll sue,' I snapped. 'I'll have him, show him up for what he is, a philandering, adulterous design-pincher.'

'Well, if that would make you feel better, go ahead.' Daisy said calmly. 'It'll cost you a fortune that you don't have in legal fees, no architecture firm will touch you again if you're seen as a troublemaker and, at the end of the day, nothing has been published here that's not the truth.' Daisy slopped milk into two mugs of coffee and pushed one in my direction. 'I actually think, Charlie,' she went on, looking me up and down, 'that what you've just done in the last half-hour is the best you could have done. You look fantastic, a professional, ready to meet with your next client.' She glanced at the clock once more and laughed 'A trifle early, I have to say but, Charlie, this is the real you. Sitting around in smelly, baggy trackies with hairy legs and a chin to match, wailing and moaning over an ex-boyfriend, isn't the right way to go about your career. You're bloody clever: this article proves that. What better way to show Dominic sodding Abraham what he's lost than by coming up with the most fantastic designs for David – Lord of the North – Henderson? And by the way, take this article with you and show it to David and Seb. Don't whinge and moan and say "poor little me". Casually drop it into the conversation and move on.'

When I didn't say anything, Daisy tutted. 'Charlie, if what you say is true, you've won an award for architectural innovation. Be *proud*. The truth will come out somewhere along the line. It always does. I never won any award for coming up with a brilliantly clever way to get "cunnilingus" into a sentence over the aeroplane Tannoy. I got the bloody sack.'

I'd been up at Holly Close Farm quite a lot over the previous weeks, taking more measurements where I was able, drawing little sketches and then, back at the bungalow adding to and amending the plans I'd already shown Josh Lee. So now I took off my jacket, rolled up my shirtsleeves and spent the next couple of hours going over these initial thoughts, ready to share them with the Hendersons later that day.

Mum had suggested, as we'd be heading back to Westenbury, we should pick up Madge and then call in at home and have a sandwich with her before heading just out of the village to where David Henderson lived.

She'd actually prepared Welsh rarebit for us for lunch. 'Your granny Madge taught me how to make this when I was a little girl.' She turned to where Daisy was helping Madge out of her red coat and matching scarf. Do you remember, Granny?'

'I certainly do,' Madge smiled. 'It was probably the one thing I got right when I was a cook during the war. Sergeant Briscoe regularly used to berate me for not having a light touch with pastry. I've bought ready-made for years now and tell everyone it's my own. Much better than all that fart-arsing around with flour and fat and lifting it out of the bowl until it's like breadcrumbs.'

Daisy and I grinned at each other, both at Madge's pretence with pastry as well as her choice of words. How many other ninety-four-year-olds said 'arse' and 'fart'?

'I don't know how you remember all that stuff back to the war,' Mum sighed. 'I can't remember anything, these days.'

'That's because you only remember what you're interested in. You're so into your pottery at the moment, that's all that matters to you.' Daisy patted Mum on the arm.

'That's a bit unfair, Daisy. I'm interested in everything you girls are up to. But, d'you know, I go upstairs and I haven't a clue what I've gone up for. Or I put the kettle on and totally forget to actually make the coffee I'd planned to make. It drives your father mad.'

When Daisy and I laughed, Mum tutted and turned back to grating cheese. 'You wait, Daisy Maddison, you'll be menopausal yourself one day. You wait until you're awake half the night with hot flushes and you go to the hairdresser and as you're waiting, sitting in the chair, the Saturday girl comes and says, "Oh, I didn't realise you've already been washed, Mrs Maddison," and I have to say, "I haven't."'

Daisy and I burst out laughing again. 'Oh, Mum, you poor old thing,' I said, going to give her a hug. 'It'll get better once you're through it, won't it? Can't be for ever, surely?'

'Well, after that, it'll be all downhill to Alzheimer's,' Mum said gloomily. 'Oh bollocks, this bloody rabbit's almost ready but I've forgotten to switch on the grill for the toast.'

Five minutes later, Daisy and I had made the toast and we were able to eat. 'Granny Madge has been telling us all about meeting a boyfriend she had called James, Mum. You know, during the war?'

'Oh?' Mum shook her head slightly and looked worried. Was this something else she'd been told about and forgotten?

'Don't worry, Kate,' Madge patted Mum's hand. 'I've never spoken about him before. The girls found his old RAF badge and a photograph of him when they were looking for my red coat.' She put down her knife and fork and said, seriously, 'The whole story is going to come out once the house is sold. I'd be surprised if David Henderson hasn't already been raking through the past.'

Mum stopped eating and looked at Madge. 'I don't know what you're talking about, Granny. *I* seem to be left out of everything these days.' She was still cross with us about making fun of her and I had an awful feeling she was going to cry.

'Why on earth would David Henderson be interested in an old boyfriend of yours, Granny?' I looked across at Daisy, who raised her eyebrows and shrugged in my direction.

'It's all a bit complicated, girls, and I need to think about it, bit by bit, before I tell you what eventually happened. The whole thing doesn't put me in a particularly good light and you'll understand why I've kept it to myself and not been able to tell Nancy the rest of it. After that first evening, James and I saw each other whenever we could, which, as you can imagine, because he was based in Cambridgeshire and I was in the middle of London wasn't all that easy...'

16

Francesca sat opposite Madge in the tiny galley kitchen the WAAF cooks had to themselves and, while Fran lit a Lucky Strike and inhaled deeply, Madge sat on her chair in her striped WAAF-issue pyjamas, legs tucked up beneath her, and simply grinned at Fran. Although not yet nine in the morning, the kitchen was already warm and stuffy, and Fran sighed before languidly walking over to the window and opening it as far as was humanly possible without falling out. She continued to pull on her cigarette, blowing smoke out of the window while watching pedestrians down below on Oxford Street going about their usual and, in Madge's eyes now that all she could think about was the previous evening and James, totally mundane Saturday morning tasks.

Fran turned and folded her arms. 'Look, Madge, I know James is rather lovely, my darling. If he wasn't my cousin I'd probably be a little bit in love with him myself.' She ground the stub of the cigarette into the ashtray on the windowsill. 'But pilots in Bomber Command are not really a good option, you know. They're either in training, waiting around to fly, flying, missing… or dead. They live on their nerves and on borrowed time.'

'He is rather lovely, isn't he?' Madge continued to grin widely, stretching her arms up to meet the ceiling. 'Tell me everything about him, Fran. I don't even know how old he is, his middle name, his birthday…'

Fran sighed and moved over to the cranky gas-fuelled geyser that was their sole means of water for tea – the water was never quite boiling and thus tea tended to be drunk through a scummy film – and refilled the heavy brown teapot that was in constant use by the WAAF cooks. 'Twenty-three; George Edward; 25 August. Look, Madge, I don't want you thinking you're in love with James…' Fran broke off from making tea and came back to sit opposite Madge. 'You've got Arthur. I shouldn't have pretended to be an officer last night in order to get you back upstairs. You two obviously needed to work things out. He looks nice…' Fran trailed off again as Madge raised an eyebrow: both women knew that, compared to James Montgomery-West, poor Arthur didn't stand a chance. 'You're not going to like what I'm about to say, Madge.'

'Say it anyway, Fran. Unless James is married with three kids, you won't put me off him. To be honest, even if he was married, I'm not sure I'd be able to keep away from him.' Madge, realising what she'd just said and how it must make her look in Fran's eyes, reddened slightly but determinedly held Fran's gaze.

'All right. James is actually *Viscount* Montgomery-West. His father – my uncle – is the Earl of Beaconscliffe, probably better known as Lord Montgomery-West.'

'Right.' Madge felt her heart quicken before dropping somewhere in the region of her stomach. 'Right. All right. I know what you're thinking now, Fran.'

'Madge,' Fran said gently, 'James' life, before this damned war, was all mapped out for him. Eton, Cambridge, some sort of business in the city and then, probably, following his father and grandfather into government.' Fran ticked each one off on her fingers. When Madge didn't say anything, but just looked at her, Fran continued, 'And then engagement and marriage to someone who will further the family line, if you get my drift, darling.'

Madge felt the bubble on which she'd floated the previous evening and through the hot, sleepless night in her attic bedroom, burst. She felt tears threaten. 'And what you're saying, Francesca, is that a poor milkman's daughter from up north wouldn't exactly further anyone's family, never mind a lord's?'

'No, I'm not saying that.' Fran's conciliatory tone was unable to mask the lie. 'I'm really sorry, Madge.' Fran lit another cigarette and then smiled. 'Look, darling, have some fun with James. Enjoy yourself. Go out for dinner with him. Sleep with him, for heaven's sake, but, I'm just warning you, either bloody Hitler or the Berkshire lot – and to be honest I don't know which is worse – will eventually take him from you.'

'Maybe what you've just suggested I do with James was all I was *thinking* of doing,' Madge snapped defiantly. 'I don't know where you've got this ridiculous idea that I might be thinking of *marrying* him, for heaven's sake, Fran. I only met the man last night.'

'You looked perfect together,' Fran smiled, relenting at Madge's tone. She hesitated. 'I bumped into James walking back from seeing you home. I shouldn't be saying this, but he was as starry-eyed as you.'

Madge wandered over to the window and, like Fran had done a few minutes earlier, gazed down onto Oxford Street and beyond to Oxford Circus, taking in the upper right section of Peter Robinson's department store whose neo-classical façade, badly damaged during the Blitz, was now boarded up and used to display the posters and hoardings that had become a familiar part of war-torn London. Despite Fran telling her to get down in case she fell, Madge leaned out further, loving the feel of the sun on her face and the heady combination of smells: of petrol from the cars and big red buses below, and the heat rising up from the warm pavements. Her heart began to beat faster as a figure below in RAF blue – one of many on this warm Saturday morning – came into view and stopped directly under their building, peering up while shading the sun from his eyes.

'Which one is it?' Fran sighed, joining her at the window. 'James or Arthur?'

'James,' Madge laughed in excitement, backing away from the window and heading for the kitchen door.

'Well, you can't go down there in your nightclothes,' Fran sighed again. 'Bad enough in a stunning black peignoir, but in WAAF pyjamas, absolutely not, darling.'

The wonderful thing about being cook in an RAF training school in the middle of London was that, unlike her counterparts on RAF bases up and down the country,

Madge was mainly free at the weekends and, if not actually condoned, the wearing of civvies off duty was usually turned a blind eye to by the NCOs in charge. Some weekends, when extra courses were put on in the requisitioned building then of course she was on duty, but this particular weekend, apart from a combined RAF and WAAF Met officers' meeting on the Sunday, where she would make and serve afternoon tea, she was free to come and go as she pleased. Madge knew that any day she could be transferred to a base where her life would not be as congenial, especially as she wasn't Sergeant Briscoe's favourite, but for now she had to enjoy what she had and make the most of it.

'Where did you go?' Daisy asked, eyes wide at the thought of Madge as a young girl, running down the stairs of the building and out onto the streets of war-torn London. 'It all sounds so romantic, but weren't you afraid of bombs?'

Madge smiled. 'I suppose people who didn't live through the war assume London was being bombed every minute of every day. During the Blitz, which was before I joined up, then, yes, London was in a mess, but by 1943, when I was stationed there, Hitler seemed to avoid London, probably because of the anti-aircraft guns, and we had weeks when the sirens didn't go off.'

'I bet your mum was worried about you being in London, though,' I said, glancing across at Mum, who'd abandoned her pudding – a Mars bar ice cream – so riveted was she at Madge's story. 'Do you remember how you were nervous at first about me being in London, Mum? You know with all the terrorist stuff?'

'Oh God, yes I was,' Mum agreed, finally finishing her ice cream and licking her fingers before moving to fill the kettle. 'Told you that you mustn't sit next to anyone on the tube with a backpack. Have you time for coffee before your meeting with David Henderson, girls? I wish I was coming with you – he's rather gorgeous, you know.'

'Come if you want, Mum,' Daisy said. 'You know Mandy Henderson now that you've had that commission from her. I'm sure they wouldn't mind one extra.'

'Not very professional, is it, taking your mother along to your first business meeting?' Mum smiled. 'Anyway, I have work to do. So, just time for a coffee and more of the James story, Granny?'

Madge nodded and smiled.

She was suddenly shy and observed James for a few seconds as he stood, looking up, unaware of her scrutiny. She walked across to him and touched his arm. He jumped slightly and then grinned.

'Did you see me?' he asked. 'I thought if I waited here long enough, you'd eventually come down this way. I was going to try to telephone you, but the box over there...' James indicated with a nod of his head the red telephone box a hundred yards away '... has a queue a mile long.'

'I saw you,' Madge smiled. She was wearing a yellow cotton dress her mum had made for her the previous summer. It was her favourite dress and she knew the colour suited her.

'You look lovely, Madge. Like a sunflower.' James bent to kiss her cheek. 'I'm afraid I've only a couple of hours. My forty-eight-hour leave finishes at five this afternoon and there aren't many trains.' He glanced at his watch. 'What would you like to do?'

Madge didn't care what they did as long as she could spend these few hours with him, holding his hand, knowing that, for the moment at least, he was safe.

'Have you been to the zoo?' he asked, stroking Madge's hair.

She laughed. 'The zoo?'

'Yes. I'm afraid it's not as good as before the war – apparently, they had to kill all the snakes in case the reptile-house was bombed and they all got out and slithered into the houses in Regent's Park – but, it's a bargain on Saturdays: half-price to all the Forces.' James grinned at her and took her hand.

She laughed again. 'Come on then, what are we waiting for? Being a right Yorkshire lass, I love a bargain.'

'Say that again.'

'What?'

'*A right Yorkshire lass.*' He laughed. 'I can't tell you how much I love your accent.'

'Well, you must be the only one round here,' Madge said tartly. 'Usually I get laughed at when I say, "I'm off for a *bath*" instead of "*barth*".'

'Are you all right walking?' James glanced down at Madge's feet. She'd abandoned her regulation-issue black lace-ups, her legs were bare and she'd borrowed a pair of Francesca's white Mary Janes.

'Francesca lent me these,' Madge grinned. 'She said I couldn't possibly wear my black uniform shoes with a yellow summer dress. I'll be fine walking, come on.'

They strolled through the streets of the city already thronged with service personnel as well as its residents, intent on shopping or simply being outside on such a glorious day when the reality of war was pushed, for the moment, from minds. Forty minutes later they were walking through the open gates of Regent's Park.

'Oh, what a mess. I'd no idea.' Madge stopped in her tracks and looked around the park, where rubble from buildings destroyed in the Blitz had been dumped on the lawns.

'Had to put it somewhere, I suppose,' James grimaced before glancing down at Madge. 'Your feet are hurting, aren't they? There's no way you're going to be able to walk round the zoo – what's left of it, anyway.'

Madge sat down on a remaining area of grass and unbuckled Fran's shoes, loving the feel of the warm grass between her toes. 'Sorry,' she said, pulling a face as she saw the blister on her right foot, 'I should have put my lace-ups on.'

James sat down beside her and examined the blister. 'Ouch, that must hurt. Stay here and I'll see if I can find us some tea. There did used to be a café in Queen Mary's gardens.' He jumped up, abandoned his jacket with Madge, and set off at a sprint while Madge gazed after him, loving the sight of his blue-shirted back as he disappeared across the rubble-strewn grass. She gazed round at the others in the park, at those who, like them, had managed to find somewhere to sit and, in an effort to calm her racing pulse, endeavoured to concentrate on what the other women were wearing. But the brightly coloured summer dresses, the pinks, reds and yellows worn instead of the ubiquitous navy and khaki, morphed into one single rainbow of colour and she had to dig her nails into the palms of her hands in an effort to calm herself and concentrate on what was in front of her.

She hadn't dreamed him then. He was just as real and even more lovely than she remembered from the previous evening. What on earth was it that was making her feel as if she'd been reborn; as if she'd been turned inside out and her skin, her nerves, every damned bit of her left tingling at the very thought of his touch?

They never did get to see what was left of the animals in the zoo but, instead, remained jealously glued to their one tiny patch of grass that had somehow managed to escape the rubble thrown so carelessly over the verdant landscape. Although not touching or even looking directly at James – Madge was too terrified of her body's reaction if she were to move closer to his arm, his outstretched leg, as he sat and talked, telling her of his war, of the sorties he'd already managed to come home from, and the terror that he felt and had to force back down somewhere in the pit of his stomach – every single bit of her was aware of him sitting next to her. It was as though there was some current, some invisible line, fizzing and connecting her to him.

As they walked back, hand in hand, towards Oxford Street, Madge felt a sense of utter desolation. What if James was killed? Tonight? Tomorrow? How could she have been given so much only to have it snatched back from her? How could she ever go back to being who she was before James? She'd been happy enough, content to meet up with Arthur whenever she'd had the chance, not upset even by Sergeant Briscoe's scathing monologues as to her tough scones and pastry. She'd been who she was: Madge Gregory, the milkman's daughter, who, once the war was over, would presumably return to Westenbury and marry Arthur as he'd convinced her she should.

'I don't want you to die,' she suddenly blurted out as they neared the West End and then reddened as she realised how ridiculous she must sound. She felt tears well and brushed them away angrily. For heaven's sake, what was the matter with her? She never cried normally. Embarrassed at her outburst, Madge stared ahead as she walked, concentrating on putting her blistered left foot down onto the dusty road as lightly as was possible.

James stopped walking and took hold of Madge's arm and, oblivious to the fact that he was an officer in uniform, turned her to him almost roughly and kissed her with such passion she thought she might actually fall to the floor. 'I'm not going to die,' he whispered softly, looking skywards into the unending blue, so that Madge didn't quite know if he was reassuring her or challenging God. 'I can't die now, Madge, now that I've found you.' He pushed her back slightly, gazing into her face before wiping an unshed tear from the corner of her eye with his thumb and smiled.

'I'm sorry.' Madge tried to smile back, but her voice wavered.

'Come home with me?'

'Home?' Madge stared at James who was smiling. 'Home where? To Eaton Square?'

James laughed. 'Much as I'd love to whisk you off there, most of the place is shut up and, anyway, that's not home.' He paused and looked bleak for a moment. 'To be honest, I'm not sure where home is at the moment. No, come down to Berkshire with me. I want you to meet my mother.'

Madge's pulse raced. 'Your mother? Oh, James, I don't think so. Why would you want me to meet your mother?'

He laughed. 'I adore my mother. You remind me of her. She'll love you, I know she will.' When Madge didn't say anything because she couldn't for the life of her imagine swanning down to some earl's house to stay, James smiled once more and kissed her cheek. 'It was just a thought, Madge. I've no idea when I'm going to have my next leave and I really do need to go back home to see my parents. My mother worries about me.'

'Well of course she does,' Madge said almost indignantly. 'Why wouldn't she?'

'So, you'll come then?' James kissed her once more and Madge thought she might just melt into him as she stood there, becoming one with him. 'It's beautiful in the country this time of year,' he smiled. 'Say you'll come? Say yes?'

'Well, then, yes, thank you. That would be lovely.'

*

'And did you?' Mum, Daisy and I leaned forward eagerly as Madge, obviously tired from so much remembering of the past, trailed off and sat back in her chair.

'I did.' Madge smiled, closing her eyes. 'Oh, girls, I did.'

17

'I think I'm a bit in love with James myself,' Daisy said as we walked down the road towards David Henderson's house. It was still raining and the pair of us were huddled under Vivienne's umbrella – filched from her room while she was out at some lady's lunch – the December wetness dripping uncomfortably down my jacket sleeve as I held its handle.

'I know what you mean,' I sighed. 'Sounds so romantic, doesn't he? You know, like someone from a film.'

'Bet he never picked his nose or farted in bed...' Daisy started to laugh.

'Well, I can't imagine Madge ever found out. They didn't have sex before they got married in those days, did they? And, as she married Arthur, I bet she probably never slept with James. What a shame. I wonder what happened to him.'

'Killed, probably, on one of his bombing raids. And Madge never got over him and probably wished she'd had sex with him after all. End of story. Right, come on, we go down here.' We turned off the road and down a country lane, and Daisy stopped in front of huge gates. 'I think this is it. Wow, what a fabulous place.'

'Hi,' an attractive chestnut-haired woman holding on to the hand of a little dark-haired tot called out to us from the other side of the gate. 'I'll let you through.'

The gates swung slowly back against the blackthorn hedge and Daisy – already intent on inspecting the vast amount of plants and shrubs on display in this fabulous garden – and I crunched onto the gravel and towards steps that led to the huge oak front door.

'Have you come about the cleaning job?' the woman smiled. 'Mrs Henderson was just saying she was interviewing at the moment.'

'Cheeky mare,' Daisy muttered. 'Does she think we look like a couple of scrubbers? You've got your best business suit on.'

I started to giggle. 'Ssh. For heaven's sake act professional or we'll be sacked before we get started.'

'He can't sack us. He *needs* us. Remember? Granny Madge's rules?'

'Hi,' I said, ignoring Daisy. 'I'm Charlotte Maddison, architect.'

'Yes, and I'm *Daisy* Maddison, landscape gardener: BSc, RHS Level 3 diploma…'

'Right.' The woman laughed and then looked mystified for a moment. 'Oh, I know, you're the two that Seb and Libby have to use for the house they're wanting to do up? All sounds a bit strange. House sellers don't usually specify who must be used to do the renovations once it's been sold, do they?'

'Well, that's our great-grandmother for you,' I said shortly. I started up the steps, Daisy following. 'Is this the best door?'

'Come on, I'll take you in. We're on a flying visit to see Grandpa.'

'Grandpa?' Daisy nudged me in the ribs. 'I thought David Henderson just had the one son?' she whispered as we followed the woman and her little girl through the door.

A very attractive man in his fifties came out of the room to the left of a long passageway, his hand held out to us. 'Come in, come in,' he said cheerfully, his face one big smile. 'You must be the Maddison sisters? I see you've met Grace?' I knew instantly where Seb Henderson got his good looks. This man was so attractive that, if I'd had a thing about older men I'd certainly be on my way to having a thing about this one. 'David Henderson,' he said unnecessarily, shaking both our hands. 'Seb and Libby are on their way. I believe your mother's met Mandy, my wife?'

'Yes, Mum's working on a commission for her for your new grandson.' I glanced at the little girl who David was now throwing up in the air, her face contorted with giggles and cries of 'More Gwanpop, more,' the second he tried to stop, and I noticed, for the first time, she had Down's syndrome.

'Long story *re* my grandchildren,' David smiled, reading my mind. 'Seb and Grace here have Jonty, my eldest grandchild, between them, and then Grace and her husband adopted Pietronella and, with her now being

Jonty's sister, we've adopted *her* as our granddaughter, too. And of course, now we have Lysander as well. And, that's why we're here, of course, so that the three of them can have your granny's wonderful farm to live in.'

The three of them? Was this to be a *ménage à trois* – Seb, Libby and Grace? Grace must be late thirties or older, I reckoned. Daisy shot me a look and raised her eyebrows.

'So, Seb, Liberty and Lysander want to be in the farm as soon as they can. You know what you young kids are like: wanting to move in before the paint's even dry. Ah, here they are now.'

'Darlings, you're here.' A flash of black trousers and scarlet sweater that I assumed to be David Henderson's wife shot past the open door of the sitting room and towards the main door we'd just entered, and within seconds had reappeared holding a yellow bundle aloft like a prized melon. 'Oh, but he's grown in just two days, the little man,' she purred and cooed as Seb and Libby followed her into the room where we were all standing. 'He looks *just* like Seb did at this age and, incredibly, like Jonty too.'

I noticed Libby and Grace exchange looks as Libby pulled off her wet coat. Was there some rivalry here, I wondered. I mean, for Grace to lose Seb to a much younger model can't have been easy. So I was surprised when Libby moved over to give Grace an affectionate hug and Grace responded with, 'How's it going, sweetheart?'

Sweetheart? Daisy and I exchanged looks once again.

'Oh, Auntie Grace, I was up four times last night with the little monster.'

Auntie Grace? Daisy's eyes, out on stalks at this new revelation, stayed exactly where they were when Seb walked in, pulling a hand through his thick black hair, and proceeded to kiss Grace just as affectionately as Libby before him.

Grace, glancing over at Daisy and I as we stood obviously gawping and trying to take it all in, started laughing. 'Mandy, Harriet – Libby's mum – and I were all at school together,' she smiled. 'I'm Libby's godmother, but I just happen to have got in there first with Seb –' I saw David Henderson wince – 'and Jonty, my four-year-old, is the result.'

If this property developing lark failed, I reckoned I could always write gritty northern dramas à la Kay Mellor based on what I'd just witnessed in this room in the last five minutes.

'Blimey,' Daisy said at last, grinning and turning to me. 'I bet you thought nothing like this ever happened in a backwater like Westenbury, Charlie.'

When everyone, even little Pietronella, turned to stare at Daisy, she blushed. 'Charlie's convinced there's never anything exciting going on up here,' she said, flustered. 'Thinks it all happens down in London. I mean, *she* had to come back north because her live-in-lover boss was actually *married* – with three *kids*.'

Every face swung back to me with interest as I went scarlet myself and glared at Daisy.

'Right, well, yes, shall we get on?' David asked, slightly irritable, reining us all in. 'There's a lot to discuss and I have a governors' meeting at the local school to go to later on this afternoon.' We obediently trooped after him as Grace made to leave to pick up her little boy from nursery, and Mandy took off somewhere with Lysander, showering little kisses on his head as she went.

'I don't see any reason why we shouldn't be able to start work on the house soon after Christmas,' Seb said as we sat down round a huge light-oak dining table, which must easily have been able to seat twenty. He moved the centre display of autumnal red, yellow and russet dried flowers towards one end of the table before placing a file of paper in front of us. 'Dad's been brilliant at working with the various solicitors this past month,' he added, turning to Daisy and me. 'He's a bit like a dog with a bone once he gets going.'

'Well, no point hanging around once you've set your heart on it,' David smiled.

'You're about to exchange contracts next week, aren't you? I know Madge has an appointment with her solicitor. I said I'd drive her down there to sign all the papers.'

David, Seb and Libby all nodded in agreement. 'I know,' Libby grinned. 'I can't believe it's all happening. And so quickly as well.' Her eyes were bright with anticipation and she took Seb's hand in her excitement and squeezed it tightly. 'You know,' she said, turning to Daisy and me, 'I really didn't want to have to leave Oxford. I loved it down there, but when I knew I was having Lysander, it was really the only option. I'm off to Leeds in September to carry on with my degree and it will be so wonderful if we're going to be living at Holly Close Farm by then. It's so much nearer to the motorway.'

'Things never go quite as quickly as you think they're going to,' I warned her. 'I can't promise you'll be living there by the autumn.'

Libby's face fell and then she tried to smile. 'I suppose I *am* acting like a big kid with a new toy, aren't I?'

Daisy smiled sympathetically at her across the table and I could see these two were going to be great allies. 'You know, there's no reason why *I* can't start on the grounds straight away,' she said enthusiastically. 'I realise we'll be well into the new year before anything can start moving with the actual building, but I can get stuck in with clearing the area.'

'Just hang on a bit,' I frowned, trying to rein the pair of them in. 'What's the point of you planting new stuff, Daisy, when it'll probably just get covered with the building site that it will become once we start on the renovation?'

'Charlie has a point,' David said, his smile placating. 'Surely the gardens should come *after* the building work?'

Daisy tutted. 'I wasn't *planning* on planting a whole load of dahlias or rose bushes where the builders are going to be working,' she said scornfully. 'I'm talking about *clearing* the land, rebuilding dry stone walls, putting up *new* walls.'

'Goodness, you know how to build dry-stone walls?' David, Seb and Libby all swivelled towards Daisy.

'Yes, of course,' she said proudly.

David turned to Libby and Seb and frowned once more. 'Look, you two, I need to know this is what you both really want. It's a massive undertaking and commitment.'

He hesitated a little and then went on, 'Mandy and I are a little concerned that you might get a bit lonely down there by yourself with just Lysander for company. It's very secluded, you know, Libby.'

'I know, I know. Perfect for studying. And we can get a dog.'

'Not with both of you out of the house all day you can't, Libby. And if Seb's away, you'll be down there by yourself.'

'I'll have you two for neighbours,' Libby beamed, turning back to Daisy and me. 'We wondered what we'd have to do with the cottage. It's great now that Mrs Booth is insisting that the cottage isn't part of the sale and that you two are going to end up down there as well.'

'Well, I'm not promising that we're actually going to end up living there,' I said, feeling slightly claustrophobic that my life seemed to be panning out in a direction that I'd not entirely agreed to yet.

'Well, *I'll* be your new neighbour,' Daisy smiled at Libby, 'even if Charlie hotfoots it back to London. And if she does, well, she can sell her part of the cottage to someone who really does want to live there, so you'll have neighbours.' Libby and Daisy grinned at each other conspiratorially and I felt a bit left out. 'Hang on, I haven't said I'm *not* going to live in my share of the cottage.'

'There you go, then,' Daisy said. 'Ready-made neighbours.'

David Henderson didn't appear to want to let it go. 'It's just after what happened there.'

'Something's happened there? What recently?' I frowned. 'Has someone been down there pinching the stone roof tiles or something?'

David frowned in turn. 'I think you'll find they were all taken years ago.' He hesitated and caught Seb's eye before continuing. 'No, I'm talking about, you know, what happened years back. Presumably why Mrs Booth moved out and hasn't wanted anyone there since.'

'I don't know what you're talking about, Mr Henderson.' I looked directly at him and he hesitated before glancing at his son once more. Oh God, what was it?

'I'm not sure that it's my place to tell you,' David said, obviously slightly embarrassed. 'Maybe you should ask Mrs Booth?'

'Look, if you know something about Holly Close Farm, Daisy and I would really like to know.' I glanced at Daisy, who'd gone slightly pale. She nodded.

'Arthur Booth, your great-grandfather, was hanged for murder.'

'Oh my God,' Daisy yelped, a hand over her mouth. 'He murdered James, didn't he?'

'James?' David shook his head. 'I don't know. Was one of them called James?'

'One of them? What, Arthur murdered more than one person?'

'Arthur Booth, Madge's husband, was tried for the murder of two policemen in the grounds of Holly Close Farm,' David said, reaching for some newspaper cuttings beneath his pile of papers. 'He was hanged in 1953, one of the last men to be hanged in this country.'

18

'We need to sort this out,' Mum said grimly when Daisy and I rushed back home after David Henderson's bombshell, immediately googling for ourselves Arthur's fate over sixty years before. Dad was away on a pre-Christmas golfing trip to Florida, much to Vivienne's chagrin: he wasn't, she'd allegedly told him archly, anywhere near ready for the first night opening of *The Importance of Being Earnest* in just a few weeks' time, and suggested he consider his priorities, as well as his loyalty to dear Oscar. His priority, Dad had apparently countered cheerfully, was five days on the razz with his golfing mates in the sunshine, and he was sure *dear* Oscar – particularly as one of the party was as bent as a ten-bob note – would, had he been still with us, be packing his budgie-smugglers and be heading to Manchester Airport with them.

Fed up of being left home alone with Vivienne and Christmas preparations, Mum suggested, faced with the enormity of our news about her grandfather, that we take Madge's car, snatch Madge back out of Heaven for the second time that day and then all meet up at the bungalow and confront her with what we knew.

'I mean, for heaven's sake, why has she kept this all to herself all these years? It's ridiculous. Right, girls, I'm off down to the Co-op to get wine and pizza, and I'll meet you at the bungalow in a couple of hours. If Madge argues the toss, says she's too tired for a second outing or she doesn't like pizza – she does, she'll just be being contrary – then say we know about Arthur and we want an explanation.' Mum was obviously riled and in fighting mode.

'Mum,' I said gently, 'we don't want to give Madge a heart attack; she *is* ninety-four, you know. Do you not think a softly-softly approach might not be better?'

'Softly-softly?' Mum snapped. 'Charlie, this is not bloody *Midsomer Murders*. It's the brutal murder of two police officers by my own grandfather.' She grabbed hold of Malvolio who, already missing pack-leader Dad, and now sensing we were also about to abandon him, was whining pitifully. 'I'm going to have to take the bloody dog with us as well or he'll eat the kitchen. I tell you, girls, *I'm* off to Costa Rica in the new year, all by myself, alone, *toute seule*.'

While Daisy stayed in the car, I ran into Almast Haven and bounded up the stairs to Madge's room. She was lying on her bed, glasses perched on the end of her nose, reading a novel, and it was almost as though she'd been expecting me.

'I wondered if you'd be back,' she said simply, laying the book down beside her.

'Oh?'

'Well, David Henderson, I believe, is a very astute man. I've spent the last few weeks googling him. There's no way he'd be helping to buy Holly Close farm without researching its history – why my darling farm has been abandoned for the last sixty-odd years.'

'He told us about Arthur.'

'I thought he might.'

'Mum's not happy. In fact, she's spitting feathers. She doesn't understand why you've kept it all to yourself all these years. She's sent Daisy and me to see if you'll come to the bungalow for a drink and pizza.'

Madge raised an eyebrow. 'And an explanation, I suppose?'

'Well, yes. But I understand, Granny, if you're too tired. I mean, we've been online and got the general gist of what happened.'

'I'm all right. I had a bit of a snooze once I got back from having lunch with your mother and you girls this afternoon. Come on, let's go and face the Ayatollah.'

It took ages to sort Madge with her stick and her outdoor clothes. She refused to go out into the cold without her red Max Mara coat, which seemed to have disappeared. I eventually found it being worn by Elsie, one of the other residents, who was convinced the coat was hers. The only way she'd part with it was to be offered Sarah the Carer's trendy red leather jacket in its stead.

'Don't worry,' Sarah smiled cheerfully as the octogenarian admired herself in red biker leathers, 'I'll be able to barter her dinner for it when the time comes.' There appeared to be a whole bartering economy at

Almost Heaven, with slippers, cardigans and newspapers being persuaded out of the wrong hands on a daily basis with compensatory sweets, buns and the promise of a game of bingo.

So, by the time Daisy – who was just about to leave the car and come looking for us – and I managed to get Madge back to the bungalow, tensions were rising and it was almost seven o'clock. Of Mum, there was no sign.

'Have we no crisps?' Daisy asked, after settling Madge in front of the fire with a glass of red. She opened the kitchen cupboards hopefully.

'You ate the last of the smoky bacon yesterday,' I said, poking round for anything in their stead. The Welsh rarebit seemed hours ago and we were both starving.

'Not guilty. *I* didn't finish them off.'

'Well, I certainly didn't: I'm vegetarian.'

'Oh, don't give me that,' Daisy snapped. 'You must have consumed every beast that ever roamed the planet in the six weeks you've been home.'

Had I only been home six weeks? It seemed more like six years. 'Well, you ate that packet of nuts we were saving for the next episode of *Outlander*. You said, when you got in from your date with that geek on Tinder, that it looked like the only nuts in your mouth tonight were going to be the KPs.'

Daisy had the grace to look embarrassed. 'I didn't say that, did I?'

'Yes. I did think it rather vulgar at the time. Where's Mum got to? She was only popping on to the Co-op before coming here.'

The kitchen door from the garden banged open and Mum appeared, looking rather the worse for wear.

'Where've you been?'

'Well, I called in at the Co-op and actually ended up doing quite a bit of shopping – they do have some good offers on there, occasionally – and who should be there but Mandy Henderson. You don't imagine people like that to be in the local Co-op, do you?'

'Don't you?' Daisy and I glanced at each other.

'Anyway, she suggested I call in for a little drink, with it being Christmas and everything, and to celebrate the commission I've just about finished for Lysander.'

'Right?'

'And so, because I've always wanted to see inside the Hendersons' house, I did.'

'We can see that. Have you driven here?'

'Of course,' Mum said scornfully. 'It was only a little drink. The thing is, I didn't like to go round to the Hendersons' empty-handed, so after I'd been through the checkout I went back down the Co-op aisles and picked up some flowers. They were jolly expensive – £30 – but then I spotted the same bunch, obviously out of date, but just £5! For the exact same bunch!'

Daisy and I exchanged looks once more. What *was* she going on about?

'So, I put the £30 bunch back and bought the £5 bunch instead. But then I realised they were actually pretty manky and felt guilty I was about to short-change Mandy Henderson – she's only used to the best, I'm sure – and had to spend a good five minutes standing in the Co-op car park dead-heading the rubbish ones.'

'Right, OK, Mum,' I said, trying to condense her tale. 'We're starving here and want to get to the bottom of the Arthur story before Madge falls asleep or even refuses to tell us. Where are the pizzas?'

'Oh gosh, yes, where are they?' Mum frowned and then hiccupped. 'Must be in the boot of the car, darling.'

'Not in the boot, Mum,' I called from the drive, thirty seconds later.

'In the car then, Charlie? On the front seat?'

'Nope. Just the dog, looking fed up.'

'Still in the Co-op then?' Mum started to laugh. 'Still in the bloody Co-op, the whole lot,' she chortled, unable to get her breath.

Daisy and I looked at each other again. 'Mum, this is a serious conversation we're about to have with Madge and you're giggling like a drain. How much did you say you'd had?' She obviously shouldn't have driven here, especially with the police on the lookout for Christmas drinkers.

'Oh, stop behaving like a couple of school prefects. It's *Christmas*, for heaven's sake. And I was upset about, you know… Where *is* she anyway? My grandmother who tells me *nothing*?'

'In the sitting room. Go easy on her, Mum, you're pretty emotional at the moment.'

'Hormones, hot sweats, Vivienne still hanging around practising "*A handbag?*" at every conceivable moment, the stress of the damned turkey and now a hanged grandfather. What do you expect?'

'Well, we *were* expecting pizza.' Daisy put her arm round Mum.

Mum started to giggle again at that and then started hiccupping, which turned into sobs. 'It's just that, well, I've realised this all happened when my mum was a little girl. She must have been about nine when her dad was hanged. *Hanged*, girls. Can you imagine how that would feel if *Dad* was *hanged*? My poor Mum. No *wonder* she was such a lousy mother.'

'And that's one of the reasons this has all been kept quiet, Kate.' Madge was standing at the kitchen door. 'Nancy went through a terrible time as a little girl. Her beloved father was dead and her childhood was ruined. And it was all my fault.' Madge's face was pale and a single tear made its way down her wrinkled cheek, carving a track through the Max Factor powder she always used. She swayed slightly as she held the door and I went to help her, but she brushed my hand away crossly. 'Come on, let's sit down. Let's have a drink. You can stay here tonight, Kate; you really shouldn't be driving the car any more this evening. I don't know about you, but I don't want anything to eat. Why don't we just talk?'

Using her stick, Madge turned painfully round, limping back to her seat and glass of wine, and the three of us trooped after her into the sitting room.

'I don't want to tell you what happened to Arthur – although I take it you've read the newspaper cuttings and Googled everything you can find about your grandfather – until I explain more about James Montgomery-West, so that you can really understand what happened.' Madge sighed, not looking at us. She constantly turned her hands in her lap and eventually said, 'I adored him, girls. I never loved any other man but him.'

19

'Gregory, you might have the day off, but you're not going anywhere not wearing full uniform.' The officer looked suspiciously at Madge's stockings. 'Where are you going anyway? You can't get too far with a twenty-four-hour pass.' Sergeant Briscoe took her duties seriously and, narrowing her already small eyes, glared at Madge. 'Bit too much lipstick on as well. You're an ambassador for the King and his government, you know, not trying to set Hollywood alight.'

'I'm going to see a friend in Ascot,' Madge replied, reddening slightly. 'I've been invited for dinner.'

'Dinner? Do you mean lunch?' the NCO snapped crossly. 'For heaven's sake, you're not back oop north now. And if you do actually mean *dinner*...' Sergeant Briscoe glanced at her wristwatch, '... then I doubt you're going to be able to eat and get back here in time. I'll be watching out for you. In fact, Gregory, you'd be better sticking your apron on and practising your Yorkshire puddings. How a girl from Yorkshire can produce what you dared to offer up to Squadron Leader Roberts last week is anyone's guess.'

'Yes, ma'am.' Madge looked at her feet in the hope that her apparent subservience might help her on her way to Waterloo. If Briscoe hadn't done with her soon she'd have to take a taxi to the station.

She obviously hadn't.

Sergeant Briscoe continued to take in every aspect of Madge's newly waved blond hair and red lipstick. 'This *friend*, Gregory, I hear you've got yourself involved with an RAF officer?'

'Ma'am.' What the hell was she supposed to say? Agree that yes, she'd fallen in love with an officer – a viscount, actually – and was now on her way to meet his mother, if only she could escape this grilling?

'A flight lieutenant, no less.' It was a statement rather than a question and, since last Tuesday, the wrong handle anyway. James, according to Francesca, who'd spoken to her mother over the telephone a couple of days ago, was now apparently Squadron Leader Montgomery-West.

'Ma'am.'

Obviously tiring of her attempts to goad Madge, Sergeant Briscoe tutted and snapped, 'Go on with you, then,' and turned on her heel, shouting over her shoulder warnings and dire consequences were Madge to be late back.

The minute she was free, Madge ran to the bathroom, patted her newly set hair and added more lipstick before grabbing her black WAAF-issue handbag and setting off at a trot for the underground. With minutes to spare she found the correct platform at Waterloo Station and boarded the train to Ascot, standing with a whole load of both American and Australian service personnel.

'Where're you going, sweetheart?' The dark-haired Yank pinning her against the window grinned down at her as he waited her reply. 'You sure look ready to fight Hitler, ma'am. In fact, you can fight my corner any day.'

'Out for lunch,' she smiled, remembering to call the midday meal by its proper handle. 'I'm going to Ascot.'

'As are we.' He raised his hand, taking in the men crowded into the carriage. 'Come out for lunch with *us*.'

'Sorry, already booked.' Madge smiled again. 'What's so special about Ascot, anyway? I'm assuming you're not all off to the races?'

'The races? That would be swell, wouldn't it? 'Fraid not, ma'am. The gee-gees are no more now that we're all camped out there.'

'Oh, I didn't realise.' Madge felt slightly embarrassed. She really must learn more about this war she was doing her bit for. If only they'd have let her train as a Met girl, as she'd really wanted, instead of wasting her efforts on Victoria sponges that wouldn't rise, she might have had more idea about who was stationed where. 'Well, thank you, anyway…' Madge trailed off.

The lieutenant laughed and ran a hand through his dark hair. 'For what, ma'am?'

'Well, you know, being here. Coming over to help us. I'm sure it was the last thing you really wanted to do.' Madge was beginning to feel a bit at a loss and she was grateful when one of the officers, seeing she was floundering under all the attention, stood and offered her his seat. She took it, smiling gratefully and, once seated, tried to calm her nerves by watching the changing countryside from the train window as it flew past, counting the myriad rusting green tractors blending into the late summer fields.

James was on the station to meet her. Like Madge, he had a twenty-four-hour pass – it had taken weeks and a whole stack of phone calls to marry the two – but unlike her he was in civvies and she was seeing him for the first time not dressed in uniform but a light-coloured pair of trousers and a short-sleeved open-necked shirt. Oh, but he was glorious. Not caring how undignified she must look, she ran towards him through the confused medley of American army personnel that appeared to be hovering, unclear in which direction they should be heading, and James swept her off her feet, swinging her round. Shy, not having seen him for four weeks since their day in Regent's Park, Madge felt totally tongue-tied in the presence of such beauty and didn't know what to say to him. James grinned down at her, took her hand and kissed her forehead. 'I've thought about you every single minute of the day,' he breathed. 'Every second, in fact…' He held her from him, taking in every aspect of her face. 'And you're more beautiful than I ever remembered.'

'James, I'm a bit nervous about meeting your mother.' Madge could feel her pulse quicken at what was ahead of her as they walked from the station.

'Honestly, Madge, there's no need. I've told her all about you. She'll love you. Come on, I've managed to wangle one of the cars – my father has an allowance because he has to go up to London such a lot – and I thought we'd go for a picnic. We can't go that far because there's only so much petrol… and I suppose you have to be back by this evening?'

Madge nodded. 'A picnic?' Relief that they were going to be outdoors on this glorious August day and not sitting down to some stuffy lunch with a whole load of confusing cutlery suffused her whole being and Madge took James's hand. 'That sounds lovely.'

'Lovely.' James repeated the word, flattening the vowels as Madge had done, and laughed.

'Don't tease me.' Madge grinned, elbowing James slightly in the ribs.

'I wasn't, I truly wasn't,' he protested. 'I can't tell you how much I love your accent. Mrs Dobson who runs our village library is originally from the north and I've spent most of the morning in there while I waited for your train, browsing through the books but really just hanging around so I could hear her speak.'

'You're daft, you really are.'

James opened the passenger door of a huge Daimler and helped Madge in. It was only the second car she'd ever been in and she sank nervously into its interior, breathing in the heady scent of the slippery leather seats as James put the car into gear and reversed away from the station, manoeuvring the heavy vehicle with, Madge assumed, the same confidence and skill he showed when in control of the Lancaster bomber.

James drove for fifteen minutes along dusty roads where huge oaks and sycamores, laden down with the fullness of late summer's foliage, met in an arch across their path, obliterating the midday sun in a cool green bower. He slowed down and braked before turning right across the main road and immediately headed down a country lane where a mellow-stoned house with walled gardens to the side came into view.

'Oh, what a beautiful house,' Madge breathed, turning back to gaze in wonder as they passed.

'The Dower House.' James smiled at Madge's animated face. 'My grandmother lives there; it's where all retiring matriarchs end up once they're booted out of the main house.'

'Booted out?' Madge was lost as to James's meaning.

'Once my grandfather died, my father inherited his title and the estate and we all moved into the main house. I was about twelve, I think. Basically, we did a swap: my parents took on the estate, my sisters and I moved from the Dower House and my grandmother moved back down there.' James seemed fairly uninterested in the whole procedure. 'Right, we're here.'

'Oh, James, this isn't where you live?' Madge's eyes were wide.

'I know.' James was slightly embarrassed. 'Ridiculous amount of bricks and mortar for one family. Mind you, once we're into September, the girls will be back.'

'The girls? Your sisters, you mean?'

James laughed. 'No, no, they're well and truly married off to suitable husbands and flown the nest. Camilla lives in Surrey, Angela is in the WAAF and Katherine's just down the road in Amersham.' He cut the engine, jumped out of the car, and made his way round to open the door for Madge. 'During the last war, the East Wing of the hall was given over to housing a military hospital tending the soldiers injured in France, poor sods. My father was a serving officer himself on the Somme and my grandfather thought it the right thing to do. Afterwards, apparently, he said never again, and so when all this lot blew up, my father, taking heed of that, agreed to the suggestion of St Augustine's Girls' School moving down from London while the war is on. My father knew he couldn't be seen not to help the war effort and he reckoned the school was better than another hospital or billets for the Yanks. My mother loves having them here. She invites them over for tea and they help with the chucks.'

'Your mother has hens?' Madge began to feel herself on familiar ground. Her own mother had always kept them and Madge had grown up with them, digging for worms and scattering their food as well as collecting their eggs twice a day before shutting them up in the wooden hen houses against marauding foxes every night.

Before James could answer, a small redhead wearing the green sweater and trousers of the Land Army, ran out from a side door of the house, a feisty-looking Jack Russell at her heels. She stopped in some confusion when she realised James wasn't alone and made to retreat towards the gardens at the rear.

'Hilda, don't run off,' James shouted in her direction and she turned, following the dog as it bounded forward to greet them. Somewhat reluctantly, it appeared to Madge, she walked towards them. 'Madge, this is Hilda; Hilda, this is Madge,' he smiled.

The girl nodded somewhat curtly in Madge's direction but didn't meet her eyes. 'I need to get on,' she said in a strong Liverpool accent, 'or Mr Morton will be after me.' She turned once more and walked off in the direction she'd come.

'As you can see, we have a couple of land girls here, too. The place gets more like Piccadilly Circus every time I come home. They're billeted up at Home Farm and John Morton, the estate manager, is in charge of them.'

'You do know she's a bit in love with you?' Madge said, feeling sorry for the girl. How must it be to feel the way she herself felt about James and not have it reciprocated?

'Is she?' James affected surprise and then smiled. 'Well, maybe a little.' He took Madge's hand and led her towards the door the redhead had just exited. A small elderly woman, dressed in black, bustled towards them and Madge stepped forwards to shake hands.

'Master James, I've done you a picnic...' So, not James's mother then: Madge dropped her arm in confusion '... and I'm afraid it's a poor one compared to what I could have done for you before we had all this rationing. Now, there's some chicken left over from dinner last night and...'

James grinned, planting a kiss on the woman's cheek. 'It'll be fine, Agnes. Really. Just see if you can find one of Dad's bottles of red, would you? I know he says he's running out, but I don't believe him. Agnes, this is Madge.'

Agnes nodded her tiny bird-like head conspiratorially and winked at James. 'Nice to meet you, Miss Madge.' She almost bobbed a curtsy before turning and hurrying away, and Madge felt herself redden in embarrassment.

Expecting James's mother to be some sort of dowager duchess dressed in Edwardian black, not, she reckoned, dissimilar to the Queen Mother, Madge was somewhat taken aback when a tall willowy blonde in men's corduroy trousers, held up and tightened against her waist with a man's leather belt, came out of the kitchen. Her chignon was falling down and she had a black smut across her cheek.

'Darlings, I didn't realise you'd arrived. I'm sorry, I was out with the hens. The wretched fox has had Bella. She's a tough old broad, though. Lost a load of feathers and damaged a wing but she'll survive. I suppose she's almost ready for the pot anyway. Now, you must be Marjorie. Jim has told me all about you.'

Jim? Madge glanced towards James, who was grinning at his mother, and held out her hand once more. Ursula Montgomery-West looked at her own dirty hands, wiped them on her trousers and, instead of taking Madge's outstretched one, moved forwards and kissed her on both cheeks.

'Welcome, so pleased to meet you, Marjorie.' Her accent was pure cut glass, exactly that of Queen Elizabeth and the two princesses, and despite the fact that she was dressed in a ragbag of farmhand clothes while Madge was in full WAAF uniform, Madge felt herself to be a country bumpkin from up north. 'Now, you two get yourselves off; you won't have that much time if you've both got to be back by this evening.' Ursula paused, looking directly at Madge but obviously addressing James. 'And, darling, make the most of the day. I suppose you won't know when you'll next have time off? I worry about him so much. This damned war.'

'I'm sure Madge will look after me.' James raised an eyebrow. 'Are we all right taking the car again, do you think?'

'Well, you're not going to get very far without some form of transport. I assume you're thinking of Sulham Woods? You really shouldn't take the Daimler again; your father will need it later on this afternoon.' Ursula frowned and then brightened. 'I know, why don't you take the estate motorcycle John Morton uses? But park it where it won't be seen or someone will be after you.'

It was only a ten-minute drive from the estate but Madge wished it would go on for ever. She'd never been on the back of a motorbike before and she adored the feel of speed, the breeze in her hair and the contact with James as she held tightly onto his waist. She pressed her nose into his cotton shirt, inhaling his scent, all her senses aroused as the machine throbbed between her stockinged legs. All too soon, James slowed down, guiding and reversing the machine into a leafy copse.

'Walk or eat first?' he asked. 'If we're going to walk, we'll leave the picnic things here.'

'Walk I think; I'm so hot and need to stretch my legs. And unless Briscoe is lying in wait for me behind one of those trees – and I wouldn't put it past her – then I'm going to take off my jacket.'

'Fighting talk,' James laughed. 'Treasonable offence, especially when you're with a superior officer. I don't seem to recall your saluting me yet today, Aircraftwoman Second Class.'

'Will this do instead?' Madge, relieved of her heavy jacket and out in the cool of the glade, reached up her arms to James as he leaned against the motorbike and kissed him softly. He responded, pulling her to him and burying his face in her hair and kissing her throat. Madge thought that if she died now she'd die happy, having known and captured this utter heaven on earth.

'Come on, on second thoughts let's take the picnic basket with us,' James smiled unbuckling the leather strap holding the basket onto the pillion. 'We might find the ideal spot and then be sorry we'd not brought it with us. And to be honest, a tramp through the woods like some sort of Boy Scout wasn't what I had in mind.'

'Oh?' Madge looked at him archly. 'What *did* you have in mind?' she asked and then immediately regretted it, aware that it was a leading question and could be construed as such. She felt herself redden and, in order to hide her blushes, bobbed down to the bike's wing mirror on the pretext of straightening her hair.

James held up his hands and laughed. 'A picnic in the woods before I'm back bombing hell out of Hitler. Come on, Gregory, take the other handle. I want to see if I can find the spot I used to play in when I was a kid.'

They walked deeper into the woods in companionable silence for a few minutes, setting the pace as directed by the weight of the picnic basket and enjoying the cool dampness of the woods after the noon heat of the late summer's day. Madge glanced often across at James, unable not to, and his eyes would already be seeking out hers. He wanted to know more about her childhood, her mum and dad, her brothers and sister; where she'd worked before she joined up. 'I want a complete picture of you,' he said, 'so that when I'm up in the air, facing oblivion, you'll be the one thing I see.'

'Your mother is quite lovely, isn't she? She obviously adores you.'

'I'm the son she always wanted after three daughters. Dad, too, obviously.'

'Oh?'

'Someone to pass on the title to... but, do you know, I reckon the war will change everything. Who knows? I don't even think about it. The future, I mean...' James trailed off, his tone bleak.

'I'm thirsty,' Madge said, wanting to change the uncomfortable direction the conversation was taking. She didn't want to talk about titles and futures, especially when the odds of them actually having a future were stacked against them.

'A few more minutes.' James came to a sudden standstill and surveyed the area. 'Yes, up here, come on...'

'How lovely.' Madge stopped and stared at the tiny glade that had opened up in front of them. Hidden entirely from view, a small oasis amongst the oaks and sycamores, the place would easily be missed entirely by anyone who didn't know these woods.

'Angela and I used to hide from Nanny in here. She'd bring us for a walk with the dogs on the proviso that we weren't to run off, and she fell for it every time. She'd be calling, shouting, eventually threatening and we were so awful: we wouldn't reveal ourselves until she was almost in despair.'

'So, Nanny didn't know best then?' Madge began to feel sorry for the poor woman.

'Nope. We ran rings round her. I'm sure she was most relieved when I was packed off to school.' James was already taking out the tartan travel rug – originally from Harrods, Madge noted – laying it down on the soft springy grass before pouring lemonade into a solid-looking tumbler for her. She drank, slaking her thirst, as James poured the same for himself. 'Good old Agnes – she's managed to filch one of dad's best bottles of wine.' When Madge looked concerned, thinking that she'd be blamed for egging him on to pinch his father's wine, he laughed. 'Don't worry, he has an absolute cellar full but won't admit it. Would you like to try it?'

She finished the remaining drops of the very good home-made lemonade – where on earth had the lemons come from? – and proffered the tumbler.

'Just try that: nectar of the gods. If there's one thing my father gets right it's his wine.' James took a small sip, savouring the ruby liquid.

'I would have thought, being in government, he'd have to get most things right.' Madge glanced across at James, trying to read meaning into his words.

'I'm sure he tries his best,' James said shortly. 'What do you think?'

The Merlot felt warm and cloying – almost, with its slightly metallic aftertaste, like blood – and Madge, unused to any wines but particularly to a rich red such as this, wasn't quite sure if she liked it or not. She took another sip, decided she could probably get used to it and, still thirsty from the walk, proceeded to take a longer drink.

'Careful,' James laughed warningly. 'If you're not used to it, it will go to your head and it wasn't my intention to get you drunk.'

Madge stared at James, loving the concern in his beautiful brown eyes. She leaned forward, brushing a piece of grass from his thick blond hair and he took her hand, kissing her fingers until she felt her stomach turn to molten gold. Whether it was the wine or natural instinct she would never know but, not caring she might appear forward, Madge pressed him back onto the picnic rug and kissed his mouth. James, acknowledging her desire, turned her over onto her back, his body covering her own, his large warm hands covering her breast. She'd gone as far as this with Arthur, of course, but always slapped down any further wandering hands, mainly because she didn't like his heavy breathing and red-faced exertions and had never felt any hunger or need to continue further to what she assumed to be his ultimate goal.

And anyway, nice girls just didn't.

But now, apparently, they did.

20

Convinced that James's mother would know she'd spent the afternoon making love to her son, Madge was reluctant to return to his parents' house with him, telling him, instead, to drop her off at the railway station where'd she'd take the first train back to London. While she didn't want to leave him – couldn't *bear* to leave him – any earlier than she absolutely had to – God only knew when she'd be able to see him again – Madge was mindful not only of Sergeant Briscoe's ire were she to be late back, but also of her own dishevelled appearance after an afternoon flat on her back in a wood.

'Darling Midge, you look even more beautiful than ever,' James protested when she told him her plan. 'You have colour in your cheeks and your eyes are bright and, if you're not careful, I shall have to drag you back into the trees and make love to you once more.'

'You wouldn't have to drag me,' Madge smiled, realising she was becoming more and more of a scarlet woman as the afternoon went on.

James turned to her as they neared the spot where he'd left the motorcycle and took her hand in his. 'Midge, this is what you wanted, isn't it? I mean, you are all right? It wasn't too... you know, too painful?'

'Yes, yes,' Madge was embarrassed. 'I mean yes, it was fine.' Oh heavens, it was more than fine; it had been absolutely wonderful. 'And no, it wasn't too painful.' She felt particularly immodest that, after all, it was she who'd asserted herself; she who'd started the whole ball rolling, as it were. Had she been too forward? What if he thought her a tramp, and couldn't wait to be rid of her, putting her on the train, determined never to see her again. Her mother had constantly warned both her daughters of the dire consequences of 'giving it away free', as if not doing so was a down payment that would lead to marriage.

James took both her hands in his. 'Midge, I know what you're thinking – that you shouldn't have let me make love to you, that I'll now think the worse of you, that you might end up pregnant.'

'I wasn't, actually,' she smiled, loving his concern. 'I was thinking how lovely it all was and why our mothers tell us to hang on to our virginity like some sort of bargaining power over men. You know, this war isn't the norm; I wouldn't even be here with you if Hitler hadn't invaded Poland.' She smiled again thinking of the incongruity of the whole thing.

'And you do know that I made sure you won't be left holding the baby? The RAF's bill for rubbers must be higher than for good coffee.' He laughed at this and Madge smiled too.

'James,' she said quietly, 'I wouldn't have had today any other way... you know... it was all lovely...' She looked up at him from underneath her lashes, determined to make him aware that it was what she'd wanted too. 'But, you know, for you, that wasn't the first time, was it? I mean, you knew exactly what to do.' Madge felt her insides melt once more as she recalled how he'd known what would give her the most pleasure.

James smiled. 'At the risk of sounding like some dreadfully spivvy lothario, then no, it wasn't.'

Madge felt the sharp pricking of jealousy: the very thought of him doing what they'd just done with anyone else filled her with pain and she bowed her head so as not to let him see.

'Listen, Midge. I've never ever felt like this about anyone before. I'm twenty-three; of course I'm not a virgin. But none of them have ever meant anything.' He sighed and took her in his arms, as he perched on the seat of the motorcycle. 'When I was eighteen, the year I left Eton and before I went up to Cambridge, I travelled to France in order to brush up my French. I've always loved languages and I reckoned being rather more fluent in French might come in handy if I were to be working on European architectural projects.' He smiled up at her. 'I'd be able to say, "*Ce sont les meilleurs plans que vous verrez jamais,*" and the French would be so impressed they'd snap me up immediately.'

'And?'

'And I stayed with some distant cousins of my mother in their château in Lyle. The French don't appear to have any of the concerns and the worries we strait-laced English have about making love. To them, it's as natural as filling their faces with a good meal and a superb bottle of wine,' He laughed. 'I spent the summer of 1939, just before this lot all blew up in our faces, being seduced by my host's widowed cousin. She taught me all I know, as well as refusing to feel guilt or embarrassment about making love, being in love or being loved.' He sighed and leaned into Madge, holding her against him. 'You know, war invades not only countries but also the mind and spirit. The chance of me surviving this bloody awful mess is remote.'

'Oh, don't say that, James, don't.'

'I need to embrace whatever time I have left... make the most of it... Do you see?' He pulled her away from him and looked deep into her eyes, and Madge felt he was looking into her very soul.

She nodded. She understood.

She reached for her jacket, straightened her hair, her tie, her stockings and applied lipstick. 'I can't come back with you,' she said once again. 'They'd all know.'

'Yes, you can,' he said gently. 'You've been on the back of a motorcycle, for heaven's sake.' He gently removed a tiny green caterpillar that was making its way along her shoulder, cupped her face in his hands and kissed her softly.

Ursula Montgomery-West was sitting at a table on the terrace overlooking what once had probably been a beautifully manicured garden but was now given over to bed after bed of potatoes, carrots and onions.

She'd changed out of her corduroy trousers and into a pink-flowered dress, and was pouring tea. With her was a tall man dressed, despite the warmth of the day, in a black three-piece suit, and a blonde girl probably a couple of years older than Madge, wearing the full WAAF uniform of a commissioned officer. Madge saluted her superior and the girl merely nodded in her direction. The man stood to shake Madge's hand as Ursula introduced him as James's father. He said very little but Madge was acutely aware of him watching her as James bounded over to the girl sitting to the right of his mother.

'Constance, how lovely to see you.' James seemed genuinely delighted to see her and bent down to where she was sitting on the rattan sofa, taking her hand and kissing her cheek. 'I thought you were stationed up in Leicester somewhere?'

'I am, but we all have time off for good behaviour.'

She glanced towards Madge, who was standing shyly, unsure whether to sit or remain standing in the presence of, not only two superior officers, but a lord and lady as well. Oh God, what was the protocol here? Should she be curtsying? Saluting?

'Your father spoke to Daddy this morning,' the girl continued, 'and said you were home, James. He called round and picked me up, knowing you'd be back from your... *picnic*...' Constance broke off and raised her eyebrows '... at some point this afternoon. It's lovely to see you, darling. Mummy wants to know if you'll come over for dinner this evening?'

'I'm not sure…' James hesitated and walked back over to Madge. 'What time is your train, Madge?'

'I'm going back up to town in an hour,' George Montgomery-West interrupted, smiling briefly. 'I'll be happy to give your friend a lift back to her base.'

'Oh, really, no,' Madge felt herself redden as all eyes swivelled towards her. 'I have my travel pass. Really.'

'Nonsense,' George barked. 'You can drive up in comfort with me. I know how full the trains are with the damned Yanks and all the paraphernalia they seem to think it necessary to carry with them. I'm driving myself, m'dear, but you'll have a much better journey than standing up on a crowded train all the way back to London.'

He continued to appraise her, not taking his eyes off her face, until Madge began to feel quite ill at ease and didn't know where to look. He knows, she thought. He knows I've made love with his son. She could see grass seeds on her stockings and longed to remove them.

Lord Montgomery-West pulled his watch from his waistcoat pocket. 'Actually, I've a meeting with Winston early evening. Going to have a drink with him first. Won't do to keep the old boy waiting. Shall we say twenty minutes, m'dear…?'

He can't remember my name, Madge realised. He has no *intention* of remembering my name. She glanced over at James, who was still deep in conversation with Constance about people of whom she didn't have a clue.

'You're more than welcome to stay for dinner, Marjorie,' Ursula Montgomery-West smiled, standing to pass over a cup of weak tea in a tiny delicate bone-china cup. Oh heavens, if they could only see her dad's blue-striped pint pot in which he regularly slurped the strong orange brew he always insisted on after a session out in the cold with the cows. If she hadn't been feeling so wretched about having to leave James once again, knowing he would be off on yet more bombing raids, she might have laughed out loud.

'Do, Madge,' James was back at her side, smiling down at her from his six-foot height. 'We can look up train times; there'll only be Mother and me if Father's hell-bent on seeing the PM. We can have a kitchen supper, just the three of us, like I used to have before I went back to school after exeats.'

What the hell was an exeat? It sounded horribly painful. Madge smiled back up at James. 'I really have to be back for eight, James. There isn't a later train, I don't think.'

'That's settled then.' Lord Montgomery-West smiled a rather cold smile before draining his cup and placing it back on its saucer with a rattle of his teaspoon. 'I'm just going up to get my valise and briefcase. I'll see you out by the Daimler, Miss... er...' He cleared his throat and took out the heavy silver fob watch once more before heading for the door. 'Fifteen minutes?'

'Thank you, if you're sure?' What else could she say? Madge herself certainly wasn't sure about spending the next hour sitting next to this rather cold, patrician man. And would he drive her right up to Oxford Street? She knew what Briscoe would have to say about that if she were to see Madge climbing out of the Daimler driven by one of Winston Churchill's ministers. Madge realised she really wanted her big sister, Lydia, here with her right now. She couldn't see Lydia being intimidated by this lot.

'Marjorie, I'm sure you'd like to use the bathroom and freshen yourself up before you leave?' Ursula stood to reach for a little bell on the sideboard. 'I'll get Agnes to show you where you can.'

'Don't bother Agnes,' James frowned. 'Come on, Madge, I'll take you.'

James, Madge realised as she said her goodbyes and saluted Constance once more, had no idea his father had manipulated her into driving back with him. He might be a bomber pilot, trained to be totally aware of potential danger up in the skies, but the undercurrents she'd felt both from Lord Montgomery-West and the Constance woman appeared to have gone straight over his head.

'Do come and see us again, Marjorie.' Ursula kissed her fondly. 'You're always welcome, you know that. At least driving back to London, you won't be late and be in trouble with your superiors. Bye-bye.'

Madge stared at her reflection in the cloakroom mirror: her eyes were bright, her face flushed. She was a fallen woman. She carefully picked the grass seeds from the foot of her stockings and removed a recalcitrant blade of grass from her hair. Then, after applying a generous dash of lipstick to her full mouth and wetting her fingers to smooth her eyebrows, she tossed her head at this new person staring back at her and thought: I don't care. I have no regrets. It's what I wanted.

Madge repeated this to James as they stood by the car waiting for his father to appear.

'Midge, darling, I don't want you having any regrets at all. You do know I've fallen in love with you? That you're all I think about? That it's your face in front of me pulling me back to England when we're over France and Germany?' He touched his shirt pocket. 'And your little cross is with me wherever I go.'

'When am I going to see you, James?'

'Soon, soon. I can't bear to *not* be with you. I'll get a lift, or bag a motorcycle or something, and come up to London. Even if it's only for a few hours.'

'Are you ready, Miss Gregory? Shall we get off?' Lord Montgomery-West appeared at their side and because they hadn't been expecting him so soon, they jumped apart almost guiltily. 'I think Constance is hoping you'll go back with her this evening, James. Hmm?' Lord Montgomery-West shook James's hand. 'Goodbye, old boy. Keep safe, won't you? Give Jerry all you've got.' He opened the boot of the Daimler, threw in his case, bowler hat and rolled-up umbrella before walking round to the passenger side, holding the door open for Madge.

'Thank you.' There was nothing else she could say. Her head was beginning to throb – too much wine, sun and, she supposed, lovemaking – and almost immediately the smell of hot leather from the car's seat assailed her senses, making her feel nauseous.

'Madge, I'll ring you as soon as I can.' James seemed totally oblivious to his father's disapproval and reached into the car, kissing her on the mouth before Lord Montgomery-West put the car into gear and moved swiftly forward.

What on earth was Madge going to talk to this taciturn man about for the hour and more it would take them to drive to London? She started on the weather – how warm and sunny it had been this third week into August – and then, catching sight of fruit trees already laden down with apples and pears, commented on their abundance and how, in a few weeks, her mum would be picking the ones in their garden and storing them in rows up in the attic. Eventually, with very little response from Lord Montgomery-West apart from a nod and an occasional wintry smile, and beginning to feel quite car sick, Madge sat back on the slippery leather seat, and determined not to say another word.

A good twenty minutes passed before James's father deigned to speak. 'How long have you known my son, Miss Gregory?' Montgomery-West took his eyes from the road and looked directly at Madge.

'Oh,' Madge replied, pleased that he was now making conversation. 'Around four weeks or so. I'm based at the Met training school on Oxford Street with Francesca, James's cousin. We're both cooks. Fran introduced us when she took me up to The Ritz and James was there too.'

'And you have become good friends?'

'Yes.' She could hardly add that, from that afternoon, she'd become his lover.

'Miss Gregory, I don't wish to pour cold water on your friendship – I'm sure that's just what the two of you have: a friendship – but I feel I need to say something here. Both James and his mother have... how shall I put it...? an overly romantic idealism about life? I can see that James has become very fond of you.' Montgomery-West slowed down and then veered slightly to the right as a large ginger cat stepped out onto the road and into their path. 'But you must realise that any notions James may have of... of taking your friendship further cannot be accommodated. Once this war is over, if he survives, James will begin to take on some of the responsibility for the estate and his position in society – although heaven only knows what the state of that society will be once this war is over. I'd hate to think – and this is for your benefit, Miss Gregory – I'd hate to think you were under any illusions as to your position with my son in the future.'

When Madge didn't respond but kept her eyes firmly on the road ahead, George Montgomery-West sighed deeply and continued, 'The thing is, your backgrounds are worlds apart. When my wife told me you were from a farming background I assumed – wrongly – your people to be landowners in the North. I have nothing against the North *per se*, although from what I've seen of it, it does appear a particularly bleak and depressing sort of place – but I cannot let my son involve himself with a... with a *milkman's daughter*. I'm sorry, my dear, it just can't happen. James will have a duty to his family – to the Montgomery-West family name – to his heritage. He will, if he survives, marry one of his own class. I'm sure you get my drift?' He took his eyes from the road once more in order to gauge the effect he was having on Madge and patted her knee.

A whole gamut of emotions passed swiftly through Madge as George Montgomery-West continued to drive, his eyes fixed on the road ahead but his left hand still planted firmly on her leg above the heavy-duty material of her uniform skirt.

'I understand entirely what you're trying to say, Mr Montgomery-West.' No way was she about to honour him with his full title. 'I appreciate your concern for me, but I think my... my *friendship* with James is his – and my – concern.'

'Unfortunately, Miss Gregory, I think you'll find it's my concern too.' He smiled that chilly smile Madge had come to expect and she moved her knee away from him in order to dislodge his hand. It didn't work. 'Going off to France for the summer when he was just eighteen was a big mistake,' he sighed. 'I'm not sure what he got up to there, although I have a jolly good idea: I find the French, despite hiding behind their Catholicism, rather loose with their morals.'

'Could you let me out please?' Madge was starting to feel really sick now as well as being near to tears. 'Please drop me off anywhere; there'll be an underground nearby now that we're heading back into London.' She wasn't going to give this man the satisfaction of seeing that his words had upset her, as was his sole intention, she knew. 'Thank you so much for the lift, but I can make my own way from here.'

'If you're sure. I am running a little late and the PM won't be too happy if I'm not punctual.' James's father deigned, finally, to remove his hand from Madge's knee. 'Miss Gregory, I'm glad we've had the opportunity for this little chat and been able to put things into perspective.

I trust our conversation will remain just that – ours. I'm sure you understand that James need not be apprised of what's passed between us this evening?'

'I understand perfectly.' Madge managed to open the car's heavy door before Lord Montgomery-West could alight and walk round to her side and do it for her, slammed it closed, hauled her bag over her shoulder and, without a backwards glance at the car or its driver, set off at a brisk step in the direction of the underground station ahead of her.

21

Christmas Eve and I longed for a man of my own. Embroiled in Madge's story about James until late the previous evening, I suddenly felt the need to be wrapped around a real man rather than the ghost of James Montgomery-West, who had been so much at the heart of Madge's past but now, it seemed, was pervading my, Mum's and Daisy's present.

After ringing Almast Haven to say Madge was staying with us at the bungalow for the night, Daisy and I had helped her to undress, found her a spare toothbrush and tucked her up into her own bed, pale and quite worn out.

Daisy and I had bunked down together in my bed, giving Mum who, after drinking more wine, seemed pretty spaced out herself, the bedroom Daisy had occupied since the pair of us had moved in.

'Madge is determined to get her story all out in the right order, isn't she?' Daisy grumbled, sitting up in bed and reaching for her iPad on the floor beside her. 'Right, what does it say here? Arthur Booth of Holly Close Farm near Westenbury... poultry farmer... married with one nine-year-old daughter... petty criminal... burglar. Burglar...?

Blimey. Madge was married to a burglar? Why can't she just tell us why Arthur ended up killing two policemen? Do you reckon it was anything to do with James, Charlie? You know, why Arthur was hanged? It just says the police had been lying in wait for him to come home. D'you know, I'm even more in love with James now,' Daisy had whispered, putting down the tablet and switching off the light. 'And fancy Granny Madge having sex with him in a wood. I honestly didn't think they did that sort of thing in those days.'

'Come on, Daisy, there were so many girls left pregnant during the war. I bet they were all at it like rabbits. And can you blame them? They could have been blown to Kingdom Come without having ever experienced a man.'

'It made me a bit jealous,' Daisy had whispered. 'Is that awful of me?'

'I felt the same, and it reminded me of being on the motorbike with Josh that time.'

'So how is the very attractive Mr Lee? You've not mentioned him for a while.'

I hadn't. I'd been meeting up with Josh fairly regularly for a drink, for heavenly food, for – let's face it – rather rampant sex, but not really admitted to Daisy, or myself, that I appeared to be getting – as Vivienne might say – my feet under his table. I knew I wanted to work with Josh as the builder on Holly Close Farm and our cottage, and had told the Hendersons and Libby as much. He'd taken me round several of his completed and ongoing building projects and I'd been really impressed with the standard of workmanship, detailed finish on the joinery and quality

stonework. Edward Bamforth, who owned most of the
fields around Westenbury, had been given permission to
build a couple of hundred houses on fields towards the
end of the village and Josh's company had bid for and
won all the contracts.

Josh was incredibly driven. He was up and out of the
house by five each morning and was always the last to
leave every one of his building sites, even though he had
managers in charge on each. He'd taken me to the site
where, only five months after work had commenced,
thirty houses were already under construction. Being
December, the workmen had knocked off once the best
of the light had gone, but the site manager and a couple
of the labourers wouldn't leave until the site had been
left each evening to Josh's obviously exacting standards.
Wearing hard hat and boots, Josh and Gatis, the site
manager, had escorted me round the muddy site but not a
stray piece of piping, broken breeze block or abandoned
wall-tie cluttered the area. Having worked on much less
tidy sites in London, I'd been impressed.

'I definitely want Josh to be in charge of all of the
building up at the farm.' I turned to Daisy.

'Don't blame you,' Daisy said seriously from her side of
the bed. 'You'll be able to have coffee breaks with benefits
once you're both working together up there.'

'You do talk rubbish,' I tutted. 'My heart, I would
remind you, is still broken. I wonder what Dominic is
up to?' I still had fantasies that Dominic was going to
appear, that he would drive up north looking for me, that
he had left Arabella Double-Barrelled and that he'd find

me on site at Holly Close Farm in my hard hat – as well as full make-up and push-up bra – in a passionate clinch with Josh Lee in the half-finished cottage. He'd push Josh roughly away, pull off my hat and, as my freed hair tumbled around my shoulders, ask my forgiveness. There were differing conclusions to this scenario. Depending on what sort of day I'd had at the bungalow, it would veer from me throwing the hat at him, laughing in his face – 'Ha!' – and driving off into the sunset with Josh on his motorbike. But too often I would be speechless with relief at Dominic's appearance and sink into his arms.

'Dominic, I would imagine,' Daisy had yawned sleepily, 'will be shagging the new office junior at Abraham Developments. Now shut up, get over to your side of the bed and go to sleep or Father Christmas won't come tomorrow night.'

'So, what are you doing tomorrow?' I asked Daisy hopefully. 'Maybe we could go over to Leeds or Manchester?'

'Clementine's,' Daisy mumbled, half asleep. 'Am working.'

'Oh.' I really didn't want to be stuck at home on Christmas Eve without even Daisy to fight or get drunk with. Was there anything sadder than being nearly thirty and holed up at home with parents, the dog and a bottle of eggnog?

'Dad and I are over to the O'Hare's for Christmas drinks tonight,' Mum said when I asked her the next morning what she was up to that evening. I'd taken Madge, still a little pale and rather uncommunicative, back to Almast Haven and dropped Daisy off at Clementine's before heading to Mum and Dad's – Daisy and I hadn't done any food shopping – to scrounge breakfast. 'We always go. Had you forgotten?'

I had.

'Vivienne won't be here this evening,' Mum said frowning. 'She's off to some drinks do herself. She'll probably come back the worse for wear, you know what she's like. Anyway, if *you're* not going anywhere, that's good.'

'Is it? Why?'

'Well, Malvolio gets terribly anxious being left by himself, particularly at Christmas.'

'The dog knows it's Christmas?'

Mum tutted. 'You know what I mean.'

I didn't.

Mum brightened. 'You could take him over to Almost Heaven and see Madge and cheer up all the other old biddies. Apparently stroking dogs will make them live longer.'

'What? The dogs?'

'No, the old biddies,' Mum said vaguely. 'You wouldn't like to make some mince pies, Charlie, would you?'

I wouldn't.

'Do the old biddies *want* to live longer in that place? And no, I don't want to make mince pies.'

'Neither do I.' Mum frowned. 'Now you're nearly thirty, Charlie, you really need to take on a bit of responsibility.

You know, whip up a batch of mince pies like other thirty-year-olds.'

'Shall I go on to the Co-op and get a couple of packets and take their lids off? I could stick some glacé cherries and some of Dad's whisky in them, like you usually do.'

Mum looked shifty. 'I didn't know you knew I did that.'

'Mum, we've *always* known you do that.' I gave her a friendly dig in the ribs as she dragged a net of sprouts towards her in an attempt to 'get ahead' as commanded by Delia.

'What the hell does she mean by this?' Mum pulled her spectacles from her head and squinted at *Delia Smith's Christmas,* opened up on the granite. 'Oh, haven't got a clue: I blame your granny Nancy – she never taught me to cook.' She frowned. 'But, I suppose knowing what we now know, I can't blame all my shortcomings on my mother. I mean, the poor thing, she was only nine when her father was hanged. How would she have coped at school? You know how mean kids can be... I mean, *hanged*...?'

'Could you stop saying that word?' I pulled a face.

'Which one?'

'*Hanged.*' Every time it was aired I could actually feel the coarse rope around my own neck. I shuddered. 'So, is Granny Nancy coming tomorrow? Have you heard from her?'

'She rang me the other day. Terrible line, but I got the impression she's going to be here. In the country, at least. Apparently, she has a new *friend.*'

'Another one?'

'You know Granny Nancy. She'll just put in an appearance when she's good and ready. She really doesn't keep in touch with Madge like she should. Maybe it's because of the *hanging*?' Mum glanced up from doing something unspeakable with the poor turkey's innards.

'Mum! Not the *H* word.' I shuddered again, doubly so as I looked at what she had in her hands.

'*I* can't say "giblets".' Mum whispered the word as if it were gynaecological, and shuddered in turn. She turned back to Delia and then started counting peppercorns from a bottle that had a use-by date of 2003. 'Why *nine* peppercorns, for heaven's sake? Why not thirteen or eighteen or nineteen and a half? Oh, feck it.' She opened the bin and threw the glistening brown mess towards it. 'I'll make the gravy from Bisto.'

'Granny Nancy's still got her apartment in Harrogate, hasn't she?' I asked.

'Yes. She wouldn't live in a backwater like Midhope ever again. Not enough expensive dress shops for her to spend her days in. I drive over to see her when she's in the country, but she rarely comes over here, apart from Christmas and when she feels guilty enough to visit Madge.' Mum paused and glanced my way. 'I thought that rather attractive boy from school had invited you to something this evening?' She finished wrapping the turkey in its sheets of tinfoil and went to fill the kettle.

'Yes, he's having a Christmas Eve party.'

'So, why aren't you going? I'd be off like a shot.' Mum peered at me through her specs and then, realising they were her reading glasses, tutted and shoved them back on to her head.

'Well, yes, I was actually quite looking forward to it, but it's fancy dress. I hate bloody fancy dress. Daisy saw him in Clementine's the other night and he told her to remind me to come dressed up.'

'Clementine's?' Mum looked put out. 'Who was he in there with? He's not two-timing you, is he?'

I have to say, when Daisy had told me about it being fancy dress at one in the morning, coming into my bedroom in the bungalow, switching on my bedroom light and waking me, I'd thrown a pillow at her and told her to tell me in the morning.

'I'm not exactly going out with Josh, Mum.'

'Oh?' She seemed surprised, and then shrugged. 'So, just having sex with him, then? Well, you do right.'

I stared at Mum as she hacked away at the bag of sprouts, discarding most of them in an ever-increasing mountain of green leaves. 'You've changed your tune,' I muttered, embarrassed. 'You've spent the last fifteen years telling me to keep my hand on my halfpenny, and myself for the man I married.'

'A mother *has* to say that to her teenaged daughters,' Mum said comfortably. 'It's what we *do*. I mean, we can't say, go out and shag everything that moves, now can we?'

I winced.

'So, fancy dress,' I said, changing the subject. 'I hate trying to make conversation with Denis the Menace or Darth Vader or... or Peter Pan.'

'Peter Pan wouldn't be too bad,' Mum said, savaging another poor sprout. 'You could go as Tinkerbell.'

'The Peter Pan I had in mind was a nude bloke with just an aluminium pan tied over his willy.'

Mum looked mystified. 'I don't get it.'

'Fancy dress?' Oh, I just *adore* fancy dress.' Vivienne, laden down with expensively wrapped and beribboned presents made her entrance centre stage. A few flakes of melting snow were nestling in the depths of her mink coat like diamonds – she had no truck with animal rights – and she kicked off her heels in obvious relief. 'We have plenty of outfits you could have a look at down at the Amateurs.'

'You two girls *will* be staying here tonight, won't you?' Mum frowned, ignoring Vivienne. 'You've never *not* been here for Christmas morning.'

'Yes, of course. We want to be here for when Santa comes. *And* you're nearer Josh's place than the bungalow –that's *if* I go this evening. As long as Dad does his usual bacon and sausage sandwiches and Buck's Fizz.' It was a Maddison family tradition that while Mum tussled with the turkey, working out how long to give the beast as well as how to actually get it into the oven, Dad was in charge of breakfast and booze.

'Well, make the most of it.' Mum said evenly. 'Next year I'm taking your dad to Costa Rica.'

'No, you're *not*.' I nudged Mum once more to make sure she got the message. 'You have responsibilities to your family here. It's the law that while you have children at home you have to continue all family traditions until they leave.'

'I thought they *had* left,' Mum said, glaring at Vivienne, who was admiring herself in the mirror, flinging an expensive-looking scarf around her – allegedly – lifted neck.

'Now,' trilled Vivienne. 'What I suggest – it really is a hoot – is that you wear just a pair of rather naughty white shorts: I did it once at one of darling Roger's parties.'

'Roger? Roger who?' Mum sniffed. 'The lodger? The dodger...?'

'*Moore*, Kate. 'Roger Moore. Superb parties he used to give.'

'So, just a pair of white shorts?' Mum asked archly. 'Nothing on top?'

'You can wear what you want on top,' Vivienne replied patiently, 'but you'll need a big black handprint on your bottom, Charlie.'

'Why?' Mum and I looked at one another.

'*Sports Night with Coleman*!' Vivienne beamed triumphantly.

Mum tutted and I shrugged, still in the dark.

'It went down a storm – showed off my best asset, which, although I say it myself, was quite a talking point forty years ago. It was a TV sports programme presented by David Coleman. You see? *Coal man?* A night out with a hot *coal man?*' Vivienne started to chortle. 'Oh, what a blast we had. Now, Charlie, I may still have a pair of white shorts somewhere – I'm sure we're much the same size. I *was* playing tennis until fairly recently.'

I began to laugh too. 'But no one will get it. No one will have heard of this David Coleman. Is he still alive?'

'Can't be,' Mum said shortly. 'Bet both he and Roger Moore have snuffed it. Now, how about dressing all in blue with a rubber chicken pinned to you and a rope around your neck?'

'Mum, for heaven's sake…' I glanced towards Vivienne. We were trying to keep our recent family history revelation quiet.

Mum's hand flew to her mouth as she realised what she'd said, but Vivienne was still away in the world of film and TV stars of yesteryear. 'Sorry, Charlie, that was rather unfortunate.'

'What was it supposed to be then?'

'Chicken cordon bleu.' Mum started giggling. 'I just thought of it.'

I'd been invited to this party of Josh's and, I realised, it would be churlish not to go. I had to put away all dreams of Christmas Eve with Dominic pouring us both champagne before opening the cufflinks I'd bought, and him then retrieving a black leather box from where he'd hidden it behind the cushion on the sofa, and then me opening the box and staring dewy-eyed at the massive five-stoned diamond ring and then…

'Bloody hell, what are you supposed to be?' Daisy started laughing the minute she came into my bedroom.

'Isn't it obvious?' I had another look in the mirror at the outfit we'd filched from the Amateurs' wardrobe down at Midhope church hall.

'Not obvious to me,' Daisy frowned, circling me to get a better look. She took in my drab brown costume, which was already beginning to make me itch. 'The hunchback of Notre Dame? Mount Everest? A loaf of Hovis?'

I tutted and attached my brown antlers to my head before turning back to Daisy...

'A tree?'

... and added the *pièce de résistance*: my big red nose.

'Ah right, got you. You look very, er, seasonal.'

I pulled off my nose, unable to breathe. 'Oh, I'm not bloody going. I look a total pillock.'

'No,' Daisy placated. 'Not a *total* pillock.'

'Do you know, I've got a beautiful little black number I bought in that fabulous dress agency across from Harrods. I should be wearing that on Christmas Eve, floating around the flat in London while Dominic goes down on one knee, instead of an effing scratchy home-made reindeer outfit that smells like someone just died in it.'

'Oh, Rudolph is a much better bet than wanker Dominic Abraham. Now come on, man up...' Daisy started to laugh again. '... *Reindeer* up, I should say and I'll give you a lift to the party and then you can have a drink. I'm so knackered after waitressing for the last week, me and the dog are going to do nothing but take charge of the sofa and the TV control and wait for Santa to arrive.'

Hmm, not much consideration gone into *that*, I thought somewhat loftily as I followed a rather attractive man in a dinner jacket up Josh's garden path. He turned, pulling a toy gun from his pocket, aiming it at me with two hands. Very James Bond.

'Glorious Twelfth isn't until August the 12th,' I laughed. 'You can't shoot the livestock until then.'

Another man in another black tux. Hmm. Oh, and there was another. Oh, slight variation: a very fat man in a white one. Hmm. And, as I stepped into Josh's house, lots of women – a couple I recognised from school – in black low-cut dresses and rather attractive black leather cat suits. And one woman, looking very chilly but incredibly sexy, in a sort of Ursula Andress-coming-out-of-the-sea sort of way. The shell in her hand was a bit of a giveaway: she *was* Ursula Andress. An obvious Pussy Galore gave me a mystified look before retreating into the sitting room with yet another man in a tux – a rather lovely midnight-blue one this time. My antlers fell slightly to one side as, taking as dignified a stance as I could, I went to find Josh.

He was putting the finishing touches to a plate of canapés when he saw me and, turning right round, eyes wide with surprise, burst out laughing. 'Right. OK, let me guess... Nope, sorry, haven't a clue. In which *James Bond* film is there a moose?'

'A *reindeer*, if you don't mind. I'll kill Daisy. She said it was fancy dress – not a *specific* fancy dress. I'm off home.'

Josh grabbed my arm as I turned and headed for the door. 'No, no, don't, don't. You look... er... fine. I've always fancied reindeers.' He lifted my nose and kissed me hard. I backed into a chair, my antlers now at sixty degrees to my head. Josh looked quite gorgeous in his black tux and tie, but his eyes glittered and I realised he'd either been drinking heavily or was on something. The latter, I guessed, and this was confirmed when the fat bloke in the white tux appeared demanding ice, a tell-tale white powder underneath his nostril.

'Charlotte? It is you, isn't it? You look a bit different with that red nose.' Pussy Galore, a.k.a. Vicky Redfearn from Westenbury Comprehensive, was peering at me, trying to work out if it actually *was* me. Vicky and I, both big into art, had been thrown together in A level art in the sixth form, but we'd not kept in touch once we'd left for university. 'Are you up just for Christmas?'

'No, I'm back up for a few months while I project-manage a property belonging to my great-grandmother. Once that's finished I'll probably head back to London.'

'Oh?' Vicky looked me up and down. 'I took a temporary job teaching art back at Westenbury Comp once I'd finished uni, and seven years later I'm still there.'

'Really?' I didn't quite know if to congratulate or commiserate with her. There was no clue on her rather deadpan features as to which way might be best, and I left it that, the word hanging in the air between us.

'These parties of Josh's are becoming quite legendary,' she said, knocking back her glass of wine in one before reaching for a bottle on the table behind me. She lowered her voice. 'There's always a *theme*... Mind you, I'm sure he's done *James Bond* before. Or was that *Mr and Mrs Smith*? Vicki frowned and shrugged. 'Between you and me, Charlotte, I was really hoping for a *Top Gun*-themed party. I've got such a thing about Tom Cruise and I have fantasies about being Charlie the flight instructor – you know, Kelly McGillis – zooming off on Tom Cruise's bike. Hell, it makes me horny just thinking about it.'

I stared at her, my antlers shocked back up to a jaunty seventy-degree angle as Vicky elaborated her erotic fantasies.

'The best one was last summer when it was *Pride and Prejudice*. The blokes were Colin Firth and although there wasn't a lake to jump in – I did suggest to Josh that we might all go up to the res at Robin Wood – he had a hosepipe in the garden that did the trick. Good do, that.'

'Charlie, you've not got a drink.' Josh was at my side stroking my reindeer bottom. He handed me a glass of champagne. 'Or there's coke, if you'd rather?'

'Coke? Gosh, no, it's Christmas,' I twittered. 'I need alcohol. You know, to get into the party spirit. You haven't got a little black dress lurking anywhere, have you, Josh? Left behind from one of your old girlfriends, maybe? And then I can get out of this bloody reindeer outfit?'

'Well, I can certainly help you *out* of the outfit,' Josh grinned lazily, reaching for the zip at my neck. 'I can't promise there's anything to replace it, though. Now, I'm going to keep the food and drink coming and then we can get started.'

'Get started?' As Josh disappeared with his tray of food, I turned to Vicky. 'As in?'

'As in, go and have a look at what's on offer. And then, knowing Josh, he'll probably have some *James Bond* porn on film. Come on, see if there's anyone you fancy?'

Shocked, my antlers shot back up to a full ninety degrees as I followed Vicky through the house. A James

Bond grabbed Vicky and, after kissing her very thoroughly, grinned and said, in a dreadful faux Sean Connery accent, 'I'm shaken, I hope you're stirred' before turning back to whom I assumed to be Octopussy, rather dumpy bare white legs akimbo as she sprawled across him.

'Terrible Scottish accent,' I tutted before obediently falling in line behind Vicky once more.

'Who? Fraser?' She gave me a strange look. 'He's from Aberdeen.'

'Right.' I was beginning to sweat – whether from the polyester reindeer suit or embarrassment at stepping round, and over, enthusiastically going for it, couples. 'You Only Live Twice' was belting out through Josh's expensive Bose speakers as a tall girl, dressed from head to toe in gold, danced by herself.

'What do you reckon?' Vicky asked almost proudly before downing more alcohol.

'I reckon I'm going home,' I said, a rictus of a smile on my face. I caught sight of myself in one of Josh's mirrors: my red nose and clenched teeth were not conducive to my copping off with any one of these pillocks, had it ever been my intention to do so.

'Oh, don't be daft. You've only just arrived. Come on, loosen up, have a drink or a line and *relax*.' Vicky looked me up and down once more. 'And don't worry about being a reindeer: once the party gets going you can get your kit off and be who or what you like.'

'Absolutely.' Josh, his pupils huge, caught up with us in the conservatory and grinned down at me. He took my hand and led me to a vacant sofa. 'So, Rudolph,' he breathed, pulling on my zip once more, 'what would make you hot? This?' Josh slipped a cool hand under the rough brown fabric and found my nipple, stroking it until it hardened under his touch. 'What would make you *moist*?'

Aagh! That word! *Moist*. Even worse than *giblets*. 'Oh, for fuck's sake, Josh,' I snapped. 'I'm going home. This is like being fifteen again and at a teenage party, seeing how far you can go. Jesus.' I stood up, righted my antlers, snapped my nose back into place and, without a backward glance, made for the front door.

22

It was snowing. Miserable sleety stuff that you don't think will settle but, when you look down at the pavement, there's a transparent covering that, make one false step and it will have you on your backside.

I skidded down Josh's drive, cursing myself for leaving my coat in his kitchen. I'd made a grand exit from his ridiculous party and there was no way I was going back in.

I came to a stop at the end of the garden, fished for my phone in my bag and tried every taxi firm in the town. Each call, if it was answered at all, was met by either rudeness or hilarity.

'It's Christmas Eve, love…'

'Right.'

'Who is this? Are you booked…?'

'Well, no.'

'I can get someone there to you in two hours…'

'Forget it. I'll have frozen to death or be in a *James Bond* porn movie by then.'

'A taxi…?'

'Yes, a taxi. You know one of those things that pick people up and take them home. You are a taxi company, aren't you?

'Yes, darling, but no taxis left… It's Christmas.'

I was frozen and utterly, utterly pissed off. Oh, Dominic, where are you? Come and rescue me from this hell. Two fat tears splashed down my face and, before I could stop them, were joined by a whole waterfall until I was sobbing. You know, that awful sobbing like when you couldn't do your maths at junior school and you can't catch your breath so the exasperated teacher tells the other girls who're gathering round, patting your back in sympathy, to leave you alone.

By this time, I didn't know if I was crying about my disappointment in Josh, for my nine-year-old self, for the sleet gathering in my antlers and making me look like a fucking Christmas tree, or Dominic. Josh, who might have been the one to get me over myself, had turned out to be a laughable damp squib. I wanted my sister.

'Daisy,' I cried and snorted down my mobile, 'can you come and get me?'

'Who is this?'

'Oh, don't you start,' I sobbed. 'It's me. I can't get a taxi and I don't want to be a reindeer or Pussy Galore. And it's Christmas. And I haven't got Dominic any more.' Great sobs rent the sleety air, losing themselves in Josh's privet hedge.

'Shit. You are in a bad way. Hang on, I've got Granny Madge here. I picked her up from Almast on the way back from dropping you off. I thought it would be nice for her to be here rather than in Heaven on Christmas morning—'

'Yes, yes, lovely,' I cut Daisy off. 'You are one very kind person, but can you just come and fetch me. Please? And bring a coat or a hoody. I'm frozen.'

The last thing I wanted was Josh coming out into the garden, seeing me like this, so I went through his wooden garden gate and hunkered down by the wall to wait for Daisy. A taxi pulled up, spilling two tuxedoed James Bonds, one Dr No, two shivering and cursing Ursula Andresses (Andressii?) and a duck (obviously didn't get the correct message either) onto the slippery pavement. Waving bottles of some lurid-looking liqueur, they slipped and slithered through the gate, desperate to get out of the wet and cold. The six-foot duck, bringing up the rear and catching sight of me, plus antlers and red nose, quacked a greeting and, without stopping, hurried after the others.

'Reindeer Rescue Team.' Daisy, wearing her panda bear onesie covered with Dad's old visiting-sick-cows-in-the-middle-of-the-night mac, wound down her window and skidded to a halt, nearly finishing me off once and for all.

'Thanks, Daise.'

'You're lucky. Madge and I were just about to get stuck into a bottle of Merlot. Ten minutes later and I'd have been over the limit. Come on, get in. I've a plate of beans on toast drying up in the oven.'

I was suddenly hungry. Beans on toast, several glasses of red and more of Madge's story sounded like heaven.

'No! You're joking,' Daisy laughed, when I gave her a précis of Josh's party. 'You didn't fancy it, then? You're a woman of the world: might have been quite interesting; enjoyable even.'

'Swinging with Rosa Klebb? I don't think so. I've never been into women.'

'How about blowing Blofeld…?'

'Don't be disgusting.' I shuddered. 'Just get me home, let me have a hot shower. Jesus, Daisy, watch that dog.' Daisy swerved and skidded as a long black dog covered in snow ran into the road. 'What the hell's the matter with it? It hasn't got any legs.'

'That's not a dog, it's a bloody badger and I've hit it. Shit, it'll have dented Madge's car.'

We were on the long unlit road that leads into the village of Westenbury, just five minutes or so from home. Sleet was still coming down as we jumped out of the car to inspect the damage both to the car and, more nervously, to the badger.

'Be careful,' I whispered. 'Aren't badgers vicious things? And full of TB? Does that TB jab we had at school still protect us?'

'I think it's dead,' Daisy whispered back, distressed. 'Hell, I've murdered something. Me, who wouldn't hurt a living thing; even swat a fly or put salt on a slug.'

'That's not strictly true, Daisy, you know: I've seen you squash greenfly…'

'Shall we ring Dad?'

'Dad? He's a vet, not a funeral director. Anyway, he'll be far too stuck into the Christmas spirit to drive here.'

'Well, we can't leave it in the middle of the road. It could cause an accident.'

'It already has. Come on, we're going to have to get it into the hedge.' Daisy and I moved towards it just as headlights picked out the cats' eyes in the middle of the road, lighting up the strange tableau of reindeer, panda and dead badger to the oncoming driver.

The car, a sporty-looking Porsche, which was definitely not the ideal mode of transport for a sleet-filled December night, pulled up and then skidded into the side of the road, narrowly missing all three of us. 'You OK?'

'Dead badger, that's all,' Daisy called more cheerily than she obviously felt. 'We could just do with pulling it into the side so it doesn't cause an accident.'

The man – tall, blond-haired and in his early thirties – opened the door and got out. He was wearing faded Levi's, a navy cashmere sweater and a navy duffel coat. He bent down to the badger. 'It's not dead,' he said. 'Just totally stunned, by the look of it.'

'Charlie, we need to get it to Dad.' Daisy, as much an animal-lover as Dad, couldn't bear to see any creature hurt. She turned to the man. 'If you could just help us lift it into the back seat, then we can take it home. Our dad's a vet.'

'Right.' The man hesitated. 'Aren't they a bit, you know, vicious? Full of TB and fleas?' Sleety snow was beginning to settle on the shoulders of his coat and he looked longingly towards the warmth of his car.

'We can't leave it here. Come on. You take its head and Charlie and I will take its back legs.'

'Right, OK, if you're sure. Just let me get my gloves.' He ran back to his car.

'I know him from somewhere,' I hissed to Daisy. 'Were we at school with him?'

'Never seen him before in my life,' Daisy shrugged. 'He hasn't got a Yorkshire accent. Nice car, though. Actually, rather nice all round. Shame we're looking like a complete pair of morons.'

'OK, let's go for it.' The man frowned. 'I need to be back on the motorway as soon as I can. Right, one... two... three.' We bent, we lifted and we hauled the thing into the back seat of Madge's little car.

'Jesus, it doesn't half smell.'

'*Rough as a badger's arse*: that's where it comes from.' Daisy panted as she banged the car door closed.

'Where what comes from?' Both the man and I looked at Daisy.

'The expression: *Rough as a badger's arse*. From a badger.'

'Right, OK, are you going to be all right? Do you have far to go?' The man looked at his watch, obviously not wanting to hang around any longer.

'Just up the road. We can put the badger in Dad's shed until he comes home.'

'If you're sure. Cheerio.'

'Merry Christmas,' Daisy shouted as he climbed back into his car.

He gave a wintry smile and a slight wave before skidding from the side of the road and heading in the direction of the M1.

'I know him from somewhere,' I said once more, as Daisy pulled into our drive. We'd both spent the last five minutes nervously glancing over our shoulder at the badger. What we'd have done if the thing had come to, God only knows.

'*MasterChef*? *Blue Peter*? Take That? I think he was in Take That,' Daisy said as she parked as near to the shed as she could and gave a worried glance towards the creature. Had it just snuffled a bit?

'Much too young for *Take That*,' I said. 'Gary Barlow must be pushing fifty now. Rather lovely, though, wasn't he?'

'Who? Gary Barlow? Oh, Badger Man? Absolutely. I bet you wouldn't have been in such a hurry to leave the party if *he'd* been on offer. Ooh, can you imagine *him* in a cream tux?'

I could.

Manoeuvring the comatose badger out of Madge's car and into Dad's shed was a nightmare.

'I now know,' Daisy panted, 'if we ever accidentally murder someone and have to roll the body up in a carpet... you know, like Richard Gere did in *Unfaithful*,... even if I had you to help me dispose of the victim... well, we just couldn't do it... far too heavy... right a bit... mind his leg, I think it might be broken... left a bit... Jesus, it smells.'

It took a good ten minutes to get the badger into Dad's shed and, by the time we'd left it on the battered old sofa he kept in there, locked the door and hurried down the snowy path and into the warmth of the house, we were shattered. And smelly.

'Badgers,' Madge said, once we'd poured large glasses of Merlot for ourselves and explained what we'd been up to, 'are incredibly clean creatures. Did you know they build a sett, separate from their living quarters, just for their latrine? No defecating on their own doorstep for badgers.'

'You sound like David Attenborough,' I smiled. 'He's about your age, isn't he?'

'Oh yes, I always had a bit of a thing for him.'

'So, while we're on men you've fancied, are you going to give us the next instalment of the James story? What happened after his father warned you off him? Was that it? Or did you see him again?'

'Why don't the pair of you go and have a shower? You really do smell quite dreadful, you know.' Whether it was the effects of the red wine that Madge had got stuck into in Daisy's absence, or relief in having escaped from Heaven for the night, it was hard to tell, but Madge seemed quite animated. 'I'll make you some fresh beans on toast – those others will be dried up by now – like I used to when you were little girls,' she smiled, 'and then I'll tell you what I decided to do about James after his father had dropped me off at the underground.'

As Daisy and I trooped upstairs to the bathroom, it suddenly came to me.

'Badger Man. I know where I've seen him before. He's the man who was standing at the back of the room upstairs at the Jolly Sailor. You know, the night of the speed dating? And then, I'm sure it was the same man – he had the same sort of car, anyway – who was driving down the lane to Holly Close Farm when I drove there with Josh on his motorbike a couple of days later.'

23

'Oh, Madge, I did warn you.' Francesca sighed and placed thinly sliced ham sandwiches and sausage rolls onto large platters ready for the steward to take into the dining room. Although it was Saturday, and the Meteorological recruits were rarely in the school rooms at the weekend, there'd been some meeting of the tutors and those in charge of the Met officers at the various RAF bases around the south going on for most of the afternoon, and both Francesca and Madge were now on duty to provide an early supper for those involved. 'And don't let Briscoe see you upset. She'll have a field day with you if she does.'

'Ssh.' Madge looked over the stainless-steel work surface to where Sergeant Briscoe was standing, ensuring anything that went into the dining area passed muster. 'I can't believe that I set off to Ascot this morning so excited to see James and now...'

'And now Uncle George has given you the hard word?'

Madge nodded and went to wash her hands at the cavernous sink. 'He made it totally clear that I was too far down the pecking order to even be *seen* with James.'

Francesca tutted and, after glancing in Briscoe's direction, patted Madge's arm somewhat patronisingly, Madge thought. 'I told you, Madge. Remember this is *my* family; I know what they're like. Totally antediluvian ideas about society and where one fits in that hierarchy. I'm really sorry.'

'If I knew what the hell *antediluvian* and *hierarchy* meant …' Madge snapped impatiently and then, with one eye on Briscoe, whispered, 'He called me a *milkman's daughter*, as if I was something he'd scrape from beneath his shoe.'

'Well, forgive me, darling, if I've got this wrong, but your father *is* a milkman, isn't he?'

'Farmer, actually.'

'*Tenant* farmer.'

'Whose side are you on?' Madge looked daggers at Fran as Sergeant Briscoe glared in turn at the pair of them. When Fran appeared to ignore Madge, seemingly giving all her attention to sprinkling the tiny ration of sugar onto the Golden Slices Madge had recently fried and left to cool on the wire, Madge elbowed her and hissed, 'And, there was some woman at the house called Constance. A WAAF officer and big friend of the family?'

'Ah.'

'What do you mean, "Ah"? Madge elbowed Fran once more. 'Who is she?'

'Constance Crawford is the girl James's parents expect him to marry.'

'Gregory, you've spent the day having the life of Riley. Would it be too much to ask you to go and help the stewards out there?' Sergeant Briscoe had appeared at Madge's side without her realising.

'Ma'am.' Madge, her heart as heavy as the loaf of stale bread from which she'd recently cut the Golden Slices, made to unbutton her white overall and remove her kitchen head gear. Briscoe would have a dicky fit if she were to venture into the dining room amongst the top brass still wearing her kitchen whites.

'What are you going to do?' Fran whispered, once Briscoe had returned to her spot at the door and was out of earshot.

Madge brushed an angry hand across her eyes to wipe away the tears that had, despite her determination not to cry, made an appearance. 'I can't do anything, can I? I can't take on and beat Lord blooming Montgomery-West, *Winston Churchill's* friend and confidant. I'll write to James and tell him I don't want to see him any more and then as soon as I can, I'm going home to my mum and Lydia, my sister. I've not been home since I left Yorkshire in January. I reckon I've got at least three days' leave owing to me.' Madge stopped to blow her nose before hissing at Fran, 'I've had enough of you damned southerners.'

By the end of that week Madge had applied for and been allowed compassionate leave, telling Sergeant Briscoe her grandmother was at death's door and her mother was insisting she return home to make her final farewells. Briscoe, she knew, would most likely have snorted disparagingly and told her there was a war on and to get on with it, but Madge had hardly taken any leave in the eight months since joining up and Briscoe signed the travel warrant with little more than an accompanying sniff and raised eyebrows. James had, apparently, rung the Oxford Street base several times, leaving his number and asking that Madge call him in Bourne, but, instead, Madge wrote the most difficult letter of her life, thanking James for taking her to meet his parents but telling him that she didn't think it a good idea for a WAAF of the lowliest rank to be getting involved with a squadron leader. As she signed the letter and addressed it, tears coursed down her face and onto her blue shirt collar until she was almost sick with sobbing.

The train journey home seemed interminable in the last few days of an early September heat wave. Every carriage was crowded with service personnel, either on leave themselves or making their way to training camps in the north, and Madge wasn't able to get a seat until she changed at Crewe before travelling on to Manchester and then to Midhope. It was almost seven in the evening by the time she left Midhope Station and walked up to the bus station, sweat trickling down her spine as she manoeuvred her kitbag from one arm to the other while she waited over an hour for the local bus to Westenbury and home.

'You're home, love. Let's have a good look at you. Goodness, don't you look smart in that uniform! Do we have to salute you?' Annie Gregory turned from her knitting and gave her younger daughter a long, appraising look.

Madge smiled. 'Not with that knitting needle in your hand, you don't. I'm exhausted. I just want to get into my own bed and sleep for ever.'

'Never mind sleeping, Madge: we want to hear everything. And now you're a cook,' she smiled, 'you can make the dinner tomorrow while I'm at church.'

'Mum, I'm no better a cook than when I left. I can make a decent Welsh rarebit and that's about it. They should have let me be a Met girl, like I wanted.'

'I saw Mrs Booth down in the Co-op yesterday.' Annie gave Madge a sideways glance in order to gauge Madge's reaction. 'Arthur's got leave too, you know. Got three or four days before he has to go back.'

'Right.' Madge's heart sank. The last thing she wanted was a tussle with Arthur. She'd managed to keep out of his way the last couple of months, ignoring his letters and telling whoever took his phone calls at the training school to tell Arthur she was on duty and couldn't come to the phone. She felt terribly guilty and knew she should finish their relationship and give Arthur a chance to meet someone else. Maybe that was one job she'd have to do in the next couple of days; there was no chance he wouldn't be calling round to see her once he knew she was home.

Madge slept for fourteen solid hours that Saturday night, falling into her narrow single bed with the blue quilted eiderdown and crying over James until exhaustion took hold and she fell into a dreamless sleep.

She woke, glad that she didn't have to wear her uniform for the next couple of days and, buttoning herself into a faded summer dress she knew would be in the heavy oak wardrobe where she'd left it last summer, went downstairs to see if Annie had left the breakfast table laid before heading off to church with Isaac, Madge's youngest brother. Isaac had always been different. At twenty-three, he should have joined up like Silas, Joseph and herself, but there was no way any recruiting officer would have passed him fit to fight for his country. He was just Isaac, happy to be on the farm with his dad and tucked up in his own bed every night. He'd been teased and bullied at school – God knows how he would have survived the wrath of a regimental sergeant major when he didn't even know his left from his right and, when nervous, couldn't speak without stammering – until Madge's dad had had enough, walked down to the school and, despite warnings from the Education Board, pulled Isaac out, just twelve and with a couple of years of compulsory schooling still to go. In a different era, Madge supposed, as she poured tea from the huge blue and white striped teapot and cut herself a wedge of bread from a large white loaf, he'd have been known as the village idiot.

'You're up then?' Granny Gregory, the one supposedly at death's door, was obviously very much alive, if not exactly kicking and, after looking meaningfully through the open door to the grandmother clock in the hall, was making her way from the front parlour where she'd been reading yesterday's newspaper and into the kitchen. She shuffled over to the chair by the window, which she'd claimed as her own the minute she came to live with them after Granddad Gregory had died a couple of years back, and sat down heavily. She was a large woman and,

Madge mused, taking in the black voluminous skirt and huge matronly bust, seemingly much larger than when Madge had left home eight months previously. 'Where is everybody? Left me alone again as usual? How about a cup of tea, Madge? Is there any left in that pot?'

Madge crossed over to the ancient age-blackened stove to put the kettle back on the hob and then, opening the kitchen door, went down the path and threw the detritus from the teapot onto the roses at the bottom of the garden. She stopped, placed the teapot on the ground and enjoyed just taking in the view down the valley from her vantage point under the ancient apple trees already bent over with a glut of late summer fruit; loving being back in the countryside after the dirt and frenzied bustle of a city caught up in war. Madge sniffed the air. It might be a glorious September day now, but some of the leaves, particularly on a pair of venerable oaks to her right, already had the tired, dusty appearance of those submitting to the inevitability of the new season ahead.

She didn't want to go back inside to be talked at by Granny Gregory – her grandmother never talked *with* one, only *at* one – she didn't want to be quizzed by her mother and Isaac, once they were back from church, on her new life as a cook and she most certainly didn't want to be hanging around waiting for Arthur to put in an appearance as she knew he must, once he knew she was also back home. And she didn't want to think about James. Had she been reckless sending James that letter? He was a grown man. He loved her. He'd said so. At least he'd said he was *in* love with her, and wasn't that the same thing? He was surely old enough to make his own mind up about whom he could love, even if that amounted to a *milkman's daughter*? She should have hung onto him, ignored Fran and his damned interfering father. She should have fought for him, not let him go at the first obstacle.

Madge wanted to garden, wanted to feel the dry soil gritty beneath her fingernails and pull up weeds rendered almost anchorless by the lack of rain these past few weeks. Forgetting that she'd intended to make Granny Gregory a fresh pot of tea, she walked down the garden to where her mother's hens were pecking fruitlessly in the arid soil for worms, and then on to the allotment beyond where her father, long before the Government's 'Dig for Victory' edict was even thought of, grew and harvested his carrots, potatoes, cabbages and onions.

Madge must have been down there a good couple of hours, using both the hand fork and the much larger full-sized fork to turn the soil, pull weeds and neaten and straighten the edges of the raised beds. Seeing the leaves at the neck of a number of her dad's onions already flopping over, she bent and pulled until she had a satisfying pile of large, brown onions at her feet.

'Madge, it's dinner time.' Isaac appeared at her side and hunkered down beside her, fingering the papery vellum skin of the onions as he did so. 'I'm glad you're back,' he added. 'I don't like it when you've gone away.'

'I've missed you too,' Madge smiled, dusting dry soil from her dress before taking off her sandals to shake the soil that had found its way into them.

'Are you back for good?' he asked hopefully. 'Can you stay?'

'No, 'fraid not, Isaac. I have to be back by Wednesday evening.'

Isaac paused, counting on his fingers the number of days from Sunday to Wednesday and then stood up. 'Come on,' he grinned excitedly. 'We've got beef for dinner.'

Beef? Where had her mother got beef from? They might live on a farm, but the herd was kept for milking and Madge couldn't see the Co-op being happy about her dad killing one of their number just because she was home on leave for a few days.

Joe Gregory, washing the cow stink from his hands and lower arms, was standing at the sink in the scullery when Madge and Isaac made their way back into the house. 'Thanks, love,' he smiled, when she placed the harvested onions beside him. 'That saves me a job this afternoon.'

The kitchen table was laid with Annie's best white starched tablecloth, and Granny Gregory was already seated, impatiently waiting to be served the inevitable plate of Yorkshire pudding. 'Where've you got beef from, Mum?' Madge sniffed the air, suddenly hungry. She realised she'd not eaten much since Lord Montgomery-West had warned her off his son and, smoothing down her thin cotton dress, she could feel her hipbones and knew she'd lost weight.

Annie tapped her nose. 'Never you mind where it's come from, Madge. Just enjoy it.'

Joe reappeared through the cellar door to the right of the kitchen, brandishing a bottle. 'Last year's elderberry,' he smiled. 'It's not every day we have a war hero back in our midst. Welcome home, love.'

Madge laughed at that. 'I don't think Sergeant Briscoe would have me down as a hero,' she said ruefully. 'More of a *menace* when it comes to my Yorkshire pudding.'

'A war hero?' Granny Gregory sniffed disdainfully. 'The boys on the Somme: now *they* were your heroes. Not some chit of a girl making scones and cakes for the top brass.'

'Ignore her,' Annie smiled, but she was cross, Madge could tell.

'There's a war hero in the *garden*,' Isaac exclaimed excitedly, getting out of his chair and going over to the window. 'In his blue uniform.'

'Mum, it's Arthur. Tell him we're having our dinner.'

'You go and tell him, Madge. He can always stay for his dinner, you know.'

'It's not *Arthur*,' Isaac stammered in his excitement. It's a *proper* RAF p... pilot with a proper hat, you know, one of those with a p... peak on.'

Madge's heart lurched and she shoved back her chair and ran for the kitchen door.

'Hello, Midge.' James didn't smile but just looked at her, his large brown eyes never once leaving her face. 'Tell me you don't want to see me and I'll turn round this very minute and drive back the way I've come. Just say the word.'

'I can't. You know I can't.' Madge walked over to where James was leaning against the wall of their outside lavatory, his arms folded. He was trembling slightly as he took her bare shoulders in his hands and held her from him, gazing into her face.

'Why did you do it?' James shook his head. 'Why did you write that letter?'

'Because, James,' Madge said defiantly, 'I was warned off you.'

'Warned off me? By your officers, you mean?' James frowned.

Madge sighed. 'No, by Fran to begin with, and then… and then by your father.'

James's hands tightened on Madge's shoulders. 'But Fran gave me your address. Told me you'd come back to Yorkshire for a few days. And my father? When? Why?'

'Mum says, do you want to bring your friend in?' Isaac was quite tongue-tied with awe. 'Do you want to come and have a bit of dinner with us? There's beef and Dad's wine.'

James held out his hand solemnly. 'You must be Isaac. Madge has told me all about you. And yes, Isaac, I'm starving. I could eat a horse.'

'Mum, Dad…' Madge ignored Granny Gregory, who was more interested in the delay over her Yorkshire pudding coming to the table than meeting any friend of her granddaughter, '…this is Squadron Leader James Montgomery-West. He's come for lunch.'

'You do know that wasn't *beef* you've just eaten.' Granny Gregory plucked at James's arm conspiratorially, glancing over towards Annie to gauge her reaction. 'It was *horse*. There, what do you think of that?'

Madge closed her eyes in horror. Her mother had just fed them *horse*?

'My favourite,' James smiled chummily to Granny Gregory. 'We used to eat it all the time in France. I don't know why we don't eat it more in England. That was delicious, Mrs Gregory, thank you. Best meal I've had for months.'

Madge started to laugh, giggling until she hiccupped and had to drink more of the elderberry wine. 'You *said* you could eat a horse.'

'He *said* he could eat a horse.' Isaac joined in with Madge's giggling. 'Outside. He *said* he could eat a horse. And he has... he has.'

Cross that her bombshell had been a damp squib, Granny Gregory went on, 'Well, lad, I'd better warn you that she makes her custard with the water she drains from the peas.'

'Stop it, Mother.' Joe Gregory was cross. 'Annie did it once, when we'd run out of milk. We've pints of milk here to make custard.'

'Well, I'll bet you'll get shot, lad, if they find you've been wasting government petrol coming up all this way to see our Madge.'

Madge glared at the old woman.

'Avoiding being shot at is what I do most nights, Mrs Gregory.' James said comfortably. 'Unfortunately, it goes with the job. And I'm actually on official duty: I'm due at the RAF base in Snaith later this evening. I just called in to see Madge here before I carry on with the journey.'

'Madge, why don't you take James for a walk to stretch his legs before he's back in the car? It's a good few miles up to Snaith.' Annie glared at her mother-in-law once more and Madge smiled gratefully at her. Her mother, she realised, disliked Granny Gregory just as much as she did. 'You could head towards Molly Carr woods.'

'I'd like that,' James smiled. 'I don't know this part of the country at all.'

'Are you really on official duty?' Madge asked as they made their way across the fields below her father's farm. Drystone walls, meticulously built long ago by artisan workers, stretched into the distance on all sides and, as they approached them, James went ahead before helping Madge over.

'Sort of.' James grinned and took her hand. 'I had to see you. I knew a train would take forever, if there even are any up here on a Sunday, so I threw myself on the mercy of my group captain – who also happens to be a friend – and asked for the use of a car. He said as long as I combined the trip and went on to Snaith to pick up three of their flight lieutenants who are being posted to Bourne, he'd turn a blind eye if I happened to stop off in some little village in Yorkshire for a cup of tea.'

'Oh, James.' Madge squeezed his hand as they walked.

'Midge, this is the most beautiful spot in the world.' James stopped suddenly. 'Listen to that lark. They both looked skywards, searching for the black, singing dot that was the soaring skylark. 'How can you ever bear to leave this place and live in a city?'

'I love London,' Madge said, surprised. 'Don't you?'

'I've had enough of it down there. The air is so pure up here. Look at these fantastic walls: the skill that's gone into making them.' James stroked the stones, almost in reverence.

Madge laughed at him. 'You've got walls in Ascot, you daft thing.'

'Ah, but not walls like this.' He stopped stroking the wall, shading his eyes against the sun. 'What's down there?'

'Where?'

'That farmhouse right down in the valley.'

Madge shrugged. 'Just one of the farms. There are loads round here.'

'Have we time to go down there?'

'Depends what time you need to set off for Snaith.' Madge hated the thought that in an hour or so he'd have to leave.

'Come on, if we walk quickly we can make it.'

24

'Holly Close Farm,' James read slowly, squinting awkwardly at the faded black lettering on the crumbling stone post.

'It's seen better days.' Madge smiled, turning to James, who bent his head to kiss her forehead. He only had to touch her, any part of her, and all her senses were instantly alert, her body craving more of him.

'I think the place is deserted,' James frowned. 'Come on, let's go in.'

'It's just a farm, James. There are loads round here. The farm lads have probably enlisted and the farmer has had enough and given up the ghost. It's hard work if you can't get enough workers.'

'Lord, look at that view.' James let go of Madge and almost ran to the fence that marked the periphery of the farmland. 'I feel I've died and gone to heaven.'

Madge smiled. 'It's just a farm,' she repeated, catching up with James and taking hold of his hand, wanting to be kissed some more.

'Midge, I want to *live* here.' James was laughing, but she knew the way that he was looking at her, his beautiful brown eyes holding such truth and honesty, he was deadly serious.

'Your dad would never allow it.' Apart from when James had first appeared in her dad's rhubarb patch earlier that afternoon, this was the first time George Montgomery-West's name, as well as his part in her fleeing from James, had been mentioned.

'Madge, my father can't stop me doing what I want. Maybe before the war... Oh, I don't know... things are different.' James frowned, pulling her to him. 'Life after this mess is never going to be the same. It can't be and... and it shouldn't be. I don't want to have been killing innocent people in France and Germany just so that I can take my place as the next Lord Montgomery-West. I don't want to live in that great pile our family has inherited for the last two or three hundred years. Madge, I want to live here, with you.'

Madge laughed at his intensity, laughed at the idea of him wanting to live in this old farmhouse.

'I can see its *beauty*. Look, there's some sort of smaller building over there.' James took her hand and together they walked over to where a small cottage built of the same mellow stone as the farmhouse lay nestled below, its south-facing aspect taking full advantage of the glorious view over the fields and valley that stretched into the distance for miles.

'This *is* heavenly.' Madge, caught up in James's excitement, led the way through the garden gate and into the cottage garden, which was beginning to look abandoned and overgrown.

'I'm amazed that this garden and the land belonging to the farm haven't been claimed by the "Dig for Victory" zealots,' James mused, trying to prop up the spray of yellow roses that had left their anchorage along the front of the cottage wall.

'Probably too isolated for anyone to bother bringing gardening stuff down here. Maybe the farmer has died and any sons or grandsons who'd have taken the place on are off with the war. It happens, according to my dad.'

'I'm going to find out.' James was quite beside himself at the thought. 'I love this place, Madge.' He bent to pick a perfect yellow rose, threading it through Madge's blond hair and kissing her softly 'And, you must know, I love you.' James took her hand and led her towards the door of the cottage, positioning her against it before bending his mouth once more to hers.

'It's not locked. Look.' Madge, leaning against the ancient wooden door of the cottage, felt it give way slightly beneath their combined weights. 'Should we go in, do you think? Although it does seem pretty cheeky wandering round someone's house and garden like this.'

'Darling Midge, there's no one around for miles.' James put his shoulder against the door and pushed, and the door creaked opened onto a flag-stoned floor. Any furniture that had once graced the cottage had been removed, but a rag rug, very much like the ones her mother would fabricate from clothes that could no longer be worn, still lay on the floor. Sunshine poured through the bank of south-west-facing windows, both warming and lighting the interior of the large room they found themselves in. 'Oh, how lovely.' James stood stock- still, gazing around him at the interior of the cottage. 'It's like a fairy tale.'

Madge frowned and then laughed. 'It's just a worker's cottage. They're all like this round here. You only think it's wonderful because it's so different from your great pile of an estate. This, James, is how the majority of people live. It's your huge hall that's the fairy tale.'

James laughed, throwing his arms around Madge, lifting her up from the floor.

'Come live with me and be my Love,
And we will all the pleasures prove'.

'Pardon?'

'Christopher Marlowe.'

Madge put her fingers to his lips, stopping his words. He took them, drawing them into his mouth, licking each one in turn, his eyes never leaving her face. She was conscious of every single breath James took, sensed every movement of his body as he gently lowered her down to the rug, raining soft kisses onto her eyes, her cheek, the small fleshy part of her earlobe and down to the hollow of her neck. He wove his fingers into her hair, pulling her slightly towards him as he kissed her mouth, tentatively at first and then, as she arched towards him, kissing him back, more deeply.

James moved his hands towards the front of her thin cotton dress, unbuttoning each little tiny disc with tantalising slowness before reaching in to the warmth of her breast, grazing each nipple, now hard and erect, with his thumb. Madge wanted him to know every part of her body and when his fingers moved down to the hem of her dress, pushing it upwards, she moved her legs apart slightly because she simply could not have done anything different. James slipped his fingers up under her skirt, making contact with the silky softness of her underwear, pushing the material aside until they were inside her, stroking softly and expertly at the exact spot he knew would give most pleasure.

Madge drew in her breath, disappointed when his fingers slipped out of her, but shocked when James moved down her body, kissing her hips and inner thighs before moving his mouth to where his fingers had been minutes earlier. Madge tensed, and James immediately stopped, sitting up to look at her. 'Tell me you don't like it, Madge, and I'll stop.'

'But, is it right? It feels lovely but...' Madge stopped, embarrassed.

'It *is* lovely, you're lovely, and it is *so* right if you enjoy it, but I don't want you to do anything you don't want to.' James smiled his lazy smile down at her.

'It felt so heavenly.' Madge knew she was giving James permission to kiss her down there again and she moved her legs once more. He took her hand, stroking the softness of her palm and then moved his body and his fingers down her hips, kissing the sharp ridge of her hip before gently moving aside the silky material of her pants with his tongue. He inserted one finger, moving his mouth and licking slowly and oh so deliciously at her mound. Madge felt her body begin to judder – it was, she thought wildly and irreverently, like that wonderful moment before a huge sneeze – and she gave a little 'oh' of surprise as her whole being exploded.

James smiled that wonderful knowing smile once more and, tilting her hips into his own hardness, entered her and, with long slow strokes that set Madge on fire once more, reached his own climax, biting his lip to stop himself crying out loud.

'I wasn't being a fantasist,' James said seriously twenty minutes later when he and Madge sat outside in the late afternoon sunshine. They were seated side by side, James stroking Madge's hair as they sat on an ancient bench facing the perimeter fence of the farm and the view down the valley, two slight dips in the stonework showing where other bottoms had previously been sat over the years. James closed his eyes soaking up the last of the heat of the day. 'When this is all over – if I survive – I don't want to be an architect in London. I mean, I still want to be an architect: there's nothing I'd rather be, although I know my father assumes I shall go into politics like him and my grandfather. I love this area, what I've seen of it anyway.'

Madge squeezed his hand but let him continue.

'I'm going to find who owns this place, Madge. See if it's for sale.'

'But your dad... he'll blame me, you know...'

She never finished her sentence as James, utterly taken by surprise, was grabbed from behind and knocked sideways off the bench and onto the grass. Madge jumped up in horror as a bundle of fury leaped on James, throwing punches wherever it could.

'Arthur Booth, get off him, you stupid, stupid idiot.' Madge launched herself at Arthur, pulling at his shirt and receiving a blow on her arm as he tried to push her off.

Taken initially by surprise, James had landed heavily on the ground but Arthur, a good deal smaller and slighter than James, was no match for him once James realised what was happening and had jumped up, knocking Arthur off him and onto the ground. James took both Arthur's flailing arms, twisting them behind his back and pinning him down so that his face was buried in the grass.

'Do you know him?' James panted angrily. 'You seem to know his name.'

'Aye, she does, an' all.' Arthur spat the words from the side of his mouth not squashed into the grass. 'She's engaged to me. She's *my* girlfriend.'

'Arthur, I am *not* engaged to you.' Madge shouted furiously. 'I never have been, and never will be. And Arthur, this is *Squadron Leader* Montgomery-West, one of your officers.'

'Aye, I know exactly who he is, Madge, and how you've been carrying on with him behind my back. And if I end up being court-martialled for assaulting an officer, it'll be your fault, you dirty bitch…'

James, livid, shook Arthur until he almost rattled and Madge had to pull on James's arm for fear he might end up killing him. 'Listen, Booth, I recognise you now,' he hissed. 'You're one of the erks on the airbase. So, listen well to what I'm going to say. You're going to get up and go back the way you came. If you ever get in touch with Madge again, or pull a stunt like that *ever* again, you'll be court-martialled and thrown in the clink and the key thrown away. Now, when I get back to Bourne, I shall file a report on the incident but I shall keep it under lock and key. Any contact with Madge or any attempt to get back at me, and the report goes straight to Group Captain Bellingham. And, Booth, I shall suggest you're moved to another base – probably the best all round for all of us.' James loosened his hold on Arthur and, as he picked himself up from the grass, James watched him, taking in every aspect of him. 'One more thing, Arthur,' James's voice was quiet. 'In your place, I'd have done exactly the same thing.'

'How did Arthur know you were down at Holly Close Farm with James?' Daisy and I were enthralled, hanging on to every word as the three of us sat in front of the fire, drinking large glasses of Merlot and eating home-made Christmas cake – from M&S – with a big lump of Wensleydale.

'Well, as James and I had walked across the fields, very near to the farm, we'd bumped into Leonard Bassinger and Walter Dyson, two of Arthur's friends from school. They'd both opted to go down the mine – you know, the one over at Almast – when they left school, so were in a reserved occupation and didn't have to enlist. I can remember it like it was yesterday, the looks the pair of them gave me as James and I passed them. I reckon they must have followed us and, once we went down the lane and through the gate of Holly Close Farm, scarpered back to Arthur's house and told him where I was and who I was with.

'And did Arthur get into trouble? Did James sprag him up once he got back to Bourne?' Daisy licked a finger and mopped up cake crumbs from her plate while Malvolio looked on longingly, strings of drool hanging from his mouth.

'*Sprag* him up?' Madge pulled a pained expression. 'What peculiar language you girls use. 'Do you mean shop him?'

'Absolutely,' Daisy said comfortably, relenting and giving the dog a slice of cheese. 'It's Christmas,' she added, when she saw my face. 'So, *was* Arthur in trouble?'

'No,' Madge shook her head. 'James wasn't the type to get people into trouble. And Arthur stayed at Bourne for the duration of the war. He was a good mechanic and James would have needed a reason to suggest one of the base mechanics be moved elsewhere.'

'I bet James was a bit nervous, though, wasn't he? Daisy frowned. 'You know, going up in a bomber that had been serviced by his love rival.'

Madge smiled at that. 'There was a whole raft of mechanics on each base. There had to be, you know, and I've no idea whether Arthur worked on James's machine.' Madge's face clouded with pain as she spoke. 'But he was certainly one of the first to know, and presumably celebrated his good luck, when *R-Rascal* went missing over Holland and never returned to base.'

Madge closed her eyes and kept them closed and Daisy and I looked at each other, not sure what to say or do next. Madge was saved from further questioning by the kitchen door banging open and Dad, obviously drunk and much the worse for wear, staggering into the sitting room. 'There's something in my shed making a hell of a noise and trying to get out,' he said, his eyes wide. 'You don't think it's one of Santa's reindeers that's got in there by mistake and can't get out…?'

Dad started laughing at the very idea, fell over Malvolio, who was still eyeing the remains of the cheese, and lay comatose for several seconds before beginning to snore loudly and deeply.

25

Surely Dominic would text me today? You know, just to say Merry Christmas?

'No, he hasn't.' Daisy, guessing my thoughts, reached for my phone. 'And don't you go thinking that just because it's Christmas Day you have any excuse to contact *him* either.'

'If you remember,' I snapped crossly, 'Arabella Double-Barrelled made him change his number.'

'Oh, don't tell me you haven't been back on to Abraham Developments website and found his new personal number.'

Blimey, that girl knew my every move. I'd done just that and knew the new number off by heart.

'And I bet you know it off by heart.'

I threw the dishcloth at Daisy and she deftly caught it and threw it straight back. She was always better at netball than me.

'What were you thinking of, you two, letting Madge drink so much red wine last night?' Mum tried to manoeuvre the turkey into the oven but failed miserably. 'You've probably pickled what was left of any brain cells she still has. You do know that we lose them at an alarming rate once we get past seventy?'

'Past fifty, if the size of that turkey is anything to go by,' I snapped, taking my frustration at Dominic's absent seasonal greetings out on Mum. 'Why the hell don't you buy a smaller turkey… or a bigger bloody oven? You have the same battle every Christmas morning.'

Daisy, bleary eyed and still in her panda onesie left off the hunt for her Cadbury's Selection Box, which Dad had hidden from us every Christmas since we were about five-years-old, and laughed. 'Oh, come on, Charlie, Christmas wouldn't be Christmas without the annual turkey tussle. Chop its legs off, Mum.'

'And who said you could invite a badger home for Christmas anyway?' Mum ignored Daisy. 'Your father must have been dealing with the damned thing for hours after you both just sloped off to bed and left him to it. It really went for him, apparently. He was already in a bad enough state after eating Hayley O'Hare's quite inedible chilli washed down with enough whisky to floor a Scotsman. How he managed to stay upright to catch the creature and tranquillise it to set its leg – legs, actually: you broke *two* of its legs, Daisy – is anyone's guess.'

'James died Mum.'

'Madge's James?' Mum gave the oven door a final whack and looked at me, eyes wide. 'How tragic.'

'Who is James? And, more importantly, who has any paracetamol?' Vivienne, floating around in a pink shell suit and devoid of her usual make-up, was looking pretty ropey, as well as all of her seventy-odd years. 'I've such a headache,' she went on, pressing two fingers to her temple in an Oscar-winning performance. 'I can't *imagine* what Graham was up to in the shed last night. It sounded like someone was being murdered: I didn't sleep a wink and it's left me with one of my heads.'

'Nothing to do with the gin you were knocking back at your cocktail do?' Mum asked drily.

'Talking of alcohol, where's Dad now?' Daisy glanced at the kitchen clock. 'It isn't on, you know: doesn't he realise it's Christmas morning and he has responsibilities? There should be bacon sandwiches and Bucks Fizz on the table by now. He's slacking...'

'So, who is *James*?' Vivienne insisted. 'Has Madge been having an *affair*? At her age?' She sniffed disdainfully, obviously hating the idea of anyone having a better love life than herself. Bad enough Nancy would soon be arriving with a new man in tow, never mind Madge getting a share of any action going.

'About time, Dad. Come on, we're all starving hungry here.' Daisy folded her arms as Dad made his entrance.

'You're like a pair of bloody cuckoos, you two...' He rubbed at his blood-shot eyes and gazed dolefully at the weals and scratches visible on both arms protruding from the YOUR DOG ONLY NEEDS THE BALLS HE FETCHES T-shirt he regularly slept in.

'Mum!' We all turned as one when the kitchen door opened and Granny Nancy walked in. Immaculately dressed in a red coat – not dissimilar to the Max Mara Madge had inherited – furry hat and long black leather boots, I thought at first Father Christmas was making a tardy reappearance.

Nancy peeled off her black leather gloves, kissed Mum coolly on the cheek and then, surveying the rest of us in our various state of undress and alcohol withdrawal, said drily, 'Lovely to see you all looking so well and full of the Christmas spirit.'

Christmas Day *started* well.

Muttering to himself that, thank God, he at least had an ally in the dog, Dad accepted he was once more about to be submerged in female-only company and came up trumps, sorting breakfast for us all, as was the family tradition. He kept Barbara Badger – 'another bloody woman - and pregnant too, by the look of her' – tranquillised in a dog cage in the shed and, once he'd given us a total rollicking for being so stupid as to handle and bring home such a savage creature, especially on Christmas Eve, even praised Daisy and me for rescuing her and showing the true spirit of Christmas to a dumb animal. Which I thought was a bit over the top, and I put down to the Scotch still circling his bloodstream.

Vivienne, who'd always viewed the very chic Nancy as some sort of competition, arrived at the dinner table so utterly dolled up, she had all the makings of a probationer drag queen. Sporting long red nails and what appeared to be a couple of tarantulas stuck to her aquamarine eyelids, she sashayed to her chair wearing the tightest of sparkly dresses and proceeded to hold court throughout lunch while the rest of us attended to her every need.

'So, Nancy, I thought you had a new friend coming with you today?' Vivienne folded her Rudolph the Reindeer paper napkin, placing it neatly onto the detritus of cheese, nuts and tangerine peel in front of her, and faced Nancy.

Nancy went slightly pink. 'Oh, I thought it would be too much trouble for Kate to have more guests. He was happy to go to his sister in Chester.'

'A man?' Dad was animated for a second. 'We nearly had a *man* here?'

'And Nancy,' Vivienne interrupted, 'isn't it wonderful news that Madge has sold her secret house? And given the cottage to Daisy and Charlotte for themselves?' Vivienne took a sip of her pudding wine, eyeing Nancy over the fluted glass and through the tarantulas to see her reaction. 'I've not been allowed to see this mystery house yet, but I believe—'

'You've done *what*, Mother?' Nancy's voice was pure steel.

'Mum, not now.' Dad glared at Vivienne.

'Nancy, I was going to tell you after we'd eaten but, as the subject has been broached, I don't see why we shouldn't discuss it now.' Madge spoke calmly and levelly. 'I'm not sure it will be of any interest to Graham and Vivienne.' Madge turned to Vivienne, who wavered slightly under her direct glare.

'Come on, Mum.' Dad virtually manhandled Vivienne from her seat. 'You can come and help me make coffee in the kitchen and then you and I can hog the sofa, the TV and the Christmas cake and watch something good while all the Booth girls discuss the mystery house.'

'Thank you, Graham.' Madge stroked Dad's arm as he ushered Vivienne towards the sitting room and a rerun of a *Morecambe and Wise Christmas Special*.

Mum poured more pudding wine. 'Best bit about Christmas pud is the wine that goes with it,' she said vaguely. 'Mum,' she went on, going to sit by Nancy in the vacated seat next to her, 'I *know* about what happened to Granddad Arthur. The girls know.'

'I think, Nancy, now that this has all come out, I need to tell you everything.' Madge had gone quite pale and her hand shook slightly around the stem of her glass. 'It was *never* my intention to tell you, Nancy, what I'm going to tell you now. I thought, all these years, I was doing the right thing by not telling you... And I *couldn't* tell you before... for one very good reason.'

'Mother, what are you going on about? What is it you never told me?' Nancy glanced at Mum, Daisy and me.

'I think, Mum, that Madge blames herself for your father's death.' Mum was trying to speak softly to Nancy, trying to get her to listen to what Madge had to say.

'He was a common petty burglar,' Nancy snapped. 'And a murderer to boot. And *I've* had to live with the shame of knowing my father stole from businesses around Midhope all my life.'

'Nancy, darling, your father adored you. You were the apple of his eye. He stole from others in order that you and I could have the things he thought we deserved.'

'Deserved?' Nancy knocked back the remains of the pudding wine and reached down the table for what was left of a bottle of Sauvignon Blanc. 'Like some latter-day Robin Hood? And did he wear green tights and a funny hat when he went a-burgling?'

Nancy, I could see, was getting drunk as well as angry.

'As I said, Nancy,' Madge was having difficulty getting out the words and had to stop talking to drink some water, 'as I said, Arthur adored you, but Nancy... Nancy, he *wasn't* your father.'

'James,' Daisy and I both said together. '*James* was Granny Nancy's dad.'

I have to give Nancy her due. She just said icily, 'And who the hell might James be? Anyone I know?'

'He was the love of my life. The only man I ever loved.' Madge was crying now, great fat tears rolling down her lined face. 'I'm sorry Nancy, I shouldn't have kept it from you, but I was really given no choice.'

'Madge,' I went over to her and took her hand. 'You don't have to do this now.'

'Oh yes she does.' Nancy was livid. 'She can't just tell me the man I thought was my father *wasn't*, without some explanation. Oh God, Mother, don't tell me this James was another criminal, worse than Arthur. How many policemen did this one murder?'

'Squadron Leader Viscount James Montgomery-West was no criminal.' Madge sat up ramrod straight. 'And I will tell you why I married Arthur Booth, and not your real father, Nancy.'

★

'Madge, darling, come and sit down.'

'Sit down?' Madge turned in surprise at Fran's words. 'And have Briscoe after me for abandoning the sinking Yorkshire puds?' She laughed at her own wit and carried on beating the creamy batter.

'Madge, just leave it…' Fran glanced towards Sergeant Briscoe, who nodded her assent, indicating she should separate Madge from her task.

'Fran, what is it? Not James? Please, not James. Say it's not him?' The wooden spoon with which she'd been intent on beating lumps from the batter fell to the floor, spattering drops in an arc around it. Automaton-like, Madge put one foot in front of the other as Fran took her hand and pulled her gently onto a chair in the deserted dining room. There was a buzzing in her ears and yet she could hear every other sound from within the training school: pans crashing to the floor from a shelf in the kitchen; one of the WAAF's loud laughter from somewhere outside the dining room, intensified and magnified until she shook her head to dispel the noise.

'I'm sorry, Madge. My mother telephoned me just now. James didn't come back last night. He's missing…'

'… presumed dead,' Madge finished dully, knowing the exact words. She glanced towards the large-paned glass windows of what had previously been the toy department of the store. The rain that had been falling for what seemed like forever showed no signs of abating. It will never be sunny again, she thought.

'Gregory, you're excused from duties for the rest of the day.' Sergeant Briscoe stood before her. 'Go to your room and rest, but I don't have to remind you that you won't be the only one to lose someone. We have to get on with it.'

Madge couldn't speak. Couldn't even utter the expected 'Ma'am.'

'Go with her, Montgomery, and then you'll need to take over in the kitchen. We still have to eat.'

Five months had passed since that hot September day when she and James had discovered Holly Close Farm and Arthur had found them both there together. Five wonderful months when Madge had fallen more and more in love with this heavenly human being and James had reciprocated that love in every way possible. She was unable to tell herself she was luckier than most: that he'd so far managed to survive the carnage in the skies over France and Germany; that she'd had him to herself for almost seven months, meeting up with her whenever he could; at the end of the telephone when he couldn't. Making her laugh with his ridiculous humour, making her cry when he had to leave her – often after stolen nights in the house at Eaton Square – after making love to her with such skilled hands, she'd given herself completely to him. Instead of being grateful for what she'd had, she felt only fury. Fury with every German who'd ever lived, fury with James's father for constantly reminding James that nothing could come of their relationship, but most of all total fury with James himself for leaving her when he'd told her that he could *never* leave her.

Madge continued to watch the relentless rain from her room at the very top of the training school, watched the grey clouds gather and roll, and knew a part of her had died too.

'Madge, Sergeant Briscoe wants to see you.' Beryl popped her head round Madge's bedroom door. Four terrible, interminable days had passed; days when Madge had risen dutifully from her bed at the usual time, carried out her tasks, walked in the rain and the dark up to the gates of Regent's Park just to remember and, shoes swimming in water, walked back to start the whole cycle once more.

'Gregory, this might not be the best time, but then again, perhaps it might. Your new posting has come through.'

'But I want to stay here. I don't want to leave London.' Madge could hardly breathe.

'Not yours to argue the toss, I'm afraid, Gregory.' Briscoe was stern, but then her tone softened. 'Look, Madge, I know what's been going on with your viscount. It could never have come to anything, you know: wartime fairy tales always fizzle out – and this was one hell of a fairy tale. You must see that?' Briscoe became matter of fact: 'Now, your posting is back up north. Presumably near your family? You're dismissed. Go on. You've a week left here before you leave.'

Madge mounted the stairs back to her room, every step an effort, but was called back down before she'd started on the second flight.

'Madge. Visitor.'

'Who is it?' For one wild moment Madge wondered if it could be Ursula Montgomery-West come to find her, to share her grief with her.

'Dunno. Sorry. Got to dash. Off to the pictures.' Nora sped off back down the stairs and into the wet night, and Madge slowly retraced her steps back down.

'Arthur? What do you think *you're* doing here? Have you got some leave?' Arthur was waiting just inside the little lobby, his hair and uniform wet through.

'Madge, I'm sorry. I've come to say I'm sorry. I know how much that officer meant to you and now he's dead.'

'He might not be,' Madge shouted wildly. 'He's missing. They don't know he's dead.'

'I'm sorry, love. He's dead. Proper confirmation came to the base today. I heard it from the group captain himself. Four planes didn't make it back the other night.'

Madge closed her eyes and then sat down on the cold stone steps. 'I've been posted. Harrogate.'

'Oh.'

'And you might as well know, because you will soon enough, I'm having a baby.'

'His?'

'Of course, his,' Madge snapped.

'They won't let you stay in the WAAF.'

'Of course they won't.' A tear rolled unheeded down her cheek.

'Will your mam and dad have you home?'

'I can't tell her.' Madge raised her eyes for the first time. 'You know what a big churchgoer she is. Biggest sin in the book, to have a baby without being married. My gran would never shut up about it.' Fat tears rolled down her cheeks and she put her head down onto her arms and wept silently.

'I'll wed you, Madge. You know I will. I'll treat the baby like it were my own. You know I would, Madge. You know it's what I've always wanted. You, me and our baby.'

Madge lifted her head and stared. 'But it wouldn't *be* your baby.'

'But it's *your* baby. I'll look after you both, Madge. We'll get married straight away. No one'll know it's not mine.' Arthur put his arms round her. 'It'll be all right, Madge. It'll all be all right.'

Nancy stared at Madge. 'Why have you never told me this, Mother? How *dare* you never tell me this?' She got up from the table and took the edge of it in her hands, shaking it so viciously that what was left on Madge's plate slid onto her lap and her wine spilled onto her new Christmas cardigan.

'Granny, leave her alone.' I took Madge's hand while mopping at her wet cardigan with a paper napkin and was shocked at how cold and frail she felt.

'Leave her alone?' Nancy was breathing hard, spittle forming at the sides of her mouth. 'I'll shake her until she tells me every damned thing. She's kept this from me for nearly seventy years.'

'At least he was *posh*,' Mum snapped, joining me at Madge's side and glaring at Nancy. 'Your father was a *Viking*, for heaven's sake.'

'A Viking...?' Nancy stared, momentarily nonplussed.

'A *viscount*.' Despite the awfulness of the whole situation, Daisy, I could tell, wanted to giggle.

'At least you *knew* your real father, Kate, and he wasn't a murderer or... or some mythical creature dragged back into the present where madam here, for some reason only known to herself, suddenly deigns to bring him.' Nancy was still breathing hard, glaring both at Mum and Madge.

'*Knew* my real father? Are you daft or drunk, Mother?' It was Mum's turn to spin like a modern-day Valkyrie. 'I *never* really knew him. You made sure of that. The closest I got to him was when he was on the top of the utility cupboard with Gin and Tonic.'

'What? What *are* you talking about?' Nancy frowned at Mum, who was dabbing at her flushed neck and forehead with her Rudolph the Reindeer napkin. 'And sage tea, you'll find, Kate, is good for hot sweats.'

'Come on, you two.' I jumped in between them. 'It's Christmas.'

'Yes, and I've always hated it.' Mum grabbed a table mat, wafting it up and down in front of her as a makeshift fan. 'I'm definitely off to Costa Rica next year, even if I have to go by myself.'

'Madge?' I stared at my great-grandmother's face. Something wasn't right. 'Mum, there's something wrong with her...'

'Oh Jesus, get your father...'

'He's a vet, not a bloody doctor.' Daisy took control. 'I'm ringing for an ambulance.'

26

'You're not going to let your aversion to joining in with Josh's Christmas swingers come between you and a damned good builder, are you?' It was a bitterly cold Monday morning in January, the first day back at work for everyone after the excesses of Christmas and New Year, much of which Daisy, Mum, Nancy and I had spent at Midhope General, sitting at Madge's bedside on the stroke ward. Daisy, dressed against the cold in thermals, and buttering a pile of toast, gave me a searching look.

'Daisy,' I said, pulling on another jumper and searching for my gloves, 'I am a *professional*. It is totally irrelevant that my builder appears to get his rocks off from dressing up as characters from films and books before indulging in group sex. Just as long as he doesn't appear on site thinking he's the Duke of Edinburgh after watching *The Crown* and expect you, me and Seb Henderson to indulge his ridiculous fantasies.'

'Ooh, if Seb Henderson is part of the indulgence, count me in.' Daisy's eyes gleamed as she crammed a slice of the toast into her mouth. 'I wouldn't mind being Princess Margaret if Seb was... what was he called?

'Group Captain Townsend,' I said vaguely. 'Look, Daisy, this is the start,' I snapped, ignoring her banter. 'Our very first site meeting with everyone on board. I want to get on with it, no messing. I'm going to do this properly and check out all the builders, plumbers and electricians Josh is working with, myself. He might be the builder, but *I'm* project manager and *I'm* in charge.'

'Blimey, you *are* up yourself this morning.'

'New year, new project, Daisy,' I sniffed, importantly. 'Dominic will not get a second thought, nor will Josh, apart from seeing how he behaves professionally. I am done with men. All I'm interested in now is my work. This is my very first project as The Lady Builder and it has to be superb. Come on, we're not going to be late on our very first day on site.' I glanced at Daisy, who was laughing and pulling a cross-eyed face at me as she'd done when we were kids, and I started to laugh myself. I *was* becoming a pompous pillock. I threw one of Madge's cushions at her head and went to give her a hug.

'You all right?' Josh had the grace to look embarrassed. He and five of his men were already waiting down at Holly Close Farm. It was only seven thirty and still dark; it seemed a long way off until the lighter mornings of spring. 'You know, after… you know…'

'I *do* know, Josh, and I am totally fine. Hey, what you get up to in your spare time has absolutely nothing to do with me. I'm sure your, er, *games* and your other little *habit* will not reflect on your professional workmanship.'

I gave him an on/off smile; he just seemed a bit pathetic in the cold light of day.

Josh reddened and glanced round at his workers, who were loading up their gear and heading for the cottage. It had been decided that, as in effect the cottage still belonged within our family and there was still quite a bit of legal work and planning to sort out with the farm building itself, we'd start there. 'Ssh, Charlie. I'm their boss.'

'Fine, but don't forget who is in overall charge round here.'

Josh gave me his now familiar grin. 'I've always liked a woman who can *dominate*.'

I looked him up and down. What a wally. 'Let's get one thing straight, Josh. You caught me at a vulnerable time when I came back home. I'm not a bit interested in any extra-curricular activities you might be thinking of. I know you're a damned good builder. And that's all. Right, shall we get going?'

Suitably chastised, Josh shouted over a small dark-haired man, around my age, who was in the process of issuing instructions to the other men. 'Charlie, this is Matis Miniauskiene. He'll be the site manager when I'm not here.'

I held out my hand. 'Hi, Matis. I'm sure we can both pull together and get this show on the road.'

Matis frowned. 'Sis show? I's a builder, Charlie, not some actor putting on shows. And where is sis roads?'

I looked at Josh. Was I going to be taken literally at everything I said to this man?

Josh laughed at the look on my face. 'Matis is from Lithuania. He's a bloody good builder, as is his brother, Gatis. It does get a bit confusing as they obviously have the same surname. You've met Gatis, manager down on the Westenbury site. Gatis and Matis Miniauskiene have more experience of building than anyone I know.'

'Right.'

'S'right,' Matis grinned. 'You leaves it all to me. No one's better.' He grinned again, showing immaculate white teeth. Gosh, he was very attractive, if you liked that sort of short dark hairy type. He suddenly turned to the labourers, who had stopped what they were doing and were laughing at something one of them had obviously just said. 'Oy, yous lot, on wis its. Sis is building sites not bloody Butlins.'

I spent the morning talking to Josh's men, had an on-site meeting with Seb and David Henderson, who assured me the final papers for the farm and land would be ready for signing in a couple of weeks, rang the hospital to check on Madge and then, realising I was famished, joined Daisy. We sat on an ancient bench facing the perimeter fence of the farm and the view down the valley, two slight dips in the stonework showing where other bottoms had previously sat over the years, and ate the ham and piccalilli sandwiches we'd brought with us.

'Funny to think Madge and James probably sat together on this seat,' Daisy mused. 'She really did adore him, didn't she? What an absolute tragedy he died.' She poured us both coffee from her flask and then stood to scan the acres of land in front of us. 'I wonder where the two policemen were actually shot?'

'Oh God, don't. I really don't want to know,' I shuddered.

'But why did Arthur have a gun in the first place? It's all a bit strange, don't you think?' Daisy peered at me over her cup, steam rising in the cold air. 'What do you think of Matis?'

'What do I *think* of him?'

'You *know*...' Daisy grinned at me, nudging me in my ribs for good measure. 'You don't think he's incredibly attractive?'

'If you find short, dark, hairy men attractive.'

'I do. Oh,' Daisy sighed, 'I really do.'

By half-past three it was already beginning to get dark and Matis came to find me, saying they'd have to finish for the afternoon. 'We's knocking off nows. Nossings else we can do.' He glanced at Daisy. 'We's off backs to the office now but going to the pubs later. Yous two wants to come?'

'Which pubs are you going to?' Daisy was animated, obviously eager to join them.

'Only *one* pubs, Daisy,' Matis admonished her. 'One pubs on a works night. Not a piss-ups during the week.'

I shook my head. I had no intention of ever again getting friendly with anyone I worked with. I let my thoughts wander to Dominic and was surprised when my heart didn't do that flippety-flip thing it usually did whenever his face swam into view. This was interesting.

'I'll come,' Daisy volunteered. I glanced both at her and Matis. Blimey. The sexual *frisson* between the pair of them was palpably crackling.

'You go,' I said. 'You won't be able to see a thing in a few minutes. I'm going to the hospital.'

'Oh, I'll come to the hospital too. I can meet the others later.' She stopped speaking as a car pulled into the makeshift car park of trucks and vans in front of the farm. 'Who's this who's just arrived?'

'I think it's Seb Henderson back again,' I said. 'Isn't that his car?'

'No, car too sporty now that Seb has grown up and got a baby, and hair too blond.' We all stood in line as if we were in the receiving line at a wedding as the man made to lock his car and then approached us.

'Oh, sorry,' he said, 'I didn't think there'd be anyone here. There isn't usually.'

'Usually?' I glanced across at Daisy.

'I'm sorry,' he said again, 'I love this place. Every time I'm up here, I come over just to have another look. I've left it a bit late today.'

'And forevers amen, matey,' Matis said dismissively, eyeing his tools and equipment as the labourers placed them neatly in the back of the truck. 'Sis farms is solds. We don't wants up-to-no-good guys wandering rounds the place. Farms solds now. Sorry.'

'Oh,' I suddenly cried, and Matis and Daisy turned in my direction. 'It's Badger Man.'

'Badger Man?' The man looked at me with raised eyebrows.

'The dead badger that wasn't actually dead on Christmas Eve?' I turned to Matis in explanation: 'It's Badger Man.'

'Oh, sorry, I didn't recognise you without your antlers.' Badger Man turned to Daisy 'Or not dressed as a panda.'

Matis frowned, trying to work out the strange vernacular of badgers, pandas and antlers. 'You knows this mans? And he's *badgering* you? We knows about guys who badgers womens. Not good.' He stepped towards Badger Man. 'Yous been badgering sese womens?' He turned back to me. 'You wants we get rids?'

I laughed at that. 'No, honestly, Matis, but thank you. It's fine.'

'I didn't realise the place had been sold.' He sighed. 'It's just that my great-uncle loved this place. He wanted to buy it and live here years ago.'

'Your great-uncle?' Daisy and I looked at one another.

'He first came across it during the war. He wanted to do it up and live here once the war was over.'

'But he didn't survive? The war, I mean?'

'My great-uncle? Yes, he did.' The man appeared puzzled.

'Oh.' Daisy looked at me again and then asked. 'He wasn't called James, was he?'

'Yes.' He stared at Daisy. 'How did you know that?'

'James Montgomery-West?'

Badger Man frowned. 'How did you know that?'

'I goes, Daisy,' Matis interrupted, obviously fed up with hanging about in the cold. 'I sees you in pubs tonight? The Jolly Sailors in Westenbury? Seven o'clocks?' He headed for the truck, leaving the three of us in the shadows of the derelict farm building.

'We *know*,' Daisy said excitedly, 'because we know *all about* James. Me and Charlie are Madge's great-granddaughters.'

'You know *Madge*?'

'Well, yes. Do you?'

'Well, not personally.' He hesitated. 'But I know all *about* her. How my great-uncle adored her, wanted to marry her and live here.' He nodded in the direction of the farm's battered wooden front door.

'Madge has just had a stroke.'

'She's still alive? Goodness, I had no idea. She must be in her nineties?'

'Ninety-four.'

'Uncle James assumed she died years ago.'

I glanced across at Daisy, who was taking it all in. 'James is alive?'

'Yes.'

'So, he didn't die? In his plane, I mean?'

'No, the War Office had never had any confirmation that he'd died. They just said missing, presumed dead. He was badly injured but turned up in some hospital in Germany and then saw the war out in several prisoner-of-war camps. Sorry, so you're Charlie and you're Daisy?'

'Other way round.'

'Look, I'm staying over tonight; I'm booked into the Jolly Sailor in Westenbury.'

'Like before?'

'Before?'

'I saw you standing at the back of the upstairs function room a couple of months ago. The night of the speed dating?' I blushed at the very thought, embarrassed that I'd taken part in the whole ridiculous shebang.

'Ah,' he smiled.

'We can't keep calling you Badger Man,' Daisy laughed.

'Oh, sorry, Corey Mackenzie.' He held out a hand and smiled. 'Do you fancy joining me to eat tonight and we can exchange stories?'

'I can't,' Daisy said, 'but Charlie here can.' She dug me in the ribs.

'OK, yes, that would be good. Thank you.' I gave Daisy a big sister look. Why the hell was she digging me in the ribs like that? 'I need to go and see Madge in hospital first. Tell her James is still alive.' I felt really excited.

'But she knows,' Corey frowned. 'Madge has *always* known.'

'Madge, you'll never guess what…' Daisy and I raced onto the acute stroke unit where Madge had been monitored since arriving in A and E late on Christmas Day.

Madge, looking every bit her age, turned her head slightly on the mound of white starched pillows, her blue eyes, now faded to the hue of washed-out denim, fluttering open at my voice. The stroke, apparently, had been in the left side of her brain resulting in a paralysis of her arm on the right as well as some problems with speech and, we'd been warned, probably some memory loss. Madge was still undergoing full assessments of both her physical and cognitive functions and her attempt at a smile, as she realised it was Daisy and me standing at her bedside, was pitiable and made me want to cry.

'You're looking much better, Granny Madge.' Daisy, always the optimist, gave me a warning nudge and I attempted a smile myself. 'We'll soon have you out of here and back at the bungalow.'

'Madge,' I said. 'Do you remember Badger Man? You know, we told you about him on Christmas Eve.'

'I think you're going to confuse her.' Daisy turned away from Madge, her voice a whisper. 'Remember, the nurse said short-term memory is more likely to have gone than her long term.'

'I'm just going to talk to you, Madge. Some of what I'm saying you might not grasp, but you're not to worry. You'll get better and remember more and more things every day. So, we – Daisy and I – met someone at Christmas. We've just met him again and you'll never guess. He's James's – your James's – great-nephew.'

Madge stared, her good hand constantly pleating and releasing the stark white coverlet on her bed.

'Girls, you're not to excite her.' Tara, the nurse in charge of the ward, had arrived to check the IV drip that was putting tPA through Madge's arm in order to improve blood flow to her brain. 'What are you telling her?'

'We've come across a relative of an old friend of hers. We were just telling her about him.'

'Well, be careful. You'll just end up confusing her. Far better to talk to Madge about the weather and what day it is or just let her know you're here for her and then let her sleep. Sleep is vital for her recovery, you know that. I've already had to ask your Granny – Nancy, is it? – to leave because she was constantly talking at her. It really isn't on, this constant battering her with information.' She turned back to Madge. 'We're going to have to watch this leg of yours as well, lovey. We need to keep it moving so it doesn't stiffen up.' Tara looked at the small watch pinned to her chest. 'Come on, girls, it's not visiting time anyway. Come back tomorrow at the proper time.'

'Why didn't she tell us James was still alive?' Daisy and I made our way along the sludge-coloured corridor to the main exit. 'God, I hate hospitals. I remember Madge saying if she ended up back in hospital with her leg, she'd never get out a second time. She never thought she'd be back in with a stroke. And, even if she does recover from this, there's no way she'll be able to look after herself at the bungalow. She'd hate to be back in Almast Haven, knowing it was going to be permanent this time. She'll just give up.'

'Granny Nancy isn't helping. Has she gone back to Harrogate?' The glass doors of the main hospital entrance whooshed open at our approach and a blast of freezing January air had us hurrying to the car.

'Jesus, it's cold. Yes, Mum texted me to say she'd gone back, but she's visiting every day. Which is something.'

'Oh, I don't know. I think she really upsets Madge.'

'Hmm. I'm not sure her visits are totally altruistic. I think Nancy's trying to find out more about what went on years ago – and I don't blame her – and what's happening to the cottage. I bet she never thought Madge would go behind her back and give it to us. Mum says we're a bit *persona non grata* at the moment: Nancy thinks we talked Madge into it.'

'That is so not true.' Daisy was indignant. 'And awful of Granny Nancy to be more worried about her inheritance than how ill Madge is. Do you think she'll get well, Charlie?'

'I really don't know. I wouldn't have thought the chances good, you know, having a stroke at the age of ninety-four.'

Once in the car we drove in silence for a minute and then Daisy turned to me. 'So, what did you think of Badger Man? Rather gorgeous, isn't he?'

'Is he? I can't say I noticed.' I shrugged and concentrated on the road ahead.

'Your nose is getting longer by the minute, Pinocchio.'

I laughed at that. 'OK, yes, *bloody* gorgeous. But, if you hadn't noticed, he was wearing a wedding ring. It's the first thing I check out now. After Dominic, I mean.'

'Oh, bugger.' Daisy sat back in her seat. 'He wasn't, was he? If I didn't fancy Matis, I'd be going after him myself.'

'You stick to the short, dark hairy ones,' I laughed. 'They're *much* more your type.'

27

Madge needed to speak. Needed to tell these two girls more about James, but her damned mouth wouldn't work. She knew the words but she couldn't form them. What on earth was wrong with her? There'd been some problem with her leg but surely that wouldn't have affected her ability to speak? Did they say they'd just met James? Or somebody to do with James? Something to do with badgers? But she couldn't remember James having anything to do with badgers. Her beloved James.

She knew the girls: hell, what were their names? She loved them, she knew that. Loved them so much. And the older one – she had a boy's name – she had James's brown eyes. The moment she'd held that baby in her arms, there'd been a connection. Where *was* James? Madge closed her eyes against the whiteness. White walls, white screens, white pillows, white coverlet. Even her hands, apart from the sunken blue veins and brown old-lady spots, were white. She wanted colours and pictures: pictures of James, not this interminable white sterility.

Here was a picture of the farm: Holly Close Farm. How she'd hated him when Arthur told her he'd bought it. Bought it for her because he knew she loved it so much and wanted to live there. Arthur had got it all *wrong*: it was James who'd loved it, not her. To her, on that hot afternoon when they'd made love in the cottage, it was just another ramshackle old farm. And although she'd grown to love the place, she'd hated living there without James. If it hadn't been for Harry, living in the cottage, Harry who became her best friend and confidant, she thought she might have gone mad. But she had Nancy, James's daughter. Nancy, who looked nothing like James, but everything like Lord George Montgomery-West, her paternal grandfather. *The milkman's daughter.* Wasn't that what he'd always called her?

How had Arthur found the money to buy the farm? Madge opened her eyes but the surrounding whiteness brought her back to a present she couldn't understand and she felt them close again, bringing myriad pictures of a past that she could. Arthur's mother, that was it. Madge had always quite liked her although she was a bit of a soppy one, never standing up to that sod of a husband of hers. What was *his* name? He'd died, hadn't he? Not long after she'd joined up. So he never knew that Arthur's mum had saved every single penny Arthur had religiously sent home to her during his three years in the RAF. Never knew that she'd given the whole lot back to Arthur so that he could buy the farm that no one else wanted.

And Harry. Darling Harry. What had happened to her best friend, afterwards?

It was he who'd brought her the letter. He'd taken his own post from the postman and carried on up to the farmhouse to bring her and Arthur's mail and have a cup of coffee with her, as he often did while Nancy was at school and Arthur 'out on business.' He'd brought her the letter.

'Letter for you, Madge.' Harry wiped his boots on the doormat and followed her through into the kitchen.

'For me?' Madge turned, in surprise. She didn't often receive mail.

'Got your name on it.' Harry laughed. 'You need to get out more, Madge. Live a little. Go into town, go into Leeds or take the train to Manchester. Arthur buys you all those beautiful dresses and costumes and jewellery and you rarely wear them.'

'Get out like you, you mean?' Madge said drily as she opened the envelope with Arthur's letter opener.

'I'm a poet. Why would I want to be anywhere but here in this glorious Yorkshire countryside in July? I'm like Wordsworth.' Harry laughed. 'I just wish I'd got in there first with the damned daffodils. They were totally divine this year.'

'There's the yellow roses around your cottage that you could write about.' Madge laughed. 'What rhymes with roses? Hoses? Noses? There you go, I'll start you off: "I chose a yellow rose, smelled it with my nose…"'

'"And tucked it in my hose"?' Harry arched an eyebrow. He was so good-looking, was Harry. Medium height, dark, almost continental looks. Arthur, Madge knew, hadn't wanted to let out the cottage to anyone, never mind a good-looking, Cambridge-educated, ex-diplomat, who'd deigned to eschew his former life in London and New York and retreat to the North in order to write. But, before his various business ventures had taken off (Madge had little idea what these might be and, to be honest, she really didn't take that much interest) Arthur had been strapped for cash and agreed to Madge's idea that they should rent out the cottage. Very wary of Harry to begin with, once Arthur realised their tenant was not interested in women, but was 'a queer, Madge, you know, a poofter', he relaxed.

'You don't miss London or New York, Harry? All the hustle and bustle of the city? I know *I* do sometimes. Goodness…' Madge stood stock-still as she read the contents of the letter.

'What is it?' Harry went to take the kettle from the range, looking round for the tea caddy as he did so.

'Goodness. Heavens… It's from Beryl, one of the WAAFs I shared a room with at the Met training school on Oxford Street during the war. I wonder how she got this address' Madge frowned, scanning the contents. 'She's arranging a ten-year reunion of the WAAFs who worked together as cooks there.'

'You must go, darling. Get out your glad rags and furs, and head for the bright lights once more.'

Madge laughed. 'Furs in July? No, Harry, there's no way I'm going to any reunion. I don't *want* to go.'

'Oh, but you must. If only to give that heavenly little ivory costume an outing.'

'I'm not sure I want to be reminded of that time.' Madge felt tears threaten. 'It was the most wonderful... and the most terrible time of my life.'

'And this isn't?' Harry took her hand. 'Madge, I know you're not happy at the moment. I know Arthur isn't the love of your life.'

'Arthur saved me.'

'From what? Doom? Destruction? Yourself? Madge, this is 1953, for heaven's sake, and I worry about you. You're too young and too lovely to spend your life holed up here with Arthur. He never lets you out of his sight except when he's off "doing business". What exactly *does* he do, anyway?' Harry frowned. 'He never gives you a moment to yourself.' He took the letter, quickly scanning the ten or so lines written there. 'It's a lunch, Madge. One little lunch at The Ritz. I'll drop you off at the station; it's only a couple of hours now by train. If Arthur won't pick Nancy up from school, then I will.'

When Nancy was just seven, Arthur had insisted the local village school wasn't good enough for any daughter of his and, without consulting Madge, had put her name down for a little private school five miles away. Madge had been furious at the time and, encouraged by her sister, Lydia, who had become a staunch Labour Party activist after Churchill's Conservative Government had returned to power in 1951, refused to go into Midhope to buy the necessary fancy uniform, equally insistent that Nancy should stay where she was. It was Nancy herself, taken by Arthur to have a look at the new school, declaring she wanted to go in the car every day with Daddy to a school just for girls and not rough boys, who won the day, and she'd been going there ever since, loving every minute of it.

'Well, I'm telling you now, Arthur won't let me go off to London by myself for the day.'

'Yes, too frightened you won't come back.' Harry drained his cup. 'Stand up for yourself, Madge. Lydia tells me you were always pretty feisty until you got married. Now you seem to have buried yourself out here in the countryside. You're going to London if I have to walk you all the way there myself.'

'I'm meeting Beryl Andrews' party. Actually, I'm not sure that she still is Andrews. She has a table booked...' Madge hesitated as the maître d' welcomed her.

'Madge. Over here. My goodness, you look wonderful.' Beryl, with whom she'd shared a room on Oxford Street, came running over, an enormous grin on her carefully made-up face. Dressed in a sky-blue dress with huge black buttons, cinched tightly at the waist with matching black belt, she was the height of fashion. A blue hat was pinned securely on the back of her now very blond hair and, despite the warmth of a London summer, black cotton gloves covered her hands so that Madge was unable to see if she was wearing a wedding ring.

'So do you.' Madge suddenly felt terribly shy and unsure of herself. Apart from parties and trips to the theatre with some new friends of Arthur's whom she wasn't convinced she liked anyway, finding them brash and vulgar at times, Madge knew that over the years since the war she hadn't been the most sociable of women. She had a whole wardrobe of the most beautiful clothes for which Arthur took her into Manchester shopping, a drawer full of silk and satin lingerie that he insisted on buying for her, and a jewellery box containing more pieces than she could ever wear at any one time.

'Now,' Beryl smiled, taking her arm and leading her into the dining room, 'there's probably quite a few girls here you won't know – they were posted to Oxford Street after you went back north. And you never kept in touch,' she added accusingly. 'It's a good job Fran knew how to find you.'

'Fran?' Madge felt her pulse race. She'd consciously not kept in touch with Fran once she'd moved back to Midhope, cutting off anyone with a connection to James. James was dead and Arthur had taken her and Nancy on, so she'd felt she owed her new husband her best shot at making the marriage work. Reliving with his cousin memories of James and how much she'd loved him would have only prolonged the agony; there had never been any correspondence between the two and that was how Madge had wanted it.

'Yes, come on, she's already here. And there's Mary and Nora, too.'

'Oh, my *goodness*, Marjorie Gregory. You look just like Grace Kelly.' Mary stood up in welcome from the table of eight women who all turned as one at her words. 'Did you see her in *High Noon* with Gary Cooper? I just *love* Gary

Cooper, don't you?' Mary's strong Birmingham accent hadn't changed a bit and Madge felt herself relax, smiling both at her voice and her enthusiasm. Mary had always been a Hollywood fan and she and Madge, when they could afford it, had spent many a happy evening down in Leicester Square in the company of Tyrone Power, Humphrey Bogart, Bing Crosby and the like.

'Hello, darling,' Fran stood, pulling out the chair next to her. 'Come and sit next to me.' Her voice, with its cut-glass vowels, was the gravely rasp of the heavy smoker. As Madge went to take the seat, Fran ground out her cigarette in the ashtray and immediately fitted another into the long black holder it had vacated.

Fran kissed her cheek and Madge was almost overpowered by expensive perfume fighting the reek of cigarettes. She stroked Madge's jacket, appreciating the cut of the expensive fabric. 'Dior, if I'm not mistaken, darling; and it fits you like a glove. You've obviously done well for yourself.'

'How are you, Fran? Are you well? You look it.'

'Well? I'm as well as can be expected, holed up down in Surrey with four chaps.' She grinned and reached for her cocktail.

'Four *chaps*?'

'Married to one and gave birth to the other three.'

'Three sons? Goodness me. They must keep you busy?'

'Oh God, no, I merely pop out the little beggars and then hand them over to Nanny so I can come up to London to shop and have lunch.'

'Don't believe a word she says, Madge,' Beryl tutted. 'I've been to stay with her, and Nanny doesn't get a look in. She's constantly bowling cricket balls for them or being rugby tackled in the garden.'

'Yes, and that's why I have to escape to London to keep myself sane every now and again. And you, darling?' Fran turned back to Madge, holding her gaze until Madge, in confusion, reached for the cocktail that had been ordered for her. 'You never kept in touch once you had your posting up to Harrogate.'

'Oh, you know me,' Madge felt herself begin to perspire. 'I was always a northern girl at heart. I'm back in Midhope.'

'And married? Any children?'

'Just the one. Nancy.'

Fran didn't say anything but continued to appraise her through a cloud of cigarette smoke.

She knows, Madge thought in a panic. She knows Nancy is James's daughter.

'Just the one? And how old is Nancy?'

'Almost eight,' Madge lied, knocking off a year in order to alleviate any suspicions Fran might be harbouring.

'You left so suddenly,' Fran continued, smiling. 'We missed you so much, darling. One minute you were with us, driving Briscoe mad with your terrible cooking, and the next you were up in Harrogate.'

'Well, you know what postings were like. Once you were told you were moving you were off, no argument. And, to be honest, I'd had enough of London.'

Fran arched a heavily outlined eyebrow. 'Really? You loved London, Madge. James, I suppose?'

Madge was saved from answering by Mary thrusting the menu under her nose. 'Now, stop monopolising Madge, Fran, we're about to order and then, Madge, I need to know all about this *heavenly* costume you're wearing.'

Madge took a long drink of her pink cocktail. She didn't know what the hell it was but she welcomed the way it went down and made her feel more relaxed. She didn't drink, as a rule. Arthur had come home with a cocktail bar one evening and it had pride of place at one end of the sitting room at Holly Close Farm. Madge thought its garish chrome and mirrored exterior ugly but Nancy loved it, especially when Arthur allowed her to make up cocktails for them using the heavy silver cocktail shaker that he kept polished with a weekly going over with Silvo. She took another sip, a deep breath and joined in with the conversation around her.

Madge looked at her wristwatch. It was the same one, despite Arthur buying her a more expensive one for her last birthday, he'd first given her when she was nineteen and about to enlist. She liked its simple lines, the way it reminded her of being a young girl again. She needed to get a taxi back to the station.

'Which train are you catching, Madge?' Fran turned towards her.

'The seven o'clock from King's Cross.'

'You've loads of time,' Fran smiled. 'I'm just popping to the Ladies; I'll ask them to order you one at Reception.

I'm staying up in London tonight; you could have stayed with me, you know. We could have had a *proper* chat then.' She'd given Madge a knowing look.

Madge smiled back. 'It's been lovely to see you all.' And it had. She'd enjoyed catching up with everyone, finding out what these girls were now up to. Two had trained as teachers and another as a nurse, but none of them appeared to have used their culinary skills learned on Oxford Street in any professional respect. Most, including herself, she realised, were stay-at-home wives and mothers. There'd been one tricky moment when Mary, after rather too many cocktails, had started to tease her about her 'terrible crush on that rather gorgeous squadron leader – wasn't he related to you, Fran?' But Fran, seeing Madge pale, had smartly changed the subject.

'Keep in touch, darling,' Fran murmured as Madge said her goodbyes and made to leave. The black cab took her along the boundary of Green Park where she'd walked on that very first night with James, and Madge felt such a sense of loss and despair she had to close her eyes in order to blot out the couples walking hand in hand, as well as images of herself and James in the past. She tried to breathe deeply and took out her lipstick, repainting her lips in an effort to calm herself. She didn't want to go home. She didn't want to go back to Arthur; he'd question and interrogate her as to who she'd seen, who she'd talked to. Nancy. She had Nancy. Think of Nancy and how much she loved her. But Nancy, she admitted to herself now, maybe for the first time, was closer to Arthur than herself. Probably because he spoiled her so; called her his Little

Princess, paraded her around their respective families in the new outfits he was forever buying her. Madge sighed, determined that this spoiling of her daughter must stop; it wasn't good for her. Madge determined to pack Nancy off to stay with Lydia's brood up the road for a few days once her school closed for the summer holidays. That would soon knock the airs and graces out of her.

As the red brick of St Pancras, and then the glazed arched facade of King's Cross stations appeared through her window, Madge adjusted her hat and gloves and gathered her bag. She smiled at the cab driver, paid him the required amount and gave far too big a tip before stepping out onto the dusty, busy street. It was Friday evening and, while most of the commuters had already made their way home, the concourse as she walked towards her platform was still busy.

So she didn't see him at first. Didn't see him as he waited for her at the gate, knowing that she would have to pass him in order to board the train.

Madge's felt her heart stop and then there was a rushing sound in her ears as she clutched her handbag and stared. She couldn't move as his eyes found hers, and then he was moving, coming towards her.

28

'Madge? Speak to me.' James was at her side, holding her arm, pulling her out of the way of passengers hurrying for the train. 'Are you all right?'

'But, you're dead. He told me you were dead?' Madge felt faint. She'd never ever fainted in her life but the rushing noise in her ears was still there and she was experiencing strange zigzag lines dancing erratically at the corner of her eyes. She shook her head to rid herself of the sensation and willed her heart, which had gone from nothing to absolute overdrive, to maintain its usual beat. 'All these years? You've been alive all these years and yet you never came to find me?'

'Madge, come and sit down. Come and talk to me.'

'I can't. I can't, James. I have to catch this train.' Madge looked feverishly towards the station clock. She had five minutes. Just five minutes with him. She gazed at his beloved face and at the angry, puckered skin that reached from below his right eye, stretching all the way down his face and into his neck.

'Madge, you can't go. I *won't* let you. There's another train – there's the next one.'

'Arthur will be waiting for me off the train.'

James showed no surprise that it was Arthur who would be there for her at the other end. 'Are you on the telephone at home? Please, Madge, I have to talk to you. I can't let you go now I've found you.'

'But I wasn't *lost*, James. You must have *known* where you could find me. It's been ten years.'

'Madge, you were married. With a baby. You'd married Arthur. How could you? Why didn't you wait for me to come back?'

'Are you for this train, madam? If you are, could you get on board? I'm about to blow the whistle.' The guard was impatient.

'Yes, I'm coming, I'm coming.' Madge turned in panic, moving towards the door of the train and then turning once more to James. She didn't know what to do. She couldn't leave him. She couldn't do this.

'No!' James took both her shoulders in his hands, pulling her right up to him so that she had to look into his eyes.

'Oh, James, your poor face.' Madge lifted a gloved hand and touched the marked, scarred and puckered skin. She pulled off the glove and stroked his cheek once again with her bare hand.

'That's not the worst of it, Madge.' He wasn't smiling. 'I'm a crock, I'm afraid.'

'What? What is it?' Madge stood back, not even taking in that the train was moving off, gaining a steady momentum as it left the station.

'Lost my right leg.' James stared hard at her in order to gauge her reaction.

'But you ran over to me. You *ran*.'

'Pretty nifty with my peg leg after ten years' practice.' He grinned the old James grin and then became serious once more. 'Madge, please, we have to talk. Telephone home. Say you've missed the train because... because the taxi was stuck in traffic. You can stay with Fran. She's staying up in London at her flat.'

Madge couldn't speak. Couldn't think of what to say or what to do.

'There's a phone box over there, Madge. Please. I have to talk to you.'

In a daze Madge made her way through the thinning crowd of travellers and commuters. She needed to know. She had to know.

Throughout the ten-minute taxi ride to Fran's house in Chelsea, James didn't say a word. When Madge started to speak, the words tumbling out and over themselves like a dropped bag of marbles, James held a finger to her mouth. 'Ssh, just wait. Wait until we get there.'

'I'm sorry, Madge, I had to telephone James and tell him where he could find you.' Fran, her usual *sang-froid* gone, appeared shame-faced. 'I just couldn't let the two of you miss each other again.' Once James had left the sitting room to find water for his whisky, she moved over to Madge and hugged her, seemingly unable to let her go. 'I'm going out for supper with Bertie Collinsworth – he's Hugo's godfather and always wants an update as to his Christian duties – so you must help yourself to a drink and get to know one another all over again.'

Madge stared at her. 'You've changed your tune, Fran,' she said slowly. 'You were as bad as James's father for wanting to keep *the milkman's daughter from up north* in her proper place.' Madge was cross and glared at Fran. 'You're ten years too late, Fran.' She put a hand to her temple, massaging the insistent thump that was starting to make her feel sick.

The tension she felt hadn't been aided by Arthur's terse response when she'd told him she was staying over in London for the night. 'Arthur, I don't need your permission to stay the night with Nora.' She wasn't sure why she hadn't said Fran. 'I'm still catching up on ten years' worth of gossip. I'll be back at some point tomorrow and if there's any problem looking after Nancy then take her over to our Lydia's or my dad's.'

'You need aspirin.' Fran frowned in sympathy.

'What I need, Fran, is an explanation.'

'Madge, I'm sorry. I was wrong to try to come between the pair of you.' Fran broke off before taking Madge's hand in her own. 'Darling, James has never loved anyone like he loved you. I'm so sorry.' She brushed away a tear. 'Good God, what is *wrong* with me? Getting soft in my old age.' She turned smartly on her Amalfi stilettoes and headed for the door.

'We'd been sent to attack the Dortmund-Ems Canal, which was an important transport link for German industry near Gravenhorst.' James had returned with his drink. 'We did what we'd been sent to do but, travelling home, we were intercepted by a Junkers 88, a German night fighter, setting the bomber on fire. The crew bailed out just as the plane crashed into a field near a farm outside the village of Zelhem, near the German-Dutch border.'

James took a sip of his drink but almost immediately replaced the glass on the polished walnut table in front of him. 'But I had your little cross.'

'Oh, James.' Madge ignored her own drink, wanting to know it all.

'But, as you see, I lost half my face and half my damned leg. Madge, I was lucky. No, really,' he said as she made to protest, 'I should be dead, like the others.'

'You *were* dead. For ten years I thought you *were* dead.'

'To be honest, I don't remember much about it. Shock, amnesia, severe fracture of the skull as I bailed out, landing badly. The whole lot, apparently...' James attempted jollity but failed. 'Anyway, I was holed up in The Netherlands in a military hospital and then taken to several POW camps in Germany. The rest of the war went on without me.'

'When Fran told me you'd been reported missing I tried to telephone your mother, but she was too upset to speak to me. I telephoned Bourne constantly until they got really fed up of me and told me to stop – they couldn't tell me anything further. And then Arthur came over to Oxford Street to let me know as soon as it was confirmed at Bourne. Your group captain friend had confirmed it, he said. He'd seen some notice up with your name on it, he said...' Madge felt feverish with trying to explain.

'Well, he would, wouldn't he?' James arched an eyebrow. 'He tells you I'm dead, that I'm out of the running, and he can seize his chance and get you back. What I don't understand, Madge, is why you *married* him. Did you love him?' James shook his head. 'I don't get it. Did I mean *nothing* to you that you could almost immediately marry someone else? And Arthur, for heaven's sake?' James stood up, knocking back his drink. He went over to the window, looking down on Russell Square, and then back towards Madge as he paced the room, as much as he could with his disability, like some caged animal.

'But, you were dead.' Tears that, until now Madge had managed to contain, ran freely down her face and she made no attempt to stop them.

'Yes, but that doesn't mean you marry someone you don't love just because you can't have someone you *do*.'

Madge took a deep breath. 'I got pregnant.'

'Yes, Arthur said the pair of you had a little girl.'

'Arthur said?' Madge stared at James, who was still moving around the room, unable to sit down.

'As soon as I was able, I drove up to your parents' house. It really hadn't changed a bit in the three years since I'd been there last. Anyway, there was only your grandmother there – I don't know where your parents or Isaac were – and she took great pleasure in telling me you were married and living at Holly Close Farm.' James glared at Madge. 'That was when I wished I'd died like the others, Madge. Holly Close Farm. *My* farm, *my* dream. I can't tell you how I'd designed and redesigned that place both in my head and then when I was able, in the POW camp, on paper. The other chaps used to tease me about it.'

'But you could have written to me. Prisoners of war are allowed. They are, aren't they?' Madge felt herself grow angry and she stood up, her heart racing, facing this man who she knew she had never, ever, stopped loving. 'You could have written and TOLD ME YOU WEREN'T DEAD.' She shouted the five words, spitting out each syllable staccato until they seemed to hang in the room, joining the dust motes caught in the shaft of late evening sun pouring in through the open window.

'I did, Madge, *I did*.' James caught her wrist, pulling her to him, forcing her to look at him. 'I was so ill for such a long time, Madge: didn't seem to be able to remember a damned thing. But somewhere, here...' James thumped his chest angrily '... there was this... this *light*, this picture of a blonde girl with big blue eyes. Someone I knew I loved, but I couldn't quite grasp the picture. It would appear and then... and then it would *disappear*... I didn't know who you were. I just knew I loved you and I had to pull through to find you again.'

'Oh, James.' Madge didn't know what to say. She had to close her eyes to eradicate the image of James, unable to remember her, locked up in a POW camp with a burned face and his leg gone.

'Eventually,' James went on, 'it all came back. I wrote to Fran, who said you'd been posted back up north and she was no longer in touch. I sent letters to every damned RAF camp in the north hoping at least one would eventually make its way to you. I asked my parents to find you, I asked Fran to find you, I wrote constantly to you at home, never quite knowing if I'd got the right address.'

'But I didn't get anything. Nothing. Nobody passed on any letters. I swear, James, I didn't know.'

'Madge, darling, I know that now. As I say, as soon as I was home and able to drive with just the one leg –' James grinned, 'bloody nightmare, I can tell you – I set off to find you. My father was furious, tried to stop me leaving the house, telling me I was...' James paused and searched for the exact words, '"a blithering idiot to be driving all that way with one leg in search of some milkman's daughter you've got the itch for." And that's when your grandmother told me you were married. I had to see you, needed you to tell me yourself, so I drove down to Holly Close Farm. And there was pugnacious little Arthur, like a damned boxer ready for a fight, telling me in no uncertain terms to get off his land. That you were happily married with your little girl.'

'And did you? Just go like that without waiting to see me?'

'Of course I didn't. Arthur Booth, even with a gun in his hand and me pretty unsteady on one leg, didn't frighten me.'

'A gun?' Madge was horrified. 'A gun? Are you sure?'

'Well, it wasn't a banana, Madge. I've seen enough guns in my life to know what one looks like.' James reached out, drawing Madge to him, stroking her hair. 'So, I drove up the lane and parked on the main road and waited and waited. And then a truck drew up and you got out.'

Madge frowned. 'A truck? No one drove much... no one had a car then... Oh, Lydia's husband. *He* drove for the mill. I must have been at Lydia's house and he'd dropped me off. But you saw me? James, you saw me? And you didn't shout out to me? Didn't *stop* me?' Madge stared at James in bewilderment.

'I couldn't do it. You stood talking to whoever'd dropped you off and then you were smiling at your little girl, kissing her face with such love. How could I march back into your life after that? You'd not answered *any* of my letters; I was crippled and with a disfigured face. I watched you swing your daughter up onto your shoulders and walk down the lane. I sat there for a good half an hour willing myself to go to you, to claim you back. But I couldn't come between you and your little girl.'

'You stupid man. You stupid, *stupid* man.' Madge was breathing heavily, almost hyperventilating. He'd been there; James had been at Holly Close Farm. He'd seen her. '*Your* little girl,' she snarled, pushing James away. 'Nancy is *your* little girl.'

Their breathing as they faced each other was the only sound in the room. A clock somewhere struck the hour. And then, James finally said, 'She's *mine*? I have a daughter?' He sat down heavily on the rather elegant chaise longue behind him and stared at Madge. 'And you didn't tell me? You kept her from me?'

'I thought you were DEAD. How many more times?'

'But why marry Arthur? Why didn't you go to my mother? She'd have helped you, let you stay with them.'

'Oh, don't be so ridiculous, James. After the number of snide remarks I got from your father about carrying on seeing you?'

'You never said.' James was angry, his face flushed.

Madge shrugged. 'I didn't want to come between you and your father. Fran, too. She was constantly telling me it couldn't work out between us. Can you imagine if I'd turned up, pregnant, on the doorstep of that great estate of yours?'

'My mother would have taken you in.'

'Oh, for heaven's sake, James. It wasn't some Victorian melodrama. I was pregnant, you were dead. I feared my mother, being the big churchgoer that she was, wouldn't have given me the time of day. Arthur asked me to marry him and I didn't know what else to do. I was in shock. I was wrong, I know that now. Of course my mother wouldn't have thrown me out. Dad wouldn't have let her. I made a mistake.'

'As did I.' James looked at Madge, his eyes never once leaving hers.

'Well, getting shot down and ending up half-dead can hardly be classed a mistake.' Madge attempted a smile.

'Madge, I'm married.'

'Married?' Madge didn't think her heart could stand any more shock but she simply said, 'Why would you *not* be?' Even as she said the words, the pain of knowing he loved and had married someone else was intolerable. How was she going to bear this? She'd been given James back for the evening and he wasn't hers to keep. She was married to Arthur. James had married someone else. A blackness so intense she felt she could touch it descended on her. She closed her eyes, breathed deeply for a couple of seconds and then, opening them, tried to smile. She reached for her things. 'I need to go, James. I shouldn't have come back here with you. I can find a hotel for the night near the station and catch the early train back in the morning.'

'Madge, I'm *not* letting you go again.' James grabbed her hand, refusing to relinquish it until she sat back down beside him once more. 'I don't love Constance.'

'Constance? You married *Constance*?' A little laugh, dry and bitter, bubbled out of her before she could prevent it 'But, of course you did,' she said, looking down at her hands, at the pink nails she'd acquired for her trip south. 'Of course you did.'

'Oh, sweet Jesus, I can't lose you again, Madge.' James closed his eyes momentarily and then reached almost blindly for her, his mouth finding hers, kissing her in the way he'd always kissed her. It was like he'd never been away: his scent, his touch, everything was just the same. He took her hand, leading her through to the bedroom and she went, simply unable not to. He turned and, just the once, asked her if she was sure. She nodded, aware that every part of her was aching for him. She stepped out of her heels and James took her foot, moving his hand upwards along the sheer silk of her stocking to the soft skin beyond until she thought she might go quite insane with desire. Madge reached for him and James suddenly hesitated. 'Madge, I'm not a pretty sight any more. It takes quite a bit of getting used to.' He was terribly embarrassed about his leg but Madge sat up, determined not to avert her eyes, helping him with the strap that secured the prosthetic above his knee. She smiled and turned her back to him, indicating that he unfasten the zip of her dress. He did so, slowly and softly moving his mouth over every bump of her uncovered backbone until she slipped out of the Dior, slipped off the bed and onto the floor and softly kissed his stump. This was James, this was his skin, and there was absolutely nothing repellent about the limb that was left in place where once his whole leg had been.

29

'So how come you live in London and yet you're always popping up out of nowhere round *here*?' I clasped my frozen hands round the hot glass of mulled wine – the Jolly Sailor had obviously had a whole load of red wine left over from Christmas and had decided, this first week in January, to go with a winter ski theme, adding cinnamon, orange juice and hot water before flogging it as Glühwein and I was appreciating both the warmth and alcohol as it began its trip around my bloodstream.

'A long story.' Corey frowned, wincing at the sweetness of the drink, and stood up. 'I think I'll have a whisky instead.'

'We've got all evening,' I said, trying to get comfortable on the high stool. The pub, post-Christmas, was virtually deserted despite, or possibly because of, the management's attempts at bringing Val d'Isère to Westenbury. I headed a cardboard polar bear out of the way and studied Corey as he went back to the bar. He was tall – well over six foot – with longish, untidy dark-blond hair and eyes of molten chocolate; really quite different from Dominic's dark hair and green eyes, I mused, and then castigated myself for sizing Corey up as potential boyfriend material. We were here simply to amalgamate what we knew about the James and Madge story. Totally irrelevant that he was pretty damned gorgeous. But totally relevant that he wore a wedding ring: never, ever again would I look at a married man.

I'd rung the hospital just before leaving the house to meet Corey, and Madge was comfortable, spending most of the time sleeping. I didn't know if this was a good sign that she'd recover or not. I'd need to Google it once I got home.

'That's better.' Corey took a long drink of his whisky, headed the polar bear back in my direction and then folded his arms. 'Right, so I'll tell you what I know and then it's your turn.'

'Just tell me what you're doing here – you know, let's get the present sorted first...'

'You're expecting a present?' Corey smiled.

'... before we delve back into the past.' I tutted. 'I think you're trying to avoid the issue.' I folded my own arms. 'I think I understand why you keep visiting Holly Close Farm, but how come you're here now, staying at this dive, and why were you on the road through Westenbury on Christmas Eve?'

'OK. So, I met my wife, Rowena, at Leeds University. We were both studying Business and Finance there. Rowena is from Manchester originally, but when we graduated we both headed to London to work in the City.'

'You've a southern accent. You're from London originally?' Oh, bugger, he really did have a wife.

'Berkshire. About thirty minutes from London. My son, Milo, was born in London.'

I smiled. 'How lovely. You have a little boy?' Oh, bugger to the power of two: he had a child as well.

'Well, he's not that little now – he's seven.'

'You and your wife must have had him fairly young?'

'Yes, I suppose we did. Rowena and I were both working ridiculously long hours, making our way up the financial ladder. A baby certainly wasn't part of the grand plan; Rowena was back at the bank when he was just two months old.'

'Blimey.'

Corey smiled at that. 'Blimey, indeed. Anyway, in a nutshell, Rowena was far more focused than me: finance and big business and being in the centre of London was never really my thing but you get yourself on the treadmill and it's going so fast you can't get off.'

'And did you want to?'

'Difficult when you've a London mortgage, a nanny and school fees to shell out for. It all gets a bit much. Anyway, Rowena was head-hunted back to Manchester and this seemed a great opportunity to get out of the London rat race.'

'Oh, so you're actually living back up in the north?'

'Rowena is. I'm not.' Corey gave a wintry smile and drained his glass.

'Oh?'

'Unfortunately, Rowena, unbeknown to me, was also having an affair.'

'She must be pretty fit, this wife of yours: racing up the slippery pole of Finance, the mother of a seven-year-old boy and still finding the time and the energy to run an extra-marital affair. It takes me all my time to hit the cross-trainer in the gym these days.'

Corey smiled but I could see he was hurting.

'I'm sorry, that was a bit crass of me,' I apologised, embarrassed at my attempts to cheer him up. I remembered how I'd wanted to hit anyone who'd tried to trivialise my break-up with Dominic.

'The plan was that I would carry on in London until something suitable came up in Manchester. By the time it did, Rowena didn't want me to move to Manchester.'

'I'm really sorry. That must hurt.'

'It does.' Corey looked at me. 'But mainly because I'm separated from Milo as well as my wife. I try to get up as often as I can to see him. I do need to find work up here – I've actually loved this area since being up here at uni – but I've no appetite for Finance any more. I keep going for interviews – had one today in Leeds and another tomorrow in Manchester – but I reckon they can see through me. I'm just not interested in money and banking any more. I've stayed here in Westenbury a couple of times because it's between Manchester and Leeds and fairly near to the M62. I can't bear soulless hotels, and your village is really quite lovely.'

I was curious. 'So, if banking isn't your thing any more, what *are* you interested in?'

'Something that I can use my hands on, maybe. I'm an artist in my spare time. I wish I was good enough, rich enough and brave enough to just put up my easel and live an artist's bohemian life.'

'You'd have to get rid of the Porsche,' I laughed. 'Bohemians don't drive expensive cars.'

'Nor do they pay school fees.'

'Get your son into a state school. That would save a bit.'

'Not fully my decision. Milo is living with Rowena and she's hell-bent on one of the top schools.'

'So why the hell were you in Westenbury on Christmas Eve? You know, the night of the dead badger?'

'I was up to see Milo for Christmas. My mother-in-law had invited me up for the Christmas period. I think she was hoping Rowena and I could sort out our differences and make a go of it...' Corey glanced up as the outside door opened bringing in a blast of icy air equal to any in actual Val d'Isère. 'I think your sister is here.'

'Yes, she is.' I waved at her as she headed, with Matis, for the bar. 'Just tell me what happened? Didn't it work out?'

'Nope. Rowena picked her moment to tell me she actually wanted a divorce, and that she and Milo wouldn't be spending Christmas with her family, but *I* was more than welcome to stay there if I wanted. It didn't come as any surprise – we'd been apart almost a year.'

'Ooh, not good.' I felt really cross with this woman.

'I couldn't see myself sitting with Sharon and Bob and their two Yorkshire Terriers on Christmas day, paper hats on our heads – and that's including the dogs: I hate little dogs, horrible yappy little beasts – and pulling crackers and reading the jokes out in turn over one glass of lukewarm Chardonnay.

'Heavens, no. I mean, our family Christmases can be a bit strange – my mum can't cook and we have our thespian Granny spouting all things luvvie – but at least my dad gets out the booze – usually top-notch stuff as well – and we can get well and truly rat-arsed.'

Corey laughed at that. 'Sounds like my kind of Christmas. So, anyway, I spent Christmas Eve with Milo, took him to see Santa, fed him and me at a rather upmarket restaurant that I'd booked for the three of us months ago and then took him back to the centre of Manchester, where Rowena is renting a flat, and stayed with him until he went to sleep. There seemed little point hanging around after that, so I set off back to London, avoiding the M62, which was closed for some reason. And then I came across a reindeer, a panda and a badger.'

'What time did you get back?'

'Around 2 a.m. I went straight back to Uncle Jim's place in Eaton Square where I've been living since Rowena and I sold our London flat.'

'Uncle Jim?'

Before I could comment further, Daisy bounded over and sat down, spilling Glühwein over her hand as she did so. 'Shit, that's hot.' She licked at her fingers before wiping them down her jeans. 'Right, where are you up to with the James's story? Matis is discussing some building work with his brother for ten minutes. I don't understand a word of Lithuanian, so, come on, let's crack on with the interesting stuff.' She beamed at both of us and leaned forwards.

'Corey was just saying he's living with James.'

'Really?' Daisy pulled a face of surprise. 'Isn't he a terribly old man by now? He was even older than Madge and she's ninety-four.'

'Uncle Jim – I've never known him as James – is pushing ninety-seven and, to say he's only got one leg, is still pretty active.'

Daisy and I stared. 'James has only got one leg? Gosh, how come?'

Corey frowned. 'Didn't Madge say?'

Daisy shook her head. 'You have to remember, Corey, we've only just found out about James. I actually don't think Madge would have ever said *anything* if she'd not decided to sell Holly Close Farm to a distant relative of hers and given the cottage to Charlie and me at the same time. She knew the murder of the policemen would be all brought up again, Nancy would find out that Arthur wasn't her real father and then the shit would really hit the fan. She's been telling us what we've called "The James Story" in dribs and drabs for several weeks now.'

'And we didn't even know James was still alive,' I interrupted Daisy. 'As far as *we* knew he'd died in his bomber during the war, Madge was left pregnant with Nancy and that's why she married Arthur. You seem to think Madge knew he was still alive?'

'Well, I don't know if she is aware that he is still alive now,' Corey frowned, 'but she certainly knew that he hadn't died after all, although, to be fair it wasn't until eight years or so after the end of the war that she was told. He was severely injured, lost a leg and his face was badly burned when he was shot down over Holland. Since I've been living with him, he's been relating the whole of The Madge Story to Mum and me.'

'Your Mum?'

Corey nodded. 'Uncle Jim never had any children of his own…'

'Well, apart from Nancy,' Daisy interrupted. 'Don't forget Granny Nancy.'

'But Mum and I didn't know anything about Nancy until recently,' Corey said. 'Anyway, as I was saying, Uncle Jim didn't have any *other* children – with Aunt Constance, I mean. My mother, Louise, was Uncle Jim's sister, Angela's daughter. My mum lost both her parents when she was just seven and was then brought up by Uncle Jim and Aunt Constance. Mum's divorced, and when it looked like Uncle Jim might need some help with Constance she went back to live with them. Having said that, he's a feisty old thing, got all his marbles and doesn't really need that much looking after now.'

'Sounds like Madge. Well, before she had this stroke, anyway.'

'Have you always known about his love for Madge and his wanting to live at Holly Close Farm?' I asked.

Corey shook his head. 'No, absolutely nothing has *ever* been said before, as far as I know. Certainly, The Madge Story is all new to Mum, too. And then Aunt Constance died six months ago and, after that, he's never shut up about Madge. That's when he asked me to see if I could find Holly Close Farm when I was up visiting Milo. He wanted to know who was living there now. He didn't seem at all surprised when I told him it appeared to have been abandoned years ago.'

'Was he an architect? You know, like Charlie? Or have I made that up?' Daisy turned to me. '*Did* Madge say that?'

'I think she said he started his training at Cambridge, but then the war came and he enlisted. Did he ever go back to it?'

Corey shook his head. 'No, he went into politics, like a load of my family before him.' He hesitated. 'You do know who my uncle Jim is?'

'As in…?' Daisy and I both leaned forwards.

'Your James Montgomery-West is Jim West.'

Daisy and I looked at each other once more. 'Sorry,' Daisy frowned, 'should we know who that is?'

'Oh, hang on,' I said, excited. 'You mean Jim West, the old Labour Party cabinet minister? I learned about him when I did politics at A level. I had to write an essay on him. He started off as a Conservative, moved to the Labour Party and gave up his hereditary peerage so that he could sit in the House of Commons. Hugely left wing? Kept diaries on his political life that have been published? Oh my God, are you telling us that Jim West was Madge's lover? Is Nancy's real father? That Jim West is Daisy and my… hang on, what is he…? Our great-grandfather? Bloody hell.'

None of us spoke for a few seconds. 'So, your great-uncle is our great-grandfather? That means you and Charlie and I are related as well then?' Daisy was trying to work it all out. 'Does it matter?'

'Does what matter?' Corey and I spoke at the same time and looked at each other and then I glared at Daisy. I knew exactly where she was going with this.

Daisy flushed: she'd even embarrassed herself. 'I mean, can we all be, you know, *friends*, if we are, let's see, second cousins once removed?'

Corey glanced in my direction. 'I really don't see why not.' He smiled. 'Right, I invited you both to dinner and I'm starving. Shall we go?'

'Go where? I thought we were eating here?'

Corey pulled a face. 'If their dinners are anything like their breakfasts, I think I'd rather not. I've always fancied that place up the road – Clementine's, is it? – and with it being Monday, and after Christmas, I actually managed to book a table.' He looked at his watch. 'We need to go.'

'That is so kind, Corey,' Daisy smiled politely, 'but do you mind if I drop out? I actually work there a couple of nights a week, plus I did come with Matis...' She trailed off, but not before she'd given me a knowing kick under the table with her heavily booted foot.

Corey stood. 'Looks like it's just you and me then, Charlie.' He smiled down at me, his beautiful brown eyes warm. Goodness, he really was rather lovely when he smiled. He passed me my coat. 'Shall we go?'

I'd never eaten at Clementine's, but always wanted to. I felt a bit underdressed in my jeans and sweater, but at least the latter was cashmere and the jeans my best ones.

'Oh, hello.' I was surprised to see David, Mandy and Seb Henderson, together with Harriet and Liberty, and another man I was introduced to as Nick Westmoreland, Harriet's husband. I shouldn't have been surprised: I'd forgotten that David actually owned the place, although it was Clementine Ahern who had made such a success of the restaurant, it usually being booked up months ahead.

'It's Seb's birthday,' Libby smiled. 'We're celebrating that, as well as starting on the building work, of course.'

'We shouldn't be too long now,' I smiled back. 'We've spent all day on site starting the initial work on the cottage and, once we get the go-ahead, Josh's team will begin simultaneously on the farm.'

'I'm very envious.' Corey extended a hand to the newcomers and he and Seb immediately started chatting. 'It was my great-uncle's dream to live there many years ago. He was a good friend of Mrs Booth's during the war.'

Bit of an understatement, that, Corey, I thought.

'Unfortunately, it didn't work out and he remained in London.'

'There is certainly some story behind the place.' David shook his head. 'We know about the tragedy of Arthur Booth's shooting of the two policemen there, but you say your great-uncle knew of the place?'

'Corey's great-uncle is Jim West.' I felt immensely proud of the connection. He'd been, in his time, an incredibly popular, if somewhat infamous cabinet minister. The last I'd heard of him was his involvement in the anti-war movement against Iraq in 2003. I was only thirteen at the time but filled with an adolescent zeal to join the march and, if Mum and Dad had let me, I'd have gone with the coachload of sixth-formers from school, who spent the day there with their banners.

'Goodness, I'm a great admirer of his,' Harriet exclaimed, wide-eyed. 'I've read all *The West Diaries*. Fancy that!'

Corey and I were shown to a small table in the Orangery and settled ourselves down with a drink and the menu.

'I've a bit of a confession to make.' Corey was smiling at me.

I looked up from trying to decide what to choose from the most delicious-looking menu I'd ever seen. 'Oh?'

'When I helped you shift that blinking badger the other night, I recognised you.'

'Oh?' I stared at Corey.

'I'd seen you at the speed dating. It was the first time I'd stayed at the Jolly Sailor and I wandered upstairs to see what was happening. I wanted to laugh because you looked so cross, sitting there.'

'I was bloody cross. I didn't want to be there.' I laughed at the memory. 'And, actually, I didn't want to be back at home either.'

'I can't tell you how much I wanted to come and sit in front of you and get to know you.' Corey took my hand.

'Really?' I squeaked, going pink with pleasure. 'Why didn't you?'

'Well, firstly I didn't have a ticket and, secondly, you were monopolised by another man.'

'Josh, the builder at Holly Close Farm. We were at school together.'

'You were with him on the motorbike on the lane at the farm.'

'Well, yes, but how on earth were you able to tell? We both had helmets on.'

'You'd taken them off and were just sitting at the top of the lane, admiring the view. I recognised you instantly.'

'So why didn't you say anything when we stopped you to help us with the badger?'

'Humping a great comatose badger into a car in the sleet is not particularly conducive to general chitchat. And anyway, I wasn't quite sure it was you: you were looking remarkably like a reindeer at the time.' Corey began to laugh at the memory. 'A rather bad-tempered one, if I recall.'

'Long story,' I smiled. 'I do seem to have become one big bad-tempered cross patch since I had to leave London. It's not really me, you know.'

'So, how come you're back in the north? Is it for good?'

'I was working as an architect in London; for a company called Abraham Developments? I fell in love with the boss. The boss was married. End of job and end of story. There, that's condensed it.'

'Do you want to talk about it? I've told you all about Rowena.' Corey stroked my fingers and little shivers of lust went through me. 'Actually,' Corey frowned, obviously thinking aloud, 'I know him.'

'Know who?'

'The Abraham Developments boss.'

'Do you?' I stared at Corey.

'Yes, tallish bloke, dark curly hair, rather a charmer?'

'That's Dominic.'

Corey laughed. 'He charmed my mother. When she decided to move in with Uncle Jim to keep an eye on him and Constance, she said she'd only do it if she had free rein to bring the house in Eaton Square up to date. Nothing had been done to it for years, walls needed to come down, new kitchen and bathrooms, the lot. Dominic – is that his name? – got the job and, to be fair, did a brilliant job too.'

I was just about to comment, somewhat shaken that Corey had actually met Dominic, when my phone rang. 'Sorry,' I apologised, 'I should take this. It could be the hospital.'

It was my mother. 'The hospital has just rung, Charlie. I can't get hold of Daisy. Nancy's here with me. I think we all need to get over there as quick as we can.'

30

It was lucky that neither of us had had much to drink. Corey and I gave our apologies to the waitress and jumped into his car. The night air was frostily cold and the January Wolf Moon hung like an old silver sixpence to our right. We drove rather too quickly back to the Jolly Sailor but, while Madge's car was still where I'd left it, Daisy and Matis, when I did a quick search of the pub, appeared to have already left.

'Is she all right?' I asked as soon as we were by Madge's bed. Mum and Nancy were sitting on either side, each holding one hand.

'Actually, she's breathing a lot better now,' Mum said with obvious relief. 'She had a bit of a bad turn an hour ago, the nurse said, quite distraught about something and desperately trying to communicate. That's when they rang us. They wondered if she'd had another stroke.'

'Granny Madge?' Her eyes were open and she was staring at Corey. 'Madge this is Corey.' I took her hand and ushered him forwards. 'Do you remember, Madge, I said we'd met a nephew of James's? On Christmas Eve.'

'Don't confuse her,' the nurse directed. 'Asking her questions isn't the best way to help her.'

'I'm sorry?' Nancy too was staring at Corey. 'If this is my father's – my real father's –nephew, then he must surely be a relative of mine? I'm actually in enough shock about this whole affair of my mother's, without being bombarded with a raft of new relatives into the bargain.'

'Hardly a *raft*, Mother. You do exaggerate,' Mum tutted as she stood and came over to Corey. 'Hello, Corey, how very nice to meet you.' She turned as she felt Madge's hand on her arm. 'Madge? What is it? Do you want to tell us something?'

'She's still very beautiful,' Corey whispered. 'Uncle Jim loved her so much.'

Madge was restless, she didn't know where to put her damned leg. And who were all these people in her bedroom? All looking grave and worried. She did hope they weren't worrying about her. She *did* know these people: there was Nancy, her little girl, getting cross about something, as usual. Her big girl now; in fact, she was getting to be quite an old lady. Mind you, she still had her skirts too short, and her heels too high. Apart from the brown eyes, she really didn't look anything like her beloved James. Where *was* he? He said he'd never leave her. But he did leave her. He had to, really. Madge screwed her eyes as tight as she could, trying to remember. She'd been to London, hadn't she? Fran had told him she'd be at King's Cross. Of course, she'd spent the night with him. Oh, but it was such heaven. Madge frowned and then opened her eyes once more. He was here! James was here, standing right here in her bedroom with her favourite girl. Confused, she closed her eyes and tried again to remember. Was she dying? Was this how you went, remembering the past; still hoping for a future? What had happened after her night in London? Oh of course, of course. She remembered it all now.

'You knew he wasn't dead. You told me he was *dead* and you *knew*.' Madge didn't care that people were looking, turning from their newspapers as they waited for their train, agog with interest at this furious woman in the beautiful Dior costume.

'Not here, Madge.' Arthur took her arm but she shook it off and marched to the car park where he'd left his Ford.

'You lied to me,' she hissed. 'And he came to find me and you put a *gun* in his face.' Madge opened the car door, slamming it shut as she sat down.

Arthur's face was white. 'He didn't love you, Madge. Nobody loves you like I do. Everything I do is for you. I bought you Holly Close Farm, you know I did.'

'But, Arthur, I didn't want it. Not without James. Nancy is his daughter. You stole her from him, you never gave him the chance to know he *had* a daughter. You never gave *Nancy* the chance to know her real father.'

'I did it for you, Madge. For Nancy. *I'm* Nancy's father. Haven't I been the *best* father a little girl could ever have?'

Madge nodded. 'Of course, of course…' then shook her head. 'Arthur, please. Just drive us home. I want to see Nancy.'

'What are you going to do? Are you going to tell her? She's not at home.'

'What do you mean? What have you done with her?' Madge was terrified.

'I haven't done anything with her, you stupid bitch.' Arthur was furious. 'She's gone to Blackpool with Lydia and the boys and Isaac. They're staying in a B and B for three nights.

'But what about school? She'll miss school.'

'And who pays the damned teachers' wages? If I want to let my daughter go off on a little holiday with her aunt and uncle for a few days…' He didn't finish what he was saying as grief overcame him and he angrily brushed at his face.

'Arthur,' Madge tried to remain calm as he drove, 'it's just that you've never wanted her to leave your side before. It's a surprise that's all.'

They drove in silence the remaining ten minutes of the journey home. Madge felt bone weary, tired in every fibre of her being. And yet, and yet, she was on fire. She was exhilarated. She had James. He wasn't dead. James wasn't dead and he loved her. He was going to tell Constance that very morning, and Arthur already knew. She was going to take Nancy, James's daughter, and go back to London and live with him there. She and James had talked into the night, making plans. And if there was a scandal, which of course there would be: all divorces were a scandal but particularly the divorce of a Member of Parliament – the divorce of a viscount – well, they would just have to face it. Together.

Madge couldn't bear to stay another night in the same house as Arthur but she couldn't go to Lydia's: Lydia was in Blackpool. And for that she was grateful: she didn't want Nancy here while she was packing their things up. She couldn't just turn up at her dad's. He'd not been himself since her mum died two years ago and he and Isaac wouldn't understand what was going on. Madge went upstairs, took off the Dior and moved to the bathroom where she started to run a bath.

'You're not leaving.' Fifteen minutes later Arthur was at the bedroom door, tears rolling down his face as Madge pulled on a pair of grey slacks and a black blouse. 'Please, Madge, don't do this to me. Or to Nancy.'

'Arthur, James is going to drive up and collect us, Nancy and me. I shan't take anything with me, none of the jewellery or the dresses. They belong to you.' Madge held his gaze as he stared at her. Would she ever be able to forgive him these wasted years, for keeping Nancy from her father, for keeping her from the only man she'd ever loved?

'He's *not* coming here. He's not, Madge. I won't have it. I won't let him take you, I won't *let* him.'

'Arthur, you can't *stop* us. This time you're *not* going to come between us.'

As the afternoon and evening wore on, there was something in Arthur's demeanour that made Madge afraid. He reminded her of a trapped animal that would bite off its paw in order to save itself. She shivered at the thought and stepped outside into the garden she had made glorious with an abundance of flowers and shrubs. She'd pruned and cut back the yellow roses around the cottage, feeding them and talking to them, bestowing them with all the love she'd been deprived of giving to James and now, on this early July evening, as she walked down the path to Harry, they beckoned and welcomed her with their profusion of colour and heady scent.

'You're back?' Harry was sitting in the cottage garden, cigarette and beer in hand, enjoying the evening sunshine. 'And how was it? Did you wow all those women with your Dior? Were they wildly envious of your sophistication and good looks?' He put to one side some papers he'd been working on and smiled at her.

'James is alive. He never died. He's not dead. Arthur knew all along he was alive.'

Harry stared at her. 'You've seen him?'

Madge started laughing and rushed over to him, hugging him, her friend who'd been her life-line since he moved into the cottage two years previously. 'Yes, and I'm going to him. He's telling his wife, Constance – he married Constance, of course he did – he's telling her and he's going to drive up and Nancy and I are going back with him to London...'

'Whoa, whoa, slow down.' Harry was smiling but cautious. 'Are you sure about all this? Who is this man? You've only ever talked to me about "James". What does he do? Where are you going to live? How do you know his wife is just going to let him go without a fuss?'

'He's an MP.'

Harry stared. 'In the government? Oh, lovey, there is going to be one hell of a scandal. You do know that?'

'He'll leave politics... He'll go back to train as an architect... We can go and live abroad...' Madge trailed off, suddenly uncertain.

'What's his full name? Who is he, Madge?'

'James Montgomery-West.'

'But, Madge, I know of him. Why did you never tell me his full name? You must have seen him in the papers?' Harry looked at her in bewilderment.

'You know I don't read the papers. Arthur won't have one in the house.'

'I bet he won't.' Harry lit a new cigarette, drawing the smoke deep into his lungs. 'Well, what about Lydia? Has she never put two and two together?'

'Harry, I've never told *anyone* about James except you. I promised Arthur when we got married that no one up here in Yorkshire would ever know that he wasn't Nancy's real father.' Madge shrugged. 'Everyone, including my family and his, assumed he was still my boyfriend, I'd got pregnant when we were on leave together and that's why we got married so quickly and I left the WAAF. It happened all the time. You know it did.'

'Why would his wife let him go? You've not thought this through, darling.' Harry shook his head. 'I'm sorry, but it's all a bit of a fairy tale.'

'James is coming to collect Nancy and me. He's going to drive up.'

'He's going to drive up here?' Harry shook his head. 'Madge, just think about it. You can't have him here,

357

where Arthur is. If you're going to go to him, take Nancy and join him in London. For heaven's sake, get yourself down there, but don't let him anywhere near Arthur.'

'You're right, of course you're right.' Madge felt feverish, suddenly panicky at the thought of the two men meeting at Holly Close Farm. What on earth had they been thinking of to assume he could just come and drive away with her and Nancy? They'd thought they were doing the right thing, being civilised about it all. 'He can't come here... I need to telephone him. Fran is helping us: I'll telephone her and she must tell him not to come. As soon as Nancy is home, we'll get the train down and stay at Fran's in Chelsea. It will be all right, it will. I know it will.'

The first gunshot had Madge out of bed, the second had her running at speed down the stairs and out into the night. Arthur, as was often the case, hadn't yet been to bed. She ran, barefoot, heart pounding, to the wooden fence that separated the garden from the farm's acres of land down the valley, her eyes straining against the summer night as she tried desperately to work out where the noise was coming from. Please, not James. Please, don't let him be dead. Not when she'd just found him again.

Madge climbed over the fence, her nightie billowing behind her in the still air, the perniciously pungent perfume of the garden's night-scented stocks left behind as she ran down the fields, desperately searching for James.

'Get back. Get back to the house.' Arthur suddenly appeared in front of her, running at speed, his breath laboured, his voice coming in gasps.

'What have you done to him?' Madge was screaming. 'What have you done to him? Where is he?' She started running again, totally oblivious to the sting of nettles at her bare feet; slipping and falling in the long grass, searching, all the time searching.

And then hands were reaching out to her, grabbing at her as she ran, preventing her from running further, pulling her to the ground and holding her firm as she struggled against their restraint.

31

'She seems a lot more settled and comfortable now,' Kylie, the nurse, said after shooing us all out from round the bed. 'I really think you can go home. And I'm sorry I called you out – I'm new on this ward and I panicked a bit.' She looked slightly embarrassed.

'Don't be silly,' Mum tutted, patting Kylie's arm. 'Madge is very precious to us and if at any time you feel she is, you know... if you think she's deteriorating then you must ring us. Night or day.'

'Am I too late?' Daisy, gasping for breath, came hurtling through the double doors and stared, wide-eyed, at the four of us standing rather awkwardly together as Kylie pulled curtains round Madge's bed.

'No, honestly, it's OK.' I put my arm through Daisy's. 'The nurse seemed to think she may have suffered another stroke and rang Mum, but it doesn't look like it now. Just stick your head round and see her and then we have to be off.'

'She actually looks a lot better than she did this morning,' Daisy opined as we all trooped along the corridor towards the main door. There was something rather melancholy about the hospital at ten o'clock at night: the café selling endless cups of filthy coffee was closed, the shop selling newspapers and sweets was closed. We walked, dividing and immediately regrouping around a lone hospital cleaner wielding a mop and bucket, and descended the steps to the car park, all wondering what we should do next.

Mum made the decision for us. 'Right, why don't we all come back to our place and have a drink? I'm sure I can rustle up something to eat for those of you who've not eaten. Or at least M&S can. And then,' she looked meaningfully at Corey, 'maybe we can finally get to the bottom of what really happened up at the farm the night of the shooting.'

'Matis is in the car, Mum.' Daisy turned to me. 'You went off with the keys to Madge's car, Charlie. Matis had to drive me over.'

Mum frowned. 'Who's Matis when he's at home?'

'One of Josh Lee's builders. I was having a drink with him.'

'Well, bring him along as well. Everybody welcome.'

'Probably best if I just get Matis to drop me off and then he can go back to the Jolly Sailor without me. This is family stuff.'

'Are you OK with this?' I asked Corey as we drove back to Westenbury. 'They can be a bit of a mad bunch, especially if Mum has a drink and Vivienne, my other granny, is holding forth on Oscar Wilde.'

Corey grinned. 'Sounds good to me. And, really, I'd much rather be spending time with you than in my room at the Jolly Sailor.'

I grinned back. 'Is that supposed to be a compliment?'

'Take it as such. Really.' He smiled again and stroked my arm. Goodness, if his arm-stroking was this good, what might his kissing be like? I had an overpowering need to find out.

'I'm assuming you no longer have the badger?' Corey asked as we walked into the garden towards the house.

'God, no. Once Dad was sober he was really, *really* cross with us for bringing it home. They're incredibly dangerous and if it had come round when we were lifting it into the car, it would have really gone for us. Dad didn't want to take it to the surgery – badgers become stressed if they can smell where dogs have been – so he kept it anaesthetised in a cage in the shed, set its legs and then, while we up were at the hospital with Madge on Boxing Day, drove it the fifty miles to the badger sanctuary over at Merepoint.'

'He sounds like a brilliant vet.'

'We think so. He did rant and rave at us for bringing the thing home; said it was the worst Christmas present he'd ever received.'

'We were pretty stupid, weren't we? Jesus, when I think about it now.' Corey pulled a face.

'Darlings, do come in.' Vivienne, wearing some sort of floaty gown, was ushering us into the sitting room as if she owned the place. 'I don't think we've met…?' She fluttered her eyelashes – literally batted them – at Corey as she held out her hand. 'Is this your builder chappie, darling? Goodness, you never said he was so good-looking.' She stroked his arm. 'Rather Robert Redford in his younger days.'

I stared at Vivienne. Had she been drinking? 'This is Corey, Granny. He's the nephew of a very good friend of Madge's from years back.

'Oh, Granny Schmanny,' Vivienne pouted. 'Do call me Vivienne, Corey.'

Jesus, was she speaking Yiddish now?

'Viv,' Mum yelled from the kitchen. 'Get back in here. Your beans on toast are burning.' She came towards us with a bottle of wine and several glasses. 'Right, family stuff this,' Mum sniffed, going back and closing the kitchen door firmly behind her. '*My* family, and I think we need a drink before we get started. Where are Daisy and Nancy? Now, you really do have to tell us *everything* you know, Corey.'

'I'm not sure which bits you know and which you don't?' Corey frowned. 'Uncle Jim has kept a diary of events.'

'Not in *The West Diaries*?' I was stunned. 'Granny Madge is in *The West Diaries*?'

'*The West Diaries*?' Nancy was pale. 'Jim West is my father? And he's written about all this in his diaries?'

'No. No, no, of course not,' Corey was quick to reassure Nancy, who was looking quite ill. '*The West Diaries* are a compilation of Uncle Jim's political career. Alongside those, he kept a personal diary, which he started when he was in the RAF and which he kept up for most of his life. He said he started the personal diary as soon as he met Madge – one night in The Ritz in 1943 – because he was so in love with her he just had to write about her. Hanging around at Bomber Command, waiting to get permission to take off, he'd spend the time writing. I've not seen them, but if they're anything like his political diaries, they'll be well written and, I assume, will be a brilliant social history of the war years.' Corey paused.

'But why didn't he marry my mother?' Nancy asked, almost crossly. 'There she was, pregnant, alone.'

'We *know* all this, Mother.' Mum was impatient to get to the bits we didn't.

'You might,' Nancy snapped. 'But I have been kept in the dark about most of this.'

Corey smiled. 'I'm sorry, I keep forgetting I probably know more than you, having had it direct from the horse's mouth, as it were.'

'Which is what *I* should have had, all these years, from my mother.' Nancy was not to be mollified. 'I just do *not* understand why she kept it all such a secret.'

'She was trying to protect you, I think, Granny.' Daisy patted Nancy's hand.

'But from what? I'm a grown woman. I can understand, after what I went through as a child – and no one who's not been through it could ever know how horrific it is to have your father splashed over the national papers as a burglar and murderer.'

'Arthur knew Uncle Jim wasn't dead.' Corey went on. 'There was confirmation at Bourne that he'd been found in a ditch in Holland, very badly injured but alive, and that he was in a military hospital before being transferred to a prisoner-of-war camp. Arthur, who'd obviously hoped his love rival was out of the picture, would have been one of the first to know Uncle Jim had survived. I assume he panicked, went straight over to see Madge to confirm his death. Apparently, Madge, pregnant,' here Corey stopped and smiled at Nancy, 'and in shock, married Arthur in order that she had a name and a home for the baby. She later told Uncle Jim she felt a good deal of herself had died when she learned of his death and went along with whatever was suggested by Arthur.'

'So, when the war was over, why on earth didn't your uncle Jim come up here to find Madge? If he was so in love with her – and Holly Close Farm – surely he'd have come looking for her?'

Corey smiled. 'He did. Unfortunately, Arthur saw him off at gun point.'

Daisy frowned. 'But he was a brave bomber pilot: a farmer with a shotgun wouldn't have frightened him.'

'It didn't. Jim went up the lane to wait for Madge to come back from wherever she'd been. He saw her with her little girl...' again Corey broke off and smiled at Nancy '... and he recalled, obviously not knowing she was actually *his* little girl, knowing that he just had to leave Madge to get on with the new life she'd made for herself with Arthur and their child.'

'Really?' Daisy and I exchanged glances. 'Surely, you do anything if you're in love.'

'You have to remember that Uncle Jim, at this point, wasn't at his most confident. He was back living at Ascot with his parents and without a job. He'd lost a leg and one side of his face was badly burned. I actually think, at this point, he was possibly going through some sort of breakdown. Maybe what today you'd call Post Traumatic Stress Disorder?'

'The poor man.' Nancy, who I'd always thought as hard as nails, wiped away a tear. 'And this was my father? Jim West? A squadron leader, a major political activist. Goodness, he could have been prime minister.' She sighed. 'And a viscount to boot.'

Daisy nudged me and grinned. This was right up Nancy's street.

'So, when did Madge realise he was still alive?' Mum asked. 'Was it when James began to make a name for himself in government?'

'I suppose eventually she would have done,' Corey nodded. 'But you have to remember this was the early 1950s. Most people didn't have TV and, if she didn't read a decent newspaper, I don't suppose his name would have come up much. It was Uncle Jim's cousin, Fran, and another WAAF, organising a reunion, that brought Madge back down to London and, after ten years, she finally discovered that Uncle Jim had survived.'

'God, there's a whole novel in this,' Mum sighed dreamily, reaching for more wine and filling all our glasses.

'So, this is the bit where it gets really interesting,' Corey smiled, leaning forward in his chair. He had a captive audience and I could tell he was enjoying telling the story. 'Uncle Jim was waiting for Madge as she was about to board her train back home. It must have been a terrible shock for her. Anyway, she didn't get on the train and they spent the night together, realised they could no longer be apart and began making plans for the future. By this time,

Uncle Jim was married to my aunt Constance: I think their respective families had always assumed they would marry and they did.'

'Any children?' Nancy asked eagerly. 'Do I have half-brothers or sisters?'

'No, I'm sorry, you don't. Jim would have loved children – he's that sort of man – but it never happened. That's another reason why he felt he could leave Constance to be with Madge: there were no children involved. And obviously, by now, Jim knew that you, Nancy, were his.'

'So, what happened? Why didn't they get together?' Nancy was agitated. 'Why didn't my real father come and be with us? With me?'

'Several reasons. That night, the very night when Madge had returned from London after finding James again, was when the police decided to lie in wait for Arthur.'

'Lie in wait for him? Whatever for?' Vivienne, who'd obviously bolted her makeshift supper in the kitchen, had now joined us in the sitting room. 'What had the poor man done?'

'Poor man? He was a common *thief*,' Nancy spat, all the years of shame and disgrace she'd endured making her almost tremble with fury. 'You must have read the newspapers, Vivienne. You're my age: you must remember it all. The litany of burglaries, the murder of two innocent policemen, the trial... the *hanging*.'

I shuddered, catching Daisy's eye. She was sitting with Mum, taking it all in.

'Nancy, dear, I don't recall *any* of this.' Vivienne put a somewhat theatrical hand to her chest. 'You were just a little girl, and as I wasn't brought up round here and am quite a *good* few years younger than you are...'

'All right, Vivienne.' Mum glared at her mother-in-law.

Nancy pushed a hand through her hair and breathed deeply. 'Arthur Booth was the stereotype of a burglar in a cartoon. If he'd gone out at night wearing a striped sweater, with a black mask and a bag with "SWAG" written on it, it wouldn't have surprised me. This area was full of textile mills and, after the war, all working to full capacity. Arthur broke into the offices at night, stealing the wages. He broke into just about every post office in Midhope, pinching stamps and postal orders.'

'Uncle Jim told me that when they searched Holly Close Farm they found huge amounts of stolen property.' Corey was eager to get on with the story. 'Arthur tried, that night, after he'd shot the policemen, to cover his tracks by burning some of the stuff.'

'But why on earth did he go from being a petty burglar to a murderer?' Mum shook her head.

'I bet he thought it was James out there, didn't he?' It suddenly made sense. 'Madge had told him James was coming for her and Nancy.'

Corey nodded. 'The police had just begun to suspect Arthur of his nocturnal goings-on and had decided to lie in wait for him that night, hoping to catch him red-handed with his loot after a night's burgling. Obviously, Arthur had no idea this was happening and the police – about six or seven of them, plain clothes as well as uniform, I believe – had spread out and were lying down in the grass, waiting. I think Arthur must have been so agitated, almost demented, at the thought of James suddenly appearing to whisk his wife and daughter off to London, he couldn't sleep and instead was patrolling his land with his gun. There's a road down at the bottom of the fields – he possibly imagined James might arrive that way – and when he came across a man in the grass and the man shouted his name, Arthur fired, assuming it was James. And kept on firing. It's a terribly sad story.'

None of us, even Vivienne, quite knew what to say. As Corey finished speaking, the door opened and Dad and Malvolio, returned from dealing with a cow with mastitis, trooped in. More wine was poured.

'So, did all this come out at the trial in Leeds? You know, was it put forward in Arthur's defence that it was mistaken identity?' Dad looked towards Nancy: she, after all, had lived through the whole thing.

'Not as far as I know.' Nancy shook her head. 'You have to remember I was only about nine when it happened, and the night of the actual shooting I was in Blackpool having a wonderful time with Aunt Lydia and my cousins. I can remember that holiday so well: the B and B down on the South Shore, Blackpool Tower, the donkey rides. Being with Uncle Isaac, as well. I was an only child and suddenly I was playing cricket with the boys, playing rough and tumble and wearing their old shorts instead of the starched little dresses Arthur was always buying me.' Nancy smiled at the recollection. 'Anyway, the press was all over the place for months, so I went to live with Aunt Lydia for the rest of the school holiday and I never went back to my old school. No one would really tell me what was going on, and I missed my dad – Arthur – terribly. Of course, eventually one of Lydia's boys told me my dad was a burglar and a murderer and he was probably going be hanged.' Nancy pulled her mouth down. 'He got a real walloping from Aunt Lydia and his dad for that.'

Poor little Nancy. Was it any wonder she'd turned into this rather brittle, defensive woman who Mum hadn't got on with, preferring to stay with Madge whenever she could?

'Obviously, as an adult, I've read the newspaper reports of the trial, but *never* have I come across any mention of James Montgomery-West. I'd absolutely no idea who he was or that he was my real father until Madge decided to drop her bombshell on Christmas Day.' Nancy appeared to be as much in the dark as the rest of us, sitting there agog as the story unravelled.

'Surely, once Arthur was…' I had to think of the best way of saying it '… you know, *no more*, surely Madge was then a widow and totally free to be with James?'

Nancy suddenly sat up straight and stared at Corey. You could almost see her mind working overtime, working out the puzzle, filling in the missing pieces.

'Uncle Harry,' she breathed, looking at Corey for confirmation. 'It was because of Uncle Harry, wasn't it?'

32

'Uncle Harry? Who the hell's Uncle Harry?' Mum stared at Nancy. 'I didn't know you had an Uncle Harry.'

'Ah,' Vivienne was almost triumphant. 'So, Madge fell in love with someone else, did she? Forgot all about this James chappie and moved on to someone else?'

'Hardly,' Nancy snapped, glaring at Vivienne. 'Harry Wilding was a homosexual.'

'A gay uncle?' Mum frowned. 'Well, you kept that one quiet.'

'Seems to run in the family – keeping secrets.' Nancy was cross.

'Well, where is he now?'

'Russia, more than likely.'

'Russia?' All heads turned back to Mum. It was a bit like being at Wimbledon.

Nancy tutted and we all swivelled back in her direction. 'Harry Wilding was a homosexual, British spy who defected to Moscow after the murders.'

Game, set and match to Nancy on this one.

Corey nodded. 'Wilding was a fairly low-ranking member of British intelligence who worked as a double agent before defecting to the Soviet Union in 1954. He served as both an NKVD and KGB operative, but for a couple of years had been trying to keep his head down a long way from London and Moscow. I think, despite his preference for men, he was probably a little in love with Madge. I've tried to work it all out but, not having anything concrete to go on apart from what Uncle Jim has surmised over the years, I can only assume Madge and Wilding probably shared a love of reading, poetry and gardening. I'm sure both the Brits and the Soviets would have known where he was laying low but, what with the murders and the police and the press crawling all over the place, Wilding upped and left. I know he ended up in the Soviet Union some time later.'

'None of this about Harry Wilding came up when we Googled about Arthur and the murders,' Daisy said. 'You'd have thought it would.'

'You didn't look hard enough, Daisy.' Nancy reached behind her to her Hermès bag, pulling out a plastic wallet of newspaper cuttings and laying the contents on the coffee table in front of us. 'This is all I really know about Harry Wilding. Madge has always refused to talk about the murders – to protect James, I suppose – but she did tell me, many years ago, a little bit about who my uncle Harry had been.'

'So, your uncle Harry was a spy? How exciting.' Mum smiled across at Nancy.

'It wasn't a bit exciting or romantic, Kate,' Nancy snapped. 'I didn't know *what* was going on at the time. I was nine years old, having to live with Aunt Lydia for reasons I didn't understand, my father had disappeared and then Uncle Harry, who had sometimes collected me from school and let me help in the cottage garden, was gone as well.'

'Did you never go back to the farm?' I asked, feeling sorry for the child Nancy.

'Just the once, to pick up some things. I ran down to the cottage to find Uncle Harry but the place was deserted. My mother would never explain anything, never told me what the hell was going on. After that, we went to live up in the Lake District for a couple of years. Madge was a cook...'

Mum, Daisy and I laughed out loud at that and even Nancy smiled.

'She got a job as cook and gardener for some old bloke in Ambleside. We lived there for six years – I went to school there – and while his garden was the talk of the town, I think he probably got fed up of Welsh rarebit and Irish stew. Madge never honed her culinary skills.' Nancy smiled again. 'When her father died, we came back to Midhope to look after Uncle Isaac. She bought the bungalow, cared for Isaac and gardened all day, her own huge garden as well as other people's in the area. Yellow roses she was into – always yellow roses. Isaac used to go with her all the time as her labourer, doing a lot of the heavy stuff. I got out as soon as I could and married your father, Kate. Not,' she sighed, 'a match made in heaven, but there we go.'

'But, I don't get it, 'I frowned. 'I don't see why having some man renting the cottage – OK, he turned out to be a traitor – could stop James and Madge being together. Was James jealous? Did he think Madge had been having some affair with him? What?'

'No, no, nothing like that.' Corey shook his head, accepted a top-up from Mum and continued. 'OK, according to Uncle Jim, before it all happened Madge was frightened. She could see Arthur was in a terrible state at the thought of losing her and Nancy, so she telephoned Fran, Uncle Jim's cousin, to pass on a message that he mustn't, under any circumstances, attempt to drive up to get her. Arthur was deranged, she said; she was frightened at what he might do if James appeared. The next thing Uncle Jim knew was when the double murder of two policemen by a burglar at a remote Yorkshire farm hit the headlines the next day. It was on the front page of every newspaper, on the radio and, I believe, even discussed in Parliament.'

'So, had James told his wife about Madge by then?'

'Yes, as soon as Madge left London he returned home to Constance and told her everything. He was, he said, going to be with Madge; that to avoid as much scandal as possible he would take Madge and Nancy and go, without any fuss, to Italy. He'd thought it all through.'

'What did your aunt Constance say? Do?'

'According to Uncle Jim she sneered, "That little trollop? The milkman's daughter you brought to Ascot to visit your mother?"'

'Cheek of the woman.' Mum was cross. 'Madge might have been a lowly milkman's daughter from Midhope, but she was no trollop.'

Corey smiled at that. 'Well, if you'd ever met my great-aunt Constance, you'd have known what a formidable woman she was. There was no way she was letting her husband go: the utter scandal of it all. To be fair to Aunt Constance, she'd stood by him when he was having some sort of breakdown after his return from Germany minus his leg and very badly burned. Constance, like Uncle Jim, had a long history of family members in Government. Her great-grandfather was a deputy prime minister at one point.'

'Goodness.' We all looked at each other at this revelation of James's wife's ancestry.

'Anyway, first of all, she told Uncle Jim she'd been to the doctor that very morning and was pregnant.'

'And was she?' Daisy's eyes were saucers.

Corey smiled. 'No, although with what happened then, she'd had no need of that little fabrication. The very next day came the news, splashed all over the front pages, of the Holly Close Farm murders. Even at that stage Uncle Jim said he would have gone to Madge and Nancy once the trial was over.' Corey took a deep breath. 'But, with the revelation that a British spy had also been living at the farm, he knew the nail was in the coffin. Aunt Constance was able to bang shut the lid and nail down the whole affair for ever.'

'I don't get that,' Daisy frowned. 'You know, yesterday's news is today's fish-and-chip paper. And I believe they ate a lot of fish and chips in the fifties? You know, before Kormas took their place?'

'Kormas?' Mum looked over her specs at Daisy. 'What've Kormas got to do with all this?'

'I was just *saying*…'

Corey came to Daisy's rescue. 'I know what you're saying, Daisy, but you only have to see what happened ten years later with the Profumo affair to realise that Constance was absolutely safe. She knew that a scandal like this could have brought down the government.'

'Oh, I know *this one*,' Vivienne interrupted. 'Profumo was more *my* era. I once went to a party at Cliveden, where all the scandal happened. Did I ever tell you? Now,' she cocked her head to one side, 'was it Frank Ifield or Acker Bilk I met there?'

'Profumo affair?' Daisy and I shrugged, not having a clue what Corey or Vivienne were talking about.

'John Profumo was Minister for War in the early sixties,' Dad explained. 'He was a married man, sleeping with a call girl who also happened to be sleeping with a Soviet naval attaché. The repercussions of the affair apparently severely damaged Harold Macmillan's self-confidence, and he resigned as Prime Minister on health grounds in, er, 1963, I think it was. The Conservative Party was marked by the scandal, which probably contributed to its defeat by the Labour Party in the 1964 general election.'

'Golly, you know some stuff, Graham.' Mum looked across at Dad proudly.

'Aunt Constance held his love for Madge over Uncle Jim's head to her dying day. Any attempt, even in the years that followed, by Jim to leave to be with Madge, and Constance would have, she told him, spilled the beans. Gone to the Sunday papers. A revelation like this: a married government minister with a love child to the wife of a double police murderer who had rented out her cottage to Harry Wilding, a spy...? The government would have come crashing down. Constance knew this, Uncle Jim knew this and Madge certainly knew it.'

'So, Madge gave him up?' Mum looked tearful. 'How tragic, how very tragic.'

'You have to remember that my mother was a key witness to the shootings,' Nancy put in. 'She wouldn't have been allowed to leave the area and flee to London and James while the trial was being prepared. The police and defence constantly questioned her about what she knew, about what Arthur had been up to and whether she was involved.'

'And in the years that followed,' Corey explained, 'with Louise, my mother, being adopted by Uncle Jim, that was another reason for him to stay with Aunt Constance. He wouldn't have taken her on after the death of her parents only to up sticks and leave her. He said he couldn't disrupt the poor child any more by whisking her off to live with another woman and her daughter abroad.'

'I just can't believe that Madge has never talked about this,' I said.

'It's sixty years ago, Charlie – a lifetime ago.' Nancy shook her head. 'And if these Henderson people hadn't approached Madge about Holly Close Farm, she'd never have sold it, never have revealed its secret, and died with it. She was trying to protect me, I think. She didn't want the past blowing up in my face again.'

'But why didn't she ever tell you who was your real father?'

Nancy looked slightly shamefaced. 'My mother knows me very well. I suppose she knew I'd be off like a shot down to London.'

'To claim your inheritance and any title?' Vivienne interrupted, giving Nancy a sly dig in the ribs.

'Do you *mind*, Vivienne?' Nancy glared, moving herself away slightly. 'To find my father and my *real* family. My blood relatives. I most certainly wouldn't have been after *anything* else.'

Daisy and I exchanged knowing looks.

'Madge couldn't have risked you doing that while Constance was still alive, I suppose,' I surmised. 'It would still have made a jolly juicy story for the tabloids.'

'But, Mum, why have *you* never said anything about Holly Close Farm?' Mum glared at Nancy with some indignation. 'You could have told me all about it. Graham and I would love to have renovated the place and lived there when the girls were little. That really was *my* inheritance, you know.'

'Yes, and Charlie and Daisy have now inherited the cottage.' Nancy arched an eyebrow at the pair of us. 'And why would I have told you about the murders? I suffered as a child at all the schools I ended up going to whenever the other kids found out who I was. I don't think any of you quite realise how devastating it was to have a father who was a burglar, a murderer of policeman, but who'd also been *hanged*, for heaven's sake. At the first school I went to, the kids used to take their skipping ropes and pretend to hang each other when they saw me. Eventually my mother took me to another school and we used different names. I was Nancy Gregory for all my teenaged years. Until I married your father, Kate, and I didn't tell *him* the truth until after we were married. He might not have married me if he'd known the truth – his parents wouldn't have wanted him marrying a murderer's daughter.'

Vivienne was nodding in agreement. 'You most certainly don't want your son to marry anyone *like that*.'

'Well, you're only one generation out, Viv,' Mum exclaimed. '*Your* son married the *granddaughter* of a police murderer.'

Vivienne's hand flew to her mouth and she gave a theatrical little 'Oh' of distress.

'Can I just remind you all that Arthur Booth was *not* my father!' Nancy's eyes glittered with anger. '*No one* here is related to any murderers, let alone *me*.'

Corey put up his hands to come between Mum, Vivienne and Nancy. 'You know, Uncle Jim has actually written all this in his personal diaries. When Aunt Constance died, he allowed me to read them. He's asked me to edit them and, once he's dead, he's given permission for them to be published.'

'I don't *think* so,' Nancy snorted. 'I don't want my name being dragged through the papers.'

'Of course, Uncle Jim wouldn't dream of publishing them without your say so.' Corey said hastily. 'I think the first thing is for you to meet your father after all these years, don't you?' He glanced at his watch. 'It's getting late. I should be going. I've an early start tomorrow in Manchester.'

'Oh, don't go,' Mum pleaded. 'We're just getting to know you. And we *are* related. Even if I can't quite work out how…'

'We have the same great-grandfather, Kate,' Corey smiled. 'Lord George Montgomery-West, the Earl of Beaconscliffe.'

'Fancy,' Mum said. 'I always wanted a family of my own, never really having had one when I was little.'

Nancy arched an eyebrow.

'Oh, come on, Mother,' Mum placated. '*I've* no siblings, *you've* no siblings, and I never really knew my own father until I was older. I think that's why I became so attached to his ashes in the utility,' she went on, tears filling her eyes. She'd got to the stage of drinking where she'd started to be maudlin. 'But now, now I've another *real* family out there, and I'd like to meet them.'

'Absolutely, Kate.' Corey smiled, drained his glass and stood, reaching for his jacket. 'I need a taxi,' he went on. 'Could you give me a number, Charlie?'

Corey said his goodbyes and followed me into the kitchen where I'd left my phone. As I reached into my bag, Corey took hold of my hand instead, pulling me gently towards his chest. He smiled and bent his head to kiss my cheek and then, oh so slowly, kissed my mouth. 'You can't imagine how much I've been wanting to do that all night,' he smiled. 'OK. Taxi?'

33

The next two weeks were manic as, blessed with unusually mild weather for January, Josh and his team were able to crack on with the building work. Because Seb and Libby were desperate to be in the farm as soon as possible, David Henderson suggested more workmen be brought in and, almost overnight, every possible relative of Matis and Gatis Miniauskiene appeared to be working on site, as well as a couple of extra local jobbing electricians and joiners, moving efficiently and effortlessly round each other, colonising the area like a bevy of intense worker ants.

'All brilliants builders,' Matis assured Josh, David and me proudly, bringing each one forward in turn and ordering them produce their credentials and building certificates for our perusal. 'Bests from Lithuania. Nons to beat thems. All excellent Bobs.'

'Bobs?'

'The Builder. You *knows*.' Matis tutted and shook his dark head at my lack of understanding. 'You not knows the little mans?'

Even Gatis' wife, Deimante, a beautiful tiny ball of energy, who worked as lollipop lady and dinner lady at Little Acorns, the village school in Westenbury, was involved, driving down the lane at the end of the school day, bringing a basket of delicious home-made goodies to encourage the men to go that extra mile. As soon as she appeared, we'd all, Daisy and I included, gather round to feast our eyes on *grybukai* – a sort of mushroom-shaped cookie – *paska* and *lietiniai* and then, after a ten-minute break, we'd be back at it for another couple of hours. Matis was a hard taskmaster and he'd have Deimante helping me to move the great arc lamps around so that the men could continue with the inside renovation of the cottage once the early winter evening set in.

At the end of most working days, we'd head for the Jolly Sailor to slake our thirsts and relax. I was beginning to feel real affection for these people, particularly Deimante, who constantly made me laugh and who was determined to improve her English so that she could train to be a teacher. Matis and Daisy were fast becoming an item and I really missed her company when she didn't return home with me to Madge's bungalow after the pub, but instead would leave with Matis to go to his rather swish house at the other side of the village, where he'd woo her – Daisy's words – with his cooking as well as – again in Daisy's words – with his bloody good kissing.

There appeared some improvement in Madge's situation. In the days after Christmas she was asleep more often than not when we visited. She would occasionally open her eyes, trying to work out where she was and who it was that was sitting at her bedside and then, as we moved into the third week of January, she was able to sit up and even begin to feed herself.

'Bit of a miracle this,' Tara, the nurse, said with a smile. 'The physio is going to do some work with her on her leg and on the side affected by the stroke. If she carries on improving, there's every chance she can go back to the nursing home in a few weeks.'

Mum, Nancy, Daisy and I took it in turns to sit and talk to her. We talked for hours about when she was a little girl, her time in the WAAF, and, of course, James, and we brought in photographs I found in the spare room in the bungalow.

With the restoration of her own place completed, Vivienne had little excuse to carry on staying with Mum and Dad and, with a huge sigh of relief on Mum's part, she finally moved back to her little town house near the centre of Midhope. Unfortunately, just as Mum was congratulating herself on getting her spare room back, Nancy felt she ought to be spending more time at Madge's bedside and had taken up residence in the vacated room.

Josh, who wouldn't let the builders leave the site until everything was neat and tidy and totally secure, tried with almost monotonous regularity to lure me back to his place 'just for a quick drink', 'a spag bol, Charlie, without the mushrooms,' or 'an update on the plans'.

'You've missed "a look at your etchings", Josh.' I tutted one Friday evening. I was tired and a bit grumpy and not particularly looking forward to my own company, but even less wanting an evening of sexual gymnastics with Josh Lee.

After the evening at Mum and Dad's when Corey had finally been able to fit the missing pieces of the secrets of Holly Close Farm, he'd returned to London to his home and work. We didn't see him for a couple of weeks – although he'd texted several times to enquire after Madge's progress – until he suddenly appeared on site just as we were packing up for the weekend with the intention of heading for the pub.

'Oh, I'm glad I've caught you,' he smiled, almost shyly. 'I didn't know the way to Madge's bungalow. Are you free?'

'Oh, gosh, no,' I gushed, delight at his sudden appearance making me come out with banalities. 'I cost a fortune.' The grumpiness I'd been feeling suddenly lifted and I realised I really, *really* liked this man. When Corey frowned, I tried to put my sensible head back on. 'What did you have in mind?'

'A drink? Food?' I've driven up from London, called in at the office in Leeds, booked into the Jolly Sailor and then tomorrow I'm driving over to Manchester to take Milo out for the day.'

I beamed. He did want to see me. 'I'm afraid there's no way we'll get a table at Clementine's this evening, the Jolly Sailor is probably the last place you'll fancy eating in, and my cooking, I have to warn you, is as bad as that of the rest of the females in my family.'

Before he could reply Josh appeared out of the dark, some heavy-duty piping slung over one shoulder. He gave Corey the once-over, sizing him up as he spoke. 'Are you coming, Charlie? To the pub? It *is* Friday evening.'

'Sorry, Josh, Corey's just arrived and we're going over to Leeds for the evening.' I turned to Corey for approval and he nodded in agreement. It had suddenly occurred to me I was in need of a really good night out in a city: I seemed to have been holed up in the countryside for ever.

'Oh, great idea,' Josh agreed. 'Not been over to Leeds for ages. We'll all come, make an evening of it.'

'Sorry, Josh.' Corey paused and then said seriously, 'Charlie and I have things to discuss *re* the new society.'

New society? Josh and I stared at him.

'Slobs.' Corey returned the stare, looking us both up and down.

'Sorry?' Josh and I spoke as one. Slobs? What was Corey insinuating? I knew Josh and I were both looking pretty dirty and dishevelled after a day helping the builders with some bricklaying and also Daisy to cut down a couple of trees that were obscuring the view, but calling us both slobs wasn't overly polite.

'Society for the Liberation of Badgers,' Corey deadpanned. 'Charlie and I need to discuss tactics for the next one.'

Josh continued to stare as Corey and I both started to laugh and then couldn't stop. 'You obviously had to be there,' he sniffed disparagingly. He turned to where the builders were packing up their things. 'Pub anyone?'

We'd driven our respective cars back to the bungalow where I'd had a bit of a meltdown. What the hell was I going to wear? I rifled feverishly through my wardrobe as well as Daisy's, but nothing jumped out at me. I really wanted to look good, and then, at the bottom of my wardrobe, I found it: the perfect thing for a cold January night: a long scarlet cashmere sweater dress, still in its Karen Millen bag, that I'd bought the day before being thrown out of Dominic's apartment. Dominic had promised to take me to The Ivy and I'd wanted to wear something special, convinced he was going to pop the question.

I smiled at myself in the mirror as I pulled the dress over my head, luxuriating in its softness. Long black suede boots of Daisy's, bright red lipstick and lots of mascara and I was ready. Forty minutes later and Corey and I were sitting in The Maven on Call Lane in the centre of Leeds, drinking Mojitos.

'So,' Corey said, once we were comfortable on the high stools and the alcohol was going down nicely, 'important question: how *is* Madge? Really? I'd love to meet her properly if she's up to it?'

'Well, no one can quite believe it. I mean, she could possibly have another stroke any time, but, typical of Madge – feisty old woman that she is – she seems to be pulling through.' She's managing to talk a bit – slightly slurred, as you'd imagine – but she's communicating by writing things down with her good hand.'

Corey smiled. 'Amazing.'

'They've done some tests and it doesn't appear to have been the worst type of stroke.'

'But even so? She's ninety-four?'

'Tell me about it. She really is a tough old bird.' I frowned. 'Do you think it's because we've all been talking about James, telling her he's alive and well?'

'Quite possibly. Do you think she'd be up to seeing him?'

'She said not.'

'No?' Corey frowned. 'Why not?'

'She said, "Not like this. I don't want him to see this ugly old woman. I want him to remember me as I was: as a lovely young girl in my WAAF uniform."'

'Oh.' Corey's face fell. 'James wants me to bring him up. You know, to see her.'

'Ooh, doesn't that send shivers down your spine? Gosh, I'd really like to be there at any reunion.'

We smiled at each other, both lost in our own thoughts and then Corey asked, 'And Josh the builder?'

'What about him?'

'He was the guy monopolising you on the speed dating evening. I recognised him.'

'I've known him years.'

'Old boyfriend or current?' Corey smiled.

'He broke my heart when I was seventeen,' I laughed. 'Now, shall we just say, if we're not careful he'll have us dressed – and undressed – as characters from *Poldark* or... or *Dr Zhivago*.'

'What?' Corey began to laugh and, by the time I'd related the story of the Christmas Eve *James Bond* party in all its gruesome detail, Corey was wiping away the tears. 'That is hilarious.'

'It wasn't at the time,' I said ruefully.

'And then to cap it all you became a founder member of Slobs.' Corey was laughing even more.

'I'm really glad you've a sense of humour, Corey.' Dominic, I suddenly realised, hadn't. I couldn't think of one occasion when we'd laughed at some daft thing one of us had said, never mind been verging on the pant-wetting state of hilarity.

We grinned at each other for a long time and then he said ruefully, 'I do appear to have lost it over the past year or so.'

'Has it been pretty awful?'

'It has. You begin to think, is it me? Did I do something wrong? Will I ever be able to trust anyone again?' Corey frowned. 'All I'm bothered about now is Milo. I need to keep on good terms with Rowena so I can see him as often as possible.'

'That's not going to be easy with you in London and him in Manchester.'

'No, that's why I've been here in Leeds all afternoon, discussing a temporary move up to the northern office.' Corey smiled at me and took my hand. 'As from next week I'm seconded up here for six months.'

'Really?' I squeaked, a great daft smile on my face. And then, not wanting to appear over eager, lowered my voice to a more appropriate level. 'Really?' I repeated, nodding my head sagely like some trying-to-be-interested politician.

'Really,' he grinned, then hesitated. 'You're not thinking of heading back to London once you're finished with Holly Close Farm, are you?'

'If you'd asked me that, even a few weeks ago,' I smiled, 'I'd have said that was my intention.'

'And now?'

'And now,' I said, looking deep into Corey's beautiful brown eyes, 'it's the last thing on my mind.

★

David Henderson obviously knew people in high places and, by the time we were into the middle of February, work had started on the actual farmhouse. The cottage was already divided into two and the skeleton of the extension – which would become large, modern kitchens overlooking the herb garden – already in place. Libby Westmoreland couldn't keep away from the site, and most days she'd wrap Lysander up against the cold and drive down to see what progress was being made. 'It's like watching a kettle boil,' I teased her. 'You need to stay away for at least a week and then you'll begin to see a difference.'

'I know, I know,' she laughed, 'but it's so exciting, isn't it?' She gave Lysander, who was entombed in his carrier on her back, a little jiggle and then gave me a knowing grin. 'And *you* seem a lot happier now than when we first started all this back in November? Is it a certain rather gorgeous man who keeps appearing on site at the end of the day?'

'Might be,' I grinned back.

Libby scrabbled in her bag and brought out some chocolate, offering me a piece. 'Well, thank goodness for that, is all I can say,' she said pointedly. 'I brought chocolate to keep you sweet, just in case it wasn't.'

'Oh? Keep me sweet?'

'Well, we were all *terrified* of you to begin with. Even David, and he's not frightened of anyone.' She paused and frowned. 'Except perhaps Mandy, his wife.'

'Oh, gosh, was I so bad?'

'Worse.' Libby laughed. 'Honest, you were stuck up, arrogant, unapproachable and, quite frankly, terrifying.'

'Right,' I said, feeling a bit tearful.

'Oh, but *now*, we really, *really* like you *now*,' she said hastily. She coloured slightly and added, 'I only just said what I said because we know you now. We know you were going through an awful time, that you didn't really want to be here.' She beamed. 'Would you and Corey like to come over to our place for supper one night? Seb really gets on with Corey.'

'How lovely, thank you.' I gave Libby a big daft smile. Corey and I were being seen as a *couple*. Could life get any better?

Apparently, it could.

Mum drove over to the bungalow with a letter that had arrived at home for me. 'It looks important – you know, official,' she said. 'I thought I'd better let you have it.'

I frowned, looking at the postcode. 'It's from London.' I opened the letter and studied its contents. 'I don't quite understand this.'

Mum peered over my shoulder at the words I was trying to decipher. 'You've been nominated for some award, Charlie. Is that what it means? A newcomer to the industry award? Oh, my goodness, you clever thing.' We both continued to read in silence apart from the occasional little 'oh' and 'ah' and 'goodness' that the pair of us couldn't keep in. 'Someone, impressed with your work for them, has put you forward for the Yorkshire Newcomer category.'

'Well, that can only be the Hendersons. I've not done any work up here for anyone else – although, Mum, I'm beginning to get quite a few enquiries for more work. How kind is that? From what I can gather it's a brand-new category,' I added, reading overleaf. 'The judges need to see not only the plans but the actual project I'm working on.'

'Look, there's a phone number here. You need to ring this woman, this Petra Wilkinson, to arrange a time when they can come and talk to you, see what you're working on.' Mum broke off. 'Well done, darling. It was all fate, wasn't it?'

'What was?'

'You know, Dominic's wife catching him with his pants down.'

'Mum!' I winced at the expression and then grinned at her.

'Well, you wouldn't be up for a Yorkshire award and…'

'And?' I raised an eyebrow in her direction as if she were a child pushing the boundaries and I were its mother. I knew exactly where she was going.

'And,' she sighed dreamily, 'you wouldn't now have met the very gorgeous, and very, very eligible Corey Mackenzie.'

By the middle of March, Madge was able to return to Almast Haven. We knew she wasn't happy at the prospect, but there didn't really seem much option: she still needed some specialist nursing care, and Mum, Nancy, Daisy and I all helped to make her room as homely as possible, arranging it with her favourite books, plants and cushions, assuring her that it was only temporary and she'd eventually be able to return home to her bungalow.

On the Monday morning of the same week, Corey, who by now was living a somewhat Bedouin-type existence moving nomadically between his new office and temporary accommodation in Leeds; his in-laws in Manchester to see his son at the weekend as well as with me at the bungalow whenever he could, said, somewhat shyly, 'I'd really like you to meet Milo.'

'Oh.' I felt a rush of pleasure as he grabbed his things and simultaneously shoved a slice of toast into his mouth before heading for the door. 'Are you sure?'

'I think so... What about you? Do you think it's a good idea?'

'Oh, Corey, I don't know.' What I *did* know was that as much as I fancied Corey like mad, that we were now in a relationship, some part of me was holding back. What if he went back to Rowena? What if he was leading a totally double life and every weekend he wasn't staying at his in-laws at all, but with his wife and son? I'd fallen for it before, hadn't I?

I could see he was feeling a bit upset at my uncertainty, but he shrugged it off. 'Up to you. Have a think about it. Actually, I *was* thinking I'd go to over to pick Milo up after school on Friday afternoon, call in to see you on the building site – Milo adores diggers and things – and then drive us down to London for the weekend to see Mum and Uncle Jim.'

'Us?' Did he want me to meet his mother as well as his son?

'Milo and me.'

'OK.' I felt ridiculously disappointed he wasn't including me in the trip south.

'Only two seats, Charlie,' he said lightly, 'or you could have come with us.'

'Another time,' I said, trying to smile. 'I'm not sure I'm up to meeting parents as well as offspring.'

34

As it turned out, it was a good job I'd not been included in Corey's trip back down to London. A phone call from a woman with a no-nonsense tone asked if it would be possible for herself and one other to meet me on site at Holly Close farm on Friday afternoon so they could take a look around my present project as well as scrutinise the plans for it.

I must have spent hours that Friday morning deciding what to wear and practising conversations in my head, not only with the judges but also Corey's son. Did I like children? Mum always said she'd only ever liked her own children and her own dogs – couldn't stand anyone else's – and I reckoned I was a bit the same. I knew nothing about seven-year-old boys apart from their tendency to be noisy and hard work. I wanted him to report back to his mother that I was gorgeous and friendly, but I also needed these judges to view me as professional, intelligent and smart. Jeans, suits, skirts, work boots and high heels were tried on, abandoned and beginning to pile up by the time I decided on clean black jeans, my best white shirt and black pin-striped suit jacket. I went a bit overboard with the make-up but tied my hair back neatly with a black ribbon. There, gorgeous and professional. I set off, crashing the gears on Madge's car. It was holding out but, rather like its real owner, I wasn't sure how much longer it would survive.

'You off somewhere?' Josh was already on site, sharing coffee and work for the day with Matis. They had the plans for the farm spread out on the table in the Portakabin office and both looked up as I walked through the door.

'Yous looking very fabs,' Matis said admiringly when I didn't reply to Josh. I didn't want him thinking I was getting dolled up to impress a seven-year-old and I certainly didn't want anyone knowing I was up for some award. Too embarrassing for words.

'It's Friday,' I said vaguely. 'Any coffee left?'

I spent the morning on a problem Josh had found with shifting an interior wall to make the kitchen in the farm much bigger and, by the afternoon, was able to work on a couple of tenders for a plot of land and an extension that had come my way through friends of the Hendersons. My business here was beginning to take off.

'Be friendly and interested – brush up on Manchester United before he arrives – but don't talk down to him and for God's sake don't snog his dad in front of him,' Daisy advised when she arrived on site from the local garden centre where she'd spent the morning. 'And you look great. Are you sure it's just a little boy you're trying to impress?' She eyed me with suspicion.

I'd told Mum not to tell anyone, even Dad and Daisy, about the award. If I went through to the next round then wonderful; if I didn't, no one would be any the wiser and I wouldn't have to bear their sympathy when it didn't go my way. By three o'clock in the afternoon I was jittery both with nerves and a surfeit of caffeine. I knew Corey had arranged to leave work at lunchtime in order to drive over to Manchester, pick Milo up early from school and then drop by for half an hour or so to introduce me to his son and show him the farm that his great-great-uncle Jim had once wanted to buy many years before. The architectural awards people weren't due until five which, I reckoned, gave me plenty of time to compose myself and swap my potential stepmother head (stop it, Charlie, I castigated myself: you're running away with yourself) for my professional head. By four thirty, and no Corey, I was feeling a bit frantic. The Portakabin was neat and tidy, architectural plans laid out with regimental precision on the desk and I was now down to visiting the Portaloo every five minutes, either to go myself, add lipstick to my already red mouth or spray Jo Malone every time one of the builders vacated it.

'What *is* the matter with you?' Daisy tutted, as I eyed the mud she'd just trailed in and she, simultaneously, eyed the new bottles of squash and packets of M&S Jaffa cakes (lime as well as orange) I'd nipped out to buy at lunchtime to impress Milo. 'He's a little boy: throw him a packet of crisps and plug him into a PlayStation and he'll be your mate for ever. Just don't snog his dad.'

'A PlayStation?' I looked round in panic. 'Where can I get one at this time?'

'Oh, for heaven's sake, I was joking. And I really don't think a seven-year-old boy cares what state the toilet is in.'

'Someone's here for yous, Charlie,' Nojus, one of the young lads, opened the Portakabin door and called in.

'Right, this is it,' Daisy grinned. 'Motherly face on, not a dad-pincher face. Go, girl.' She pushed me to the door.

It had been a mild, beautifully sunny, almost spring-like day and, as I walked down the steps of the Portakabin and made my way round to the makeshift car park, daylight was only just beginning to fade. The melodic notes of a blackbird, hoping to woo a mate with his song, were being delivered at full voice from his vantage point on the roof of the farm, while the fields and woodland around were already gearing up to take on the mantle of the coming season.

I stopped, searching the plethora of cars and trucks for Corey's Porsche. A large black Evoque was parked by the end of the lane, a tall figure, totally dressed in black to match the car, leaning against its closed door. My heart started pounding, making such a commotion in my chest I felt it might actually leave my body.

'Hello, Charlie, how are you?' The man smiled his heart-breaking grin and walked towards me.

'Dominic? Oh my God,' I whispered. 'What are you doing here?'

'Hello, darling. God, I've missed you.'

'Oh, Dominic.' I ran towards him and he wrapped his arms round me, lifting me off the ground and kissing me with such force we nearly fell over. I breathed in his

Dominic smell while he pulled the ribbon from my hair and buried his hands in its length.

'Let me have a good look at you,' he smiled. 'You look wonderful. The north obviously agrees with you.' He bent to kiss me again.

'Hang on a minute,' I snapped, pulling away, 'What the fuck are you doing here, Dominic?'

'Realised I couldn't be without you, Charlie.'

'Oh? And when did this realisation suddenly hit you? When you were at home with your wife? While you were buying ice creams for your kids? When you were in the middle of a Sainsbury's – oh, sorry, you only ever went to Waitrose, didn't you – shop? When you were taking the bins out in – where's that place you were holed up in? – Haslemere, that's it…?'

'Aw, come on, Charlie, I know what I did was dreadful, but it's all in the past. I've left Arabella…'

'… or was it when you took my designs for the Islington job and passed them off as your own in order to win that award?'

Dominic bent down, wrapping his arms around me tightly, stopping my ranting with a long kiss. I vaguely heard the sound of a car pulling into the drive and, as I struggled to pull myself free, saw a little face peering out of its passenger window at me and the car swing round and head off at speed the way it had just come. And then Daisy descending on us, her face a mask of anger, her voice furious.

'What the hell do you think you're doing, Charlie? Corey's just arrived with Milo and driven straight off again. He's seen all of that.' And then turning her anger on Dominic, she punched his arm, shouting at him as she might Malvolio with a rabbit. 'Put her down, you wanker. Down, this minute. Drop!'

35

'Come on, Charlie,' Dominic's voice was languid. 'Take me somewhere for a drink – if there is anywhere in this backwater – and we can talk.'

'What you *can* do, you moron,' Daisy was still wild, 'is bugger off back down the M1 where you came from and leave my sister alone.' She turned on me. 'Or did you *know* he was coming? You did, didn't you? That's what the lipstick and the Jaffa cakes and the posh pong in the Portaloo were all about?'

'Posh pong in the Portaloo?' Dominic gave a bark of laughter.

'Jo Malone, actually,' I snapped. 'And no, Daisy, I didn't know he was coming. If you must know, both of you, I'm waiting for the judges of a rather prestigious design award to arrive. I didn't want to say anything, but I've been nominated for best newcomer to the industry, Yorkshire region.'

'Oh, Charlie, that's wonderful.' Daisy's eyes gleamed. 'Just get rid of this *person* here.' She turned and gave Dominic such a withering look, he actually began to, well, wither. 'Go and get your lippy back on – it does seem to have disappeared, for some reason – and then you're good to go.'

'Er, actually, you can't get rid of me.' Dominic had never withered for long. He folded his arms and smiled. 'I *am* the judge. Or at least one of them. I got here early to explain… you know… about what happened in London. Come on, sweetheart, we've half an hour or so before Petra arrives.' He turned his back on Daisy and said in a low, caressing voice, 'I've missed you so much, Charlie. Forgive me?'

I stared at him. Oh, but he was *so* good-looking with his dark curls, his green eyes and long black eyelashes and olive skin. But his smile didn't quite reach those eyes, there were no laughter lines – probably because he never howled with laughter at ridiculous nonsense; probably because… I stared at his face, at his smooth forehead… 'You've had Botox,' I said finally. 'That's what's different. Or is it a face lift?' I peered up at the flawless skin, at the immaculately white capped teeth and it was like looking at Barbie's Ken.

'Don't be ridiculous, Charlie.' Dominic reddened slightly and I knew I was right. 'Come on, Charlie, this isn't you,' he wheedled. 'I'm here, I'm back, let me show you how much I've missed you.' He reached for my hand but Daisy glared at him and, instead folded his arms once more, obviously thinking better of it.

'*You're* one of the judges?' It was suddenly hitting me what he'd said. '*You* are?' I could feel my heart begin to pound once again.

'That's right.' Dominic almost smirked. 'I was invited onto the ad hoc panel a couple of years ago and when I saw *your* nomination, well, I obviously put myself forward to be one of the judges for your category.'

'But you *can't* do that.' Daisy and I spoke as one. 'That's the biggest conflict of interest I've ever heard of—' She broke off as a car came at speed down the lane and shot into the parking area.

'Ah, that'll be Petra. Now, don't forget, Charlie, Petra knows you used to work for me, obviously, but not about... you know...'

'That you used to be shagging her? That you shacked up with her? That you never told her you were married with three kids?' Daisy was wild. 'That when your wife threw her out of your apartment – oops, sorry, *her* apartment, wasn't it – on a cold Friday night in November with just five black bin bags, Charlie also lost her job, the job that she adored...' A diminutive woman of about Mum's age got out of the silver BMW and walked over to where the three of us were standing. '... or that when Charlie's work in – where was it, Charlie? Islington? – when that was nominated for something, you very conveniently forgot to mention that it was *her* work?'

'Daisy...' I put a warning hand on her arm but she shrugged it off. Dominic, behind his winter tan, had gone quite pale.

'I appear to have arrived in the middle of an argument.' The woman frowned before thrusting a hand in Daisy's direction. 'Petra Wilkinson, one of the judging panel for *Design Today*.'

'*This* is the architect,' Daisy snapped, ignoring the hand and indicating with her own that it should be me the woman was addressing. 'And this *person* here, who apparently has come to judge as well as yourself, couldn't judge himself out of a paper bag, never mind when he should lay off the fake tan.'

'Could I possibly get one word in here, Daisy?' I snapped. 'Actually, several will be needed.' I turned to Petra Wilkinson. 'I'm so sorry, but you've had a wasted journey. I do hope you've not come far?'

'Ramsbottom,' Ms Wilkinson said. 'You know, in Lancashire?'

'Vaguely. Well, as I say, you've had a totally wasted journey. I'm afraid I *know* your other judge.'

She raised an eyebrow. 'As in the biblical sense?'

'I'm not sure there was anything remotely *biblical—*' Daisy interrupted.

'Will you shut up, Daisy? As I was saying, Ms Wilkinson, Mr Abraham and I were in a relationship for almost a year up until November. As such, I'm sure that precludes him from any judging in your awards? But, more importantly, I have one thing to do and then I've got to go.'

'Go?' Go where?' Daisy stared.

I turned, aimed and thumped Dominic hard, right in the solar plexus, and he jumped back with a little 'oof' of surprise, holding on to his toned abdomen. 'I should have done that four months ago,' I growled with satisfaction. 'Now, if you don't mind, I'm off to London. To find the man I've fallen in love with. *If* I'm not too late.'

I swept back into the Portakabin, gathering my bag, my warm coat and the keys to Madge's car while ringing Corey's number as I did so. He wasn't answering. I pressed redial and left a message and then another.

'What's up? Who are all those people outside?' Josh, Matis, Gatis and Deimante were inside, eating some little delicacy that Deimante had produced to celebrate it being Friday, and stared as I rushed round, finding what I would need for the journey. I had to find Corey. Had to explain why he – and oh God, his son – had just witnessed me kissing the life out of Dominic.

'I love that man,' I announced. 'I'm going to find him and tell him.'

'Not Josh then? He nots the ones?' Deimante pulled a sympathetic face and stroked Josh's arm.

''Fraid not. Bigger fish to fry. I'm off to London to tell him.'

'Yous off to London to cook some fishes?' Deimante frowned.

'No, to tell Corey I love him. Whether I'm in with a chance any longer, I've absolutely no idea.'

I ran outside to Madge's car. Daisy was still deep in conversation with Petra Wilkinson. Of Dominic there was no sign. I fastened the seat belt and turned the ignition. Nothing. I tried once more. Still nothing. 'For fuck's sake...' I jumped out, rocked the car a bit in the hope that it might dislodge something, anything, jumped back in and tried again.

'Starter motors,' Matis mouthed through the closed window. 'Knackereds. No goods to mens or beasties.'

'Right, fine.' I jumped out in a temper and gave the car a kick. If I'd had a branch to hand I'd probably have given the car a good beating in the manner of Basil Fawlty.

'Could one of you give me a lift to the train station? I'll get the train instead.'

'We takes yous,' Deimante was at her brother's side. 'Gatis is promising me days in London for evers. We takes yous,' she beamed. 'We all goes, and Gatis and me, we goes see *Jumper Boys.*'

'*Jumper Boys?*' I was momentarily distracted from my mission of getting to London before Corey fell in love with someone else. Or Milo decreed me far too flaky as potential stepmother material.

'S'right. Gatis and me, we loves Frankie Valli: "Big girls don't cries, bi-ig girls sey don't cry iy iys,"' she sang, totally out of tune. 'Yous knows the one?'

'Yes, Deimante, I do, but, honestly, I'll get to London much quicker by train. If someone could just give me a lift over to Wakefield to get the train.' I was almost hyperventilating at my need to see Corey. To explain.

'Matis and I'll take you.' Daisy was at my side as Petra Wilkinson drove off with a little wave in our direction. 'Don't worry about the award – I've explained everything to Petra. She's really nice and she'll be in touch again when she's discussed things with the panel.'

'Daisy, that's great, but not the most important thing in my life at this moment. Come on, Matis. Please?'

36

The train pulled into King's Cross station just after 9 p.m. Not having an advanced ticket, it had cost me an arm and a leg, but I didn't care. I'd constantly tried to ring Corey during the two-hour journey but to no avail. Daisy had chatted to me on my mobile as we headed south and she too had tried to ring his number in case it was just me he was avoiding but, again, to no avail – he just wasn't answering.

And Dominic? Dominic had had the nerve, the audacity, the *conceit*, not only to put himself forward as a judge of my architectural abilities but thought he could just reappear and pluck me from my new life and start again where he'd left off. I shook my head at the thought. What a total... I shook my head again... there weren't enough expletives to describe how I felt about him.

Walking through the concourse towards the taxi rank, the irony of it all couldn't fail to hit me: the last time I'd been here I'd been fleeing from one lover and now, here I was, four months later, running towards another. What if Corey wouldn't see me? He had been badly hurt by Rowena and was finding it difficult to trust another woman.

The only plan I had was to make my way to Eaton Square in Belgravia. I had absolutely no idea how big it was or at which number Corey was living.

The taxi set me down at the east end of the square near a large classically built church with a clock tower. Almost 10 p.m. Surely Corey and Milo would have made it back by now? I walked, scanning the parked cars for his silver Porsche but, although there were all manner of upmarket cars, including Porsches in black and white, I couldn't see Corey's.

This was ridiculous. I was beginning to feel a bit panicky but I kept on walking, pulling my coat around me against the cold night air. I'd not thought to bring my gloves and the heeled boots I'd been wearing all day were starting to pinch my toes. A black cab pulled up at the side of me and, without hesitation, I accosted the elderly woman as she alighted the taxi.

'Excuse me, I'm so sorry to bother you. I'm looking for someone who lives on the square, but I've absolutely no idea of the number.'

The woman looked me up and down with suspicion, as well she might.

'James Montgomery-West?'

She stared at me and then shook her head. 'I'm sorry, dear, I've really no idea.'

'Jim West? The old MP?' The woman's companion touched my arm. 'Over there.' He pointed his walking stick. 'The one with the dark green door.'

'Thank you so much.' Oh golly, what did I do now? Sit on the step until Corey's car arrived? I walked up the steps, took a deep breath and knocked. Nothing. I took the huge metal ring held in the lion's mouth and set it reverberating into the night air once more. A light went on behind the glass skylight of the door and, after a couple of seconds, there came a shuffling noise and then the door opened.

'Hello?' An old man with longish white hair, faded brown eyes and a disfigurement down the left-hand side of his face eyed me with interest.

'James?'

'Yes.'

'Er, well, the thing is, I'm Madge Booth's great-granddaughter. I was, er, hoping Corey might be at home?'

The man stared. He seemed unable to say anything. After what seemed an eternity he took my hand in both of his. 'Yes, you are. I can see that you are. You have Madge's beautiful face.'

'Who is it?' A woman's voice reached us and then the woman herself appeared at James's shoulder. Tall and stylish, she was probably in her mid-sixties. 'You all right, Uncle Jim?' She frowned, trying to work out if she knew me.

'This is Madge's great-granddaughter.'

'Your Madge?'

James nodded, still clasping my hand and smiling down at me.

'Oh, come in, come in.' Corey's mother smiled. 'You must be Charlie? Corey has talked so much about you. But wasn't he supposed to be with you? I thought he was taking Milo to see the farm?' James finally let go of my hand and ushered me inside, pressing me forward as we followed Corey's mother through a beautiful, classically decorated hall and into a sitting room on the right. She threw a log onto a fire that had obviously been allowed to die and I realised it really was getting quite late.

'Is Corey not here?' I scanned the room for signs of another man and a small boy but, apart from a cut-glass tumbler of amber liquid and a novel open and book-marked with a pair of spectacles, there appeared to be nothing that might give any clue to their being there.

'Charlotte, do come and sit down.' James moved the book onto the arm of the sofa and patted the spot it had vacated.

Louise Mackenzie glanced at the clock on the mantelpiece above the open fire and then looked searchingly at me. 'No, they're not here yet. Didn't you see him up in Yorkshire? I don't understand…'

The sound of a door opening and running feet had us all turning in that direction. Louise smiled and walked towards it. 'Oh, I was getting worried.'

'Granny!' A small boy, blond and brown-eyed – a mini Corey if ever I saw one – shot through the door, knocked the book flying and flung himself into Louise's arms. 'We broke down, we were sat for *ages* on the side of the motorway and then the police came and it was really good and then we were pulled away and the problem was that Dad's phone had broken down too…' He came to a halt as he realised I was standing there.

'Where's Dad now?' James drew Milo towards him and planted a kiss on his head.

'He let me in and then he's gone back to see the breakdown man and take the car off the van. Come and have a look, Granny. Come and look at the breakdown van.' All the time he was speaking, Milo was staring at me, trying to work out who I was and I felt myself redden under his scrutiny.

Milo gave me one last stare and then grabbed Louise's hand and pulled her from the room. I felt sick with nerves. What if Corey didn't want to see me? I turned to James, suddenly shy. This was James, for heaven's sake: Madge's James. It was a bit like meeting someone from a novel. Or The Beatles. I was totally tongue-tied, nervous of Corey's reaction when he knew I was here but, at the same time, vivid pictures of Madge's stories about James were passing through my brain like an animated Victorian zoetrope, rendering me unable to make conversation with the man himself.

'You know, I loved your great-grandmother very much. I adored her.'

James's words seemed to break the spell and I went to sit next to him. 'Oh, I know, I know. And she was the same. You must know that. She's been very poorly, but now you really *must* come up to Yorkshire.' From being unable to say one word, it now seemed I couldn't stop.

James patted my hand. 'I think I must. I'm an old crock, but I have to see her again. Just once more.'

'Oh, it doesn't have to be just the once,' I warbled on. 'You've both got *loads* of time left. *Loads* of years left to meet up again.'

James laughed. 'We'll see. Now, would you like a drink? And then perhaps you'd like to tell me what happened this evening? I think something obviously has. With you and Corey, I mean?'

I told James all about that afternoon and what had happened with Dominic while Louise gave Milo supper and put him to bed and Corey helped the RAC man to unchain the Porsche, made him coffee and then took himself off for a shower. The only communication between Corey and myself had been when he popped his head around the sitting-room door, nodded curtly in my direction and said he'd be down in ten minutes, before heading upstairs.

'You have to know that Corey has been through a lot recently, motoring up and down the motorway to see Milo, changing jobs, realising that his marriage was over. When he met you, he fell in love all over again but, as I'm sure you've noticed, he's put up a lot of barriers since Rowena went off with someone else. I suppose seeing you with your ex this afternoon resurrected a lot of the bad stuff.'

'But I wasn't *with* him. The moment I saw Dominic – my ex – I *thought* he was all I wanted. It took two minutes, really and truly, just two minutes to know he most certainly *wasn't* what I wanted. He wasn't Corey...'

I broke off as the sitting-room door opened and Corey came in, fresh from the shower. He rubbed at his wet hair with a huge navy towel, his feet bare beneath the faded Levi's.

'You'll need ice with that,' James said, as Corey poured himself a large whisky. Corey nodded, walked back the way he'd just come and James stood and smiled. 'Just tell him what you've told me, Charlotte. If you're anything like your great-grandmother you're as honest as they come.' He bent down and kissed my cheek. 'I do hope you're going to stay for the weekend. There's still so much to catch up on.' He reached for his stick and walked towards the door, patting Corey on the shoulder as they passed in the doorway.

'Are you sulking?'

'I never, *ever* sulk.' Corey frowned. 'Can't bear sulkers. I get a bit mad, lose my temper, but it only ever lasts two minutes.'

'You drove off pretty quickly.'

'That was my two minutes of temper.' Corey sat on the floor and rubbed at his hair once more. God, he was gorgeous. Tired, rumpled and cross. But bloody gorgeous. I longed to go over and sit on the floor next to him.

'So why didn't you come back? You know, if this temper thing of yours is only a two-minute window.'

'What and let Milo get *another* eyeful? I'd no idea where you were going with it all. We might have driven back down the lane and you could have been horizontal with your ex by then; or up against the Portaloo, swinging from the rafters or pole dancing around the scaffolding.' Corey gave me a wintry smile.

'Don't be ridiculous.'

'Ridiculous? Charlie, you were *going* for it.'

'But you realised it was Dominic? My ex?'

Corey frowned. 'Is that supposed to make it all right? I told you I'd met Dominic Abraham before. I think he was wearing the same all black outfit when he seduced my mother into spending ridiculous amounts of money with him.'

'But, Corey, I had absolutely no idea he was going to suddenly turn up. It was as much a shock to me as it must have been to you.'

'You were looking pretty glam. Not your usual working gear.'

'I wanted to look nice for Milo.' I sighed. 'Do you think I could have some more of that whisky?'

Corey poured me a couple of fingers, added ice and sat back against the sofa. 'Go on.'

'And, I didn't tell anyone except Mum, but I was also waiting for a couple to arrive from *Design Today*. I'd been told I'd been nominated for a design award.' I shrugged. 'Dominic just happened to be one of the judges.'

Corey laughed mirthlessly. 'Very convenient.'

'I didn't *know* that. Look, Corey, do you think I'd have thumped Dominic, messed up my chances of winning an award and embarrassed myself trailing round London looking for you if I had any feelings whatsoever for that pillock?' I shook my head, suddenly defeated. 'I know how it must have looked, I know it must have been awful for you trying to explain to Milo, but it meant absolutely nothing. Actually, yes it did...' I stood up, drained my glass, and reached for my coat. 'It meant... it meant I knew I was in love with someone else.'

'Where are you going?' Corey lay back on the floor and closed his eyes.

'I'm off. There must be a hotel somewhere round here.'

'It's Eaton Square. Bloody expensive round here.'

'Well then, I'll sit on King's Cross station and wait for the milk train back home.'

Corey opened one eye. 'The milk train? Didn't they stop in the 1960s?'

'Whatever.'

'So,' Corey said, closing his eyes again, 'do feel free to leave; the door's not locked. But... this, er, this... *someone else* you say you're in love with. Anyone I know?'

'Might be.'

'Who's sulking now?' Corey started to laugh. 'Come here, you idiot.' He opened his arms and I went over and lay down on the floor with him. He wrapped his arms tightly round me and I closed my eyes. He smelled so right, felt so right. It was, I knew, going to *be* all right.

37

On the Sunday morning we set off back north in convoy: James and Louise in Louise's car and Corey, Milo and me in a hired Audi.

I'd spent two days in Eaton Square and fallen more and more in love with Corey Mackenzie, as well as being welcomed and made to feel totally at home by Louise, James – I couldn't think of him as Jim – and even Milo, whom I'd apparently won over, not just with my skill at sorting some complicated Lego model, but with the fact that I used to sit next to Man United's newly acquired striker at primary school when I was seven.

James. What can I say about James? He was everything Madge had ever said about him – and more. At ninety-seven he was still amazingly alert and on the Saturday afternoon, while Corey and Louise took Milo up to Hampstead Heath with a neighbour's dog, James and I had continued our chat from the previous evening, condensing the sixty-five years since he'd last seen Madge into a couple of hours.

'Please come up and see Madge, James.'

'Do you think it's what Madge wants?'

'To be honest, she did say she wanted you to remember her as she was, you know, as a young woman...'

'She'll always be young and beautiful to me.' James had held my eyes and not said anything for a few seconds. 'I want to see her, Charlotte, you know, while I can...?'

I'd nodded. 'I know,' I smiled. 'I know.'

By two in the afternoon, James and Louise were booked into the one decent hotel in Midhope and, after giving Milo lunch there, Corey and he set off on the forty-minute journey across the M62 back to Manchester. I'd phoned Mum and told her James was with me and I was going to take him over to Almast Haven to see Madge.

'I think you need to tell her, Mum. You know, warn her. We don't want the shock to kill her.'

'And she'll need her best dress and her lipstick on...' Mum was excited. 'My grandfather. I'm going to meet my grandfather... What about Mum? Should I be getting your granny Nancy over there... you know, to meet her father at last...?'

'I wouldn't, Mum. I think at this stage the fewer people the better. Just tell Madge James is coming to see her and then, and then... oh gosh, I don't know, we'll just have to play it by ear.' I was so nervous, excited, but terrified of Madge's reaction. What if she refused to see him?

Madge sat ram-rod straight in her favourite chair, her eyes fixed on the closed door of her room as she waited.

She'd said she didn't want anyone with her, had sent Kate downstairs to the lounge with all the old dodderers. She needed to see James alone.

It was four thirty. Tea-time. She could hear the trundle of the tea-trolley as it clattered its way from the kitchen along the corridor to the lounge where the residents would be eagerly anticipating the fish-paste sandwiches and lemon drizzle cake. Anything to break the monotony of a long Sunday afternoon, made even longer by the lengthening days as Easter approached.

Just once more. She had to be with James just once more.

Madge kept her eyes on the door. Five minutes had passed since she'd last looked at her little wristwatch; an hour since Kate had told her James was coming to see her. She glanced towards the window, allowing herself just a few seconds away from her constant vigil on the door. A weak sunshine was continuing to light the sky to her right. She was glad: rain and cloud wouldn't have been right.

The door opened and he was here, his still-tall frame – now somewhat stooped – filling the space, those brown eyes immediately meeting her own.

James.

'Hello, Midge, darling, I'm here. I'm here for you now, my love.' He walked over to her, placed the tiny gold cross in her lap and then, taking both her hands in his, bent to kiss her.

The years fell away, taking with them the frailty of old age and, as Madge kissed him in return, she was nineteen once more and with the only man she'd ever truly loved.

Acknowledgements

My thanks, as always, to my agent Anne Williams at KHLA literary agency and the fabulous team at Aria.

The story of Holly Close Farm is one I've wanted to write for a long time. Years ago, when my husband and I were looking for the perfect house, we came across a farmhouse for sale. We didn't buy it for a number of reasons but the story of a farmer, Alfred Moore, who'd once lived there, fascinated me and I did a lot of reading around his case. He was a petty burglar who was hanged at Leeds in the early 1950s for the murder of two policemen at the farmhouse. While the tale of Charlie and Madge at Holly Close Farm is nothing whatsoever like the Alfred Moore story, I would like to acknowledge the influence this case had on the telling of my story of Holly Close Farm. Particularly as, I know, there are family and friends of Alfred Moore who still believe he was innocent of the murders.

Hello from Aria

We hope you enjoyed this book! Let us know, we'd love to hear from you.

We are Aria, a dynamic digital-first fiction imprint from award-winning independent publishers Head of Zeus. At heart, we're avid readers committed to publishing exactly the kind of books we love to read—from romance and sagas to crime, thrillers and historical adventures. Visit us online and discover a community of like-minded fiction fans!

We're also on the look out for tomorrow's superstar authors. So, if you're a budding writer looking for a publisher, we'd love to hear from you. You can submit your book online at ariafiction.com/we-want-read-your-book

You can find us at:
Email: aria@headofzeus.com
Website: www.ariafiction.com
Submissions: www.ariafiction.com/
we-want-read-your-book
Facebook: @ariafiction
Twitter: @Aria_Fiction
Instagram: @ariafiction

Printed in Great Britain
by Amazon